MY
HEART
IS
NOT
MY
OWN

MY HEART IS NOT MY OWN

Michael Wuitchik

PENGUIN
an imprint of Penguin Canada

Published by the Penguin Group
Penguin Group (Canada), 90 Eglinton Avenue East, Suite 700, Toronto, Ontario, Canada M4P 2Y3

Penguin Group (USA) Inc., 375 Hudson Street, New York, New York 10014, U.S.A.
Penguin Books Ltd, 80 Strand, London WC2R 0RL, England
Penguin Ireland, 25 St Stephen's Green, Dublin 2, Ireland (a division of Penguin Books Ltd)
Penguin Group (Australia), 707 Collins Street, Melbourne, Victoria 3008, Australia
(a division of Pearson Australia Group Pty Ltd)
Penguin Books India Pvt Ltd, 11 Community Centre, Panchsheel Park, New Delhi – 110 017, India
Penguin Group (NZ), 67 Apollo Drive, Rosedale, Auckland 0632, New Zealand
(a division of Pearson New Zealand Ltd)
Penguin Books (South Africa) (Pty) Ltd, 24 Sturdee Avenue, Rosebank,
Johannesburg 2196, South Africa

Penguin Books Ltd, Registered Offices: 80 Strand, London WC2R 0RL, England

First published 2013

2 3 4 5 6 7 8 9 10 (RRD)

Manufactured in the U.S.A.

LIBRARY AND ARCHIVES CANADA CATALOGUING IN PUBLICATION

Wuitchik, Michael I. (Michael Ignatius), 1952–, author
My heart is not my own / Michael Wuitchik.

ISBN 978-0-14-318798-1

1. Sierra Leone—History—Civil War, 1991–2002—
Fiction. I. Title.

PS8645.U47M9 2013   C813'.6   C2013-903759-4

Visit the Penguin Canada website at www.penguin.ca

Special and corporate bulk purchase rates available; please see
www.penguin.ca/corporatesales or call 1-800-810-3104, ext. 2477.

ALWAYS LEARNING   PEARSON

TO SHELLEY, NATALIE AND DANIEL

Part One

ONE

Nadia is in her robe, legs curled beneath her, a glass of cocoa warming her hands. Finnegan remains on his mat beside her chair—he thumps his tail a couple of times but doesn't get up. A candle casts a soft glow from the mantel. On her lap is a package; the wrapping paper is battered and torn. Dirt-smudged. Tattered corners. Like a Christmas parcel that has come a long way by surface mail.

"How did it go?" she asks. Something isn't right; the filthy parcel in her hands and the look in her eyes—a look that brings a knot to my chest. Even Finnegan seems off—he hasn't risen to greet me.

"It went fine. There were lots of questions. Receptive audience. The psychiatry residents took me out for drinks and sushi afterwards—I think I overdid the sake."

Nadia's patience makes the silence all the more heavy. My head aches. She'll want to talk—I want to go to bed. The grandfather clock ticks behind me—tick tock, tick tock. Still she waits, her dark hair in disarray. Her complexion is pallid, as if no blood flows beneath her skin. She sits completely still, the only thing moving is the steam rising from the cocoa to just below her nose. The knot expands into something black and foreboding, and I struggle to make sense of it. I see it then, in her eyes. A tension. Nadia is afraid.

She stands, approaches me, her robe coming suddenly open—the shock of her nakedness making her vulnerability complete. Finnegan finally moves off his mat to stand beside her. She places the package in my hands. It is addressed to me. The sender is a Corporal John Lewis, Canadian Forces, United Nations Integrated Office in Sierra Leone.

"This came for you today. Open it, John, it must be important." She tries to smile for me, but her lower lip trembles.

The parcel feels heavy and damp.

"Nadia—"

She turns the package in my hands. "Here—there's an envelope taped to the outside."

I feel pins and needles seeping into my right hand. I force myself to breathe, trying to will the familiar numbness away. My fingers are clumsy, fumbling with the envelope.

It contains a single page, handwritten.

Dr. Rourke,
I work with the UN Mission in Sierra Leone. A priest
in Buedu, near Liberia, gave me this diary. The priest knew

of my interest in the plight of refugees from the war—he said he found it in an abandoned church and hoped I might help. I read it, and found your name mentioned in a few places. The writer doesn't identify herself, but seems to have known you at Connaught Hospital during the dark days. I've had a colleague back home do a search on your name—shouldn't be too many Canadian physicians named John Rourke. I thought you would want to have this.

I have to warn you, it's pretty heavy going.

Corp. John Lewis,
Canadian Forces, UN Mission, Sierra Leone

PS. The priest had no idea what happened to the woman who wrote the diary. The records here are abysmal—I couldn't trace her. Sorry. J. L.

Nadia has been reading over my shoulder. Her face is rigid, her eyes round and unblinking. Slowly, I will my fingers to pick at the bands of tape securing the brown paper wrapper. It comes apart too easily, as if the tape is tired, its job done. Inside is a book with a brown leather cover. The smell of mould sucks the oxygen from the room.

"What is this?" Nadia whispers. Her hand grips my knee. I wish I was alone.

I don't trust my voice—all I can manage is a long sigh. There is something old-fashioned about the leather cover—something I recognize from long ago. I look from the book to Nadia. Her eyes are softer now, wistful, as if her thoughts are elsewhere. I fan the pages and the mustiness thickens the air. It feels damp, the moisture reminding me of *her* skin. I close my eyes, afraid that Nadia will see what I am seeing, feel what I'm feeling. My fingers stop on a random page.

"Aren't you going to read it?"

The handwriting is neat, the letters exact—almost childlike. The ink, once blue, has faded to dull grey. The voice on the page is unmistakable—it is a voice that stops my breathing.

After some time we go north on the way to Kabala. Every day I carry Jolie's baby on my back. I know she is hungry but that baby is so good all the time—Lord Jesus she give me strength! She come to me for a reason, a reason I do not understand. I see all the other girls separated from their families, cryin and wantin to die. We all suffer so, but that baby, she is what keep me alive.

We are all walking now, stayin away from roads, like passing devils in the dark. When we go through a village the people stay inside or go hide in the bush. The rebels destroy everything they cannot steal for themselves. They kidnap boys and girls—spoil them with drugs and guns and make them do such bad things they can never go back. There is no way they can go back.

When the people look at us I can see what they think. To them I am a rebel woman now. Damaged goods, I will never be the same.

In my hands is her diary—the diary of Mariama Lahai.

I rub my fingers along the grime of the leather. Nadia is on her knees in front of me, her robe still open. Her grip on my leg tightens. When she speaks, her voice is tentative, as if she is out of breath. "John? Whose diary is it? Is it the Sierra Leonean nurse, the one whose picture you have?"

"Yes, it's her. It was 1999, the year our medical group was evacuated from Freetown. My God, its been ten years. She ..."

My own words sound hollow to me—I'm trying to reassure Nadia, but I feel off balance. Unsure. "This part of her diary must have been written after I was airlifted out. She …"

"Might be still alive," she whispers, almost inaudibly. She nods slightly, her eyes darting from the diary to me and back to the diary. Her face crinkles and strains, as if the muscles under her skin can't settle on what she's feeling.

Slowly, she rises to her feet, drawing her robe together, tying it tight to her waist. She takes my face in both of her hands and kisses me. Tenderly. She turns, and without saying another word Nadia walks up the stairs to our bedroom. Finnegan follows her. In a few minutes, the two of them return. She is dressed—jeans, a shirt and sweater. "I'm going for a walk," she says. With that, she opens the door and the two of them go out, into the night.

The candle burns low on the mantel and still I sit with the diary in my lap, lost in thought.

I met Mariama over a mango. She was sitting on one of those white plastic chairs in the open breezeway of Connaught Hospital, waiting for her shift to start. I had just finished mine and was waiting for my lift to the expats' compound. Freetown was on edge—everyone remembered the rapes and lootings from only two years before. The hospital was still full of amputees and war-wounded—and it was just a matter of time before it all started again.

"Mind if I join you?" I asked. She was so beautiful, I had trouble looking her in the eye. Tall, with high breasts and powerful hips, she had an elegance that was natural and unassuming. Her skin was the colour of rich chocolate and her hair, glistening with oil, was wound in tight plaits.

"You are welcome to sit here," she said formally.

"My name is John Rourke."

"Yes, Dr. John, I have heard of you. I am Mariama. Mariama Lahai. I am pleased to meet you."

"Can you call me John?"

She smiled shyly and said, "You are a doctor. Please, I will call you Dr. John."

Mariama took the ripe mango between her lips and started peeling it with her teeth. She held the fat end in her palm and stripped the narrow end of its skin, spitting the peels onto the ground beside us. She sucked the pulp from the pit before taking off more skin, spitting out the peel and sucking the newly revealed mango flesh. She had a way of tilting the fruit over her mouth so as not to spill a drop on her crisp white uniform.

She caught me staring. "I'm sorry," I said. "I've never seen anyone eat a mango that way."

She arched an eyebrow and her wide brown eyes held mine. "How do you eat a mango, Dr. John?"

"I, I peel it with a knife."

"Oh, I see. Here we do not walk with knives in our pockets, so we must use our teeth to eat a mango."

It was, I would soon discover, Mariama's way. She would use whatever was at hand to do whatever she needed to do. As a nurse she was the same—bright and resourceful. Once, we saw a little girl who had lost an eye and was in danger of losing her arm. It was a day when, of all things, we had a shortage of gauze. One of the expat nurses started swearing, saying, "How are we going to pack this with no fucking gauze?"

Mariama smiled, patting the frustrated nurse's shoulder. "It is okay," she said. "Women's pads. We have so many boxes, we will use women's pads."

And so we did. I was with the little girl and her mom and Mariama when she woke from surgery. I took the bloody pad from her eye and looked to Mariama—she just reached into her pocket and handed me a new one. "Still no gauze, Dr. John, but this works just fine," she said.

Later, I checked in on the girl before leaving for the day. The mother was asleep on the floor beside the bed. Mariama was sitting with the girl's head resting in her lap, gently stroking her hair.

"Mariama, your shift ended hours ago—you should be home."

She smiled and tilted her head toward the girl. "I am happy here, Dr. John. In a while I will go."

It was her way—her beautiful way.

Above me, the Vancouver night sky is clear and I can see the red twinkle of Mars in the east. I'm not alone—Dante the raccoon is watching from his perch. He likes to sit in the crotch of our big Douglas fir, eyeing the human who insists on standing in the cold outdoor shower, anytime, day or night. I remain motionless, my mind and most of my body numb. A physiological paradox: if I stay long enough under the stream of freezing water the feeling in my hand will return.

Tonight it's taking longer than usual. I've been better these past few months; I've had fewer episodes, and even those have been over quickly. Until today. Mariama's diary has changed everything.

Damaged goods. There was nothing damaged in the Mariama I knew. Pride seeped out of her like sweat from skin. You could hear it in her voice, see it in the way her eyes held you, and in the way she walked—her back straight, head held high.

She was particularly good with other women. One night, when we were on shift together, I was called to do a Caesarean section. The mother was small and exhausted and the baby was stuck in a posterior presentation. An older midwife who was trying to teach Mariama how to turn the baby was struggling and overwhelmed. When I arrived, she threw up her hands, asking me to do the C-section "quick-quick." Mariama, who stood across from me, looked disappointed but hid it from her teacher. Her eyes found mine and held on—"we must try," she seemed to be saying.

I massaged the woman's abdomen and quickly found the fetal head and buttocks. I applied pressure and the baby started to shift. Mariama put her hands on mine, following my lead, and then I let go and asked her to do it. She was a natural, an artist sculpting clay. The mother was older than Mariama, but that didn't seem to matter—Mariama cooed something in Krio, her tone so soothing it was like a lullaby. The mother locked her frightened eyes on Mariama's and relaxed. It was as if the two of them were in their own world, apart from the dingy case room with its grey walls and the panting sounds of other women.

When the fetus turned, Mariama smiled. "There, now," she said. "The baby move, Dr. John. It will not be long now." She held the mother's hand during contractions and massaged her abdomen with palm oil in between. Mariama was right—the baby was born within the hour.

The water envelopes me, and I'm so deep into its cold that my thoughts, finally, diminish to nothing at all. My watch tells me I've been standing here for over half an hour. The stars have disappeared and the sky is completely black. Dante tires of waiting—he comes down from his tree and drinks from the coolness swirling about my feet. Dante is showing his age— he moves a little more slowly now and tufts of silver-grey run the length of his snout. Tonight he doesn't acknowledge my presence, just rubs his paws in the wet and waddles over to the compost.

The light is off in our room above, but I know Nadia is awake. She waited up for me, *knowing* the parcel in her hands had come a long way, *knowing* it would bring back the trauma of Sierra Leone. When she returned home from her walk, the candle on the mantel had burned itself out and I was three-quarters of the way through the diary.

"How is it?" she asked. When I looked up, she saw my eyes and her breath caught. "Oh, I'm sorry."

"I have to finish it. I'll be up soon."

She nodded, patted my hand and climbed the stairs. This time, Finnegan stayed with me, curled at my feet.

Nadia and I have been married five years, and I haven't seen or heard of Mariama in ten. Slowly, I've been getting through it all. The troubled sleep, the numbness in my hand, the flashbacks and the guilt are much better now. I tell my patients to handle things in manageable doses, compartmentalize, deal with what you can and tuck the rest away. Even my own story, the parts I haven't told anyone, couldn't have prepared me for what I've read in Mariama's diary.

Nadia and I have never told each other our own stories—hers about Croatia during the war, mine about my last days in Freetown. We've kept the hurts secret. She has her compartments, I have mine. I rationalize it is because we love each other, want to spare each other—the pain of the telling too high a price to pay. And so we've managed to live together, never fully understanding what the other is afraid of.

I towel myself, waiting for the sensation to return.

"It's starting to rain," I say, as I slip into bed.

"Shh. I don't want to talk."

She's naked. Nadia rolls toward me and pinches my nipple gently, her nails electric against my skin. I turn my body until I feel the warmth of her breath against my chest.

"Are all Croatian girls so forward in bed?"

"I've never been in bed with one, so I don't know," she says. "Stop talking."

Her smell deepens as she snuggles closer. She slides down and takes me into her mouth, all of me, and I grow hard as her head moves, and it is so good I relax and leave it to her. The rain patters on the skylight above us—the rhythm of it matches hers.

"You like it, don't you?" she whispers.

"Yes. I love the rain."

"I meant your cock in my mouth."

I laugh. "I love that too."

"Inside me," she says, moving up on the bed. "Man on top. I want you to come inside me."

I move over her and she draws me in. She is already wet, and she clenches her legs tight about me, pushing back with tiny panting breaths. As I come, she meets every pulsing spurt with a little thrust of her own, and it is as if every nerve ending in her body is centred in her cervix, demanding everything I have to give.

I cradle her head as we look up toward the skylight. Two expressionless faces are reflected in the glass.

"You tortured yourself longer tonight," Nadia says finally. "I don't know how you stand it."

"I like the cold." I don't tell her that the numbness in my hand returned when I opened the package from Sierra Leone. It's an unexplained condition that has plagued me on and off for years, since the day I left Freetown.

"You're awake half the night and spend forty-five minutes in a freezing shower? It makes me wonder what you're washing away." Her voice sounds small and fragile.

"I was thinking about Mariama's diary and about the doctor, Momodu, who left the mask with me before he disappeared."

"Momodu is the man in the photo on your desk, the man standing beside this Mariama?" she asks.

This Mariama? I wonder if Nadia intends to sound harsh. "Yes."

"The mask is very ugly," she says. "I'm surprised your clients don't get distracted by it."

I sigh. "Well, I promised Momodu I'd keep it for him, and I know you don't want the thing in the house."

She says nothing, but her silence underlines what we both know: the mask connects me to a place that Nadia prefers I'd leave behind.

"You never talk about your time in Freetown, John."

I stifle the temptation to remind her that she never talks about the war in Croatia. "I think I was there for the wrong reasons. I was addicted to the adrenaline."

Nadia stares at my reflection for a long time. There is a tap, tap, tap on the skylight above us. "It's raining again," I say, welcoming the sound. Within seconds the downpour is pounding the glass and our reflections are washed away.

Nadia's movements, when she undresses, are utilitarian, reflexive, like a breath repeated. The way she puts on her clothes is something else—like stripping in reverse, but more mindful. Bras go on without her ever taking her eyes off the mirror. Tights are rolled over her long legs with a slow, unfolding caress. She tilts her head in a characteristic gesture, inspecting her work. She buttons her top from the bottom up, another tilt of the head, a hand brushing over a breast. Today it's jeans and a khaki silk shirt.

She manages her life in the same way—her actions are always mindful. The fridge is checked before going for groceries, cheques are never written without balancing the chequebook, the gas tank is filled before going on a trip in the car. It's not an obsessive attention to detail so much as a vigilance about maintaining order and her place in the world.

She catches me staring. "What?"

"I don't know what I enjoy more: watching you taking your clothes off or putting them on."

She smiles. "Why don't you decide while getting me a coffee."

We share a running joke that our marriage is built upon two pleasures: she watching me cook, and me watching her get dressed.

She comes down the stairs with the smile still playing on her lips. "The sounds and smells of Saturday," she says brightly. "I like this!"

We sit down to an omelette with red peppers, green onions, cheese and shreds of fresh basil. I add sausages because I like watching her eat them. She taps her tongue to one until she's sure the temperature is just right. Oblivious of greasy lips, she chews, slowly, with her eyes closed.

Our eyes connect over coffee cups. She winks playfully at me. There's something about Nadia's eyes—a need for joy that is ferocious. She grew up near Vukovar, the site of a Serb massacre of Croats in 1991. Early in our relationship I'd asked her about it. The first time, her eyes looked so sad we just hugged, saying nothing. The second time, she mumbled something about moving on and that I also needed to move on. She has no family—no parents, no siblings, not even a cousin. It's as if Nadia came from a place that ceased to exist.

Once, I asked if she would like to go back with me. I'd worked as an emergency physician during the siege of Sarajevo, and I was interested to see the rebuilt city. It was said to be beautiful again. We could spend some time there and go to Vukovar and maybe find her old friends. Nadia looked at me with the kind of blank expression I've seen only in psychiatric patients—a stare so vacant and devoid of emotion it frightened me. I was stunned that the person looking back at me was actually my beautiful, vibrant Nadia.

I don't ask about the past anymore, and neither does she—until now, when it was delivered to our door, in a brown paper wrapper, from Sierra Leone.

TWO

"Dissociative. Describes sensations of floating and lightness—especially when thinking about death. Mother committed suicide. Angry when asked about her father. Borderline features, manipulative, unstable moods, history of chaotic relationships, seductive ... oh, stupid!"

"Who are you calling stupid, Dr. Rourke?" The diminutive form of Bonnie Church stands like an exclamation mark in the doorway. Bonnie is the lifer on the Inpatient Unit. She took the job fresh out of nursing school and never left. Twenty years.

"Remind me to stop leaving my door open," I say, pointing to a chair and switching off the recorder. "I'm just mad at myself. I'm dictating my assessment of the client you referred. I forgot to review her meds."

Forty-something and petite, with short, spiked black hair and painted eyes, Bonnie has the look of someone better suited to a career as a barista than as a nurse. Unconventional and androgynous. Her legs are so short, her feet hang above the floor when she sits. But what Bonnie lacks in size she makes up for in personality—she is the most assertive person I've ever met.

She smiles, shaking her head. "An interesting oversight for a psychiatrist with your reputation. So you *are* human." Bonnie clicks through the colours of the fat pen that hangs on a cord from her neck. One irritating click after another. We're on different teams, so Bonnie has rarely been in my office.

"I wanted to thank you for standing up for me," she says.

A couple of weeks earlier, Bonnie had given an interview to a local newspaper about suicide. Our department head, Dr. Christopher Smith-Charles, wasn't in when the reporter phoned, and one of the clerical staff directed him to Bonnie. The headline that ran the next day screamed "Psychiatric Nurse Blames Incompetent Mental Health Bureaucracy for Suicides!" Dr. Smith-Charles issued a formal denial and said his head nurse had been misquoted. The reporter contacted Bonnie and asked her what she thought of Dr. Smith-Charles's denial. The headline to his follow-up piece read, "Nurse Stands By Comments—'Well what would you *expect* the department head to say?'"

"My pleasure, Bonnie. You said what we all feel—you just have more courage than the rest of us. We all know this place runs because of you."

"Well, that may be," she says, blowing on her nails theatrically, "but I had to promise I wouldn't do any more interviews." She clicks her pen for emphasis. "So, how did you and Carrie North get along?"

I chuckle and lift Carrie's chart. "Let's see. In your rather colourful letter of referral, you asked for—let me quote you—'Anything you can offer to get Carrie off her ass and stop apologizing for being born.... Client is approaching middle age, morbidly obese, the survivor of serial relationships with abusive men and over-prescribing doctors.' Your point about over-prescribing doctors makes my failure to ask about her meds look even more incompetent. So, thank you very much!"

Bonnie's smile is so broad her ears wiggle. "We all know it's the nurses that do the heavy lifting—your fuckup isn't anything I haven't seen before. Besides, I can tell you what drugs Carrie's taking. The real question is, do you have any tricks up your sleeve to get her to stop apologizing? Women like that make me want to have a sex change." She clicks her pen three times in succession and rolls her eyes.

"I'm seeing her again tomorrow. I have an idea to try something a little unorthodox. She'll either sue me or thank me."

"Thanks. I owe you."

Her eyes shift to the African mask on my wall. It is carved from wood, dark, with protruding eyes. Hanging from the mask is a long skirt of raffia. Bonnie walks across the room and stands close enough to inhale the scent of the wood. She tilts her head, twitching her nose like a rabbit.

"Not a typical wall-hanging for a psychiatrist's office. Where'd you get this?"

"My strange friend? A doctor in Sierra Leone gave it to me years ago. This man in the photo," I say, pointing to a picture on my desk of Momodu Camara. "I worked in a hospital in Freetown during the civil war. I went there after Sarajevo. My friend Dr. Camara had to escape—the rebels were hunting him. He had me promise to keep it for him. Since then, I've done a little reading—the masks are usually kept in a sacred bush that only members of a secret society are allowed into."

The numbness returns, seeping through my hand like ink through water, distracting me.

Bonnie runs her hand through the raffia and then puts a strand to her nose and sniffs. "This reminds me of the cedar strips you see on Haida masks," she says.

"It's raffia. Comes from a palm tree."

"My grandfather is a Haida elder—he'd like this," she says. She glances toward me. "Many of the West Coast First Nations had secret societies, and the masks were part of all that. Another part of our culture the residential schools and missionaries tried to cleanse." She sighs and lifts both hands toward her chest. "Sorry. I don't mean to preach. We're getting the traditions back, that's what matters."

"No need to apologize."

A small medicine bowl is carved into the head of the mask. Bonnie rubs her fingers along the rim and puts them to her nose. "I'm pretty sure this brown stuff is dried blood."

I have to smile. "No one has ever noticed that before, but I'll bet you're right. I wouldn't want to advertise it around the hospital, though."

Bonnie's head swivels toward me, her eyes wide. "Yup, my grandfather would love this." She pauses and looks back to the mask. "You have interesting friends." She strokes the wooden lips, using a finger as if she's applying lip gloss. The lips are smooth and purple-black. "I think they used something simple for this," she says.

"Simple for what?" I feel my body tighten, afraid she's going to put the mask on her head.

"The colour of the lips," she says, almost to herself.

I rub my hand. "Shoe polish maybe."

It's getting late in the day, but Bonnie returns to the chair. Clearly, she has no plans to leave anytime soon. The knuckles on my right hand are white. She is so sincere, I don't have the heart to ask her to go.

"It must have been pretty bad, when you were in Africa," she says. Her eyes are steady, unblinking.

I try to hold her gaze but eventually look away. Bonnie isn't one to rush through silence.

"I was in general medicine, which in Freetown was emergency medicine. I arrived at the peak of the war. Lots of civilians with arms or legs hacked off by rebels. Many of them were kids and teenagers. I did whatever needed doing, I guess. All the expat medical people were airlifted out when things got bad in January of 1999. I hung out in Ghana for a year or so after they pulled me out, not ready to come home, and not ready to go back to a war zone either."

Bonnie leans forward. It's as if her face is the mask looking back at me—drawing me in. I'm aware of her hands moving forward, reaching toward my desk. When I finally break from her gaze, Bonnie is holding the picture of Mariama and Momodu. She studies the photo so intently her eyes squint. I miss the clicking of her pen. "Do you keep in touch with your friends?" she asks, in a voice that seems far away.

The feeling in my hand is completely gone. She wants to know about Mariama and Momodu. She waits, her expression so beguiling I'm unable to resist. I'm tempted to tell her about

Mariama's diary, but I close that door quickly—what I read there is too raw. "I don't even know if they're alive," I say. "Over the years, I've searched death certificates, the UN Refugee Agency, contacted old colleagues—nothing."

"It must have been very traumatic," she says.

I shrug. "Time heals, and it's been a long time."

"And quite an adjustment for you, shifting from emergency medicine to psychiatry."

"Harder to kill someone with just your head, I suppose." I continue to rub my hand—I wonder if Bonnie notices. With an effort, I pull the other hand away.

"Oh, I'm not so sure," she says. She clicks her pen and looks over again at the mask. "There is something about it, isn't there? Like the old Haida masks—the longer you look at them, touch them, the more you want to hear their stories." Bonnie regards me quietly, tilting her head, as if trying to see me from a different point of view. She clicks her pen and asks, "Have you been to any of the rituals they do with these masks?"

I smile again. "You're like a dog with a bone, Bonnie. No, I haven't participated in any secret rites. Strictly members only. I remember once, though, I did a clinic in a town called Kabala. The Poro members entered the town one night. It was pitch black, and all the noises of the village stopped. No men talking, dogs barking, babies crying. It was silent. And then we heard this shrieking, crying sound, like an animal dying a slow, excruciating death. I'll never forget it. We had no idea what it was. And something like heavy breathing that seemed to come through the wall. My door opened and the French nurse in the room beside mine rushed in— white as a ghost. She climbed into bed with me, sobbing. Our guard, Maliki, came in off the porch looking scared to death."

Bonnie reminds me of a child watching a Disney movie—perfectly still, feet dangling from the chair, her eyes wide. She nods her head, encouraging me to go on.

"Maliki closed the windows, blew out the candles and said, 'You look outside, you be bewitched.' Then he sat on the floor and waited."

"What happened?" she whispers. The light on my phone blinks. I'm tempted to take it—I'm not sure how much I want to tell Bonnie. I let the call go to my voice mail.

"Our house was on a narrow street across from the chief's house. Christ if the whole chanting lot of them didn't stop right in front. Sounded like they were on our porch. The drumming was so loud the walls were shaking. I was sure they were going to break down the door. It was so strange; one minute there was all this freaky noise, and then the sounds just faded away. The creepiest thing I've ever experienced. That was it for Suzanne, the French nurse. After that, she refused to be alone in a room with any of the Sierra Leonean staff. Just lost her nerve. She left the country within days of our getting back to Freetown."

Bonnie takes out a cigarette and rolls it between her fingers as if drawing the nicotine in through her skin. "That's some story. And your friend, here, on the wall? Didn't it scare you after that night? Sort of remind you of it?"

"No, not really. The mask isn't intended for me."

"Uh-huh. Who is it intended for?" she asks.

Her question triggers a memory—a dark night, sporadic gunfire. "Momodu's father. He was killed by the rebels."

Bonnie shrugs, as if to say, "Well, maybe, maybe not," then stands and walks to the mask again. "Strange, isn't it? Some fellow in a secret society carved this mask believing it should be in this sacred bush place, and it ends up …"

"Hanging on my wall."

Our eyes meet.

"John, what are you thinking? You look a little distracted."

"Oh, nothing really—I come from a superstitious family. I try to avoid taking these kinds of things too seriously."

The mask is behind her, over her shoulder—the two sets of dark eyes are staring back at me. The hairs on my neck bristle.

She walks to the door, pauses and turns toward me. Her face is drawn. "Don't underestimate what you have hanging on your wall," she says quietly. "It's not something to be taken lightly. There is a power there."

THREE

This morning, as I was leaving for the hospital, Nadia looked up from her breakfast and asked, "Do you mind if I read the diary of your friend?"

I did mind. I wanted to read it again, keep it to myself, so I tried to dissuade her. "It's not light reading, Nadia."

She held her coffee cup with two hands, her expression tentative, weighing what she wanted to say. "I don't have to."

I've never told her that Mariama and I had been lovers—and she has never asked. But if she reads the diary she will know. I don't feel guilty, exactly. I met Mariama years before I met Nadia, and we both came into our relationship wanting a clean start to everything. No one else's fingerprints on the mantel, just our own. And the rules have worked, because we share the same obsessive need—always looking forward, never looking back. But now my omission feels like a betrayal. I don't know what to say.

I was putting my coat on when she tried again. "I don't know how you do it."

"Do what?"

"Listen to those people all day when you get so little sleep."

"I don't mind. Everyone has a story. I often tell my patients that you have to go through the dark to find the light—I guess that applies to all of us."

Her eyes held mine—one of those knowing, wifely looks. And then she came to me and we held each other a long time. "I'm here for you, too, Nadia," I said, kissing her hair.

"I know," she said, but her eyes said something else.

I hesitated. "Okay. Make a pot of tea and read it. But as I said, it's heavy going. Let's talk about it when I get home."

I must find food. I take the baby off my back and hold her. Why does she not cry? My own belly hurts and my lips are dry and the smoke from the fires burns my throat. She is newborn—still she do not cry! I wonder if she knows there is evil around us—rebels roaming the streets like so many devils.

I come to Kroo Town Road in the afternoon and there is no light from the sun—only the yellow glow from the background sky. It is strange to see no one on these streets. Where did all the people go? I sit with the baby in my lap and my back to a wall. A burned out truck shields me from the road. So quiet.

The quiet have a sound to it—like breathing—like hearts beating, trying not to be heard. I know where they are! I can feel them breathin behind the closed door at my back. Women and children and babies in arms, too scared to cry. Almost too scared to breathe.

For the first time I want to cry—only inches of wood between me and the people inside. I feel so alone.

"Dr. Rourke, are you listening?"

"Sorry?"

"Have you heard anything I've just said?"

For a moment I wonder if I should bluff my way through it, try to make the most of a wasted session, but she deserves better, and I stop myself.

"I'm sorry, Carrie, to be honest, this has been a difficult week. Can we reschedule? I can shift a few things. I'll call you later today with a time. I promise you'll have my undivided attention."

She blushes. "Oh, I'm so sorry, Dr. Rourke. You don't have to work your schedule around me. I know you're extremely busy."

It wouldn't be so bad if Carrie was the first patient to accuse me of not listening, but she's the second one this week. She rises to leave.

"I have a bit of homework for you," I say, "something to think about for next time."

"I hope it doesn't involve a lot of writing," she says with a little laugh.

"The amount of writing depends on what you do. Between now and our next appointment, I want you to write a list of the things you think you need to apologize for. Then go ahead and apologize for as many things as you possibly can. Don't hold back. Buy a little diary and write them all down—every one. Can you do that for me?"

She blushes again and tilts her head. Quizzical expression—the kind that asks, "Is my psychiatrist nuts?" "Okay," she says. "I'll do my best."

Carrie closes the door so gently it sounds like another apology. Paradoxical intention isn't to be taken lightly—and it's not something to use in a session where the therapist is distracted. I walk to the window and wonder how I've let this happen.

Below me, the weak winter sun has given way to darkness, wind and rain. The street lights have come on, casting the city in a palette of yellows and greys. Everyone hurries—a young woman with a wind-inverted umbrella, employees from the bank, a clutch of students rushing for the bus.

In the midst of it all, a single, wet, hatless head bobs in the sea of umbrellas. Unlike the others, the head moves slowly, oblivious to the rain. As the throngs part around Carrie North, an empty space follows in her wake. I wonder if she feels alone, like Mariama in the smoky yellow light, with her back to a breathing wall. I wonder how far Nadia has read in her diary.

I met Nadia in January 2001, almost two years to the day after I was evacuated from Freetown. I was beginning my psychiatric residency at St. Peter's Hospital—my default position after leaving emergency medicine.

When I pulled into the hospital parking lot, a well-meaning security guard pointed out the quickest way to the Psychiatry wing: through the Emergency entrance, straight ahead. I walked through the automatic doors, and the old familiar smells hit me: antiseptic, fear, blood. A slim, dark-haired nurse caught me as I collapsed. She moved me so adeptly into a wheelchair no one took any notice.

"Wheel me outside," I said, too abruptly.

"No, you must see a doctor. I saw you losing—"

"Please," I said, catching her eye. "Just wheel me into the fresh air and I'll be fine."

She hesitated, her eyes resting on my ID tag: Dr. John Rourke, Dept. of Psychiatry. She wheeled me outside, dodging the stretchers and smokers, and parked me in a small Japanese garden. I tried to stand, feeling embarrassed. She insisted I take a seat on a bench.

"I'm fine now, thank you," I mumbled. I looked at my watch. "Damn. I'm late. Do you know another entrance to Psychiatry?"

"You must sit for a minute," she said firmly. Tall, with olive skin and flowing black hair, she was beautiful—but her beauty came with an asterisk, a reticence, something in her eyes, or in the little crow's feet that framed them, like the winsome sadness of fall leaves.

I gave in and felt myself relax. "You're from Croatia," I said.

She cocked her head to the side, the kind of look that asks, "Do I know you?" For a moment I forgot where I was and where I had to be—I felt my heart pound, the energy sudden and unexpected.

"I was in Bosnia," I said. "In Sarajevo … in the nineties."

She didn't blink, just nodded her head. "The nineties" was a sort of code—it meant we'd both been there during the Balkan war.

"I am Nadia Varga." She looked back at the hospital. "I should go back inside. This is my first day. I think you are fine now?"

"Yes, thank you, I'm fine. It's my first day too. You wouldn't know a way to Psychiatry other than through the Emerg, would you?"

She looked confused and pointed back to the Emergency doors. "But Psychiatry is not far—this is the quickest way."

She didn't know that I'd become a Pavlovian dog—trained to feel nauseated at the least hint of antiseptic. "I just need a walk in the fresh air. I'm a little jet-lagged, and I haven't slept in a while."

She shrugged. "I think you can go along the street, there is a sign at the other entrance."

"Thank you," I said, already walking away. "The air will do me good."

Over the next several months I rarely saw her. Occasionally, we bumped into each other in one of the cafeterias, but she was always with a group of nurses. We exchanged polite hellos and little waves. Her eyes were confident, but there was also a reticence behind her smile. It was something that drew me to her—a subtle mystery.

One day, I was out for a walk in the Japanese garden, enjoying the new spring colours. At first I didn't notice her—my eyes were drawn instead to the maple that had broken into a brilliant lime green.

"You like this tree too?" She was sitting on the bench, a book in her hand: *97 Ways to Make a Dog Smile.*

"*Acer shirasawanum* 'Aureum,'" I said. "Otherwise known as full moon maple. In Japan, it's the most cherished of all maples. Have you had to rescue any more doctors in distress?"

"No, most doctors do not faint at the smell of blood." She smiled and patted the bench beside her. "I like to come here. How do you know the name of this tree?"

"I have a weakness for Japanese maples," I said, sitting down. "In Japan, one of the translations of *momji*, a name given to maples, is 'baby's hands.' Parents will sometimes pass a new baby through the leaves of a maple to give it luck."

We sat quietly for a while, she looking at the maple, and me looking at her. I had never met a woman with such an expressive face. She had a way of crinkling her nose, her tongue lingering on the tip of her lips. But it was those tiny crow's feet around her eyes that drew me—little not-yet-wrinkles that spoke of something beyond the smile. There was so much to her—so much I wanted to know.

I pointed to the book in her hand and asked if she had a dog.

"I am thinking of getting one," she said. "But I live alone, and nursing shifts are twelve hours. It is just an idea." She shifted her body toward me as if to say, "Enough about dogs."

"Why did you choose psychiatry?" she asked. "You were in emergency medicine before coming here?"

I felt suddenly off balance. "How did you know?"

She tilted her head, considering me quietly for a moment. "Nurses," she said. "You must know there are no secrets in a hospital." A rolling of the eyes, as if that explained everything.

I wanted to tell her how I used to have confidence in my hands, enjoyed putting the paddles to someone's chest and telling others to stand clear. All the times in Sarajevo and Freetown, making split-second calls that saved lives, or didn't. The urgency of emergency medicine in a war zone: no wound too grotesque, no smell too ghastly, no day too long. Good work if you can get it, but it spoils you for the inane routines of shopping malls, of doing lunch, of hanging out with friends who've never lived the life.

So I told a half-truth. "Burnout," I said, using a term that is so overused it is virtually meaningless. "What about you? Where did you learn your nursing?"

"Vukovar," she said quietly. She might have said Auschwitz, or Hiroshima. And so we came to an unspoken pact—I wouldn't push her to tell her story, and she wouldn't push me to tell mine. The game of "don't ask, don't tell" would become our folie à deux, a way of protecting each other, keeping each other out of harm's way. It was an understanding for which we would pay a heavy price.

She stood suddenly. "Tell me again, please—what is the name of this beautiful tree?"

"Full moon maple."

The crow's feet relaxed and her eyes softened. "The name is as pretty as the tree. It is nice meeting you, Dr. Rourke. Now I must go."

"I hope you get that dog," I said.

She smiled and touched my hand with hers, and then she was gone. She had survived the war in Bosnia and didn't wish to speak of it. It was part of the mystery of her, a colour I didn't have a name for, and it didn't matter, because her brown eyes and sad aura awakened something in me that had been dormant for years—it was the moment I fell in love with her.

FOUR

Mariama's diary rests like an open bible beside Nadia's empty chair. The little string for marking places hangs limply, the thread-worn end touching the table. Beside it are a teapot and a cup and saucer. The cup is almost full; the rim is lined with a kiss of lipstick.

I call out, but there is no answer. Not a night for walking, but Nadia will walk in any weather if she is upset. I open the diary at the page with the string.

I do not know the date. I am tired. Today I think maybe if I take the drugs too I will make the bad feelings go away. But then I feel those fingers squeezing me. Jolie's baby. She has saved me so many times. Now even the rebels think she is special. Sometimes at night the rebel girls watch me and ask to hold the baby. It is so strange to see. Girls who kill someone the same day ask at night to hold this baby. I even hear them sing the songs their mammys sing to them when they were small. They see how quiet the baby is and it make them quiet too, like she is a good luck charm.

Jolie's baby. My hand loses its strength and I put the diary down.

I look at Nadia's chair and Finnegan's mat and feel gripped by loneliness. I put the groceries away, open a bottle of wine and turn on some music. Loud. "Adult Alternative" on the internet station. Somehow I manage to start cooking. One of her favourite meals: spaghetti with mushrooms and double-smoked bacon with a green salad. Nadia likes to perch on a bar stool and watch me cook while we talk about the day. The stool stands empty, leaving me to slice, chop and peel alone, the sounds of the knife echoing loudly. The old wooden floor creaks beneath my feet as I move about the kitchen, a lonely sound, something I notice only when she is not here.

The wine is tasteless and goes down too easily, and I'm through half a bottle when I notice the "new message" light on the phone is blinking. The number on the display has a 232 area code. Sierra Leone. I play the message: *"Dr. Rourke, an old friend awaits you. The mask want to come home. It is time."* A voice I don't recognize. Male. West African accent and probably middle-aged. I've heard the tone before. It's the voice of someone who is used to telling others how it is, and how it's going to be. A Big Man.

I pour another glass of wine and press the "play" button again. A friend of Momodu? If so, why wouldn't he identify himself? And how did he get my unlisted number? And why, after hearing nothing at all in ten years, have I received something connected to both Mariama and Momodu in the same week? A coincidence? Over the years, I've gradually come to the conclusion that they are both dead—probably dumped into unmarked graves.

I dial the number with my left hand and listen to a canned recording in the formal English of Freetown: "*The person you are dialing is either away or their phone is switched off. Try again later.*"

I hear the door open and close. I jot down the number and delete the message. Finnegan saunters into the room, shakes a couple of times and goes straight to his mat. Nadia follows, towelling her hair. She's pale. Mascara runs down her cheeks and I know it's not from the rain.

"Nadia—"

"I read it," she says, wiping her face with the towel. She glances at the food on the cutting board and shakes her head. "I'm not hungry."

"I'm sure she's no longer alive, Nadia. The way the diary ended, and where she was …"

She takes a sip of my wine, her eyes wet. "John, I know this was another time. But things, important things, happen for a reason. I know you believe this to be true. Why was this book sent to you? Why now?"

I shrug. "It was found in a church by a priest and sent to—"

She cuts me off. "What will you do with it?"

"Do with it? I don't know, put it on a bookshelf maybe. What can I do with it?"

"She loved you."

"Nadia, it was only one night."

"It was more than that to her. What was she to you, John? Do you think of her as 'just one night'?"

"Nadia—"

"No. Of course you don't. She is part of you still—I can see it in the way you look away from me now. This is not a book you can put on the shelf!" She pauses, and when she finally speaks she sounds far away. "And she is not a woman I think you can forget."

The fear in her eyes reminds me of a look I've seen before, in the eyes of the mother of a dying girl. The feeling in my gut is the same as it was then—helplessness. "Nadia, that life is behind me. You know I want what I have with you. You know I love you."

Her skin is uncharacteristically grey. "I'm sorry you made dinner. I just want a bath now." As she leaves, she turns and releases a long, sighing breath. "Her voice …" Nadia shrugs her shoulders, turns and walks slowly up the stairs.

This is where I should take the book and place it on a shelf somewhere. I should walk up those stairs and tell Nadia that I did love Mariama, and, no, I don't love her anymore, and, no, I don't want to return to that horrible place. I should tell her that of course I want to know what happened, and that I hope Mariama survived. And I should tell her that I love her, and only her. From his mat, Finnegan watches me. Even he seems to be saying, "What are you waiting for?"

I know what to do and say because it is exactly how I feel. Saying it should be as easy as breathing. But telling Nadia would take courage—something I left on the floor in Connaught Hospital years ago. There is so much more in the telling, so much I'm too gutless to even think about, let alone tell anyone—including my wife. That compartment is locked tight. I close the diary, leaving it marked at the same page. I avoid the stairs. I walk outside into the garden, strip off my clothes and turn on the shower.

This is where I'll stay, until long after the water runs cold.

FIVE

I remove a file from the bottom drawer of the filing cabinet. The label, "Sierra Leone photos," is so faint I can barely make it out. I drop the file on my desk—it has been so long. Across the room, the mask stares at me. "Open it," it seems to say. "Open the damn file!"

I have a busy day ahead—a full slate of clients and a talk to prepare. I should be reviewing the stack of charts on my desk, but the phone message of yesterday plays and replays in my mind. I'm sure it wasn't Momodu Camara, but there was something in the accent that reminded me of him. And why did he use those words—*the mask is ready to return*—as if the thing had a life of its own?

The top picture is of the three of us, Momodu, Mariama and

me. We were in Makeni. My friends look weary and ready for bed. We're on a bench on the verandah of our bungalow. They're still in their scrubs—I'm wearing a T-shirt and khaki shorts. I have the manic expression of someone fuelled by adrenaline—a three-day-old beard, wired eyes.

The town was under the control of the Revolutionary United Front, the RUF. Our medical NGO was officially neutral, and the rebels were happy to receive the free medical care. It was two weeks of sixteen-hour days, feeling strangely alive in a world of suffering. Malaria, cholera, gunshot and machete wounds, emergency obstetrics—we did whatever needed doing.

Our head was a Frenchman, Dr. Pierre Poulan. He had discouraged Momodu from coming on the mission. Dr. Momodu Camara was thought to be a high risk for kidnapping by the RUF. Unlike the expat docs, if Momodu was taken, no foreign country would risk its own by going to look for him. But Momodu insisted on coming along. While in Makeni, he spoke only English, Krio and Mende. If someone spoke to him in Temne, the language of the north, he just shook his head and pretended not to understand. I learned later that Temne and a related Kuranko dialect were Momodu's first languages. When I asked him why he hid his real identity, he shrugged. "We Africans are a complex people."

The second photo is of Momodu standing in front of one of the wooden Krio houses near Connaught Hospital in Freetown. I called them gingerbread houses—turn-of-the-century and leaning like rickety old men. Momodu is tall and muscular, and the bulk of his thighs stretches the fabric of his jeans. He poses formally, looking straight at the camera, just the hint of a smile. Although my friend was gracious to everyone, there were times when even he took on the persona of the Big Man.

Below this are two photos of Mariama sitting on my verandah in the expat compound, holding her first glass of red wine. The most beautiful lips I had ever seen. The first time I saw her lips, I wondered what it would be like to kiss them—the photo was taken just prior to finding out.

There are a few random pictures taken from the hip—beggars, child soldiers, thugs—whatever I could shoot without drawing attention to myself. Everything in Freetown in 1998 and '99 foretold disaster. The United Nations rated the country the worst place to live on the planet, and the most dangerous. Pessimism had metastasized into a dread so pervasive that seasoned war correspondents were turning down postings to Freetown. As the days went by and the rebels closed in on the city, even the beggars became pushy. "You give me! You give me!" they shouted.

A photo of Momodu standing with a waitress in a dingy chophouse. He's wearing his hospital blues and smiling broadly. A handsome man, Momodu had a way of holding on to the lighter moments with a belly laugh that was infectious. The chophouse smelled of fried fish, old beer and stale cooking oil. We went there just to get away for a while. Beggars stared through grey windows, their eyes psychotic with hunger. There was only one item on the menu, the chop of the day: fishbones, skin, bits of flesh, white rice and yellow sauce. I wondered if the cook ever threw the bones out or just recycled them in the next day's chop.

Despite the smells and the miserable food, it is the plastic napkin holders that have stuck with me to this day. Made in China, in pinks and blues. They were always empty, but they remained on the tables. I didn't know if they were a sign of hopefulness or hopelessness. I told Momodu the napkin holders were a symbol for the entire country.

"You seem quiet today, my friend," said Momodu, as we sat at the table farthest from the hungry eyes.

"Dreading the walk back," I said, thinking of the gauntlet of beggars outside the door.

Momodu glanced toward the window and nodded his head. The young waitress asked if the chop was okay, her fingers delicate on Momodu's shoulder. He patted her hand with his and smiled. Just the bill, he told her.

"It will get worse before it gets better, John," he said. "You must keep your gear together. Freetown will erupt again. When they say you go, then you go. No questions."

"And what about you, Momodu? What will you do?"

He picked at a piece of backbone, sucking the skin and cartilage. "When the time comes, the decision will be made for me, my friend," he said enigmatically. "Now we go. We have patients waiting for us, and I must guide you through all these citizens on the street."

The waitress returned with the bill. They exchanged some words in Krio, smiling and touching again. He placed some leones in her hand, covering it with both of his. She, less than half his age, offered him a lingering smile.

We left the chophouse and the crowd descended upon us. Amputees, victims of the last RUF foray into Freetown, swatted each other with stumps and crutches. As they closed in on us, an old woman in rags, her eyes desperate and pleading, reached a bundle over the outstretched arms. I almost took it, but Momodu held me back. It was a baby.

"If you take it, she will run," he said.

One man took his crutch and prodded me. "You give me! You give me!" I looked to my friend and his eyes blazed with anger. He raised both arms and spoke in a booming voice. They stared at him, backing off, their eyes downcast. As Momodu slowly led me away, I glanced back at the quickly dispersing crowd.

"What did you say to them?"

"Ah, John. This war is destroying the traditional ways. Nothing is respected anymore. I just tell them to go home."

I close the file of photos and return it to the drawer. I touch the mask given to me by my charismatic friend—a man who foretold that things would get worse before they got better.

And they did, in ways I couldn't have imagined.

SIX

A bus stops in front of the restaurant window. The advertisement on the side catches my eye: a girl in a green bathing suit, something about sunscreen. Above her, the passengers seem oblivious to the world around them—expressionless faces, some reading news-papers, girls tapping on cell phones, an old man, ear squished against the window, fast asleep. It triggers a memory—children in blue and green uniforms, little girls with tightly plaited hair. A minivan—a *poda-poda*—lying on its side in the middle of the road. Blown-out windows, diesel fumes and thick black smoke.

A chair is pulled out and someone stands over me, saying my name. "John? Can I join you?" It's Bonnie, patting my shoulder. "I waved to you from the street. You seemed to be looking through me. You're pale, John. Are you okay?"

"Hi, Bonnie. Uh, why don't you pull up a seat. I think I've had too much coffee."

She drops her bag on the table, goes to the counter and orders green tea. She returns with a steaming mug and takes the seat beside me. "I'm impressed with your taste in restaurants," she says, taking in the clientele. Theresa's is the café of choice on Commercial Drive for those inclined to political posters, body piercings and tattoos with their scrambled eggs.

"My roots. I worked in a place like this to pay for medical school. I come on days off when Nadia's working. It's all a bit left-coast and sanctimonious, but I like the people." Bonnie removes her leather jacket—there is a single eagle feather embroidered on the back. "Actually, with that spiked hair of yours, you fit in pretty well yourself. Done any newspaper interviews lately?"

"I was a little heavy on the product this morning, wasn't I?" she says, patting her hair. "No interviews, although I'm thinking I'm more cut out for skanky tabloids. What do you think?"

"My imagination soars at the possibilities."

She sits facing me, waiting.

"Okay, Bonnie, you have permission to speak. What's on your mind?"

She sighs. "Thanks for seeing Carrie North again for me."

"Uh-huh. Did she tell you about what a pathetic listener I am?"

"Yes, but she also said you offered to make it up with a new session. She said, 'Imagine! A doctor as busy as Dr. Rourke apologizing to me!' And she was right—most psychiatrists would have shrugged it off, or told her she was projecting." She offers me a warm smile and pats my hand.

"I haven't been at my best lately, have I?" I try holding her gaze but can't—my eyes escape to the crowded street.

"Well, maybe not your best. Preoccupied?" she asks. "I'm not interested in hearing your confession, I know you're a private person, but if you ever want to talk …"

"An interesting choice of words, Bonnie. My older brother is in the priesthood. Perhaps there's a family trait you're picking up on." I surprise myself—I've rarely spoken about my family to anyone but Nadia.

She nods her head as if affirming something to herself. "So, there's a family trait of making oaths—your brother made one about chastity and obedience, and you've made one about doing everything you can to help the sick."

Despite the tension, I smile. Bonnie is drawing me out again. "I promised my father I would become a doctor. He was a priest himself, before he emigrated from Ireland."

She puts her cup down and stares at me. "Your dad was a priest? He was a *Catholic* priest?"

"Yes, a Catholic priest. In Ireland there really aren't any other kinds."

"And your mom?"

"A nun."

Bonnie's hand goes to her mouth so quickly she smacks her lip. She hesitates, waiting for me to say I'm kidding.

"A *Catholic* nun," I add, struggling to keep a straight face.

"Oh my goodness! What was she like?"

Another surprise. "People don't usually ask me that. She died giving birth to me."

Her eyes soften, and again I feel the warmth of her fingertips. Am I imagining it or does she seem a little more feminine today? We remain quiet for a moment, no need to fill in the spaces. "I'm sorry," she says

"That's only part of the story. I think my dad saw her death as inevitable—a curse for breaking his oath to the Church. He lived two lives, one as a priest and one as a man. When he destroyed one, he destroyed the other. The long and short of it is that he learned to take his oaths seriously."

She remains quiet—the consummate listener—and there is something about how she does it, and how it makes me feel. I'm a grown man, someone who practises psychiatry for a living, and yet it's like I'm that infant whose mother has died birthing me and Bonnie knows just what to do.

Finally, she says, "I'm glad I bumped into you today. Having tea with you isn't to be missed."

"I guess it's an interesting background for a psychiatrist."

"It's an interesting background for anyone." She rubs her finger along the rim of her cup, her eyes so intent on the contents I wonder if she is going to read the leaves for me. "Everyone knows you're a gifted psychiatrist, John. So you're going through a tough stretch—people will forgive you for that. But I think you're an emergency physician at heart. You're drawn to collisions and train wrecks. Most psychiatrists like a little more order in their day."

"Yes, and what else do the leaves tell you?"

Bonnie smiles, but her eyes seem focused beyond me. "Well, I suspect that your tolerance for disorder, or your hunger for it, is one of the reasons you're a better doctor than those other guys." She glances at her watch. "Oh, shit, I'm sorry—got to go."

She slips out of the café, her tiny form swallowed by the crowd. I linger on, buzzed on caffeine and Bonnie's words. She has a knack for taking me to places I don't usually go. She was right—being an emergency physician was easier than psychiatry. The job was simple enough: assess, mobilize and move with the adrenaline. No time to second-guess or be torn by self-doubt. Psychiatry is more about unfinished business and small steps— the job is never really done.

A waitress with two nose rings and tattoos covering her shoulders, arms and neck wipes my table, glancing meaningfully toward a couple waiting at the door. I apologize and tell them the table is all theirs.

I step into the crowd, zipping my jacket against the rain. Ahead of me a homeless man shuffles along with a shopping cart full of bottles. He's wearing a black leather Bulls cap and an oversized army-surplus camouflage coat, done in desert colours. He pushes the cart into a crosswalk against the red light. One of the bags falls onto the asphalt. Bottles roll, blocking traffic.

I'm tempted to put my head down and walk by like everyone else. A Canada Dry bottle rolls at my feet. "Hey, buddy, it's dangerous out here," I say, squatting beside him. I reach for the bottle. He smells of Listerine and mouldy socks. He's on his knees, reaching under a car for a plastic Coke bottle. Horns honk. A young man in a BMW rolls down his window, filling the street with the bass beats of hip hop.

"Bums!" he shouts at us.

"Why don't you go start a hockey riot?" I yell back.

He lifts a middle finger and his tires screech.

"Got to keep everything nice 'n' tidy," the man with the Bulls cap says to no one in particular. He places a bottle into a bag while two more fall onto the asphalt.

"Looks like that bag is broken," I say. By now the traffic light has changed, triggering a rush of pedestrians into the crosswalk. We stuff the bottles into the cart and reach the sidewalk. "You going to be okay with that load?" The crowd parts around us— we have plenty of space.

"Get these to the recycle. Keep things tidy," he repeats, not looking at me. He's younger than me, probably mid-thirties. A clump of greasy hair flutters below the brim of his cap. "Spare a quarter or smoke?" he asks, still looking away.

"You hungry?" I ask in return, noticing a wrinkled piece of cardboard in the cart: Hungry. Down on my luck. God bless.

We walk back to Theresa's and take an outdoor table. He removes his camouflage coat and hangs it over the handle of his shopping cart. He orders ham and eggs and coffee. White toast. He smothers it all in ketchup. As I leave, he pulls a cigarette butt from his pocket. Two drags are all it gives him. He butts the tiny stub against his jeans, grinding the ash slowly.

Neat and tidy. That's how the man with the ball cap and home-in-a-buggy wants his life to be. Flat. When the feelings come, drink them away. Or take a cold shower.

SEVEN

"You're rubbing your hand, John. Should you see the neurologist again?"

We're in the garden, enjoying a burst of sunshine. Finnegan is fast asleep at our feet. He snores so loudly his head shakes. Misty ribbons of steam rise up like ghosts from the slate patio. I've prepared a lunch of cheeses, smoked salmon and a baguette. Nadia is drinking Perrier, I'm having a glass of wine. Her eyes are as full of love as eyes can be.

"Nadia, you know it's always the same. A paresthesia with no known cause—we've ruled out central nervous system causes, we've run toxicology tests, ruled out inflammatory diseases." I roll my eyes—what's a little numbness anyway? "I can live with it."

We haven't spoken about Mariama's diary since the day Nadia read it. If we talk about it, we'll have to think it through, deal with the feelings, do something about it. I've rationalized that I've never met a carpenter who lives in a completely finished house—there are always windows to be trimmed out, or siding to be finished. Plumbers must have leaky taps.

Nadia tilts her head—her way of telling me she has something she's going to say and wants me to take it seriously. Lately, she has been making it difficult to keep the vault locked tight. It's as if she's growing into a new space and is giving me a choice: grow with her or be left behind.

"John, you are so good to me, and so loving, but sometimes you are too far away. I see you standing out here in the cold. You stay under that freezing shower and you're as still as the tree. It frightens me."

"We both have one, don't we? A story we're not comfortable telling." A wave of guilt washes over me. "I'm sorry, that's—"

"Unfair?" Her hands remain in her lap. "No, it is not unfair. I have a story too," she says. "We've both known that since the day in the garden." She pauses so long, I think she'll change the subject. She offers me a nervous smile. I hate seeing her this way—so vulnerable she looks like she could break. Her eyes glance up and to the side and a veil of sadness falls over her face. A hummingbird drops down from a tree, hovers inches from her head and rises back up to a feeder. Nadia takes no notice. She reminds me of someone at a train station, reading the options, fast trains, slow trains, trains going east and west. Which one to take?

"I will tell you first," she says. "It is only fair." Nadia settles back in her chair. She looks up and to the side again, looking back in time, searching for the beginning. She sighs and holds me with her brown eyes. "It was November 21, 1991. I was finishing my nursing training. I was working in the hospital in Vukovar. They, the Serbs, made a siege of the city for three months. I think you know of this?" She asks the question but doesn't wait for my answer. "Always they shelled us. The hospital was well marked, but it did not matter. The Serbs pounded and pounded. There was no place to go, and little to eat. All we had was turnips and potatoes. The shelling and gunfire lasted day and night. Every day, we waited for the Croatian army to come—for anyone to come. Maybe the UN, or the United States. Surely someone. But no one came."

She fights tears and her chin quivers. It's too much.

"I'm so sorry, Nadia. I knew it must have been hard, you don't have to tell—"

"My boyfriend's name was Goran," she interrupts, not hearing me. "Goran," she says again, as if tasting the name on her lips. "It means 'mountain dweller.' I was twenty, he was twenty-five. He was a reporter. Every day, he sent out radio reports about the siege. Every day, I nursed the wounded. Civilians. Children. Our fighters."

For an instant, I see her as an old woman telling the same story, her jaw set and her eyes wistful, the sort of eyes that seem to be permanently looking back in time. "Goran sent out a report about a street battle. It was a great victory for us—the Croats humiliated the Serbs. He described how our fighters hid in the cellars—on purpose they let the Serb tanks move in. The Serbs could not lower their gun barrels low enough to hit the Croat gunners. They destroyed the first and last tanks, trapping the ones in between. Someone described it as a killing field of tanks."

There is something in her eyes—a wildness I've never seen before. She reaches for my wineglass and stares into the bowl of red liquid, sighs again and places the glass back in front of me. "We could hear it all from the hospital. I washed and dressed wounds and changed bedpans and smoked cigarettes and waited for him to come back to me. When he returned, I couldn't calm him. He was too excited about the victory. His eyelids did not even blink—it was like he was still a witness to the killing, watching it over and over. Twice, we started to make love that night. Twice, he couldn't do it—it was as if he had spent himself on the danger.

"The next morning, he was so frightened. 'The Serbs won't forget this defeat,' he said. He said I must get out when I got the chance. Get out any way I could, with the Red Cross maybe, but get out. But I was young too, and I loved Goran. We argued. I was learning to be a nurse and was needed every day. He was one of the few reporters getting the word out. It was our time. I have never admitted this, John, but it thrilled me in a way. Do you think that is possible? That such a horrible thing can be thrilling?"

Somewhere in the distance a siren wails. "Yes," I whisper, knowing full well that such things can be thrilling. What did Bonnie call it? My *hunger for disorder*. But Nadia's question was rhetorical—she doesn't hear my answer. A cloud casts a shadow over us, and Nadia holds her arms across her breasts.

"When the Serbs took the city, they came to the hospital. Three hundred people were taken. Civilians, medical people, wounded soldiers. We knew what was going on everywhere in Bosnia, what they were doing to women, and we were so afraid. One group was offered a chance to walk out of the city. Goran's ID gave him away; he was the reporter who had too much to say—the voice. He was sent with the others, the ones who weren't paraded for the foreign press as they left the city. I knew as he turned his back I would never see him again."

"I'm sorry, Nadia. I suspected something like that, but I didn't know."

She folds her hands, her knuckles white. She looks at me, really looks at me, for the first time. "There is more, John. I was pregnant. I found this out after Goran was taken away." She pauses, her eyes remaining on mine. "I had an abortion. The only part I had left of Goran, the only piece of him, and I killed it."

I reach across the table. Her hand is cold. "Nadia—"

"I had no hope," she says. A sob rises from deep within her. She pulls her hands away, wiping her eyes with her sleeve. "None of us had any hope—I was so young. I couldn't bring a child into that. I just couldn't.

"I spent the rest of the war in Zagreb," she continues. "I registered my name with an organization that located refugees all over the world. And I waited. I heard stories of people finding loved ones in Australia and Britain. Everyone tells you to never give up hope. Then in 1993 a mass grave was found near a pig farm outside of Vukovar. Such graves were being found every-where. I knew what they would find there. It would take three more years before his remains were identified.

"There," she says, with a weak smile, "I've told you my story. I've cried for years, and it is behind me. I won't live as a bitter woman." She cuts a piece of cheese and tears off a crust of the bread. She chews listlessly, as if doing even that takes all her energy.

I drink my wine and watch her eat. She smiles. At first, I find it superficial—she can't really feel like smiling. And then it comes to me: Nadia's smile doesn't come from a place of spontaneous joy, it takes courage. It's a mask of sorts—she is like a mother who has lost a child but finds the strength to smile for the mourners at the funeral.

"What?" she asks. "You are so deep in thought."

"I'm thinking that I love you more at this moment than I ever have."

Ever so briefly, there is a wisp of fear in her eyes. "And I love you. Next it is your turn to talk. But let us enjoy the sunshine—it reminds me of home."

There is something different about her. Her colour seems higher, fuller.

"You haven't drunk anything today," I say, pouring myself another glass of wine.

Her smile cuts to my heart. "I'm pregnant."

EIGHT

It's a short day, and by noon I've seen the last. My Saturday morning at the East-End Clinic is about people wanting drugs, or wanting off drugs, or asking for refills of lost prescriptions. Bonnie and I put in a half-day every two weeks, and I love every minute of it. Some of the patients tell me of unwanted voices, or recent sexual assaults, or ask for help with a meddling social worker or a harassing landlord. They call me Dr. John and bring me little gifts—heart-shaped rocks, eagle feathers, an old Cowichan toque.

The clientele is largely First Nations, and most come to see Bonnie. Here, the woman who functions as head nurse in a hospital-based psychiatric unit morphs into a spiritual healer. She's about smudges and healing circles and putting her people in touch with long-lost relatives or getting them to join dance and drumming groups. We joke that she has more eagle feathers than I do, but I have a few more rocks.

I've discovered that Mr. Neat 'n' Tidy comes with a proper name, Art McLeod. Today, Art walked in with some nasty skin lesions that Bonnie dressed. I recorded a diagnosis of schizophrenia and wrote prescriptions for antipsychotics and antibiotics. One of the volunteers will have it filled and become Art's new buddy.

"I'm sorry for rushing off the other day," Bonnie says, as we work on the last of the charts.

"No worries, Bonnie, it was nice to see you." I throw a chart on the pile and face her. "So, what do you have planned for today?"

"I'm going to a sweat. We have a healing circle, mostly native people, but some whites come too. Everyone's welcome. John, why don't you come along?"

"You think it would do me good, don't you?"

Bonnie taps her feet together and nods her head. Her appearance today is more masculine again. Harder. "Yes, I do. No one judges. There'll be some drumming and chanting. The heat draws out the toxins, both physical and psychological."

"No masks?" I don't really mean it, but the words slip off my lips.

She smiles. "No masks. The people come for different purposes. Some do it to help them stay straight. I go because it's who I am."

"Maybe another time. I have to prepare for a talk I have coming up, and if I don't do it tonight I'll be winging the whole thing in front of a room full of people."

"I saw the poster. You're doing the after-dinner speech at the World Psychiatric Congress this weekend."

"No big deal. They want me to talk about being a physician in a war zone, with some colour about African secret societies thrown in."

"No shit. Can I come?"

I glance up, thinking she's pulling my leg. She's not. "Bonnie, you really do need a social life. I'm not getting ambitious with this talk: I just don't want to fall off the podium or otherwise embarrass Smith-Charles. He's already been in my office twice to warn me that all the big names in psychiatry will be there."

"John, they asked you precisely because you're the faculty member who's least likely to embarrass them. I've heard of some medical students actually auctioning tickets on eBay."

"No shit yourself! Well, if you're so hard up, let me give you Nadia's ticket—she's working nights this weekend."

She taps her feet and faces me squarely. "You're relaxed here, aren't you?" she says.

"I like wearing my jeans to work. And I like the people." And my hand has never bugged me here, never felt numb.

"You gravitate to the underdogs."

"I guess we both do."

"John, I'm half native."

I have to smile. "And my parents were Irish immigrants—the sort who wrote the book on being underdogs."

I mount my bike and pull onto the street. I dodge a shopping cart full of bags of empty bottles over top of which is draped a camouflage jacket, once desert tricolour, now so filthy it is uniformly grey. Mr. Neat 'n' Tidy tips his leather ball cap—the gesture of a man having a good day.

My route takes me past the milling denizens of Hastings Street and the camera-toting tourists at the head of Burrard. Along the seawall, I think about becoming a father, what it will be like to have a son or daughter to take to Stanley Park. I have no doubt that Nadia's decision to tell her story about Goran was prompted by the news of her pregnancy. It was as if she thought, "Okay, we need to grow up and put the secrets behind us."

I hadn't expected the speed or size of the changes. Her skin glows and her hair shines and her eyes have greater depth. She carries herself differently and speaks with an authority that wasn't there before, and even when she's unsure of something she has a way of denying it. It isn't to say that her cracks and vulnerabilities are gone—if anything, they, too, are more transparent. She is moving forward, creating such a wave of energy I feel rocked by her wake.

She has always been bright and easy to read, but something has changed, something that has me looking on in awe. It feels intimidating, like I'm the rookie here and she is way ahead of me. And so, when she speaks of painting the house and fixing the fence, I wonder why I didn't think of those things.

I'm ready to be a father, but I've spent so much of my life living selfishly. Until Nadia came along, my life was all about finding the edge. My father found his cliff edge—it was my mother. "She brought out the *alive* in me," he said once. I've always wondered about the irony of his words. I don't really know what happened when she died—Dad didn't do well talking about it. His eyes went grey when he described the "horrible bleeding" that led to a late C-section. She left a space he was never able to fill. My brother found his comfort in God. I found mine in long hours and bursts of adrenaline.

Ever the superstitious Irishman, my father carried his guilt like a cross to his deathbed. "John, I broke a promise with the Church—I don't want broken promises to become the curse of this family. Promise me, son, promise that you will never break an oath." And so I promised him, and I wonder if I'll be any better at keeping my promises than he was.

I reach English Bay, buffeted by the wind. A gale is forecast, and waves crash the beach. Other than a few joggers, I'm alone. I need to get home and prepare my talk for the conference tomorrow, but my mind leaks thoughts about women pulling me forward: Bonnie, Nadia, Mariama. My father always said that things come in threes. Mariama's diary. The strange phone call. Nadia's pregnancy. I wonder if they are connected.

Or maybe I'm becoming like my father—superstitious.

NINE

"I knew the worst cases by their smell: a mixture of disinfectant and rot. Untreated infections. Stale blood. I could close my eyes, but I couldn't block out the stench—it had become part of me."

The conference planning committee had asked me to describe life as a physician in a war zone; a mix of personal experience and local colour. Despite the topic, they emphasized that it was an after-dinner speech, so I should strive to keep it as light as possible. "Remember, there are non-physicians in the audience," they cautioned.

Untreated infections. Stale blood. I'm wondering if I'm laying it on a little too thick.

Seated at the head table below the dais, along with the guests of the World Psychiatric Congress and Canadian Psychiatric

Society, is our department head, Dr. Christopher Smith-Charles, and his wife, Gladys. Christopher has been fretting about my speech. He is standing for nomination as head of the international organization. Earlier in the day, he did his best to impress upon me the gravity of the event. "Rourke, you do know you represent both the department and the university? I can't say I was too thrilled to hear you were giving a talk on voodoo. For God's sake, watch what you say up there, will you?"

I prefer Nadia's advice. "John, you will be wonderful. Just smile at the head table once in a while—I want the father of our child to have a steady job." She actually straightened my tie as she said this—something she has never done before. I found it touching, and reassuring, like a child going off to school with a hug from Mom.

I probably shouldn't have brought the mask, which I've placed as a prop on a pedestal beside me. Ghastly nose, eyes and lips, and four feet of raffia skirt. The effect is that of a bizarre alter ego watching over my shoulder. One of my medical students suggested I bring it: "Dr. Rourke, the mask is brilliant! You have to bring it to your talk!" And an overzealous convention employee insisted that the house lights be dimmed, leaving only the mask and me illuminated by spotlights. At the centre of each of the tables, a candle flickers, casting a yellow light on the audience.

I'm enjoying myself—the adrenaline. I focus on a group of medical students who've been relegated to the seats at the back of the room. They seem eager, and I find myself departing from my text. It's as if a place long closed off to me opens, and the memories there stream into consciousness, unbidden. Connaught Hospital in Freetown, Sierra Leone, on January 6, 1999, the day I was evacuated. The audience fades. Emotion seeps into my voice.

"We moved among the panicking crowd—patients waited in the hallways, the courtyard breezeway, anywhere they could find a place to stand or sit or lie on the floor. Many were children and teenagers. Beaten. Bleeding. There was a young mother, the stump of one arm bandaged with a bloody rag, nursing and rocking her baby—rocking herself. Some, the lucky few, were on stretchers; the majority were sandwiched into whatever space they could find on the floor. Some were moaning. Some quiet. Others were completely still."

I become aware again of the darkened conference room. Dr. Smith-Charles's wife has her hand at her mouth. The woman beside her is nodding to me. "Go on," she seems to be saying, "I want to hear more." The room is quiet. Waiting. My breath catches, and I can hear the tension in my own voice. "The rebel forces of the Revolutionary United Front, the RUF, had advertised their assault on Freetown as 'Operation Kill Every Living Thing.' They might have called it 'Maim Every Living Thing'—I'd seen women who'd experienced multiple rapes in Bosnia, but nothing could have prepared me for what I saw that day."

I pause, so far from my prepared text I don't dare risk a glance at my department head. Christ, it's an after-dinner speech; people expect some humour with their coffee and crème brûlée—what was I thinking? *Don't stray too far ...*

Somehow I've segued into a description of the secret societies. "Secret societies are not the exception in West Africa, they are the norm ..."

Vaguely, I'm aware of several eyes shifting from me to the mask. I feel a sense of calm. I'm not altogether sure what I've been saying, but the audience looks content. Dr. Smith-Charles is nodding. He is smiling.

"Think of the role of parents in our culture. Or that of teachers, the local hockey coach, the police, church and peer groups—all of these play a part in socializing young people in Western societies. In West Africa, the secret societies are the primary means of teaching right from wrong, respect for elders, the importance of truthfulness and honesty. The senior Poro elders are as powerful as the chiefs. This is why the RUF's mistreatment of elders, women and chiefs was considered unconscionable to the local society—and why, after the war, there has been widespread acceptance in rural areas about going back to traditions."

I pause, glancing at the mask beside me. I feel so disoriented, I have no idea how I've moved on to the topic of secret societies. "This is also why those of us who practise Western medicine should be mindful of the power of traditional medicine and beliefs when working in places like West Africa. You've been a great audience. Thank you."

Even Dr. Smith-Charles and his wife put their hands together in applause. The lights come on and I breathe easier. I remember Nadia's advice and smile toward the head table. It feels good, and I wish she were here.

The master of ceremonies, a Dutch psychiatrist who gave a talk earlier in the day entitled "Designer Drugs Revisited: When Less Is More," draws some laughter when he makes a point of walking well clear of the mask on his way to the podium. "Well, I am sure there are many questions and comments, although, this being only an after-dinner speech and not a formal paper, perhaps we can keep the questions limited."

"It was more informative than most of today's formal papers, sir!" yells a French delegate from the floor. "Let there be as many questions as the audience pleases!" A few of the medical students break into applause, which triggers spontaneous chatter and shushing for quiet.

Chastised, the master of ceremonies invites anyone with a question to use the microphones on either side of the ballroom. I relax as several people approach. The first questioner, a delegate from India, asks if I myself am a Poro member. "If I was, I wouldn't tell you, would I?" I respond. Laughter. Others are interested in the prevalence of mental illness in West Africa and the role of witch doctors in contemporary African society.

By now, I'm feeling good enough to chance a quick glance in Dr. Smith-Charles's direction. He's smiling broadly. The lineup at the microphone is down to one woman. She is a psychiatrist from New York and an authority on gender issues. I'd noticed her earlier in the day—very attractive, with a head of lush curly blond hair toned down by a pair of tiny reading glasses.

She reaches for the microphone, and with her free hand she brushes her hair behind her ear. "Dr. Rourke, thank you for enlightening all of us on this topic. I'm interested in the female secret society you refer to as Sandei, or Bondo. Can you comment on the practice of female genital mutilation, which I believe is fairly common in West Africa?"

Suddenly, I feel lightheaded, aware of all the eyes in the room, hundreds of eyes, fixed on me, waiting. Nothing comes to me—my mind is a void. The room becomes quiet, expectant. I try focusing on the back—a mistake, the medical students are leaning forward, unmoving, like gargoyles on cold church ledges. My throat is dry. The silence is like a noise pushing all other thought aside.

"Well, I, uh, can say with some confidence that removal of

the, uh, clitoris as part of the initiation which they call Bundu is very common. Especially outside of Freetown." I gasp the words, each one sounding frightened and weak. Sweat stings my eyes. Someone yells, "We can't hear you!"

The conference ballroom fades and I'm somewhere else, in a darkened hallway in Connaught Hospital, with a girl on the floor, her legs opened wide. Jolie was her name, maybe fifteen, having contractions. There were filthy bandages where her hands had been. Raped. Bleeding. I see the healed clitoral scarring— she was circumcised, a Sandei woman, no different than the majority of Sierra Leonean women. I sense the blond woman backing away from the microphone, a weak smile on her face. She's given up on me.

The Dutch host stands beside me, clearing his throat. "Dr. Rourke?" I scour the podium for my notes, trying to collect myself. Every second seems an eternity. I see another woman, very beautiful, with skin the colour of rich chocolate, her tightly plaited hair, black and oily, shimmering in the evening light. We're lying together, our bodies sweaty in the cloying heat. Mariama's eyes are closed. I can see a scar, where Jolie's had been.

"Dr. Rourke?" The accent brings me back to the stage, to the room full of waiting people. Below me, Dr. Smith-Charles sits very still, his body so stiff he seems not to breathe. His wife studies her table napkin, her head bowed as if in silent prayer. Beside her, the head of the World Psychiatric Congress stirs his coffee, his hand moving in relentless circles. I look to the MC and nod—enough already. The grateful man gestures to the stunned faces and suggests another round of applause.

I'm surprised when a small crowd of well-wishers quickly gathers at the podium. Keeners, each one with something nice to say. "Wonderful talk, haven't been to Sierra Leone, but I've been to Kenya on safari. Do you plan on returning?" "Really liked how you used the mask as a metaphor. I was wondering what you think of contemporary metaphors and schizophrenia." "It's my first trip to Vancouver and I don't really know anyone. Would you care to join me for a drink?"

Finally, Dr. Smith-Charles stands before me. Christopher is an impressive figure—white hair, bushy Santa Claus eyebrows and a ruddy complexion. I feel bad for him—his eyes seem a little rheumy, as if this has all been just a bit too much. We face one another, each waiting for the other to say something. What I see in Christopher's eyes isn't what I expected—it is more caring father than harsh department head.

"Rourke, nice talk, that," he says eventually. "Seemed well-enough received, until the questions."

I shake his hand and thank him. I've let him down. I try to explain, but don't know how to start. He touches my arm, nods in a kind way and returns to the head table, where everyone is preparing to leave. Dr. Smith-Charles shakes everyone's hand, speaks in hushed tones, poised—the behaviour of a department head.

I pack my things, grateful Nadia isn't here to witness my humiliation. A gentle tap on my shoulder—Bonnie's warm, smiling face looks up from her five-foot frame. Her hug is fierce. "Careful," I say. "I just got my breath back, I don't want to lose it again." Her smile exudes so much warmth I feel embarrassed. "Was I that bad?"

"Don't worry about it, John. It looked like you got a little tired at the end, but by then everyone was ready to hit the bar, so no worries."

"You're too nice. I had a panic attack in front of two hundred people. Out of the blue."

"John, none of us have any idea what you've really been through. I admire you for just getting up there. How about a drink? There's a bar next door. They're open-minded, they'll let you in if you're with me." She grabs my arm with the strength of a football player and turns toward the door.

"Uh, Bonnie, there's a wee problem. I can't leave the mask here."

She smiles, giving me a conspiratorial wink. "You and your bizarre friend will fit in just fine where we're going."

TEN

It's a gay bar—the Mirror Image. The place is small, with a granite bar, a few booths, some tables and a dance floor. Seventies disco music, too loud; something that reminds me of John Travolta in a white suit. A strobe light projects hundreds of stars, moving right to left along walls adorned with mirrors and red textured wallpaper. I follow Bonnie to a booth and place the mask on the table against the mirrored wall. The music changes to something slow, and two women get up to dance.

"Your talk was wonderful," Bonnie says, patting my hand.

There are so many mirrors it's like being in one of those clothing store dressing rooms where you see a cascade of images of yourself. Reflections of the mask and me—hundreds of them. "No place to hide, is there?" I say.

"People who come here are happy they don't have to," she says sagely.

"Man," says the bartender, "there's drag queens and there's drag queens." He nods toward the reflection of the mask. "I like your friends."

"Where can I get my hair done like that, honey?" asks someone walking by.

Bonnie is all smiles. "See, I told you it would be cool," she says.

I order an Irish whisky, she asks for a Coke.

"I loved your talk." It's the woman from New York who asked me about female circumcision. She's with a female medical student I recognize from one of my lectures. The student smiles and throws me a little wave.

"I'm not sure I answered your question."

"Not an easy topic," she says, offering yet another supportive smile. She nods to Bonnie and returns to her table.

Perhaps for the first time all day, I feel relaxed. "Strange world, isn't it? Within an hour of feeling humiliated in front of my professional peers, I'm being accepted in a gay bar. Thanks for bringing me here."

Bonnie swirls her ice cubes and smiles. "I guess we have some catching up to do. I'll start. I'm a two-spirit woman, John. Do you know what that means?"

I've been so wrapped up in myself, this takes me completely by surprise. I've wondered if Bonnie is a lesbian, but two-spiritedness in indigenous culture can mean much more than a matter of sexual preference. "Well, I think it means you have both male and female gender traits. You see the world from both points of view."

She smiles, nodding her head. "I'm not transgendered, but it's what you might call a gender variant. Biologically, I'm a woman. And I'm attracted to women. But, yes, I also have a male perspective. It's probably more common to have two-spirited males who have a strong female side, but I am who I am. In the time before contact with whites, I would have been a warrior woman. Two-spirited people, whether biologically male or female, are often visionaries or caregivers. Medicine people of some kind."

I'm struck with the realization that Bonnie's "look" is more female than the other day at the East-End Clinic. It's as if she's always in a state of transformation. "Wouldn't you be more comfortable living in an aboriginal community?"

Bonnie looks into the mirror and seems to study the multiple images of herself. "Most two-spirited aboriginal people choose to live in the city. It's very sad, but the white and Christian influence on generations of our culture has destroyed our own people's acceptance of ourselves." She gestures around the room. "I fit in better here than on a reserve, and, no, I haven't come out at work. Bringing you here is as spontaneous as I get." She pauses and touches the lips of the mask with her finger. "Well, that was until now, anyway. I think I'm finally ready."

"Why now, Bonnie?"

She smiles. "I had a vision during a sweat a while ago. I saw myself, a two-spirit woman in traditional dress, with powerful white people, like Dr. Smith-Charles. It's time to own who I am."

I swallow the last of my whisky and motion to the bartender for another. Bonnie sits on her Coke. Her expression becomes serious. "John, when that woman asked you about female circumcision, I was like the rest of the audience, hanging on your every word. Suddenly you struggled a bit. You were away somewhere."

"Away. That's a good way of putting it." I look into the mirror, taking in the multiple images of the mask and me, each image smaller than the one before it. "One minute I'm acting the hero physician, actually enjoying myself, the guy who survived an epic stint in an African bloodbath. Then I'm trying to hide the fact that I'm having a panic attack in front of two hundred half-drunk psychiatrists."

"You were speaking so easily until that moment. It was something about female circumcision, wasn't it, a specific memory?"

"Yeah. The question triggered a flashback to my last day in Freetown. I was with a nurse, Mariama Lahai—the one whose photo is on my desk. We were kneeling on a filthy floor examining a young woman who had been brutally raped. She was full term and going into labour."

"Jesus, John. I can't imagine."

"Despite everything going on, I noticed she had been circumcised. She had a scar; it's what I saw when that woman asked me about female genital mutilation. And her eyes—Bonnie, I think I could have handled it but for her eyes—they did me in. It was horrible." Bonnie's gaze is so intense it's as if she's looking into me, trying to see it all for herself. After a moment, I continue. "I was evacuated that day. We just got in a helicopter and left."

Bonnie stares at me, her lips move, but she struggles to speak. "And the nurse? Mariama? You don't know what happened to her?"

I hesitate—I'm talking too much—the territory is foreign to me.

"What?" Bonnie asks. "What is it?"

"Something came in the mail last week. A parcel, sent to me by a Canadian peacekeeper. It contained Mariama's diary."

"Jesus! What did it say?"

"She was captured. The rebels and a group called the AFRC, rogue government soldiers who switched sides, took the hospital the day I left. It was very bad—I really don't want to talk about the things she wrote. Mariama was an attractive young woman. They were raping and butchering mindlessly. The diary entries come to an end four months later, and I have no idea what happened to her."

She stares at me incredulously. "Oh, John, I had no idea. I'm so sorry."

"She was like you in a way."

Bonnie tilts her head and squints, as if to help her see my meaning. "Like me?"

"Powerful. She had an aura of some kind, a sort of presence. When I followed her along the corridor that day, there were all these desperate people holding out their hands, asking for help—Mariama had a way of reaching out, touching them with her fingertips, reassuring them."

Her eyes darken over the rim of her glass. The music is so loud I feel the bass beats thump in my chest.

"What will you do?" she asks.

"Do? What can I do?"

"You were in love with her! You've closed yourself off from all this, haven't you? You have Mariama and Momodu's photos on your desk beside your wife's. Did Nadia read the diary?"

"Yes, she read it. She was so upset she could barely speak."

The music stops. "Oh, John ..." Bonnie is staring at the mask.

Without the pulsing beat of the music, it has stopped vibrating. It sits, perfectly still, on the table between us. Bonnie's face is so rigid, I wonder if she's having a seizure. Finally, she relaxes and her head nods affirmatively. "Remember I told you my grandfather was in a Haida secret society? I know a little bit about masks, John. I don't think this was carved for tourists."

"Yes, and?"

"This mask was made for a purpose. It's meant to be used for something."

We both stare at it. "Used for what?" I whisper. The eyes draw me in, the darkness there as deep as space, like two black holes with no beginning, no end.

"This is a powerful mask," I hear Bonnie say, as if from a great distance away. "Powerful masks are either for good or for bad. I wonder what this one is for."

ELEVEN

I hail a taxi and ask the bearded driver to take me to St. Peter's Hospital. The mask rests on the seat beside me. My head is pounding.

"Do you want Emergency?" the driver asks.

"No, the main entrance will do fine."

Our eyes meet in his rear-view mirror, and I wonder if he can smell my boozy breath. A can of air freshener rests in the seat pocket behind him—he's smelled worse.

The commissionaire at the desk recognizes me. "Working late, Dr. Rourke?"

I smile, feeling awkward with the mask in my hands.

He nods, as if saying, "No need to explain—you're the psychiatrist."

I hold my breath until he's behind me. The Psychiatry wing is two floors up. I've never been here in the middle of the night—the lights seem brighter, the hopeful sayings on the waiting room walls stand out a little more: "Listen to your doctor—trust in yourself." "You can't change the beginning—endings are optional."

My office door is wide open. Music playing—something Asian sounding. I think of calling Security, but then a tiny Vietnamese woman strides out of the room pushing a cart—mops, a broom, a feather duster. "Mrs. Nguyen," her ID badge says. The cleaning lady I've never met.

I point to the desk. "My office," I say.

"All done, no problem," she smiles, her eyes on the freakish thing in my hands. The cart is as tall as she is, but she easily manoeuvres it out of my way, giving us a wider berth than she needs to.

I turn off the light and let my eyes adjust to the reflected colours of street lamps and passing headlights. I attempt to re-hang the mask on the wall, but my arms feel weak—it's as if they are unwilling to do what I'm asking of them. With a grunt I mount it and pull myself away, retreating across the room to the window. Even after all these years, there is no escaping it—the mask smells of Africa, dank and raw and vibrant.

For most of the decade I've been away from Sierra Leone, the mask has lived on my wall. Before that I'd kept it in a wooden crate, never particularly drawn to it. Initially, I found it odd that Momodu attached such importance to the thing. I dismissed his interest as superstition. The only attention I've shown the mask is to give it an occasional dusting. I've even thought of taking it down, finding the old crate in the basement and stuffing it away.

I sit on the sill, back to the windowpane, watching as the lights from the street weave across the wall and the mask; here a green, moving left to right, and there a yellow, moving right to left, and over it all a blinking red. It's as if the mask is coming alive before my eyes. My thoughts turn to questions of fate and the mysterious phone message and the women who've suddenly taken an interest in the things I can't seem to wash away.

As I look at the macabre thing on my wall, I remember the night it came into my life. It was in December of 1998, just days before we were evacuated. The tension in Freetown had everyone on edge, and on this particular night I was awakened by shouting and sporadic gunfire. I sat up, sensing another person in the room.

"Stay where you are," said a voice in the darkness. I could make out a black silhouette standing very still by the bed. The voice belonged to my friend Momodu Camara, and he was afraid. "John, I must go into the bush, I am no longer safe in Freetown. I would like to leave something in your safekeeping. It is very important to me and to my family. Will you promise to keep it?"

"Of course, Momodu, but—"

"And will you promise to return it when it is time?"

I hesitated—this would be a difficult promise to keep. "Okay, I promise, Momodu, even though I don't fully understand."

"It is a mask handed down from my grandfather to my father, and from my father to me. It is very important, John—I do not have time to explain. The rebels have murdered my father. The mask is safer with you, my friend. If we meet again, I will ask you for it. If we do not, trust the Kuranko."

I heard something being placed on the chair by my window, followed by movement toward the door.

"Momodu, wait! It's far too dangerous out there. If we evacuate, you can come with us."

"I must go, there is no time to explain. Keep your light off and stay in bed. Keep di bodi safe, my friend. Remember, trust the Kuranko." The door opened and Momodu was gone.

I had a fitful night, rattled by strange noises and bizarre dreams in which I saw a mountain and animals of some kind made of sticks and dried grass. When I woke, I sensed a presence. It was quiet—no gunfire in the distance, no yelling, just the cackling of chickens out in the yard. In the chair by the window shone two circles—the light of the rising sun streaming through the eyes of the mask.

For the first time in Sierra Leone, I felt truly afraid. I was out of my depth in a culture that seemed from another age, another world. I'd promised to return the mask if I ever had the opportunity to do so—a promise that already weighed heavily.

There was something else about that night that I hadn't expected; it was the last time I saw Momodu Camara.

I walk around to my chair and notice the light blinking on the phone—a 232 area code. *"Dr. Rourke, an old friend awaits you. The mask want to come home. It is time."* The voice is the same. And the message is identical—it's as if someone is reading from a prepared text.

I try the number. After two rings, the familiar voice repeats yet again: *"The person you are dialing is either away or their phone is switched off. Try again later."*

I feel something I've missed, a quickening. The mask

draws me, a force I can't resist. I stand before it, sensing—from a great distance and over the span of many years—chanting and drumming and a sound that is neither animal nor human. My hands, no longer my own, are drawn forward. I touch the wood and my fingers tingle—there is an energy there that feels strangely familiar. *There is a power there*, Bonnie said.

Without thinking, I do something I've never done before—I put the mask on my head.

TWELVE

She takes my hand and quietly leads me, as I imagine a geisha would do, up the stairs. She has three candles already lit, and the flames cast a wavering light as we enter the room. We come to the bed, and she turns, pulling off her top and dropping her jeans and panties to the floor. Her eyes on mine, she reaches forward and undoes the buttons of my shirt. It has started to rain, the tapping on the roof the only sound but for our breathing. I lie on my back and for a brief moment see my reflection in the skylight above me—I seem boyish and vulnerable.

She slides her body on top of mine, and again she takes my hands, one on each side of my body, stretched out, Christlike, as she brushes against me, her nipples painting long strokes against my skin. Nadia is weeping, but still she moves, and her tears fall like raindrops onto her breasts. My hardness reaches up to her, but she takes her time, lowering a wet nipple into my mouth, and then the other, and in the skylight I see her reflection, her butt arching upward and her hair falling in a long cascade about my face.

She doesn't let go of my hands. I can feel the heat of her sex moving, her wetness enveloping me like a hot glove, and then, finally, sucking me into her. Her rhythm is slow, unhurried, the movement of a lover who knows you.

But it is her hands that I feel, and her tears. It is as if she's determined to learn something new about me, and us, and she's going back to what first-time lovers do—hold hands.

We've been spooning quietly for a half-hour. Nadia has her arm draped over my chest, and her breath feels cool on my neck. My headache has gone and I feel spent and relaxed.

"How did it go tonight?" she asks finally.

Prior to coming home, I dreaded the thought of having to talk about my evening of horrors. Somehow our lovemaking—her touch—has changed that.

"The talk went well, but the question-and-answer was a disaster. I had a panic attack."

"A panic attack. You? What happened?"

"It just hit me out of the blue when I was trying to answer a question. Bonnie was there. After the talk she took me out to a club she knows. We had a few drinks—or I did anyway. I think it's called the Mirror Image, a gay bar—lots of mirrors."

Nadia reaches for my hand again. Squeezes it. "I think it is your turn now," she says gently.

My turn. Nadia wants to hear what mattered to me before I met her, and what matters to me now. She is like a mother bear sniffing the air for danger, and she won't rest until she *knows* what's out there. She's committed to a new way forward—no locked compartments, no "you can have your secrets if I can have mine." She holds my hand with both of hers and communicates by the strength of her grip that, tonight, there will be no letting go.

For a moment I actually think of begging off with a headache, or going outside to the shower again, following my well-worn path. In that instant, I notice the diary resting on the bedside table—a book written by someone who never had the luxury of excuses.

I know she wants to hear about Mariama, one of those impossible-to-satisfy expectations that couples have of each other: tell me about your past, I know it will hurt me, but I must know. She wants me to begin with the tough parts—leave nothing out, as she did with her story about Goran.

I owe it to her. I turn on my side to face her—for this I need to see her eyes, and she needs to see mine. I clear my throat. "It was near the end. Freetown was burning, the rebels were in the outskirts of the city, and everyone was afraid. Soldiers were changing sides; people loyal to the government were being butchered. Our area was still controlled by soldiers from a collection of West African states, mostly Nigerian soldiers fighting the rebels.

"A few of us went to Paddy's, a raunchy bar in a suburb called Aberdeen. There was a table of journalists—hardened guys who had covered Cambodia and Bosnia. One of them had asked for an assignment to Freetown. He'd only been in town a week and he was returning to London. 'This won't end well, it just won't end well,' he kept saying.

"When we returned to our compound, Mariama and Momodu and a few others were there. Everyone was worried about what was coming. Many Sierra Leoneans had already fled to Guinea."

Nadia remains quiet. Her brown eyes are soft in the candle-light, but her focus is somewhere beyond me. I wonder if she's thinking about Goran, or Mariama's diary.

"Mariama and I became lovers that night." I can feel the numbness seep into my right hand. I don't rub it, or worry about Nadia noticing. It is, I'm beginning to realize, part of my story.

"I was on the way to Connaught Hospital the next day, on the main road, close to the National Stadium. We were in a car with a Red Cross flag and red crosses scrawled on cardboard in the windows. On a normal day, the streets near the stadium were crowded, bumper-to-bumper traffic and people everywhere. This wasn't a normal day. There were no civilians. The only living creatures were jacked-up soldiers at the checkpoints, a few feral dogs and vultures feeding on corpses at the side of the road.

"Abbas, my driver, slowed the car as we rounded a corner. In front of us, in the middle of the road, there were flames and thick black smoke. A *poda-poda* full of women and school-children had taken a rocket-propelled grenade. I can still remember the sign on the back, above the blown-out windows: With God, All Things Are Possible."

The candlelight flickers behind Nadia's black hair. She lies perfectly still, her expression serene. "The vehicle, what did you call it, a *poda-poda*—what happened?" she asks.

"The schools were closed, but these children were wearing their uniforms, some in green, others in blue. Maybe so they wouldn't be mistaken for child soldiers. They were trying to break through to the Nigerian-held area in Aberdeen. But it didn't matter—I'm sure the RPG was fired by the Nigerians. There were bits and pieces of children, blues and greens mixed with red—and the women. Abbas wanted to keep going, but I screamed at him to stop the fucking car.

"I got out and walked toward the wreck, Abbas yelling at me every step of the way. It was already stinking hot, and the closer we came to the burning vehicle the hotter it got. A mother and a little girl were the only ones alive—both critical. Little pink bubbles came out of a hole in the girl's chest whenever she exhaled. The mother was missing a leg. She stared at the bloody stump in that distant, vacant way I've seen so many times.

"I looked at the little girl, and the mother's eyes followed mine. I knew what she was thinking—it was the moment of wishing she could trade places with her daughter."

Nadia's eyes are closed. Her cheeks are wet.

"Nadia, I don't need to—"

"What happened to the mother? Could you help her?" She uses a corner of the bedsheet to wipe her eyes.

"We heard yelling from up the road. It was getting louder. Closer. The girl struggled to breathe—the bubbles were getting smaller. The mother's eyes stayed locked on her daughter. She didn't want to lose sight of her for a second.

"I knew the mother had a chance. I got her into the back seat just as a jeep full of Nigerian soldiers arrived. A soldier ran up to me, took his rifle and started butting me with it—'You de go! Go! Go!' he screamed. His face was so close to mine, I could smell the dope on his breath. I told him to go fuck himself. I was sure, maybe hoping, I'd be shot. I ran back once more and heard him take off the other way.

"The little girl was lying there, her head on the asphalt. She was gone. I might have carried her to the car and put her in the back with her mother, but I didn't—somehow I couldn't bear to see the mom look into the unseeing eyes of her daughter. So I left her there. Rather than give her back to her mother, I played God. I left the little girl's body on the roadway."

Nadia shakes her head, runs the back of her hand across her cheeks. "You did what you needed to do. You were in danger. I know what I'm talking about—"

"Nadia, that's one of the memories that plays and replays at night. All those times you've asked me, 'Are you awake?' The nights when I go outside and turn on the garden shower, just standing there, unmoving, letting it run cold. It was such a hot day, the kind in the tropics when the heat and the smells choke your skin. I try, but I can't wash it away.

"That day on the roadway did something to me. It was open season on anyone connected to the government. Nine journalists were murdered—some purposefully hunted down, others executed for being in the wrong place with a camera in their hand. Sierra Leoneans even have a name for it: the second coming of the demons."

Nadia nods her head gently. I pause, wondering again if she's thinking of Goran. "There is something else, I think," she says, her eyes piercing mine. "There is more." She strokes the palm of my right hand with her fingers.

"Yes. There is more. We made it to Connaught Hospital—a nurse wheeled the mother to the O.R. The waiting area was chaos, with people banging on the metal gates, begging to be let in. I felt a tugging on my arm. It was Mariama—she insisted I follow her. The corridor was thick with people asking for help. She led me through it all, stepping over bodies, reassuring people with a few words and a touch of her fingertips.

"Mariama stopped at the end of a hallway. In front of us was a pregnant girl. She was lying on the floor beside the corpse of a boy, a child soldier. The only light came from Mariama's lantern and a window. I'll never forget the light—it was yellow and wavy, from the fires outside. The girl was fifteen or sixteen, pretty, with a lovely name—Jolie.

"She just stared into the darkness. It was as if she was in some kind of trance. Her *lappa* skirt was stained with blood. Where her two hands had been were filthy, bloody bandages. I knew without asking what her tormentors had asked: 'You want short sleeves or long?' She must have said long.

"Across from us, an old woman was sitting against the wall. She pointed her finger at me and said something I didn't understand. 'What is it? What is she saying?' I asked Mariama. It was the only time Mariama looked rattled. 'She say the girl is cursed,' she said. 'This Jolie is cursed.'

"Everything I loved about emergency medicine, the fine line between getting it done and falling off the edge, the adrenaline, the second wind, failed me then. So many times, in Sarajevo and in Freetown, I'd thrived on the rush—become addicted to it. But something was different now. It was as if I was bleeding out, and my hands had no life to them.

"I looked to where Mariama was directing her light. Jolie had been raped—she had vaginal tears and she was bleeding. She was close to full term and her baby was transverse. There was no way she was delivering vaginally. She had a weakened pulse and we were out of blood. Even in that dark moment, Mariama looked at me with that gentle smile of hers and said, 'If you get the baby out, maybe you save one of them.'"

It's the scene that gripped me, unbidden, a few hours ago in front of a room full of people. I'd told Bonnie part of the story; now I'm about to tell my wife the part that I've buried the deepest—the part that has hurt the most. I take a breath. Above us, rain patters on the roof. The candles burn down to the nubs and Nadia remains silent.

"We were out of antibiotics. No time to go looking for anesthetics. 'You be in Africa now, Dr. John,' Mariama said. 'You be in Africa now.'

"Nadia, I was so overwhelmed I … I actually considered using a decapitating wire to get the fetus out to save the mother. Can you believe it?

"Mariama touched my arm, trying to get me going. 'A lower-segment C-section, Dr. John,' she said. 'You don't need no anesthetic, you don't need no nothing, 'cause this girl and baby gonna die if you don't do something now. There be nothing to lose.'"

Nadia's eyes are wet. Her lips move, mouthing that it's okay.

"Beside us lay the body of the dead child soldier. A bottle of whisky was propped against his pocket. Mariama took it and dipped the scalpel into the bottle—then she used the whisky to clean the skin. Nadia, she even put the scalpel in my hand. I held the blade over the girl's skin, but it just hung there—I didn't have the guts to cut. I froze. I … oh, Jesus …"

"What, John? What is it?"

"When I feel my right hand go numb, I always feel this

pressure on the top. I've never been able to make sense of it. Or I've never had the courage to see the obvious. But now I know—it's Mariama—I can still feel her hand on my wrist ..."

For the first time in my telling, Nadia moves. Her hand comes to her mouth and she sighs, her head nodding slightly. The little crow's feet around her eyes stand out, and it is like she's using every ounce of strength to hold on.

"Mariama took the blade from me then. 'Let me,' she said. She made the cuts for me. She cut the abdomen, cut the uterus and held it back. 'Take the baby now, Dr. John,' she said. I put my hand through the uterine opening and found the baby's feet. When I lifted her out, she was limp. Unresponsive. A girl."

"John—"

"I didn't think she would survive. We were losing the mom. That's when I abandoned them, Nadia. My boss, Dr. Poulan, came running just after I handed the baby to Mariama. He said a helicopter was waiting. He looked at Mariama and told her he had full confidence in her ability to close a C-section. I told him I would close. I pleaded with him to give us a half-hour. Poulan refused, said the chopper wouldn't wait and I was putting the whole expat team in jeopardy. I pleaded with Mariama to come, but she wouldn't. She said, 'This is my home, and I will stay.'

"I left Mariama to sew the skin, and to try to resuscitate the baby. I left them in the heat and squalor of that hallway. I turned when I got to the end of the corridor. There she was, in the lantern light, sucking on the baby's nose and mouth and spitting the mucus on the floor. Time and again, she covered the baby's face with her mouth, blowing—it was like she was trying to will life into that tiny body. In the midst of all that dying and suffering, Mariama stayed focused on that one little baby. I think it is the most amazing act of courage I've ever seen."

Nadia's eyes find the diary on the bedside table. When she speaks, her voice is quiet and reverent. "It is the baby in the diary. The one Mariama cared for after she was captured, until the diary ends."

My hand feels warm. For the first time in days, I feel a sense of relief. Is this what closure feels like? We've been married five years, and we're finally getting to know the places we've closed off to each other. My smile broadens, and this time it feels genuine.

But Nadia, the woman who insists on living with a smile on her face, isn't smiling. Her face is twisted with pain.

I reach out to her. "What? What is it?"

"This is where you go when you are standing in the freezing cold. She has been in your mind all these years!"

"I haven't been thinking of her—I've been blocking it all out, for Christ's sake!"

"Which is even worse. If she didn't mean anything, you wouldn't have to."

"Nadia, I'm not going anywhere. I love you, and I'm happier here, now, with you than I have ever been. That story is behind me, like yours is behind you."

Her head dips, shaking quickly from side to side. "No! You do not understand! My Goran died. He was buried in a pit. They found parts of him—parts of him! Mariama's voice is alive—it is only the book that stopped. You will always wonder. The questions will drive you crazy."

"Nadia, she's dead. She wasn't the type to lose her diary—it was part of her. She didn't lose it in a church—she's dead."

Nadia does something completely unexpected then. She laughs bitterly. "I'm sorry, John, but I remember something my mother told me. She always said, 'Remember, Nadia, there is one thing about men. They know nothing about women. And the men who think they know the most? They know the least of all!'"

"Nadia—"

"John, I am pregnant. Do you know what that means? It is the most vulnerable time in a woman's life. Nothing else comes close. Why do you think that is? Because our baby means as much to me as you do—even though I haven't even met her." Nadia pauses. She takes in a shuddering breath and lets it out in a long sigh. "I will protect her, John, and I need you to be strong. Strong for the three of us."

THIRTEEN

Carrie North turns to leave. She bumps into Bonnie coming the other way. She starts to apologize—and catches herself. "Oh, dear," she says.

Bonnie is quick with a "No worries! I'm so short, I get run over several times a day."

Bonnie closes the door and places two coffees and sandwiches on my desk. "Now, that was interesting," she says. "Carrie's been in my assertiveness group for weeks and I haven't got anywhere with her. She walks out of your office and she stops in mid-apology. What'd you do?"

"High level psychiatry, Bonnie. Paradox. I prescribed the symptom—told her I wanted her to apologize for as many things as she possibly could. Keep a record and bring it in to me. Fifteen apologies the first day, ten the next. None the last five days. She said she couldn't keep it up—she was tired of apologizing. Wants to get on with her life."

Bonnie takes the plastic top off her coffee. "Now I know why I sent her to you. You should get caught not listening to your clients more often."

I shake my head and pull the lid off my own coffee. "Frankly, I still feel like a schmuck for that. Has it ever happened to you?"

"What, not listening or getting caught out by the patient?" She smiles and runs her hand through her spiked hair. "I cannot tell a lie. No, I've never had a client accuse me of not listening to them. It's what I'm paid to do—kind of like being an airline pilot: once you're in the air, deciding not to fly the plane is no longer an option."

"Thanks."

"Well, you handled it perfectly. I think she feels an apology should mean something, and, coming from you, I guess it did. Carrie even talked about it in our group."

"Get out!"

"Said you were amazing. Two of the other women asked how they could get referred to you." She takes a bite of her sandwich. Her eyes deepen as she looks at me. "I don't bring free sandwiches and coffee to just anyone. You said in your voice mail you wanted to talk. What's on your mind?"

I stand and walk to the window—I don't like my desk between us. "Speaking of breakthroughs, after I saw you the other night, Nadia and I had a long talk." I tell her the parts I held back at the Mirror Image. About Mariama's hand on mine when I held the scalpel, and how I froze and she made the cuts to Jolie's abdomen, and how all I did was lift the baby out. And I tell her about Nadia's terrible look of desperation—the kind of expression that seemed to say, "I can't compete with that woman."

"Nadia has taken sick days, something I've never seen her do. She hasn't said why, she just put in a call to her ward clerk and said she wasn't coming in. When I get home, it's the same thing—a cold pot of tea on the table by her chair, the diary face down and open at her place. She's read it more times than I have. At first, she wouldn't talk about it. Later, she said she was reading it 'because I need to understand. Something like this doesn't arrive for no reason.' She's become obsessed with it."

Bonnie remains quiet. She drinks her coffee, chews her sandwich and nods her head. Her eyes never stray from mine.

"Over the last few days, she's started asking me questions. What was Mariama like with other women? Was she from a poor family? Did she ever hurt anyone, say anything disparaging about anyone?"

Bonnie listens with such intensity, her eyes suck the words out of me. Finally, I have nothing left to say. "Well?" I ask.

"Well what, John?"

"What should I do?"

"About what?"

"About how to reassure her. How to help her believe I'm committed to her and that I'm not going anywhere."

Bonnie stands and walks to the mask on the wall. She is so short, it reminds me of a little girl looking up at a stern parent. She turns, and her expression is warm and caring. "I suspect Nadia is at home asking the same question, John. What should *she* do?"

Scrawled on the back of a hydro bill on the kitchen table is a note: "I'm out for a walk with Finnegan, left some fish to thaw in the sink. Back by 6. Love you, Nadia."

I pour a glass of Argentinian Malbec and take it to the living room. The diary is in its usual spot, open on the table beside Nadia's chair. Although I've read the entire diary a few times, every time I pick it up the now-familiar dampness and musty smell awaken my senses.

Only the baby keep me alive. Even the other girls, the ones who fight and carry guns, they come and say, "Mariama let me hold you baby." Sometimes they ask to carry her as we march through the bush. But I say no—we have taken the same long walk. If the baby go die, then I go die too.

"What part are you at?" Nadia stands at the doorway to the kitchen. Finnegan approaches me, wagging his tail, and I rub his ears.

"Where you left off. I think they're somewhere close to the city of Bo."

"John, close the book." There is something in her voice and the set of her jaw—the fear of the past few days is there, but the emotion seems coloured by something else. I recognize it from a week ago—that new-mother surety she has.

"How much do you love me?" she asks.

I don't hesitate. "With all my heart."

"Then you must go, John. Go back to Sierra Leone."

"What? Nadia, you're pregnant, we're expecting a baby. There's no way. Now you're letting this get to you."

Her eyes soften. "John, you must do this for us. Find Mariama. You'll never really rest until you find her. I've read her diary—I've read it again and again. It will haunt us forever. She is in your head at night. She is even in your hand." Nadia's eyes are dry. She sits beside me, taking my hand in hers. "And now she's in my head—I want to know too. You've never given me any reason not to trust you." She pauses, the hint of a smile. "Go and find out, and take that stupid mask with you."

"Nadia, you told me yourself—you're vulnerable. There's no way I'm—"

She shakes her head. "You forget—I have a lot of experience being vulnerable. I don't want you to hold my hand because I'm pregnant. We both need to show each other there will be no more secrets." Finnegan walks across the room. Lays his head on Nadia's knee. She rubs his ear. "Look how loyal he is. He's worried too." Her eyes find mine. She smiles again, and the bravery of it chokes me. "John, I cried when I heard the news about Goran, but I was so relieved to know the truth. It is better than not knowing, and I will not live that way again. It will be difficult, and I will probably change my mind a few times. But today … today, I know it is the right thing to do. Do it for all of us."

Part Two

FOURTEEN

The heat and humidity assault my senses. As I stumble off the Airbus, I'm struck by the darkness around me. Welcome to Freetown, the dimly lit sign says. There is no electricity outside of the airport. The terminal building and single runway are the only sources of light.

The inside of Lungi Airport hasn't changed much—jostling porters, urine-coloured lighting, a single functioning baggage carousel, exhausted passengers trying to figure out the options for getting across the estuary into Freetown: a seven-minute helicopter to Aberdeen for eighty dollars; a "speedboat" into the darkness for forty-five; a ferry that is notorious for being overcrowded. In the past few years, the helicopter has crashed and various boats have sunk. *Welcome to Freetown.* I decide to take a chance on the helicopter.

Passport control runs smoothly enough, but luggage retrieval is another story. Bags fall off the overloaded carousel. A drunken passenger yells at a porter, demanding to see someone in charge. I shove my way to the carousel and arrive just in time for my duffle. A sweaty fellow approaches and demands his "fee" for unloading the baggage. I ignore him, my eyes fixed on the carousel, watching for a wooden crate. If curious hands have opened it, I'll have a lot of explaining to do.

A porter grabs my bag, but then another man, smaller, and showing no sign of fatigue, barks something in Krio and takes it from his hand. "I am Ussef," he says confidently. "How many bags, sir?" Ussef has the physique of a bureaucrat who spends his time behind a desk.

"Just one more, a crate," I say. "Oh, here it comes."

"Uh, you do not travel light," he says, eyeing the crate. He whips it onto a cart, piles the duffle bag on top and hesitates. "What is in this box?" he asks. Written in bold letters on all four sides are labels reading "Echo-Diagnostic Equipment for the People of Sierra Leone."

"An ultrasound machine," I say, irritated that the man would make it his business. "Which way to the helicopter?"

"Stay close to Ussef, it is crazy here," he says.

My new best friend manoeuvres us to the front of the line for baggage clearance. The uniformed officer ignores the people ahead of us and checks my luggage tags. Next is another hand-luggage check—again Ussef takes us to the front of the line. "Next we go through Customs," he says, still keeping his eyes on the crate. "Do not worry, just follow Ussef."

Too embarrassed to make eye contact with any of my fellow travellers, I wonder if I should hire Ussef as a fixer for the duration of my stay. He leads me through the dim light to the Customs line and seems to make a point of picking out the inspector on the end even though one closer to us is available. He pushes the cart toward the inspector and looks at his watch—he doesn't have all night. The inspector places both hands possessively on the crate and looks me in the eye. "Your mission in Sierra Leone, sir?" he asks. His uniform cap is askew and his officious tone is comical.

"I'm a tourist," I say.

"No NGO, no sponsor?" he parries. Tourists to Sierra Leone are as rare as lions and elephants.

"No. I was here during the war. I'm visiting some friends."

He stares at the packing crate at my feet. I consider offering him some leones, but play a pretentious card instead: "One of my friends is a medical doctor. I'm bringing this as a gift to the people of Sierra Leone."

Ussef is already picking up my other bag, smiling at the Customs inspector, brother to brother.

"Welcome to Sierra Leone," the man says.

As we walk away, Ussef and I exchange glances. "Good work, Ussef, I—"

Another glut of passengers is pushing and shoving in front of a man holding a sign with the word *helicopter* on it. My heart sinks.

"No problem, no problem, give me one hundred and fifteen US dollars," says Ussef.

"I thought it was eighty."

"The price went up yesterday," he says, not blinking an eye.

I hand him the money and Ussef takes my gear and drops it at the head of the line. Yelling, "Ticket! Ticket!" he reaches toward a man who is dealing with five other people, all pushing, all yelling at once. A slip of paper and the money pass between them. I feel a tug at my arm, a money-changer with a wad of leones fanned across his fingertips. I offer him fifty US dollars. The man hands me 215,000 leones in greasy five- and ten-thousand-leone notes.

Ussef returns with what looks like a luggage tag. He boldly scrawls "#1" on the paper. He smiles, his job done. "See, you the number-one passenger, you de go first! You need a driver in Freetown?"

"What, you drive too?" I have no more queues to wait in, so I take a moment. Ussef's eyes are friendly enough, but there is something else—a familiarity or breeziness about him. He seems out of place in the noise and chaos of Lungi terminal.

"My older brother, sir. Hussein. He has reliable trans-port. In Allah We Trust Taxi Co. Take this," he says, forcing a business card into my hand. "You de call Hussein for sure. Say Ussef send you. Now di helicopter is waiting. Make sure you call Hussein!"

As the rotors gain momentum, the body of the lumbering Russian-built Mi-8 helicopter shudders so badly I wonder if the thing is going to fall to pieces. Ten years ago, we took off in an Mi-8 from the Aberdeen side, three doctors and four nurses from six countries and a crew of Ukrainian mercenaries. None of us spoke—we were still in shock from the horror unfolding below. As the helicopter lifted off, an empty vodka bottle clanked down the aisle from the cockpit. They can have their vodka, I thought at the time—they're staying.

Times have changed, in an odd sort of way. The crew is from an Eastern European country, and they wear crisp white shirts with epaulettes. They seem sober enough. We are invited to wear headsets and watch a brief video—it extols the beauty of the women and beaches of Freetown. The message is all about going forward—invest your money here, fun to be had, deals to be made.

I feel weary. The last ten days have been a jumble of preparation, explanations and self-doubt. Dr. Smith-Charles was gracious. "Take the time you need, get your affairs in order and come back ready to work," he said. I suspect he felt he had little choice in the matter; it doesn't do for the department head to have his psychiatrists succumbing to panic attacks.

Bonnie was her mystical self—trying without success to get me to "prepare" by attending a sweat lodge with her and some of her two-spirit friends. Bonnie is convinced that looking for Mariama and returning the mask are somehow part of the same journey. And it was she who convinced me to disguise the mask in a crate labelled Echo-Diagnostic Equipment. "If you don't find your friend Momodu, you can't just give a mask like that to anybody," she instructed me. "Keep it hidden until you *know* the time is right." When I asked her how I would know, she shrugged and said, "You'll know."

At the airport, Nadia and I held each other forever. She seemed strong. When we finally separated, she put her hand on her tummy and smiled. "Well, I'm at eight weeks now, and the kicking is supposed to happen between sixteen and twenty-two. But don't wait that long, John."

"I'll be back before the baby kicks," I promised.

When I turned toward the departure gates, I felt like I was walking in my sleep. Numb. Her pregnancy isn't a theoretical thing anymore.

"I'll be fine with Finnegan," she said. "Now it's your turn. Find the answers you need. Come back to me."

The ancient helicopter descends into the Aberdeen peninsula. I realize, yet again, that I have little else apart from Mariama's diary to guide me. The diary describes her journey as a captive with the RUF and then stops, *in medias res*, in a backwater I'd never heard of—Buedu. I doubt there are any detailed maps to where I'm going.

We hover, and the darkness gives way to the pale yellow lights off Lumley Beach. The pilot switches on the landing lights and the helicopter starts its shuddering descent. The woman beside me, who told me earlier she works for a Christian NGO that specializes in "sustainable water wells," grabs my arm, her eyes closed as if in prayer. The wheels touch down with a twist and a crunch that reminds me of setting a dislocated shoulder. I touch the woman's hand. "We're down," I say. "Good luck with the water wells."

Something in the seat pocket catches my eye, a book, *James and the Giant Peach*. "A little boy embarks on the fantastical journey of a lifetime," the jacket reads. I drop the book into my backpack, a light companion for Mariama's diary.

FIFTEEN

Connaught Hospital is smaller than I remembered it. Walls that haven't seen a coat of paint in years, blown light bulbs, filthy windows. The waiting room is quiet and smells of disinfectant and sweat. Today, it is three-quarters full, with patients sitting stoically on long wooden benches. They face the front with tired eyes. A few lie on the floor, fast asleep.

The hallway is gloomy, but it's not the dark place that it was. I walk to the end, stop at the barred window. The glass has been replaced. No stains, no blood on the floor, no bodies, no light from the fires of Freetown—nothing to hint at what happened here. My eyes are drawn to the wall—no old woman with sunken eyes pointing her finger toward me. Just a dirty wall.

I drift from ward to ward. Everything is so much smaller than my memory of it. It's as if the entire hospital has shrunk in size. The wards have twelve net-covered beds to a room. Nurses sit behind desks facing the beds, like old-fashioned schoolteachers. The wards are arranged around an outdoor breezeway, a place for relatives to sit and wait.

I receive puzzled looks—another curious white stranger taking photos, a slum tourist in the Third World. I sit on a plastic chair coloured by years of red dust and sun-baked sweat. I wonder if this is one of the chairs Mariama and Momodu were sitting on when I took their photo.

"Can I help you, sir?" A young nurse addresses me with the earnest expression of someone new to the profession.

"To be honest, I'm a little lost. I was here during the war. I'm looking for two colleagues, a nurse named Mariama Lahai and a physician, Dr. Momodu Camara."

She smiles. She must have been in her early teens during the war—but old enough to carry a gun. "I see. Just one minute, please, sir. I will go for Sister Clare."

Ten minutes later, she returns with an older nurse. Sister Clare is all business. She dismisses the younger woman with a curt wave.

"How di mornin?" I ask.

"I am fine," she says, using perfect English. "When were you here?"

"In the late nineties. We were evacuated in January of '99."

"Hmm, okay," she says, as if the date explains everything. She has the face of a woman who is kind by nature but who has seen too much—a statue pitted by the elements.

"I'm sorry, I don't remember you," I say.

"I was an army nurse, stationed in the Wilberforce Military Hospital. Who are you looking for, please?"

"A nurse who was here at Connaught, Mariama Lahai, and a local doctor, Momodu Camara. Mariama would be in her mid-thirties now, Camara in his forties."

Sister Clare looks away, searching her memory. Slowly, her eyes trace back to mine. "As you know, Sierra Leonean doctors have always been in short supply. I do remember that name from the war. Dr. Camara came to the Military Hospital a few times. Very well respected."

"Yes?" I smile encouragingly, but it is all I can do to keep from screaming at her to hurry up.

"I have not heard his name mentioned for all these years," she says. "I do not know. The rebels needed doctors, but if he survived I have not heard of his return. I am sorry."

Her eyes shift to the book I'm holding—a book with a worn leather cover. Slowly, her hand reaches for the wooden crucifix that hangs about her neck, her thumb rubbing the body of Jesus. Staring at the book, she says, "It was a very difficult time. The rebels and AFRC took the hospital and most of Freetown. The people stopped coming here for a while because there were no doctors to care for them."

"And the nurses?"

"You have heard of Maskita?" Again, her eyes hold mine.

The name makes me feel sick. "The field commander of the RUF," I say, no longer trusting my voice. "Why?"

"He was in Freetown," she says. "I saw him when he came to the Military Hospital." She pauses, studying me. "Maskita was a thin man with empty eyes. When he came, we hid our military uniforms and just dressed like nurses. He took whomever he wanted. I was able to escape, but many of my sisters were taken."

I can't look at her. I've read Mariama's diary so many times, I feel as though I know him. Maskita epitomized the narcissistic African rebel leader. A psychopath.

My next question won't form itself, but Sister Clare reads my thoughts. "It is quite possible that your friend was taken then. The rebels took young women as bush wives. If the girl happened to be a nurse, all the better, as far as the rebels were concerned—a nurse had many uses. You may have heard of what happened. The women were passed among the rebel fighters. Sometimes the women bore arms." She pauses, perhaps to let me say I've heard enough.

"What happened to them?" I *know* what happened to them.

Sister Clare places a hand on my arm. "Most became sickly with malaria, gonorrhea or cholera. If they were too sick, they were abandoned or beaten to death. The lucky ones were shot."

"And if they survived?"

Sister Clare's demeanour softens—no longer the officious head nurse of a few minutes ago. Her voice has the sad quality of someone telling a story that has no happy ending. "Some returned to their home villages, but not all were accepted. Our culture is not easy on women. I am ashamed to say, it was better for the rebel men who handed in their arms after the war than it was for the women whom they captured. I am sorry."

"I know that Mariama was taken," I say. "This is her diary, she wrote about her experience over the first four months. But I don't know what happened after that, or where she would have gone."

"A refugee? A few were taken in by other countries." Her tone suggests she doesn't believe it.

"I've checked the lists—she didn't leave as a refugee."

Her eyes are kind, but the good sister isn't one to soften the message. "They took so many," she says, "especially if they were pretty."

SIXTEEN

I find the little chophouse Momodu and I used to go to. There are no amputees hanging about the entrance, just a street vendor selling ball caps. To the right is a shop advertising cell phones and SIM cards—a money-changer lurks in the doorway. He clinks a handful of coins to announce the stacks of Sierra Leonean notes he will have stashed close by. To the left is Aminata's Tailor-Shop—two ancient Singer sewing machines and bolts of brightly coloured cloth stacked to the ceiling.

Inside the chophouse, things have changed. They have a menu: pizza, fried fish and an assortment of Lebanese dishes like chicken kebabs, beef kofta and tabbouleh. The walls are adorned with posters of the palm-lined boulevards of Beirut. I order the chicken and a Star beer. The little Chinese-made napkin holders are stuffed with clean napkins. Progress.

I place Mariama's diary and the photo on the greasy table-cloth between a knife and spoon. The picture is the one I had on my desk of Mariama and Momodu sitting on plastic chairs in the breezeway in Connaught Hospital. Mariama, painfully beautiful, is wearing a white uniform and one of those old-fashioned white-and-black nurse's caps. Her hair is plaited in tight rows. The ease of her posture gives no clue of the tension outside the hospital gates. In her hands is her cherished leather-bound diary.

On the night before the picture was taken, we were alone on my verandah. Armed security guards paced nervously at the compound gate as gunfire crackled in the distance. Mariama held the book on her lap, her thumb running along the spine.

"You carry that book everywhere, Mariama. What is it?" I asked.

She lowered her eyes, her fingers lightly tracing the leather cover. "This book contains my life," she said. She emphasized the verb, as Sierra Leoneans often do.

Maybe it was the light, or that I was a little bewitched, but as her finger moved I thought I saw an image in the leather, a face, neither male nor female. As a boy, I'd seen something similar on the cover of one of my father's favourite books—something about St. Francis of Assisi's writings on the virtues of poverty. "The cover ... Where did you get it, Mariama?"

She looked at me, tilting her head, at first saying nothing. Finally, she said, "A nun, Dr. John. It was a nun give me this—she said it was blessed."

"In your hands, I think it *is* blessed. It's a small book for such a big life," I said, putting my hand on hers.

"I write every day. Sometimes a little poem, but mostly it is about my work. It is not such a big life. I live like every Sierra Leonean—I work and I pray that I will have rice for tomorrow."

After Nadia read it for the first time, she went walking in the rain, took a warm bath and didn't speak for an entire day. Then she started reading it again, from the beginning. Nadia had heard Mariama's voice, and she couldn't get it out of her head. I wonder if it's because she identified with Mariama, identified with being a young woman and a nurse alone in a war zone. I've even wondered if Nadia would have had me come here if she *wasn't* pregnant.

I take a long swig of the beer and open the diary to the entry of January 7, 1999—the day after I abandoned Mariama.

I am cleanin the baby when the rebels come.

Young boys, twelve, thirteen, fourteen. White rags on their heads, eyes glassy and wild. They come holding rifles low on their hips. Ignorant boys. Some have blood dripping from their heads—blood from the cuts they make for to rub the brown-brown. They ask, you have brown-brown here? Stupid, we do not even have anesthetic and these boys are askin for brown-brown to rub in their heads.

They back off when they see Jolie lying on the floor with her belly open. It is so strange—those boys so tough with their guns and machetes but they are afraid of a woman who die givin birth.

When Dr. John go, I blow in that baby's mouth and nose so

long my lips get sore. So many need my help, but I shut them out
of my mind. I do not know why, but something make me stay.

> The mammy's eyes stare at her baby,
> Her life already gone.
> What did she do for such a curse?
> What did her family do?
> She is too young.
> What did she do for such a curse?
> Nothing. She do nothing at all.

I close Jolie's eyes and I want to close my own. I am so scared
my body is fixed to the floor. So much yellin and cryin all around
me. No one know what to do.

Dr. John, he de beg me to come with him. He have such wild
eyes when they force him to go. Before, he was always so calm—
the more people come through the door, the calmer he get. But
not today. I do not know what happened when he see Jolie on the
floor. He forget who he was.

I think how nice he treat me and I want to go too. If I go, who
will look after the babies? Who will care for the mothers? I na
nurse—nursin is what I do. Oh how I want to get up and go! But
my feet stay like roots in the floor.

When the baby cough and open her eyes she look back at
me. It is like she see me then. She already seem old, like she know
things a baby cannot know. She is not my own but I see my own
mammy in her eyes. Why do you wait? That is what she is saying.
Why do you wait?

I remember Dr. Poulan say go to the Military Hospital. What
was that man thinking? That I take a helicopter like the foreigners
and fly?

I hear screaming and gunshots from close by. The rebels must be shootin people who get in their way. I take the *lappa* off a dead girl and use it to wrap Jolie's baby on my back. Even with the screamin so loud something make me look down in the dark. Dr. John's medical bag. Thank you Jesus! That man is so nice, I know he leave that bag for me. I run from the yelling sounds, stepping over the dying and already dead. Soon that hospital will be empty. No one go come when they hear the doctors gone.

What can I do? It is like the whole world is sick and dying. The rebels hate anyone who have an education—no one is safe. Outside, Lightfoot-Boston Street glows red from the fires. Smoke fills my lungs and it is so difficult to breathe. I cannot think. On my back I carry the baby of a dead mama and have nowhere to go. By the nursing school my legs take me past bodies and burnin cars. Oh the smells—everywhere I smell death and fear. I go toward Congo Town, but soon I hear voices. Men's voices. My throat fills with a lump—young boys with rags on their heads and guns on their hips. Lord Jesus, they are like devils appearin through the smoke.

I have seen what those rebels do to women in the streets. Where can I go! Beside me is a car that is still smoking. It have a burned body inside, a man, still holdin the wheel like he is going to church. I hold the baby and climb in the back seat, prayin she will make no sound. Lord Jesus, I pray, help me now! Those boys come so close I can hear them breathing outside the door.

As I lie on the seat another smell come to my nose—the smell of Jolie's new baby, right there in front of my nose. The sweet smell of new skin that only a new baby can have. Thank you Jesus. I breathe the smells of that baby and she give me new life! Like a miracle, we see each other and a smile come to my face.

Something scrape the outside of the car, make me look up. It is a rebel boy, staring through the window—his eyes go from me to the dead man at the wheel. I hear a hard sound—I think his gun is scrapin the door. When he see the baby there is a flash in his eyes, like something from another time come back to life. Slowly his face change—he no longer look like a rebel, just a boy with a rag on his head. He look like he want to go cry.

"Dey all dead," I hear him say to the others. "Dey all dead." And then he is gone—back into the smoke he go.

> Walking for hours,
> Listening for voices in the dark.
> Smoke and death and blood on the streets,
> Freetown is dyin that night.
> Even the smoke seem sad.

Somewhere in the dark I hear Nigerian soldiers—they are on our side, but some are as bad as the rebels. In the hospital I see what they do. They shoot anybody they like, so I hide from all the men I see. I am so afraid the baby will go cry when the rebels or soldiers come close. But that little girl seem to know—she suck on my finger and stay quiet, like she know.

Bodies litter the streets. Most are civilians, shot and cut with machetes and left to rot in the heat. I hear stories from patients but nothing prepare my mind for what I see in those streets.

Everybody have their houses closed, so I tap on the window shutters. "I have baby! I have baby!" I say.

"Go away, thirty people in this house!" someone whisper through the door.

I try again at the next house. "I have baby!" I say. That baby is so calm. It is like she know not to cry so the rebels nor know where we are. But she cannot help it when she is hungry. She go cry like a little lamb. Not loud. Not screamin. Little cries just for me.

I find a house with a sign that say Mary's Tailor Shop. "*Kushe, ow di bodi*, me na nurse, you get rice?" I say, tapping on the shuttered window. An old woman open the door. "*Kushe* auntie," I say, "please, me na nurse and have baby."

Thank you, Papa God, she let me in! When they close the door behind me it is so strange—I am holding Dr. John's bag and feeling Jolie's baby squirming on my back. Many people lyin on the floor, different families, young and old. They all talk at once. Everyone have a story to tell.

One woman say her son go last week for rice and nor come back! Another say the AFRC put three families in a house and light it with kerosene. When families lock themselves in, the soldiers just burn them alive. If people come out they shoot them. "Burn you! You like di government, now you burn!"

Finally I see a woman with a baby. "I de beg you, I need you feed this baby," I say.

She is sitting against a wall, one baby asleep on her lap, another on the floor. She look at me with tired eyes—I know it is hard for mamas with no rice to have milk for their babies. "Give her to me," she say, "my breasts are full."

"She has not sucked before. Her mammy is dead," I say.

We lie on the floor and the woman I do not know takes that baby and gives her her breast. A big smile light up her face. "She has good suck," she say. "You baby could get milk from a stick, she suck so good."

"I do not know what I will do," I say.

She look at me with kind eyes. "I have two sucking babies. I cannot help you after tonight."

All the time there is fightin outside and everyone lie on the floor because of the bullets. It is night and even with the fighting close by I want to sleep.

I think about Dr. John. We are so different, Dr. John and me. I see the look on his face as he and Dr. Poulan go run to the helicopter, like his heart is about to stop. They say they go come back in a week, when the rebels are driven out of Freetown.

Dr. John was not like the rest. Some of the foreign doctors cannot drink the water we drink, or they think we have too much starch in the food, or it is too hot in the sun, or they sweat too much, or the skin on their hands peel because they wash so often with the special soap they bring. Dr. John was so different—he is not a black man, but he was so different from the whites too. Sometime I even remind him to wash his hands.

> I never have a man who love me like he do.
> He put his tongue in my ear,
> Askin to come in.
> You come in! my eyes say to him,
> You are welcome to come in!

> I never have a man who love me like he do,
> Smell my skin like he do,
> Look in my eyes like he do,
> Taste me like he do.
> I never have a man,
> Who love me like he do.

Only our women treat another woman like that, when they plait the hair of another, rubbin in palm oil, massaging the skin. In Sierra Leone the nicest thing a woman feel is havin her head in another woman's lap, the other doin her hair, making it glow so it reflect the stars in the night. To feel the comb parting each strand and feelin the heat of the sista close, her hands pullin each knot close to my head.

Dr. John is so different—he make me feel like a woman do.

When we lie on the floor I think of the good things that happen, before the rebels come.

One day we had a little girl come from Hastings way. She suffered from a bomb blast that took her eye and do damage to her arm. Dr. John was so nice to that girl and her mammy, he act more like a nurse. He know the little girl is going to lose that eye, but when he take the bandage off he make sure he was standin on the side of her good eye.

When she see him he make her smile. "How's my little *pikin?*" he say, holding her hand. She just smile and her mammy smile too. He bring his face so close she do not even know it is only one eye she see him with!

Later he do surgery to fix her arm. He tell me to make sure I go get him before she wakes up. When she open her eyes he was already there, sitting on the bed. "How's my little *pikin?*" he say again. He sit on the bedside and act so nice, I think the mammy just fall in love with him right there. That little girl forget she have only one eye, he treat her so nice.

"You must be thinkin of you man." It is the mammy beside me, her babies asleep on the floor.

"You have a man?" I ask.

"He is with the SLA, fightin in Bo," she say. "What will we do if di rebels take us?" She is staring at the window like she is tryin to see all the way to Bo. We hear terrible stories of what the rebels do.

No answer comes from my mouth. We hold each other's hand and say nothing. Sometime women know and do not need to speak the words. We know.

January 8, 1999

The tailor family give me some rice but have nothing else to give. It is still dark when I take the baby and go. We try for Kingtom Bridge, but Congo Town is no man's land. So many bodies, young and old, men, women and children. The Nigerians take any young men that are not in the army and accuse them of bein rebels. They take them to the middle of the bridge and throw them off! So many bodies float there, like the garbage that flows through Kroo Town slum in the rainy season.

Someone say there are thousands waiting in the National Stadium with no place to go. I try for go there, but the Main Road is too dangerous. I see some Nigerians coming the other way and they say keep goin, do not stop.

I go hammer on doors or shuttered windows and say, "Me na nurse! Can you help?" Some go open the door a little and say the mammy have malaria, or they have a girl who was raped. In Dr. John's bag I find pills for malaria. And I have gauze, and paracetamol for pain. Women with sucking babies smile when Jolie's baby latch on to their breasts—"Wah!" they say. "Dis baby have good suck!" Some give me rice but have no room for me to stay.

> We sleep behind some houses,
> Trying to close our ears
> To the fightin on the streets.
> Everywhere the devils walk,
> Even in sleep, I hear them creep.
> I feel sure we will die this night.
>
> We sleep behind some houses,
> So close to the latrine

It is like having shit for a pillow.
Even the smells of Freetown burnin
Are better than where I put my head.

We sleep behind some houses,
Listenin to men's voices
Whisperin in the dark,
Or screamin and shootin their guns,
Or cryin for mercy,
Or sayin, "Swit girl, you come here now."

A night when mercy is like clean air
There is none in Freetown.

It is Jolie's baby that keep me alive. I put her by my face and the same thing happen as before—the sweet baby smells make me forget the latrine behind my head. I am the first person that baby ever see and already we look at each other like old friends.

When she sleeps I think of my own mammy, dead ten years from malaria. My mammy teach me to pray to Jesus and teach me the traditional ways—Sandei ways. My mammy was a *sowei*. She tell me if I find a man I must respect him, but she say my strength will come from other women. Those rebels have no respect for the traditional ways, and that bring curses as sure as I am lyin on that ground.

January 9, 1999

On the third day I can find no women to feed the baby, but I know what the women in poor villages do. When someone give me cooked rice, I take it and add water, mixing it with my hands to make a mush. I find a ripe banana and boil it for juice. I tickle the baby's lips with my finger and when she suck I put little bits of porridge there. She open her eyes longer today. Only a few days old, but already she seem like an old soul.

In one house it is only young children, none older than eight years. Ten children, from two families, all the mammys and pappys are dead. One child is burned, and each one is hungry and afraid. I tell them to stay inside. But what will they do? They have no food and there is nothing for the baby and me. All I can do is put dressings on the girl with the burn. I give her antibiotics from Dr. John's bag, but I know she will have an infection in a few days. Her pain is so bad, but she does not complain. I tell her to go to Connaught Hospital when the fightin stop—if not she will die for sure.

When we go, I look back at these children. *Pikins* with no one to care for them. They watch us leave but they do not speak. They are like kittens with no mammy, all sitting tight, their eyes wide with fright. I know the rebels have so many children the same age, same eyes, same hearts.

I do not know which way to go. Aberdeen have the ECOMOG troops, but the way is blocked. I cannot go toward Kissy Road, I have seen too many amputees and women raped come from there. I will go up the hill to Wilberforce. I know they will take me as a nurse at the Military Hospital. It is so dangerous, but what else can I do?

I make my way up the hill, toward the fighting. It is like going into the fires of hell, but that is what I do.

"Sir, is the chop not good?"

It is the Lebanese manager of the restaurant. She wears a hijab—her wrists sport an expensive-looking watch and gold bracelets. Behind her, the young waitress, a Sierra Leonean, looks frightened, as if her job rests on my opinion of the food.

"Uh, it's very good," I say. "I'm just not hungry now." The manager is about to turn on her heel when I say, "Did you stay here during the war?"

"Sir?" She runs painted fingers along her hijab, looking confused.

"Here. In Freetown. Were you here during the war?"

"I went to Beirut," she says. "Most of the Lebanese left. Only a few stayed. Freetown was not a good place to be."

"No," I say. "It was like the fires of hell."

SEVENTEEN

The outdoor bar-restaurant is just off the beach. Ocean breezes. Expats drinking beer. Lebanese men sucking on water pipes. Plastic tables and chairs in yellows and blues. A double-leg amputee waits in a battered wheelchair, a begging cup between his stumps. He's fast asleep, his chair as close to the hotel entrance as the security guard will allow.

Along the roadway, prostitutes slink about in the darkness— scantily clad wraiths appearing and disappearing with each set of passing headlights. The ones who've been beckoned wait patiently in the restaurant with their choosers. The women twirl fingers in their hair or look into little mirrors, bored. The men eat noisily, drink beer, ignoring the women sitting beside them. One couple gets up from a table. The man, overweight and red-faced, walks toward the hotel. The girl, maybe fifteen, stumbles behind him on stilettos that are two sizes too big.

I'm on my second Star beer, missing Nadia and wondering if I've made a huge mistake. Sister Clare reminded me of her—a survivor, honest to a fault, a believer in reality therapy. I'm the only man sitting alone. The waiter asks what NGO I work for. None, I say. Mining company? No, I don't work for a mining company either. He looks doubtful. NGOs and mining companies account for ninety percent of the foreigners in the country—the rest are from the World Bank or criminals moving drugs or diamonds. I feel silly—I'm not sure myself why I'm here.

A girl waves from the street. She is a caricature: stilettos, short skirt and a top that struggles to contain her breasts. She places a hand under each breast and lifts them, like a market trader offering pieces of fruit. I look away, my eyes drawn yet again to the card Ussef put in my hand: In Allah We Trust Taxi Co. What do I need a taxi driver for? I don't even know where I'm going. Should I just get a ride to Buedu, to where the diary comes to a sudden end? The odds seem so poor. If there is a grave, it won't be marked.

I flip open my new Sierratel phone and dial the number on the card. A gravelly voice answers on the first ring. "Hussein," says the voice.

"*Kushe*, my name is John Rourke. I have your card from Ussef."

There is a pause. "Okeh."

"I'm at the Family Kingdom Hotel. I may need a driver. Can we meet?"

"When?" Hussein is clearly not a man of many words.

"How about tomorrow morning?"

"I will be there." The line goes dead.

It's 7 P.M. in Freetown, about noon in Vancouver. I dial home. There's a long delay before the first ring. I anticipate the sound of Nadia picking up, and then the "Hello, John, is that you?" I wonder what I'll say if she asks me to come home. Or how I'll respond to a voice that sounds lost. The recording comes on, the message so clear I could be next door. My own voice. *"Hello, you've reached John and Nadia. We're not home right now ..."* I tell her I love her and I'll try again in a bit. Cut off with the beep.

I feel a hand on my right shoulder. The hand lingers a moment and then the fingers graze my neck. The touch is gentle. It belongs to a young woman in her early twenties. She could be pretty, but the makeup hardens her. Her small breasts spill out of a low-cut top. Black tights. Red lips and sparkles in her purple eyeshadow. There is no twinkle in her eyes.

"What you nem?" she asks. It's more of a command than a question. Her tone reminds me of the child soldiers during the war: pushy, demanding attention. Many of the bush wives, unwanted in their home villages, ended up here in Freetown as prostitutes. The young men had AK-47s to trade for motorbikes—the girls had nothing but themselves.

"Christopher," I say on a whim. I'm tempted to add "Smith-Charles." "Where you from?"

She looks away. "Kono," she says.

"Why you don't go home?"

"I look like a farmer to you?" Her fingers linger on my shoulder. She's close enough for me to smell her bubble gum. Four men with British accents at a table full of beer stare at her from behind. One of them catches my eye and points to the girl's behind. He gestures obscenely with his beer bottle.

"Are you hungry?" I ask. Her eyes settle on the partially finished chicken on my plate. "Go ahead," I say.

She tears off a drumstick and eats noisily. Soon, her lipstick is smeared with chicken grease, but she doesn't seem to mind. I rise from my chair and she pauses, suddenly unsure. "You can finish it," I say. I pay the bill and ask the waiter to give the girl a Fanta.

"Do you want her to come to your room, sir?" he asks.

She eyes me expectantly—a young woman in a push-up bra with a drumstick touching her lips. The waiter pauses with notepad in hand, as comfortable pimping the girls as he is offering another beer.

"Just get her the Fanta."

The amputee in the wheelchair jiggles his cup with a little thrust of his pelvis. He glances from me to the girl as if to say, "You give to her, you give to me." He looks vaguely familiar, but to him I am just another *waiteman*. I hand him twenty thousand leones. I wonder if the security guard is going to put his hand out too, but he simply nods his head. "Have good sleep, sir," he says.

My room is an oven. I find a fan in the closet and struggle with the mosquito net. I lie naked under the net, willing sleep to come. The bathroom shower drips, and I can hear a television from the room next door. There is a strange squirting sound, something like *phwoosh*, from somewhere in the darkness. Fifteen minutes later, I hear it again. *Phwoosh.* I take my headlamp and walk toward the sound. Along the wall below the window is an automatic insecticide dispenser, programmed to give the room a squirt every quarter-hour. I disconnect it while holding my breath.

I pick up Mariama's diary and settle down to read it under the net with the headlamp. I'm jet-lagged and promise myself I'll read only for a few minutes. The air is so humid, the pages feel dry to my fingers. Her voice and the images she describes fill my head, and I despair at the futility of coming here. An hour turns into two, and when I finally put the book down, sleep doesn't come.

I weigh the advantages of malaria over cancer and think of the men ogling the girl in the low-cut top, waiting for her to finish the chicken. They remind me of crocodiles, waiting and watching. I think of Nadia, courageously sending me away, and how motherhood, or becoming a mother, suits her. Women have been doing this forever. How will I do?

I fall in and out of sleep, obsessing about Ussef's brother, Hussein. He had an abrupt tone. I wonder what it would be like to travel into the interior with him, away from the civilization of Freetown, toward the borders, from where the rebels came.

And what will I tell Hussein if he shows up? After all, I don't know where I'm going.

EIGHTEEN

At 9 A.M., the outdoor Royal Hall at the Family Kingdom Hotel is crowded with expats from NGOs and mining companies. On weekends, the place is a venue for wedding receptions and beauty pageants. For patrons who might not otherwise get the hint that this is a place to have fun, hundreds of disco balls hang overhead like stars. There are several gaudily painted ceramic parrots, a black-and-yellow eagle, Christmas lights in random places and artificial flower arrangements that never wilt in the tropical heat.

A sputtering, choking cough shatters the morning calm, and everyone looks toward the parking area. The racket belongs to an ancient Mercedes-Benz, so rusted and filthy with red dust I can't make out the colour. It shudders to a stop behind one of the many brand new SUVs. My heart sinks—In God We Trust Taxi Service is scrawled in yellow paint on the front and back windscreens.

The driver's door growls open and a one-armed man, his face soaked in sweat, springs into the parking lot. He takes a handkerchief, pats his dripping forehead and gives a vigorous wipe to both headlights. Like a chauffeur who has just touched up the boss's Rolls, he stands back and admires his work. He turns and spots a pretty girl sitting under the sign marked Family Kingdom Hotel: Reception. Unimpressed with his leering smile, she blows a bubble with her chewing gum and retreats to the office.

Rebuffed but undaunted, the man surveys the rest of the compound, spots me sitting alone in the restaurant and waves. His face is kindly and scraggly and brimming with confidence. He waves to me as one would to a long-lost friend.

If there is a God, I think, let this not be Ussef's brother. The man tucks his handkerchief under his stump and strides toward me.

"Ah, *ow di bodi?*" he asks, smiling.

"Di bodi fine, tenki," I say.

"You need transport? Mohamed A. Lee at your service!"

His eyes are warm and expressive; despite my misgivings about the car, I like the man. "John Rourke," I say, shaking his hand. "Are you from In Allah We Trust Taxi Company?"

"Ah, yes, *tenki.* Allah, God. *Ngewo.* All di same, eh?"

"Why is the name on the car different than the card?" I ask.

"What card?"

"The card Ussef gave me at the airport. It says, 'In Allah We Trust Taxi Co.'"

He looks puzzled, his eyes shift from the card to me and back to the card. He shrugs. "Ah, you see, I am a businessman. You cannot have Allah and God at the same time. So Allah on the card, God on the car! I have my bases covered." He smiles and asks, "Ussef? Who is Ussef?"

"Your brother. At the airport."

Mohamed's eyes move off into the distance as if searching the horizon for a glimpse of Ussef. "Ah, yes, Ussef. My brother! I am a Muslim man. Everyone is my brother." He flashes a smile of yellow teeth. Old friends.

"You're not Hussein?" I ask. A voice from long ago reminds me that nothing in Africa is as it seems.

"I am Mohamed, my friend." His expression is that of a patient schoolteacher, repeating something yet again to a very slow student.

We walk to his car, but I'm beginning to think our conversation will be a short one. Mohamed is a random taxi driver hoping to pick up a fare. I should have known—most taxi and trucking companies in Sierra Leone are named after God, Allah or the Blessed Mother in some way.

"Where you want to go? I know Freetown like nobody else!"

"I don't think your vehicle will make it," I say, taking in the bald sheen of the front tires.

"Ah, as you can see, it's a Mercedes! A 1966 220b, one of the few in all Sierra Leone. German engineering, front and back."

If it's a 1966, it must be one of the few remaining in the entire world. I try the handle on the passenger side. It doesn't move. Mohamed reaches through the rolled-down window and opens it from the inside. "She need a little grease, no problem," he says.

A big car, heavy. I wonder how he can afford the fuel. "Not Freetown," I say, "the provinces. I need someone to take me into the provinces."

He takes a breath, holds it momentarily and slowly exhales. A fare to the provinces isn't to be taken lightly. "The provinces," he says, drawing out the word. "Where in the provinces?"

I hesitate. "I'm not really sure."

"You want to go to the provinces, you need a driver, but you don't know where you're *going*?" He takes out his rag, swats at the hood a couple of times and leans against the car—the demeanour of a businessman preparing for a protracted negotiation.

I wonder why we're even discussing this. The car, big as it is, is so rusted it looks like it could collapse under his skinny frame. "I'm looking for some friends I lost during the war," I say finally.

Mohamed slips a toothpick between a couple of crooked teeth and sucks. He regards me thoughtfully, picking away, sucking and swallowing.

"Okeh, okeh, okeh," he says. "You need one part driver, one part detective. *Insha'Allah*, Mohamed's the man for the job. But I must double my price, for double the job. I think fifty American dollars a day, plus petrol."

A loud popping sound announces the arrival of a green Nissan, probably no older than a 1995. If the car has a muffler there's a hole in it.

A spiderweb crack in the Nissan's windshield obscures the driver. In Allah We Trust Taxi Co. is printed in block letters on the front and back. A man steps out, studies a piece of paper in his hand, looks directly at me and returns the paper to his pocket.

He starts toward me. When he sees Mohamed, he slows his pace.

"I am Hussein," he says. No smile. Eyes that refuse to meet mine, like two flies buzzing, refusing to land. Ignoring Mohamed, Hussein stands directly in front of me. Too close. His teeth are rotten and his breath smells of cigarettes and something oily, like kerosene.

"Your brother is …?"

"Ussef."

I look toward Mohamed, who remains perched on the hood of the Mercedes. He shrugs as if to say, "Okay, wrong brother."

Hussein waits. By now, his breath has won—I take a step back, trying to clear my head. I wonder what it would be like to drive anywhere with this man. His eyes continue to shift, never settling on mine.

"When you want to leave?" he asks.

"Leave?"

"You want to go to the provinces? When you want to leave?"

I hadn't told him I wanted to go to the provinces.

I glance again at Mohamed. He's chewing away on the tooth-pick and scratching his stump with his good hand. He watches Hussein as one might watch a snake.

Still Hussein stands before me. He reminds me of a customs inspector, officious, no time for small talk. "Uh, sorry," I say. "I've got a ride already. I won't need you, Hussein. Thanks anyway."

His face is a mask of cool neutrality, but his eyes, finding mine for the first time, betray his anger. Even now his eyes shift, but the movement is subtler, like a tick. I step back, sensing he's going to spit at me. He turns and without saying another word marches back to the green Nissan. I can see the piece of paper sticking out of his back pocket, the one he was looking at when he got out of the car, the size of a photograph.

Hussein drives away, leaving a cloud of diesel smoke hovering in his wake.

Mohamed continues to lean on the filthy Mercedes. A man with honest and expressive eyes who drives a relic on wheels that might not make it out of the parking lot. I start to laugh. Could I possibly be any farther from home?

I know what I should do—go to the Lebanese and rent a new SUV with a driver who is used to Western clients. The peace of mind would cost $150 US per day, plus gas. At 4,400 leones to the dollar, I would need a suitcase to carry the bricks of cash.

Mohamed waits, eyes on mine, sucking on a fresh toothpick. For him, a fare to the provinces is a rare opportunity—a week or two with me would net him what he'd be lucky to make in six months. I really have no idea how well Mohamed knows the rural areas outside of Freetown—many people here spend their lives never leaving the city. If we follow Mariama's diary, it will mean a journey into the backwaters that were the rebel strong-holds during the war. Areas I've never been to and know nothing about.

The eyes have it—I will go with Mohamed.

"If you can fix the door handle, and you don't mind helping me figure out where we're going, we have a deal," I say.

Mohamed rubs his stubbled chin, weighing his options. I have no doubt he's thinking he should ask for more money. Finally, he nods decisively and holds out his hand. "Okeh, no problem. Mohamed A. Lee go where di work is."

NINETEEN

Kissy Road. I'm questioning my sanity. When Mohamed isn't leaning on the horn, I hear a strange noise from the front right wheel. A death-rattle clanking that I can feel through the floor.

"Mohamed, that doesn't sound good—should we have it checked?"

"Ah, Mr. John, every wheel in Sierra Leone sound like that. No problem!"

Whenever we descend a hill of any size, he turns off the engine and coasts. "I save you petrol money, eh, Mr. John."

"You're giving me whiplash, Mohamed. I think you should keep the engine running."

"Okeh, okeh, okeh. This is Africa, Mr. John," he says,

bouncing his stump on the steering wheel. "Petrol is too expensive. This is how we drive."

Freetown is choked with slow-moving traffic. Throngs of people spill onto the streets. It's Sunday, and the Christian women stroll in their best outfits—dresses, tops and head ties done in matching colours. We drive with our windows down, but our progress is so slow there is little or no breeze to cut the stifling heat. It's the dry season, and the ditches on either side of the road are putrid with raw sewage and rotting garbage.

With every stop, I'm offered something from passersby: bananas, oranges, leones for dollars, cell phone cards, little plastic bags filled with water. "What you need? What you need?" yell the touts working the stalled traffic.

We're looking for the God Is Good Chophouse. Corporal John Lewis, the Canadian soldier who sent me Mariama's diary, has agreed to meet us on the way out of town. Mohamed says he knows the place, although he was surprised that two white guys would meet there.

Whenever there is a break between vehicles and people, Mohamed tries to make up for lost time. At the intersection of Fourah Bay Road and Kissy Road, two women with platters on their heads, one stacked high with baguettes, the other with a pyramid of bananas and oranges, appear from behind a dump truck. Mohamed blasts the horn and veers to the right, stubbornly keeping his foot on the gas. The two women swear and swivel their hips out of the way.

"Mohamed, we're in no hurry—you can slow down!"

"Yes, Mr. John, okeh, okeh," he says, making no effort to do so. Luckily for the citizens of Freetown, Mohamed doesn't like to downshift, so when he does ease off the accelerator, he lugs the engine, stalling or almost stalling the Mercedes. The honking from behind is relentless, but he takes little notice.

The streets of Freetown. Filthy. Chaotic. Crowded. Teenage girls out for strolls, many holding hands. Colourful signs: Jesus Loves Me Tailor Shop; Have Faith Pharmacy; HIV Forgives No One—Use Your Condom. Red-bereted policewomen directing traffic. Rotting banana and mango peels, plastic bags and bottles, boys using NGO-issued wheelchairs to move cases of Coke and lumber—anything, it seems, but people.

"You like music, Mr. John?" Mohamed asks, noticing my irritation. "Dolly Parton? Shania?" He reaches into the glove box and pulls out a cassette, steadies the wheel with his stump, shoves the battered piece of plastic into the player and turns up the volume.

We listen to Dolly's "Coat of Many Colors," Shania's "You're Still the One" and a nameless church choir crooning "Jesus Touch Me One More Time." The tired cassette repeats itself and Mohamed sings along. Only three songs on the tape, and my driver is content to rewind and repeat, rewind and repeat. He apologizes that he doesn't have any Celine Dion. No worries, I assure him. By the time we've made it halfway through Freetown, Jesus has touched us several times.

"You hold that book tight," he says, glancing at Mariama's diary.

"A friend's diary. She's one of the two people you're going to help me find."

I tell him about Mariama and how I'm sure, if she's alive, she hasn't been in Freetown for years.

Mohamed listens intently. "She was here, in Freetown, when the rebels come in '99?" he asks.

"Yes, Mohamed. She walked these very streets."

We go behind the houses, like rats in the dark we go. When I say me na nurse, it open the doors. Malaria, cholera, madness from fright, not sleeping, nothin to eat. I tell them to boil water, but they are afraid to show smoke from a cooking fire. If they look for food the rebels go catch them and say, "Go walk in front—take di bullets from your Nigerian friends."

None of the women want to go out and be taken as a bush wife or be raped by a gang of soldiers. But they have to go because the men get taken to fight. I hear stories of people seeking vengeance on a neighbour. They tell the Nigerians their neighbour sympathize with the rebels. The Nigerians thirst for blood so much they take the neighbours and shoot them on the spot.

Everything is worse for the women. Why do they hate the women so? Last year, when the government soldiers join the rebels, they take all the pretty girls to a place they call the container. They keep the women in the containers that come off ships, raping them, keeping them in the heat till they die or they be no good anymore. They throw the bodies in the ocean when they are done with them, like garbage.

I walk in the dark, but it is difficult to hide, there is so much light from all the fires of Freetown. Slowly I go, making my way to Wilberforce and the Military Hospital, up the hillside, avoiding the main roads. I listen for helicopters and watch for the white jeeps the foreigners drive. But no one comes. The people are too afraid to come out in the open to bury the dead. Only the dogs and vultures show themselves, so hungry and mean lookin, feedin on the bodies.

I come to a corner and do not know which way to go—everything is wrecked from fighting. "Help me sista, help me," I hear someone say. It is an old man crawlin in the ditch. I want to run, but the man look in my eye. "Help me sista," he say again. I na nurse. No way I can walk by that old man.

"*Ow de do*, Pa?" I say. "*Ow di bodi?*"

"*Di bodi fine*," he say. "A rebel hit mi back with his rifle. Di pain so bad."

I see the way the man is trying to crawl along, only his arms are moving. His legs are dead. Jesus Lord, I have nothing for this old man.

I am bending over him when a truck come upon us. Four fighters with rifles and guns with bombs on the end. Rebels. They stop and point their weapons at me. Those boys are so jacked up they have the meanest eyes I have ever seen. They are smokin ganja weed and lookin crazy. They see me and laugh.

"Heh sista, you come here now," one say.

I feel my stomach come into my mouth. Two wearin no shirts, just bullets hangin down and rags on their heads. The others wear half soldier clothes, half mufti.

"Me one of you, me na nurse, me one of you!" I say. Jesus forgive me for this lie.

The oldest one give me an evil look. "Why you here if you na nurse?"

"I come for my sista's baby," I say. "My sista is dead."

"Throw it under the truck, we nor need no cryin *pikin*," he laugh. He is serious. That man want me to just throw Jolie's baby away. I think I go run then, but I see no place to go. Just a ditch behind me with so much muck and trash. Those boys are watchin me like they want me to run.

"You go now," I say. "This pappy need my help."

The rebel in charge lose his smile. "You say you one of us. Why you help that old man?"

He does not wait for me to say anything more. He push me

aside and walk up to the old man on the ground, one hand on his gun. His face is calm like he is relaxin and reading a book. He put his gun so close, I see the old man close his eyes tight. The rebel shoot him dead, like he shoot a wild dog diggin in the trash. The rebel look at me, a smile on his face, the old man's body still shakin on the ground. I fight to breathe.

"You nor one of us sista," he say and point the gun at me. I close my eyes. Dear Jesus, I pray, take us home now. I feel Jolie's baby give me a kick—one of that baby's feet just give me a little poke like she nor want to die on that dark road. I open my eyes and look at him straight. His gun is so close I can smell it.

So I tell another lie. "Me na Maskita woman! If you hurt us, he go kill you!" I say. I hear of the evil rebel commander named Maskita, or mosquito. I know this rebel be more afraid of Maskita than the Nigerians.

The rebel tilt his head like if he look at me sideways it will help him decide. "Why you here if you Maskita's woman?" he ask.

"I tell you. I come for my sista's baby. Then I get lost hidin from the fightin. And me na nurse. I am one of you." We hear shooting just up the road and the rebels all start to fidget with their guns.

"Get in then Maskita's woman. You go see you man soon enough. He at the Military Hospital."

"I de go bury my sista first. I will come soon," I say, feelin my legs shake.

He raise his rifle and I know he will shoot me dead if I do not move quick. So I climb in the back of the truck, holdin Jolie's baby so tight she is almost part of me. One of the rebels watch me the whole time like he starvin for woman heat. He just stare and stare. The others ignore me. They look so drugged and afraid, I do not think they know their names. Jumpy as scared dogs, lookin at the burnin houses, fingers on the triggers of their guns, sometimes shootin I don't know what at—just shootin and makin crazy sounds.

Those guns make such noise I think my head will explode. An empty bullet touch my leg, hot like a burning coal, but I nor move. I think of those girls in the containers and I make myself as small as I can. I pretend not to see the rebel who keep starin at me. He make me think of the commander Maskita. What will I do when I see that man?

The farther we go up that hill, the more afraid I get. It is night-time, but the sky glows red from fires—the whole world is burning. We stop at rebel checkpoints along the way. At every stop I see bodies. The fighters have girls with them. Girl soldiers, some as stoned as the men and boys. Some just scared and empty eyed, and some nor scared at all. I think they all expectin to die soon. When I say, *"Ow di bodi"* in Krio, or *"Bu wua, bi sɛ"* in Mende, they cast their eyes aside like they do not want to see me.

My stomach feel sick when I see the sign for the Military Hospital at Wilberforce. We go by groups of women and girls standin by charcoal fires, cryin and afraid. They look so tired, like they have no sleep for days. Some have bruises and blood on their faces and faraway looks in their eyes. Rebel fighters stand around with guns—cruel smiles, sunglasses on their heads, posin like cocks before a hen.

I see him then. Sittin on the verandah—a man enjoyin his Sunday afternoon *poyo* with some officers. He have the nicest uniform, all clean, and a red beret on his head like he is dressed for a parade. I think maybe I should run. If they go shoot me and Jolie's baby it will all be over.

I feel someone grab my arm. It is the commander of the truck. "You nor want to see you man?" He is smilin. The officers stop talking and look at me. "Commander, this chicken say she you woman."

Ugly as a wasp. The beak of a mosquito. Thin as a stick. Wearin that fancy uniform. That is a man in love with himself. All the other rebels are so filthy, holes in their mufti clothes, everybody wearin something different. Maskita have such a clean uniform even his boots shine. He is wearin sunglasses on his head, the kind that reflect you back. I stand alone and scared, my *lappa* shakin like a tree in the wind.

He look at me a long time, his eyes so empty I think there is no soul in that man. Everything go quiet, like the world come to a stop. All I see are those eyes looking through me—I can feel him seeing inside my head.

"So you mi woman," he say. He is talking to me, but he have a way of wantin everyone to hear his words.

I do not answer, I am too busy prayin to Jesus. For the first time all day Jolie's baby start to cry! I know she is hungry, but that is not why she fuss. It is Maskita. He have a smile on his lips and bits of milky palm wine drippin from his pointed chin. The other commanders and young boys and women all wait in the dark—everyone look at Maskita and me and no one is sayin a word. I feel like I have no clothes, nothing to hide me from those evil eyes.

"Me na nurse," I whisper. "I go help you." I sound like a weak woman, and right away I know that is my mistake. This man love weakness like other men love sexin.

His smile get bigger then. He look at the others and they smile too. "A nurse," he say. "We can use a nurse, but we have no need for the *pikin*. Throw it away."

Some of the men laugh. I feel so sick in my stomach.

"I will not do that," I say. "You can kill me too."

Everything go quiet again. No shooting, no bombs, no birds—no sounds at all. Even the baby stop crying. Maskita is the Big Man—he will take no from no one, and not from a woman in front of his men.

He look at me for a long time, his face like a mask, as cold as ice. I feel sweat run in a little stream down my back. I look down

and see the baby's eyes, wide like a grown woman's, seein me. Her
fingers wrap around my thumb and squeeze. It is the strangest
thing, but I feel that little girl is telling me something. Even Maskita
seem weak when I look in that baby's eyes.

"Bring the two women over there, the mammy and daughter," I
hear Maskita say. They bring a girl, maybe fourteen years, and her
mammy, about thirty. The girl have her mother's beautiful face and
smooth skin. From their clothes and fine foreheads I know they
are Limba women. Proud women. Today they are afraid. I feel sick. I
know what this man will do.

A boy push the woman and girl with his gun. The mammy's
eyes are big and wet with fear. She remind me of Jolie. I remember
when Dr. John look in Jolie's eyes he change. When he see the
stumps of her arms and her torn private parts he was still okay—
still a doctor thinking about what he need to do. But when he look
in Jolie's eyes, that is when he lose his way. Now the mammy have
the same look, like she is fallin, letting go and not comin back.

Maskita is like a snake, his thin tongue on his lips as he size
up his prey. "Which one, nurse?" he say to me, loud for everyone
to hear. "Which one will have short sleeves? We see what kind of
nurse you are, eh? If you keep the *pikin*, one of these will lose an
arm, and you can stitch her up. Or you can throw the *pikin* under
the truck and they can go free, to love our soldiers with both arms."

"No, please," I say, "I de beg you, please, sir. Please do not do
this!" I feel warmth running down my legs. I stand straight so he
do not see the wet. The mammy and daughter hold each other,
sobbing, the mother whispering something to her daughter, callin
her Jemi. She keep saying, "You be okay, you be okay Jemi girl."

"Please, I de beg you! I beg you! I do what you want, I na nurse,
I can help your soldiers. Leave these women be! Let me keep di
pikin, she is newborn and have no one else. I beg you!"

"You waste my time," he say, waving his hand like I am a fly. "I do what I want with you. Now you need a good lesson." A smile return to his face. He look at one of the young rebels, a cocky boy of maybe fourteen years. "You! You be the young one's age. I let you have the first go. Mount the young one, have your fun." He say this, keeping his eyes on mine. Those eyes feel like worms moving under my skin, makin me sick. He want me to be sick, I know, a man like that want to own a woman, to get into every part and own it.

Two rebels drag the girl from the mammy and turn her on her hands and knees like a dog. The young rebel sneer at the girl and twist his cap to point back on his head. He slap the girl and laugh with the others—but something else is on his face. Fear. He pull his pants down and try to mount the girl, but he is too small. The others laugh loud and the boy get angry, slappin the girl again like it is her fault he cannot get big. The girl, Jemi, and her mammy are both cryin now and the mammy fight to pull the boy away from her daughter.

I feel the baby's hand, still holdin my thumb. Her eyes go big, like she know these men are so bad. The boy is still slapping Jemi and now I see he is getting big. He look at Maskita and nod his head, a smile coming to his face. I can take it no more.

"Stop!" I say. "I de beg you to stop! The mammy, I pick the mammy!" I am on my knees cryin. "The mammy. Let the girl go!"

The world go slow again. Everyone look at me. The girl is on her hands and knees. The mammy is beside her, so scared. Maskita is staring at me with those evil eyes. I will not forget that moment, that moment when I look at the mammy and I try to say I am sorry. I am sorry. But the words will not come. So I mouth them. I am sorry, I de beg you, forgive me!

Maskita point to a young rebel with a machete standin by the mammy. "Killerboy," he say, "use the cutlass on the mammy."

The one called Killerboy grab the mammy and lay her on the

ground. "Short sleeves or long?" he shouts. One of the rebels put her hand over a ditch. She take a deep breath and try a little smile to her daughter, but the girl cannot see—she is crying and lookin away.

"Long," the mammy say, lookin at me with a sad smile that say, "It is okay, a mammy always protect her babies."

The girl scream when the blade come down. The mammy, she just look at her hand in the ditch then close her eyes.

Maskita lift his arm and point his finger at my face. "Okay, nurse, fix her arm. You na one of us now. You na one of us."

Jesus Touch Me One More Time.

As the tune switches back to Dolly's "Coat of Many Colors," Mohamed sings along yet again, his voice soft and emotional. My driver sings with the commitment of a man who might have written the song himself. But he gives Dolly her due. "You know what she means, Mr. John?"

By now I've heard the tune so many times, I have a pretty good guess what Dolly was thinking. "I think Dolly's message is that money and clothing don't make the person," I say. "It's what's in your heart that counts."

Mohamed slaps the steering wheel with his good arm. "That's it! That's what she's getting at. *Insha'Allah*, even with no money you can have a big heart."

Mohamed is a believer.

After a few false turns in a warren of alleyways, Mohamed finds the place—a chophouse squeezed between Good God Auto Spares and the Battle Axe Ministry Evangelical Church.

I had expected to dislike Corporal John Lewis—a man's man, a guy who looks you in the eye and gets to the point. After all, he is a member of the UN-sponsored mission to train the new Sierra Leonean military. But he carries one of those leather shoulder bags—the kind that has been in fashion in Vancouver since the seventies. And he wears glasses in narrow frames worn well down on his nose. He's a nerd's nerd. He sits stiff-backed, blue beret neatly folded beneath a shoulder loop, so proper I can't imagine the man with a rifle in his hands.

"Thank you for seeing me on such short notice," I say.

"Glad to be of help." He waves to the waitress and asks for menus. She tells us there is only *plassas*—rice with sauce. We order the *plassas* and Star beer. She brings the beer, flips off the tops, places a napkin on each one and gives us a basket of short baguettes. Corporal Lewis glances across the room to Mohamed. "Your driver?" Mohamed is drinking a Coke at a corner table.

"My driver. He seems honest enough." I don't like the way Lewis arches his eyebrows.

"You're really going to travel across the country with him?"

"What did you think of the diary?" I ask.

He doesn't blink. "Rough read. And I must say, I didn't expect to meet you here. The war's been over since 2002. These people don't have phone books or street addresses. Word of mouth is the only way to find someone. Do you have a good vehicle?"

Corporal Lewis knows the answer to his question—he was waiting outside the chophouse when we arrived.

"I'm hoping for the best," I say. "So far, we've made it to the edge of Freetown. I'd rather trust the driver than worry about the vehicle."

Lewis gazes out the window. He lets out a long sigh and says, "I wish you luck. But if you're going all the way to Buedu, you really do need a good vehicle. There's nothing there except for witch doctors and voodoo—it's off the grid."

"In your note, you said a priest had given you the diary. Any chance he knows something about my friend?"

"He may have, but he died soon after he gave me the book. Malaria." He takes a swig of beer and uses his napkin to wipe his forehead. "I've spent time in the area—the Sierra Leone Army has a camp near the border. Buedu was a rebel hotbed—nothing nice happened there. Now the secret societies run the show."

I leave my *plassas* untouched. He eats all of his and wipes his plate with a baguette. Corporal Lewis's decision to look me up and send me the diary was a spontaneous act of kindness—but beyond that he has no idea how I might find Mariama. Being the straight-shooting fellow he is, he doesn't hide his skepticism about whether I will find her. And so we talk about hockey and his tour in Afghanistan and the beauty of Sierra Leonean women. He gives me his cell number and the number for his satellite phone. "Whatever you do, don't hesitate to call if you get into a jam out there," he says. His seriousness unnerves me.

As we leave, Corporal Lewis waits by his brand new white UN Land Rover. I reach through the window of the Mercedes and pull on the door handle. Stuck. Mohamed mumbles, "like this," and reaches across from the driver's side. The door springs open. I wave to Corporal Lewis—no worries, just a door.

Mohamed revs the engine and pops the clutch—too soon. We stall. He gets it on the second try and we rock forward. I wave again.

Clasped tightly in my other hand are Corporal Lewis's two phone numbers.

TWENTY

"You look at that box a lot," says Mohamed, catching me glancing into the back seat. "What is that thing?"

"Echo-diagnostic equipment."

"Yes, that is what the box say."

I detect a note of suspicion. I feel protective toward the contents of the wooden crate. When it was on my office wall, some people didn't seem to notice it at all. Others avoided looking at it, like submissive dogs refusing to make eye contact. Bonnie was different; she was captivated, acting as if she were alone in the room with it—drawn to its mysteries. My two-spirited friend was convinced that the mask on my wall was made for a purpose.

"You read English, Mohamed?"

"I ... oohwee!"

He swerves the Mercedes, narrowly missing a man pushing a monstrous cart with oversized truck tires. The cart is filled with sand. The man, bathed in shimmering sweat, breathes rhythmically, like a woman in labour.

Mohamed slaps his hand on the wheel, smiling broadly. "Driving in Africa—it not for everyone, eh, Mr. John? You need to be quick! Of course I read English, how could I be a detective for you if I do not read?"

"Alright, Mr. Detective—and again, please call me John—how would you go about finding a nurse, early to mid-thirties by now, who disappeared from Connaught Hospital in January of 1999?"

"January 6?" he asks, staring ahead.

I feel sick—it seems that January 6 is carved into the soul of every Sierra Leonean. "Yes, the day the rebels came."

Mohamed takes a new toothpick and contemplates my question. Like a golfer with a pre-shot routine, he follows the same tooth-picking sequence whenever he tackles a tough problem: steady the wheel with his stump, use his good hand to hold the toothpick, dig, make a quick sucking sound, swallow.

"Ah, I am sorry for your friend." He hesitates. "Was she pretty?"

My heart sinks yet again. "Yes, very."

"Good, now we're getting somewhere, Mr. John. I think she was not killed on that day. If they catch her, they make her a bush wife, guaranteed—so she might have lived for a short while."

She might have lived for a short while. "Well, I know she lived for a few months. In this book, her diary, she made several entries. She was captured and taken all the way to Buedu. That's when the diary stops, a few months later. It was found in a church. Mariama told me she was from the south—maybe we should start there."

"Buedu," he says, saying the word as if it tastes bad. "Mr. John, that is almost Liberia. It was the rebel stronghold, bad fightin there for many years. But I don't think we start there. Women taken by the rebels were damaged. Many families did not take the women back. If she go with di rebels all the way from Freetown, maybe she come back to a place she likes, or a place where she know the women. That mean we look everywhere along the way she go."

I put my arm out the window—even the breeze is hot. The seat is a sponge sapping my energy. Mariama's captors didn't stick to roadways—it was too dangerous. I wonder if Mohamed's optimism is more about the fare to the provinces—the longer we take, the more money he'll make. I keep seeing Corporal Lewis's arched eyebrows and the way he wiped his plate—the actions of a man who knows what he's talking about.

January 12, 1999

Maskita say I am one of them.

No I am not. I do not kill. I do not rape. I do not burn people in their houses. I have respect for the traditional ways.

I was twelve years on the day the *sowei* cut the string. I was so afraid that day. All I wear is a white *lappa* about my waist and a white head tie. My breasts are bare. I see all the women in the village and the other girls like me, everyone come to the Bondo bush under the cotton tree.

There is so much noise I cannot think. I eat the special rice they give me and listen when my mother warns me not to eat anything given by anyone but my auntie. You never know who is a witch, waiting to come inside your womb. So I drink all the herbs they give me and feel my head spin. Again and again they sing my name—

> Mariama, Mariama, why are you here, Sandineh?
> Why are you here?
> To become a woman, Sandineh …
> The butterfly's wings will fall off at dawn,
> Mariama, Mariama, you will be a woman …

All through the night the singing and dancing go on. When the light comes in the east, the *soweis* lead us down to the river to a place the men are not allowed to go. They bathe my body in the water while some sing the Sandei songs from shore. They cover me and the other girls with white paint. I feel like a leaf being carried in the river's flow, from one woman to another I go. We have been in the sacred bush for weeks preparing for what is to come. I just want to sleep on the cool dirt at my feet, but there is no sleep on this day. The river flows over my body and I feel other women touching me, singing over me, and I let myself be carried from one to another.

When they plait my hair it is with the comb my grandmother used so long ago.

> My head in the lap of another,
> Her hands working palm oil
> Into my skin and hair.
> Mariama, Mariama, why are you here, Sandineh?
> Mariama, Mariama, to become a woman.

Strong fingers making my head glow warm,
Pulling my hair so tight
I think it will come out of my head.
Oh, what a feelin this is,
Knowing others will turn their heads to see!

The butterfly's wings will fall off,
Mariama, Mariama, you will be a woman.

When they shave between my legs I know my time has come.
It is difficult to be afraid when so many women are so happy. They
say if you cry you do shame to your family. My mother is there, but
she pretends not to see me. I know she will feel my pain when the
sowei makes the cut. Over and over I pray that I will not bring her
shame. She is the mammy queen, the most respected woman for
many miles. As her daughter I cannot bring her shame.

Some women I do not know come into the hut and lift me
between them. My eyes look up to the cotton tree as they carry
me out, holding me so close I can feel their heat and sweat and
hearts beating under their breasts.

I look up and the tree glows red from the flames of the fire like
a placenta carryin blood to the branches. Now I know why they
call it the mother tree. Aaah! But those strong fingers make me
want to cry out! I turn and can see only women, so many women,
the chanting and drumming pounding in my head—everything so
loud I close my eyes.

I can feel the hands holding me up, my legs apart like a mother
about to give birth. I know this is the time the witches can come
in, so I must not fight, I must not cry. I feel a hand between my
legs and a pain like a burning branch. First one cut, then another,
burning me, my blood running free and hot between my legs like
the river carrying the leaf. The pain makes me so sick I want to

scream! But I know my mammy is watching, feeling my pain like she is birthin me again. I shut my eyes so tight it squeeze the hot tears that run like blood down my face. I do not cry out—no, I do not cry out.

Mariama, Mariama, the butterfly has flown away.
You are a Sandei woman now.

TWENTY-ONE

Kissy Road surrenders to Bai Bureh Road, the busy route that leads out of Freetown toward the provinces. Allentown, Wellington, Hastings—colonial names along the RUF's route of horror into Freetown. The first few amputation victims I saw at Connaught whispered "Bai Bureh" as if just the name spoken out loud could unleash another outburst of unspeakable slaughter.

"What's that haze up there?" I'd noticed it earlier, a reddish-orange cloud in the sky ahead of us.

"Ah, you hear of the harmattan wind? In the dry season, the dusty winds come from the deserts to the north." Mohamed picks away at his teeth, occasionally glancing toward me. "You have a wife, Mr. John?"

"Yes, her name is Nadia."

"Ah, and children?"

"One on the way," I say.

"You have a child coming here?"

"No, it's an expression. Nadia is pregnant."

His toothpick hangs on his lower lip. "Hmm. You are like an African man, Mr. John. Children are women's work, eh?"

I promised Nadia I would be home before the baby kicks, a few weeks at the most. "I don't have long, Mohamed. If we don't find my friends soon, I have to go back."

He swerves, flashing his lights at an oncoming truck. "Mr. John, Sierra Leone is not an easy place," he says. "Many things go on—you do not know. This Hussein, why did he come to get you?"

"I met his brother at the airport, a porter named Ussef. Or I thought he was a porter. What did you think of him?"

He picks away for a moment. I wonder if he's heard me.

"We have a Krio proverb, Mr. John. In English, it says, 'When you raise a leopard, you should not be vexed when he eats your goat.' I don't know how that leopard find you, but you make the right choice with Mohamed A. Lee."

Despite the heat, I feel a chill. "I don't know either," I say. Ussef had seemed nice enough, although I found it strange that he could pull me, unchallenged, to the front of so many lines.

"Mohamed, I also had a doctor friend, Momodu Camara. I think he was born in Freetown and educated in London. He returned here in the nineties. In the first week of January, he showed up in my room one night to tell me he was leaving. That was the last I saw of him."

Mohamed's toothpick seems to catch in mid-pick. "This doctor, you are sure he was born in Freetown?"

"Well, I'm pretty sure. Why?"

Mohamed stares straight ahead, as if the road suddenly deserves his full attention. Finally, he asks, "This Momodu, where were his people from?"

"I don't know, but his grandfather was from the north."

"Did he have marks on his skin, on his back?"

"You mean, like Poro markings?"

Mohamed slowly turns his head toward me. His eyes seem darker, as if the whites are gone. "What do you know of such markings?"

"I read a lot, Mohamed. And I often saw them on men and boys I treated. I know the markings are part of the Poro initiation—they signify the teeth of the bush-devil eating the boy so he can be reborn as a man. Momodu had Poro markings on his back. Why do you ask?"

Mohamed's eyes have returned to the road ahead of us. "The cloud is getting darker," he says, ignoring my question. "Too dark for a harmattan wind."

I'm distracted by a sign for a mental hospital. Last night I'd reread Mariama's entries about what happened here. There are little rickety shops with cloth sellers, pharmacies and phone stores, ditches filled with trash, uniformed schoolgirls holding hands, dust and diesel fumes. I smile at the people and they smile back. Nothing speaks of the horror Mariama experienced here.

After Maskita's men cut off the hand of Jemi's mammy, the earth start to shake from bombs. Everyone panic. Maskita say he change his mind. He tell me to leave the mammy and get in the truck with Jemi and some other soldiers. I say I cannot go until I sew the mammy's arm. Even with bombs exploding so close he look at me and he laugh. He laugh so hard the spit fall like a rope from his lips.

"She lucky I nor cut both arms," he say.

They push me and the baby and Jemi into the truck. Behind us I see Jemi's mammy sitting in her own blood, watchin us go. She waves the bloody stump like she is forgetting there is no hand attached. I scream at the women closest to her and plead with them to get some rope or a belt and tie a tourniquet above her elbow. Jemi does not look back.

Ah! I feel something is missing. The bag I have carried across Freetown, Dr. John's bag, is still sittin on the ground. I am afraid if I run they will shoot me. "My medicine bag," I say to a rebel standin by the truck. "I need my bag for nursing."

He look around—everyone is walking away. Two of the women are helping Jemi's mammy. The rebel tells me to stay in the truck and then he go get the bag for me. I think maybe he feel shame for what they do. As we are about to leave, Maskita and one of his commanders come to the truck.

"You go for a long ride nurse," he says. "If you smart you help the Revolutionary United Front. When you help the RUF, you help the people." I am happy because I see Maskita is not coming. He put his commander, Abu, in charge and tell him to take us all the way to Buedu.

Before we leave, Commander Abu ask Maskita somethin that give me a bad feeling. "She you wife commander?" he ask Maskita.

Maskita look at me a long time like he is reading a dinner menu. Slowly a smile come to his face. "She not ready yet," he say. "Maybe when you get to Masiaka Junction you call me. If she ready you call me."

The fighting is so bad we take three hours just to Bai Bureh Road. This is always a busy place—so many people, crowds like ants and no place to walk. Tonight I see no one on that road. Just rebel boys and AFRC thugs. The rebels stop near the mental hospital. I see so many bodies the ditches run red with the blood.

Commander Abu come back and yell, "Out! You stay here tonight and do as you told."

Some of the rebel soldiers are girls. I smile when I see the first one, but she laughs in my face. She is a tall girl, maybe eighteen, cold and strong like a man. Her T-shirt and soldier pants are tight to her breasts and legs. Every boy look at her with fire in his eyes. A boy tells me she is called Madonna, the bush wife of the rebel named Killerboy.

"Look boys, new chickens," she says, a smile on her face.

The girl named Madonna holds a rifle like the men and boys do, and her eyes remind me of Maskita. It is like she has no soul.

I can feel Jemi close to me, whimpering like a puppy. "Do not show them you scared," I whisper, "it make them bold. We must stay strong."

But Jemi is only fourteen. A few hours ago she saw her mammy cut and lying in her own blood—the hand that had plaited Jemi's hair left in the ditch. Jemi tell me she become Sandei woman two years ago. A boy in her village already pay the bride price, and now she is so afraid the rebels will spoil her. I have been with men, but we have ways, Sandei ways, so our husbands will think they are the first. But no one forget rape. If we are raped we don shame our family—no one will forget that.

The spoilin start in a ward in the mental hospital. Six empty beds. I think the people from those beds end up in the ditch outside. I know what the rebels go do, so I put the baby on a bed in the corner, then wait close to the door. I hold Jemi in my arms. "Stay close now," I say. "Whatever they go do, you stay close."

The one called Killerboy come in with five others. They throw us on two beds, side by side. Killerboy have such wild eyes—I have never seen eyes like that. He have so much hate and anger and excitement it seem his eyes will blow out of his head. When he lie over me I close my own eyes and pray.

They all take turns. Two hold each of us, then they switch. They do things I never hear of before. Later I learn they see these things on videos from Nigeria and America. Sometime the boys hold up their hands pretendin they have a camera. They have no shame, holdin the pretend camera up close like they filmin the sex.

Why do they do that? We do not have sex like that in our country. I have never heard of the things they do. I feel such pain. I can smell those boys and men, the smell all over me and Jemi, the smell in my skin like it suffocate the air out of me.

I feel for shame. For shame.

After a small time I just close my eyes and stay quiet. I know those boys like it more when we cry. So I do not cry. Sometimes I even look straight in those boys' eyes. They do not like that. Or I stare at the grey roof, or the fan that do not work, or some spider in the corner. Anything but what they are doin to me.

At first Jemi scream and scream. She scream for her mammy and scream from the pain and scream from the shame.

Those boys like us to cry, but they do not like a wild banshee like Jemi. "Go quiet!" Killerboy yell at her. "Go quiet or we cut out your tongue!"

But Jemi's eyes are mad with fear and she continue to scream. I know what those boys do if she do not go quiet. I open my eyes and see Killerboy staring at Jemi—she vex him bad in front of the others. His eyes come to me. A strange thing happen then—I see him but I do not feel fear. I do not blink, I just stare him back. It is a moment when the world go slow. Tears flow from my eyes but I keep them open and stare him back.

I reach over to Jemi between those beds and I find her fingers there. My hand takes hers and I hold it strong. I hold it so strong I think I go pull it off. I feel her hand grippin me back, her fingers twisting in mine. Just when I think Killerboy go scream at me too, Jemi become quiet. I do not look at her, my eyes are still with Killerboy. Oh, Papa God, it is like she put her screams into her fingers and I hear them there! The pain she feel for herself and her mammy and all the fear she feel inside, I feel in her hand. It is the only thing I feel.

Still I stay quiet—those boys do not hear a sound from me or Jemi. Even Jolie's baby remain quiet in the corner. That baby knows, she stay quiet like she knows what to do!

Soon they leave us alone. I think they like crying girls, but they do not like madness. Thank you Jesus. But we hear girls in other wards, and it is the same thing. We hear them scream, then they go quiet.

Jemi and I lie on the bed in the corner. I hold the baby so close I feel her fight to be free. She is hungry. I know I have to find food for this baby, so I put on my *lappa* and shirt and go out like nothing has happened to me. I go to the cooking fire where the rebel women sit, and they look at me quiet. They know. One woman is feeding a baby and I ask, "Can you feed my baby too? I de beg you, can you feed my baby?"

She dip her head. "Bring her," she say, "bring di baby."

While the baby feeds I go and wash by the well. In my whole life I never know a smell like those men and boys. I wash so hard I hurt my skin. I sniff every part of me and if I smell those men I wash some more.

When I am done I fill a bucket and put it on my head. The women give me a cloth and soap for Jemi. I see some palm oil by the fire. I point and say, "I de beg you, some oil, just small-small?"

The mama who feed Jolie's baby give me a cup and say, "Okeh, we do not have much."

I go back to the ward and find Jemi still lyin in the dark crying. She sound so small, crying like a little child. She is bleeding and dirty and lying in that filth like she do not ever want to move again.

"Jemi I de go wash you now," I say.

She stare at the roof like she is afraid it de go come down. I wash that girl from head to toe. Not hard like I wash myself, but gentle, like I am washing Jolie's baby. I put soap near her nose so she smell something different than those boys. After I wash her with soap I rinse with clean water and then dry her skin. I dip my fingers in palm oil and touch it to her—slowly I rub it in her skin. I even put some in her ears, maybe it help to stop hearing the sounds of this day.

There is a Sandei song we learn, a song about being by the fire and cooking rice. It is a song about the sisters looking in each other's eyes and knowing things without needing to speak. I sing the words and Jemi becomes quiet again.

"I see you, I see you now," I sing. "Put your head in my lap, put your head in my lap and feel my fingers in your hair, feel the palm oil run into your skin, feel my fingers in your hair."

I sing for a long time, and after a while Jemi do what we do with the Sandei songs, she repeats what I say. "I see you, I see you now. Put your head in my lap." Her voice is light and she sound so nice, like a young girl singing by a well.

Something sweet happen then. I hear the voices of women and girls in the next room, and the room beside that, all repeating what I sing. "Feel my fingers in your hair, feel the palm oil run, feel my fingers in your hair."

It is the sweet sound of our mothers, and of their mothers, singing to their babies, telling us to be strong.

January 13, 1999

I look in Dr. John's bag and, thank you Jesus, that man have three bottles of ofloxacin, the drug the doctors give for gonorrhea. I swallow some and give some to Jemi. I know that soon Dr. John's medicines will be running low. I know I need to find more, or make some traditional medicine when we go into the bush.

I cannot write any more today.

TWENTY-TWO

"Your friend, Momodu Camara. What did he say when he left you?" Mohamed is working the toothpick. Ahead of us is an overloaded truck.

"Mohamed, can you get by this guy? I think the rear wheel is about to fall off."

"Momodu Camara. What did he say when he left you?"

"He just wished me well." I have no idea why, but I'm hesitant to tell Mohamed about the mask.

He directs a doubtful look my way, leans on the horn and pulls into the oncoming lane. Thumping his stump against the wheel, Mohamed coaxes the Mercedes to go faster. Pedestrians carrying wood and charcoal, scooter drivers and goats scurry out of our way.

"And the nurse? What was she good at?" he asks, pulling back in front of the truck.

"Who?" I can barely think after all the near misses.

"What was she good at, the nurse you look for?" He glances over at me, annoyed, as if to say I'm not trying hard enough.

"Mariama? Well, she had a way with women, even women much older than herself. She was loving and kind, but at the same time seemed to carry some authority with other women. They listened to her. And she was good with babies."

It was Mariama's first helicopter ride. September 1998. The hospital in Kabala was overrun with civilian casualties. Dr. Poulan asked for volunteers, repeating several times that our safety couldn't be guaranteed. After a year in Freetown, I was ready for a change. "I'll go," I said.

Momodu Camara nodded his head. "I will go too. Kabala is close to the home district of my grandfather," he said.

"You won't have an opportunity to leave the hospital, much less get any visiting in," said Poulan, looking around the room. "The army is holding the town, but the situation is pretty desperate, I'm afraid. One of the nurses there has gone missing. We can spare a nurse from here, if one of you wishes to join the mission. Keep in mind the rebels like to take Sierra Leonean medical staff. If they are close by, you are a target. So don't go if you are not up to it." Poulan seemed almost apologetic as he looked about the room.

Mariama shyly raised her hand. "I do not mind going," she said.

Momodu and I smiled. Of all the nurses, Mariama had the largest presence—the charisma of someone much older. Earlier in the day, we'd worked side by side as the emergency triage team. A soldier began yelling, pushing to the front and insisting that he be treated first. Some older women started shouting him down, and soon there was a near riot of people screaming at each other. I was about to call for Security when Mariama waded into the throng, touching hands and speaking quietly. Like magic, she brought calm to those around her.

We left for Kabala in a UN helicopter with four Gurkha soldiers. Mariama had the window seat beside me. After we had taken off, I attempted some small talk, but she was having none of it. "I have never been in an airplane before," she said, her gaze fixed on the shifting landscape below.

"You still haven't. This is a helicopter," I said, my humour lost on her.

One of the soldiers in the seat across from us didn't take his eyes off her for the entire flight, but she seemed oblivious, a happy sightseer, her nose inches from the window. "Have you been to Kabala before?" I asked.

"I am from the south," she said, in a way that suggested further explanation was unnecessary.

When we reached Kabala, the Gurkhas tensed, fingers over triggers, safeties off. The pilot circled the hospital so long, I thought he wasn't ever going to land. Finally, he touched down in an empty courtyard. My stomach tightened—there were no patients standing about, no groups of relatives anxious for news. No one. Two of the Gurkhas remained with the helicopter and two followed us into the hospital.

Inside, it was the same—no lines of patients waiting

to be seen, no staff to greet us. The only movement was the little bits of paper and plastic blowing about the corridor. I followed Momodu into a ward. "Jesus, Mary and Joseph," I said, mimicking my father's half-prayer, half-swear. IV and blood transfusion bags dripped beside empty beds. Lifeless bodies lay on stretchers. Tray tables were laden with cold cups of tea and half-finished plates of rice—it was as if someone had set lunch for the corpses. The only sound was from a teakettle boiling dry on the nursing desk.

"They've gone to the bush," whispered Momodu, unplugging the kettle. He stared at the nursing desk for a moment then grabbed my arm. "John, we are in danger here."

We raced out into the open. Dust and litter swirled about as the pilot restarted his engines. Standing their ground in front of us, the four Gurkhas aimed their semi-automatics down the street. I felt a chill: advancing toward us was a small group of men and boys carrying rocket-propelled grenade launchers and Kalashnikov rifles—white rags on their heads, shirtless. Rebels. The rotor blades of the helicopter whirled at full speed and the pilot yelled at us to run.

"Mariama," I yelled into the din. "The nurse, Mariama—where is she?"

"She was inside with us," said Momodu. "If we get on, they'll leave without her."

The soldiers backed toward the helicopter, shooting into the air. Momodu grabbed my arm and pulled me toward the aircraft. I was about to step up when one of the soldiers pointed behind me: it was Mariama, running from the hospital, her arms clutching something bundled in a blanket. In the midst of the noise and dust, she handed the bundle to me and scrambled aboard. We took off with the door open, Mariama wedged between Momodu and me.

She opened the blanket, oblivious to the slant of the helicopter as we careened over the treetops. It was a newborn baby, the bloody umbilicus still attached and tied off with a piece of string. Mariama cooed and hummed a little tune as she wiped the cord with some alcohol she had in her bag. "His mammy die," she said, as she massaged the baby's chest and back with palm oil. "His mammy die." Mariama didn't once look at the scenery on the way back to Freetown.

We watched her, captivated. Tough Gurkha soldiers in helmets and flak jackets and two doctors—the six of us touched by the tenderness of a young woman toward a baby she had known for ten minutes. Finally, when the baby's skin glowed from palm oil and his eyes seemed to find hers, she put a finger into his mouth.

"What will you do with the baby," I asked.

Mariama scrunched her eyebrows as if I had asked an odd question. In Sierra Leone, there was no formal adoption service.

"Dr. John, we will go back to Freetown and I will find a mother who has lost her own. There are so many, it will be no problem," she said.

I looked up and caught Momodu's eye. He was smiling, I assumed at my stupidity. Later, he said, "John, I don't know who showed the most love, that nurse to the baby, or you to the nurse. Be careful, friend, she is a lot of woman to love."

"Ah, now, as you say, we cook with gas! *Insha'Allah*, there is a small-small chance she survived! She may be in Guinea, or Côte d'Ivoire, or even here. In our country, it is true that many women die in childbirth. Midwives are highly valued. If she was smart, she became a midwife to help her sisters. Yes, she has a small-small chance."

Guinea? Côte d'Ivoire? It could take years to find Mariama. And what of Momodu Camara? *I'll be home before you feel the baby kick*, I had told Nadia.

"Now we begin the search," Mohamed says. "We go to every clinic on the way to Kabala, which is the road to Guinea. If she is in the north, we will find her, it is the place of my birth, you know."

"Mohamed, you're from Kabala?"

"Ah, no, but close by. I know Kabala well."

"And my friend Momodu Camara? How do we find him?"

"So many Camaras in Sierra Leone, Mr. John. They are everywhere you look. How does your friend spell his name, with a *C* or a *K*?"

"Camara, with a *C*."

"Ah, then his family come from the north. And you say his grandfather was from the north—it will be somewhere near Kabala, I think. Kamaras with a *K* live in the south."

Despite Mohamed's optimism, a gloom falls over me. Everyone I see who is over twelve is old enough to have felt the fear Mariama and Jemi felt, and still they return my smiles. They chatter and laugh and argue. I wonder if Mariama is alive, and if she has something in her life that allows her to smile again.

Mariama could be anywhere between here and Buedu, or even in another country. Most likely, she's dead. And Momodu has a surname as common as Smith or Jones. What are my chances of finding either of them?

Ahead of us is the strange cloud. Even Mohamed seems mystified by the brooding horizon of black—a horizon that darkens by the hour.

January 14, 1999

Today we move. There is no truck, so we walk. All the women but the one called Madonna do the carrying. She and the men and boys carry only weapons—machetes and guns. The harmattan winds blow and the air is thick with dust and smoke. Village after village, house after house, is destroyed by the fighting.

By Waterloo we see something that make me sick. A girl's head stuck on a pole. The rebels laugh and say that will happen to us if we try to run. They say the Small Boys Unit do that. Boys only ten and twelve, so young they do anything Commander Abu say.

In Waterloo the rebels steal everything the traders have to sell. I see some boys put two or three hats on their head, and the rebel women carry big bundles of dresses and tops. These rebels are from the south near Liberia and they do not care about the people here—when there is too much for us to carry they burn everything they cannot take.

When the night comes we have no strength left, but those boys are the only ones to rest. "Make my rice," they say. "Fetch me water." Before the war if a twelve year old tell me to make his rice I would slap his face. But this is a different time. We make the rice and sauce and fetch the water and serve the boys first. We eat when they want no more.

Every girl who is not taken as a bush wife have to sex any man or boy who wants her. They choose any girl they like, any time they want. The Small Boys Unit is the worst. They choose Jemi all the time. After what we see, we are all afraid to say no. Commander Abu and Killerboy and Terminator, they all have turns with me, many turns. I do not say a thing, but now I look them in the eye. They do not like that.

Jemi and me and the other new women do cooking, carrying and finding wood. I see some girls shot dead when they get caught trying to run away. And some they do worse to. It will bring a curse to do such things but these rebels get so drunk and stoned they do not care about curses.

The girl soldiers carry guns and go on raids with the men and boys. "Yaya," they say. The girls change their clothes and go into villages first. They pretend they are refugees asking for help, but they are looking for government soldiers and where the chief lives and where the food is kept.

When they come back they even tell the commanders where the prettiest girls live. Whenever they go on yaya raids I feel afraid. They go crazy with drugs and the things they do are worse than the devil's deeds.

TWENTY-THREE

I'm wondering how the Rolling Stones would go over. A bit of "Jumpin' Jack Flash" or "Get Off of My Cloud." I ask Mohamed if he ever gets tired of hearing the same songs. He seems surprised by my question. If the music is good, why would you tire of it?

When he isn't singing, Mohamed engages me in his second-favourite pastime—suggesting new business ventures. His know-how and my money are the secrets to success. Freetown needs good hotels. And the country could do with a fleet of fishing trawlers. "We can compete with the Portuguese! Or we can start a bus company, or a brewery! Look at the success of Guinness!"

Despite my irritation at his driving habits and repetitive music, I find Mohamed's optimism infectious. There is something about the way he interacts with people in the markets—he has a self-confidence that I wouldn't expect in a taxi driver.

The front-end noise still worries me, but Mohamed dismisses my concern. His view is pragmatic: this is Africa, if there were no noise, there would be no car. The farther inland we go, the hotter and dustier it gets. We're driving north and east with a simple plan—try to retrace the route described by Mariama in her diary and check in at every health clinic along the way. We ask after a nurse or midwife named Lahai, and a physician named Camara, spelled with a *C*.

In Waterloo and Newton, the local staff of foreign NGOs apologize—there are one or two Lahais in the area, but no one fitting Mariama's description. There's a family of Kamaras with a *K*, but they are farmers, not doctors. The clinic in Jama Town is closed, so Mohamed asks the chief. No nurses or doctors. Would I pay for a hospital so they can attract qualified people? he asks.

At Masiaka Junction we have a choice: north toward the cool hills of Kabala, or east and south to the diamond fields around Bo and beyond. To the north the sky is black and ominous, to the south a welcoming palette of blues.

"Mariama wrote about being near Makeni, and later taking the road north to Kabala," I say.

Mohamed works his toothpick vigorously. "Hmm. The fighting was very bad in the north. During the war, many thousands of civilians crossed the border to Guinea. You say they find her diary in the east, in Buedu?"

"Yes, it was found in a church."

Mohamed shakes his head. "She was in the bush a long time. Most women die after not too long with the rebels. If she live, maybe she come back to the north. It is not far, Mr. John, I think we de go north, to the land of the Fula and Kuranko."

"Mohamed, you said you are from the north. Are you Fula?"

"No, Mr. John. Not Fula, I am a Kuranko man."

I hesitate. I don't have a day to waste, but the thought of coming so far and missing her is too much to bear. *Trust the Kuranko*, Momodu had said.

"Alright, north it is—toward the black cloud."

February, 1999. I do not know the day.

We walk with the rebels for two weeks when they take Jemi on a yaya raid. We are in a village that has been deserted. They go early in the morning. Before they leave they eat some drugs. I see Commander Abu give some to Jemi. She look scared but she do what he say. I stay in the camp with the baby and some new women and small boys to guard us.

All day they are gone. I hear shooting from far away. We are all scared because when the rebels come back they are always jacked so high. The sun is setting red in the harmattan dust when they return. They have more boys and girls and women. The women are carrying food and clothes and anything the rebels want.

I see Jemi walking behind Commander Abu. She is wearin a new dress and a gold chain around her neck. She looks happy and is laughing with the others. It is the first time I have seen her laugh.

"Jemi," I say. "Where did you get that dress?"

She look at me with eyes as grey as old cooked rice. "Where you think Mariama? Why you look at me that way? Go get Commander Abu and me some chop!"

I get the food and bring it. Jemi and Abu are sitting in the
house of the chief. Two days ago they kill him and two of his
wives. Jemi does not look at me when I give her the rice. She laugh
with Abu but I know there is no happiness there. Before she was
so scared, a young girl spoiled by these men. Now she have that
empty look in her eye, the rebel look. It make me so sad to see.

That night I find a rocking chair and rock Jolie's baby for such
a long time. The look that baby give me is so different than what I
see around me. Funny how she give me strength, but that is what
she do. I pat her back and rub palm oil into her skin and sing what
my mammy sing to me so long ago. I thank Jesus for the day
Dr. John hand me that baby across Jolie's open belly. If he did not,
I think I be dead already.

February, 1999

Maskita, he have ways to make his soldiers be true. When the
RUF take prisoners, the commanders like to catch a boy and his
mammy. When they bring the mammy I see what they do. "You
sex your mammy or we shoot her!" they say. If the boy say no the
commanders shoot them or shoot the mammy. Sometimes they
have a boy sex his mammy and they go shoot her anyway. When a
boy do this they make the boy a soldier—give him drugs, give him
food and girls. Those boys be loyal to Maskita then because they
know they never going back to that village. Never going back to
their family. They always be a rebel now after what they do.

Those boys are so angry they will kill anyone. The youngest
are the worst. They turn the country upside down. They rape their
mammys and sometime even kill the chiefs. I do not know why, but
they want a country where the young are in charge. No rules, no
traditional ways, just guns.

Sometime on yaya raids girls or boys see brothers or sisters or their mammy and they pretend they do not know them. Many nor see their family for years. If they come to their home village many pretend they nor know anyone in that village. When they leave the village they are never going back. Never.

I see the same thing all the time. The rebels go on yaya raids and take food and new boys to fight—and new girls to cook and carry and have sex with. When a rebel take a girl as a bush wife, then the raping stops and the girl will be loyal to her husband. This is what happen to Jemi. Commander Abu take her as a wife and the raping stopped. The commanders' wives have a lot of control in the camp.

Maskita is a very smart man.

February 26, 1999

Yesterday I help bury a boy who wear a watch from a yaya raid, so I know the date today.

After some time we go north on the way to Kabala. Every day I carry Jolie's baby on my back. I know she is hungry but that baby is so good all the time—Lord Jesus, she give me strength! She come to me for a reason, a reason I do not understand. I see all the other girls separated from their families, cryin and wantin to die. We all suffer so, but that baby, she is what keep me alive.

We are all walking now, stayin away from roads like passing devils in the dark. When we go through a village the people stay inside or go hide in the bush. The rebels destroy everything they cannot steal for themselves. They kidnap boys and girls—spoil them with drugs and guns and make them do such bad things they can never go back. There is no way they can go back.

When the people look at us I can see what they think. To them I am a rebel woman now. Damaged goods, I will never be the same.

The women left in the villages have nothing to say, no greeting, just turn their backs like we are not there. The old men look at us with judging eyes. If I say I see you in Temne or Mende they do not see me back. Already we are like shadow people, the ones who walk but do not live on this earth.

Some of us are sick with malaria and everyone walk slow. I carry a bag of rice on my head and Dr. John's bag in my arms. It is heavy but I nor let that bag go. As we walk I watch for plants for medicine. One day I find *njikoi*, the leaves are good for bleeding. Sometime when we stop I find *gbanbgei* root. When I was a little girl my mammy show me what to do. The juice from *njikoi* is put right on a bleeding wound. *Gbanbgei* root can stop malaria from coming on and keep the stomach moving.

The rebels get used to me walking about looking for plants. Sometimes we stop in the afternoon and the commanders go sleep. The youngest boys are left to watch but they fall asleep when the sun is high. I watch and think maybe one day I will just walk in the bush and none of them will see me go. I must be so careful—I remember what I see in Waterloo. I do not want to die like that.

When we walk Madonna stay close by. I do not know why, but she always walk behind me. One time, when we stop, she look at Jolie's baby and ask, "Mariama why you not give that baby a name?"

"When the time is right," I say. "I will know when the time is right, or she will tell me."

The rebels all take new names. They are ashamed of doin the things they do with the names their mammys give them. They take names like Sexy. Blood. Rambo. No Mercy. Hurtin Unit. Names they see on videos from America or Nigeria, names that make them feel like big men.

I feel sure they bring on a curse with names like that.

Sometime in March, 1999

Near Makeni there is lots of fighting. Everyone walk so slow, afraid of what the next turn in the path will bring. Killerboy and Terminator walk in front, the muscles on their backs wet from sweat. Killerboy wear pants from a soldier he kill. The pants are still brown with the dried blood. He never wear a shirt, just straps of bullets like teeth down his back.

Early in the day we come across some dead rebels. The bodies have holes in their chests. Everyone whisper, Kamajors! They take the hearts for medicines to make them strong. All the time we hear the same—if a Kamajor kill you, he eat your heart, or use it for secret medicines they carry.

It is so quiet—no birds, no women singin in the streams, no farmers in the fields. Every one go slow. Today Madonna walk in front of me, her gun on her hip just like a man. I see her finger is always ready to shoot. She wear men's trousers, tight around her hips. That girl don't try to hide from the men, but they are afraid of her all the same. Funny thing, I walk behind Madonna and I feel safe—she is so mean but I feel safe behind that girl.

Boom! All of a sudden there is shootin all around—Kamajors! Terminator is screaming and shooting into the bush. The Kamajors are the only enemy the rebels fear. They have special medicines to make them invisible—the bullets pass them by! In the north they call them Tamaboros, members of the secret hunter society. The rebels shoot at trees, they shoot at everything, cause the Kamajor or Tamaboro hunter have magic to turn themselves into anything at all. I see a boy named Hot Number empty his gun at a rock on the side of the track. When he stop to reload he start to cry like a baby he is so afraid.

Commander Abu is firing his gun past me, all the time yelling at me, "Hit the ground, hit the ground woman!" I grab the baby from my back and squeeze her tight. I do not fall, just stand in the open, the bullets flying past my head.

I see two rebels hit by a bomb, the explosion is so loud my head hurts. Then I feel the baby kicking and see she has started to cry. I fall to the ground, squeezing her to my chest, covering her ears and looking in her eyes so she can see me close. Madonna is standing strong, screaming filth like a man, shooting and shooting into the trees. I think that girl is a better soldier than most of the boys.

That is when I feel him. A man in the bush, not far behind us. He is the strangest man I have ever seen, wearing a wig on his head and a hunter's shirt with cowrie shells. He look like the devil himself. I smell a stink so bad—I have never smelled anything like that before. He seem nor afraid, like he is watching a TV in a parlour in Freetown. He is working slowly on his gun like he has all the time in the world. Maybe he have no bullets left, but it does not vex him, he just take his time.

He looks at me like he knows who I am. He sees me lying on the ground with the baby and he does not move—it is like we are all alone in the trees. I want to run. Maybe he will help me escape, but I am afraid. There is something strange about him, like he knows something I do not know. Maybe he is a chief.

There is much shooting and people screaming. My legs will not move. They say if you do a Kamajor wrong he will make you have your period for the rest of your life. None of the rebels see him! All this shooting and he is standing there like a stone in the river watching me. He nod his head, so calm, he remind me of a man in the market saying, "Hello, I'll buy some oranges and bananas."

I nod my head back, I see you, but I do not move from that spot. He is so scary in those crazy clothes. I hear the boys crying. Killerboy and Terminator, crying like babies. "Help me, help me!" I want to go run away, but I stay still, holding Jolie's baby. Killerboy and Terminator look so young now. Yesterday they were raping new girls. Now they are like little boys, lying in their own blood. Killerboy have a bad leg wound. He is staring at his leg like it surprise him to bleed so bad.

I am a nurse, so I stay and go help those boys. Maybe I stay because I do not know if the hunters are worse than the rebels. But I stay. I see something that surprise me. Madonna is looking scared. She is Killerboy's bush wife and if he die she will have no protection. Any man can have her. Her gun will be no good then. If she shoot a rebel she will be shot too.

Killerboy is bleeding so bad I do not know if I can stop it. His foot hangs by bits of broken bone and skin. I look at him and know he is going to lose that foot. He is the one who cut off the hand of Jemi's mammy, now he is losing his own foot. He bring a curse for his evil and now the curse come home.

Jemi is standing beside me and I see the ice in her eyes, as cold as Madonna. "Help me to tie this around his leg. We need to stop the bleeding," I say. She nor move. She stand still like a palm with no wind, her eyes empty. "Help me tie this or he bleed to death!" I say again.

Madonna look at Jemi like she dead if she do not help me. Then Jemi come to and we take Killerboy's belt and make it tight on his leg. Killerboy fell in a ditch when the bomb hit and the wound is dirty with mud. I tell Jemi to pour water on the wound and then I find some *njikoi* leaves to chew. I squeeze the juice from the wet leaves on the wound and wrap it with gauze from Dr. John's bag. Maybe I cut off his foot tomorrow, but now I hope he just die.

I feel a shadow come over us. Commander Abu is standing above me, blood dripping from his fingers, staining his gun red. "What your name witch?" he say. He one of the men who rape Jemi and me for four days and now he ask me my name.

"Mariama Lahai," I say. "I am not a witch, I na nurse."

He stares at my face like he never see me before! What did he think, that the women he rape have no names? "Mariama Lahai!" I scream at him again. "That is my name. Sit down and I will wrap your wound." He look at me like a man look at a river wondering if the water is fit to drink. "Sit now, let me see your arm. If I am a witch I would have cursed you many times by now. You will die of poison blood if you do not let me clean your arm."

He is lucky, the bullet take some flesh but did not hit the bone. "I must stitch this arm," I say. "We have no anesthetic."

He tell a boy to mix some ganja weed and cocaine. Abu suck so hard on that I think the smoke go come out of his ears. "You a witch for sure, you stand still and no bullets hit you. Maybe you be a Kamajor witch," he say.

I look him in the eye like I am nor afraid. "You can believe what you like and you can kill me. I na nurse and I can fix your arm. So you want to kill me now, or after I fix your arm?"

We stare at each other some more and I say to Jemi, "Wash the commander's arm." Jemi do what I say. Before putting in the stitches I squeeze some more juice from the *njikoi* leaves on his wound. I pull the stitches tight, maybe I pull too tight, but I pay him no mind.

What can he do if I bring him pain? Take away my name?

TWENTY-FOUR

The cloud descends upon us, a blanket of dust so thick I'm sure the Mercedes is going to choke to a stop. But she sputters along defiantly. It's midday, and every vehicle with working headlights has them on. I thought I'd seen overloaded vehicles in Freetown, but they were nothing like the wobbly-wheeled wrecks coming out of the north.

"Guinean traders," mutters Mohamed. "They buy cheap goods in Guinea and sell them for more in Freetown."

Every couple of kilometres, we pass a truck that has broken down—flat tires, broken axles, or just carburetors that have asphyxiated in the dust. "What do you think?" I ask the filthy windshield.

"I am thinking of my country chicken," says Mohamed.

"Your what?"

"Ah, my country chicken," he says. "She misses me. She hate it when I leave."

"I thought that was just someone you met last night at the guest house," I say, happy to have something to take my mind off black clouds and broken door handles.

"Ah, she just a girl I meet, not my usual chicken. In Krio we say 'country fowl,'" he says, pronouncing it *foal*.

"You mean a girlfriend?"

"Mr. John, you have no country chickens in your country? They are natural, they eat whatever there is to eat, oranges or bananas on the side of the road, local rice, anything they find, and they never get sick. The city girls, they do it for money, you have to buy them things, they want to change their hair every week, or have new clothes—but the country chickens, they do it for love." Mohamed pronounces *love* like it has five *v*'s.

"Does your wife know about your country chicken?"

"Of course, Mr. John. It make her angry, so I say I love only her. But my country chicken want me to marry her too. It is a big problem for me. She is sweet like a ripe mango, and she always open her wings to Mohamed. Ah! She have wings like you cannot believe! Mammy and pappy business, that what we call it in my country. I'm Muslim, you know; I can have four wives, but I have no money."

"I hear more than one wife always brings trouble," I say, trying to calculate the real price Mohamed must be paying for those glorious wings.

"Ah, yes, trouble. *Palava*, we call it. They say too many wives causes *palava*. Mr. John, you know more about our culture than I thought. Like the cloud ahead of us: *palava*." He chuckles. "Let me know if you want a country chicken, Mr. John. Mohamed will get one for you, anytime."

"I thought you said the country chickens do it for love, Mohamed."

"Yes, you must tell them you love them. And you must say you will visit again. But a bit of money or a small gift go a long way in our country. There are many girls in Makeni, Mr. John. You say so, and Mohamed will find you a nice country chicken."

Killerboy's leg swell with infection so bad he have terrible pain. On the second day he have a fever. He wake up screaming, callin his mammy and talking to the dead. We have no morphine but the rebels have lots of drugs. They give him ganja to smoke or rub brown-brown into his head. I know they need to cut that leg off, but I keep quiet. If I try and he die maybe they will kill me too. So I wait. The others do not come close to Killerboy. If he is cursed they do not want the curse on them.

On the third day they go on a yaya raid. I am left with some women and new girls and some of the Small Boys Unit. I know they go shoot me if I try to escape. I am alone with Killerboy and even the other sick ones leave us. Killerboy is in a very bad way and I know he will die this day.

I am washing his face when he look at me strange. His breathing become quiet and even the sweat seem to dry on his head. "Why you do this Mariama?" he ask.

"Why I do what?" I say.

"I rape you before. You see me cut the hand off Jemi's ma. If you do not give me a cool cloth no one will know. If you give me no water and leave me in the sun, only you will know. If I get better maybe I rape you again. Why you help me like this?"

"What you real nem? What nem you have before you become a rebel?" I ask him.

He tilt his head and look at me like he do not understand. Slowly his eyes close. "Ibrahim," he whisper. "Mi nem Ibrahim."

When Killerboy lay over me at the mental hospital his eyes were evil things. They were the eyes of a devil. Like the masks the Poro use. Now I am sitting over him, my eyes above his, and I see no mask, no devil there. "I help you because you have a mammy somewhere wonderin where her Ibrahim is. If you de go die, you going to heaven or hell, there is nothing I can do about that."

Killerboy close his eyes like he do not want me to see the sadness there. I feel his chest move like he is fightin for breath. Even that is not the chest that came over me, blocking out the light at the mental hospital. Today his chest is like his breath—small-small.

He die before the rebels return. I am afraid they will call me a bad nurse or say I witched him, but no one say a thing. Commander Abu break the camp and we leave Killerboy's body on the ground like the ashes of an old fire.

TWENTY-FIVE

"Mohamed, this is a little fast, please slow down!"

Ahead of us, two picture-postcard bundles of innocence stand to the side of the road. They are maybe eight or nine years old, carrying platters of bananas and oranges on their heads. Suddenly, there is a thumping sound from the rear end—metal on metal—the kind of grinding that can only mean something has broken or is about to break. The Mercedes begins a bumper-to-bumper, bone-grinding shudder. We careen to the right, the cherubic faces and platters of fruit directly in line with the Mercedes star.

"Mohamed!" A subtle bump, like a headlight striking a branch on the side of the road. The Mercedes skids on the gravel and comes to an abrupt stop. Oranges roll like tennis balls on the asphalt behind us.

"That was close," Mohamed says, as we both get out.

"Close? Mohamed, I think we hit—" I stop in mid-sentence. Behind us the two children, unhurt, are picking up the scattered fruit. Their mother cuffs them both about the head, but the real object of her wrath is Mohamed. She screams at him. I don't need an interpreter to know she'd have killed him on the spot if he had hit her kids.

Mohamed smiles and shrugs. He opens the trunk and grabs a pipe wrench, shoves a rag under his stump and slides under the rear end of the car. I hear hammering, muttering in three languages, and the word *Allah* repeated several times.

Vehicles of all sizes and states of road-unworthiness whiz by as a crowd gathers to gawk. Apparently, speeding trucks barely missing their kids is no novelty, but a perspiring white man is. The people smile and put down their loads, content to encircle me and the Mercedes and wait.

I try smiling back, muttering my usual *"Kushe, ow di bodi?"*

"Di bodi fine," they all say, smiling back.

A kind old woman points to a stump of wood in the shade of a tree and motions for me to sit down. She calls to a young girl who is standing close by. The girl has a yellow jerry can balanced on her head. Effortlessly, she lowers the can and pours some water into a gourd offered by the old woman. I hesitate, running through my physician's checklist of all the reasons I shouldn't drink the water. The little girl smiles shyly. The heat and good manners and gentle smiles win the day. The water is cool and tastes of ash—the old woman has offered me water that has been boiled.

"Tenki," I say.

"Bi siε," she answers in the Mende dialect. Thank you.

Finally, Mohamed slides out from under the car, so caked in red dust and oil I feel a wave of guilt that I didn't offer a hand. "Just a U-joint," he says.

I glare at him, dumbfounded. Although my mechanical aptitude leaves me challenged by door handles, I'm pretty sure he means a universal joint. We must be miles from a garage.

"Mohamed, what …?" I'm so flustered I can't phrase the question. There can't be a single Mercedes dealership in the entire country.

He pulls out his cell phone and dials. Again I wonder what I was thinking, hiring the driver with the friendly eyes and happy-go-lucky disposition. I'm soaking wet, the asphalt below my feet is sticky from the heat and we're not going anywhere soon.

The entire trip was a mistake. Hopeless. I feel angry at, of all people, Nadia. I couldn't believe it when she said I needed to come here. In the week before I left, she changed her mind several times, as did I. Maybe what she really wanted was for me to find my voice and say no. Perhaps I took up the challenge too easily—jumping at the opportunity to head out on an impossible quest to find an old lover, return a mask and bury the past.

Mohamed stands before me, and his expression suggests he, too, is wondering what he's got himself into. Behind him, I notice a path through the elephant grass that lines the road. Mohamed calls after me, but I ignore him. I need a little time away from him and the broken-down Mercedes. When he fixes the car, if he fixes it, I'll thank him and have him take us back to Freetown.

I step onto the trail and pull out my cell phone. The whole thing was a long shot. Nadia and I can paint the baby's room together and get on with the task of becoming parents. I dial our number. "Call Failed," says the display. I'll try again later.

The pathway in front of me is invitingly cool. My legs take me forward, away from the heat and frustration and staring faces. Within twenty metres of entering the bush, I'm in another world.

The elephant grass is so thick that soon the sounds of the roadway are lost behind me. Wary of snakes, I hesitate, wondering if I should turn around. Ahead of me is a well-used path of hard clay. If I stay on the trail and follow it back, I can't get lost. This is Mariama's world, I reassure myself. She might have walked this very path a decade ago.

The way is littered with mango pits covered in ants and banana peels and footprints like newly formed fossils in the drying clay. The smells are of shit and wood smoke and leaf litter—the same things she would have seen and smelled every day of her long walk. Impenetrable green surrounds me, pulling me forward.

My mood lifts. For the first time, I am on her ground, feeling her world close in about me. I fantasize about rounding a corner and glimpsing a woman with a bag of rice on her head, a doctor's bag in her hand and a baby on her back. I will my legs to slow down, tell myself to turn around, go back to the roadway and wait for Mohamed to fix the car, but still I move forward, the pathway drawing me deeper.

A sound enters my consciousness, something repetitive, a pulse of base notes—the thump, thump, thump of wood pounding on wood. Women's voices. Relaxed. Joyful. Sounds that in Africa usually mean a well or a cooking fire. I step into a clearing and the thumping stops. A small village—no more than a dozen huts.

Before me, chickens peck about in a garden of cassava and sweet potatoes, while goats graze untethered, their eyes listless in the late afternoon heat. An old woman, bare breasted and wearing only a thread-worn *lappa*, pokes at the coals of a cooking fire. Smoke rises lazily about her, the greyness giving her an aura of timelessness—I wonder if she is really alive. Beside her is a young woman, tall and strikingly beautiful. The pole she's been using to pound cassava hangs suspended in mid-air. Bundled in a *lappa* tied to her back is a baby, limp with sleep and the rhythms of her mother's supple body. Another young woman, her *lappa* bunched between her thighs, squats over a pot of rice.

The women stare at me; three statues around a three-stone fire, the only movement coming from the smoke rising between them.

I try the Mende greeting. *"A wua naa, a wua sie."* Hello, are you there? Thank you.

They're probably Temne, but bits of Mende and Krio are all I have.

"Bu wua, bi sie," they answer. *"Kahui ii yee na?"* How are you?

"Kaye gbi ii Ngew ma. Kahui ii yee na?" I answer in the traditional Mende way. I am well, by the grace of God. How are you?

The women laugh and shriek with delight. The pretty one with the baby asks something, which I guess to mean "How is your family?" I respond with *"Kaye ii Ngew ma."* Thanks be to God, the Mende phrase that covers just about everything. They laugh yet again.

The older woman pulls on a T-shirt and says something to

the pretty one. The young woman bends forward and scoops together a bowl of rice, chicken and cassava. She offers it to me with a shy smile. I start to back away, not wanting to take their dinner. The old woman beckons in a welcoming way. She issues another instruction to the young mother, who darts into the hut and returns with a spoon for me.

They squat around the fire, passing the larger rice pot among them, mixing the fragrant cassava and bits of chicken with hands yellowed and greasy with palm oil. Taking turns, they roll the mixture into little balls, popping them into their mouths. I relax, suddenly feeling very hungry. The cassava is spicy, the texture smooth and oily. I still have food in my bowl when the young woman takes the shared cooking pot and scoops another piece of chicken into mine. She has eyes to get lost in, round like saucers, matched by the most beautiful pair of lips—lips that remind me of Mariama's. They start to giggle—I've been staring at her. She stares back, smiling, her confident eyes holding mine.

Behind her, the weakening sunlight washes yellow-green on the palms along the horizon. To some unheard cue, insects begin an afternoon chatter—the sun will disappear soon. The three women talk easily, occasionally glancing my way, passing the big pot, mixing, rolling and popping the little balls into their mouths. A small mutt, scratching at fleas, lazes at my feet. Flies crawl over an open wound behind the dog's ear. No one seems to notice.

I wonder how many women have squatted here, bathed in yellow light, cooking rice and cassava and chatting about babies and malaria and strange men. There is a good chance the RUF occupied this very village, but there is nothing, no graffiti, no broken buildings, no drug-addled boys, to break the bucolic spell.

I think of Mariama's diary. These women, the younger ones, could have been taken by rebels—they would have been in their teens, old enough. The older woman might have been passed by, one of the women who remained quiet, staring at Mariama as she walked in a line of rebels with Jolie's baby.

The younger one with Mariama's eyes bends at the hips, using her hands to roll another ball of rice—a woman in the prime of her life, supple and sexy and so terribly beautiful with her baby at her back in the smoke of her cooking fire. Until this moment, I've never seriously considered the possibility that Mariama survived. Nor have I allowed myself to imagine finding her, perhaps in a village like this, a woman whose eyes don't look away, whose oily fingers roll balls of rice in a shared pot and whose hips bend with the lithesome ease of a young willow.

Three stones around a mound of smoking coals—charred rocks that may have occupied this very spot when the old woman was herself young and supple and carrying a baby on her back. My breath catches, and my eyes shift to the older woman.

"Mariama could be alive," I say. "She could be squatting over a fire just like the three of you."

The women look at me quizzically. I force myself to my feet. "*Mua lɔɔ gboma*," I say in Mende. We shall see—goodbye.

They say the same, nodding quietly, the old one again standing perfectly still, the young one with the baby somehow making her eyes sparkle through the wisps of smoke.

I walk through the clearing and glance back at them—they wave, like schoolgirls, giggling again. My pace quickens and the hard clay at my feet feels familiar. Strangely, it is not Mariama's voice I hear but Nadia's. She is committed to the belief that everything happens for a reason, and I have no doubt now that the U-joint was meant to fail and that I will not be telling Mohamed to return to Freetown anytime soon. I feel a quickening, my senses so alive I can smell the mango pits and banana peels without seeing them.

A few moments ago, I was resigned to failure. My journey was misguided—the folly of one who doesn't know where to look because he doesn't understand what it is that he's lost. And I still don't—but I've found something unexpected, a feeling in my gut that I can't ignore. Hope? Perhaps, but I've been so jaded for so long I'm not sure I'd know what that is.

The wall of green closes behind me and the pounding of cassava resumes, like a fading heartbeat, as I walk through the failing light.

I step out of the bush, disoriented. It takes a moment to recognize the dust-covered Mercedes, surrounded now by a spontaneous, bustling, evening market. Local people, sensing that cars and trucks will have to slow down for the broken vehicle, have set up cooking fires and food stalls on either side of the Mercedes.

There are people everywhere—children selling water in those tiny plastic bags, women squatting over bowls laden with yams and red rice. Aromas of roasting corn and bush-meat thicken the evening air. Women and men gather in separate clusters, locals and truck drivers, drinking palm wine from porcelain and plastic mugs.

Mohamed is eating with a couple of truckers; a yellow jerry can of palm wine half-empty at their feet. He sees me, his whiskered face breaking into a big smile. "Mr. John, have some *poyo*," he says, pouring me a mug of the frothy liquid. He sets aside a kerosene lantern and makes room for me on a log beside the Mercedes.

Mohamed has pulled off a minor miracle. He called one of his "brothers" in Freetown who had a friend who knew someone else with a yard of rusting hulks used for spare parts. The friend has already dispatched a mechanic with a used U-joint; Mohamed thinks he can replace the thing at first light and have us on our way by noon. I'm in shock—I couldn't have had it fixed as quickly in Vancouver.

"Mohamed, I feel very bad for how I acted."

"Ah, no problem, Mr. John. I think you were too hot," he says, beaming from ear to ear. "Mohamed see your face was red. You must drink more water."

"You did well, Mohamed. Thank you."

"You were gone long time, Mr. John."

I feel a little sheepish. "I came upon a small village," I say. "Three women were cooking. One, with a baby, was very beautiful. They were very nice and fed me cassava and chicken."

He tops up my mug. The *poyo* has the consistency of skim milk but tastes like watered-down lime juice and coconut milk.

"It was a small village?" he asks, eyeing me over his cup.

"Yes, their cooking fire was toward one end. It was by the largest house."

"There were no men around?"

"No, I think their men were probably off chopping wood," I say.

He cackles one of his dry, throaty laughs, the grease on his chin reflecting the light of a nearby fire. He's eating roasted duiker, the miniature deer favoured as bush-meat in Sierra

Leone. Mohamed is so incredulous, he seems to be eating in slow motion.

"What?" I ask. "What's so strange?"

"Mr. John, African women need no man to cut wood. Next time, you nor go by yourself, you get into trouble. I think the beauty with the *pikin* be one of the chief's wives. You lucky he not come and accuse you of doin woman damage!"

He takes a big bite of greasy duiker and, chewing noisily, says in Krio, "You be in Africa, Mr. John. Nex tim you de go walk in di bush, you de tek Mohamed."

Nadia picks up after the first ring. "Hello?"

"Nadia! It's me."

Even with satellites, there's a second's delay. "John, yes, I hear you!"

Another delay as we both wait for the other to speak. I feel like a teenager calling a girl for the first time. I have my wife on the phone and I have butterflies in my stomach. I should have written down what I wanted to say. "I've tried calling a few times. Did you get my messages?"

"Yes," she says. "How are you?" She sounds tentative, fragile.

I'm leaning on the Mercedes, the back end up in the air. We've put the crate in the trunk—the back seat is my bed for the night. "I'm fine, Nadia. Hot, getting a little tired of rice and mystery sauce, but fine. And you?"

A pause. "I miss you. Isn't it getting late there?"

"And I miss you. It's around ten. I'm about to go to bed." Around me, the darkness is almost complete; the dust of the harmattan has extinguished the stars, and the only light is the pale orange of the few remaining charcoal braziers that have been left to burn out. "Where are you?"

Pause. "Where am I? John, I'm at home, you called me here."

"No, I mean where are you sitting?"

She giggles. Girlish. The sound calms me. "I'm in the living room, in my chair by the mantel."

"Good. What are you wearing?"

Another pause. "My blue uniform. I'm getting ready to go to work. I'm on nights. Why?"

This time the pause is from my end. "I just want to picture you, as you are. You look good in blue. What's the day been like?"

"Wet. Miserable. A day for my duffle coat. How about you? Where are you?"

She wants me to describe the town and hotel I'm staying in. "Oh, Mohamed found this place on the road to Kabala. The people are very nice." I look into the back seat of the Mercedes, wonder where I'll put my legs. "Not the Ritz, but I'm quite comfortable."

"Hmm. I can only imagine. You're so clear, John. You sound like you're down the street."

"Go figure. Everyone says the cell phone reception is great throughout Sierra Leone."

"How is it going?" she asks. I hear something in her voice and the butterflies in my stomach turn to worms.

"To be honest, until now I haven't been very optimistic. We stop at every little clinic we can find, ask if they know a Sierra Leonean nurse or midwife in her early thirties or a physician named Momodu Camara. Lahai is a very common name. Lots of Mariamas too. We get asked for tea, but that's about it."

"You say 'until now.' Why? What's happened?"

How do I tell my wife I feel alive again, buoyed by the eyes of a beautiful young woman?

"John? Are you still there?"

"I met some women in a village close by. They had all survived the war, and they seemed, well, surprisingly happy. I realized they could just as easily be Mariama. It's possible that she and Momodu made it through somehow. But when I let myself think that, I get discouraged again, because if they did, why have they remained among the disappeared?" The silence on the end of the line echoes back to me. I think she's crying. "Nadia, how are you?"

Another pause. "A little sick in the mornings. But okay."

"I should be there with you, shouldn't I? I miss you, Nadia."

"Do you?"

"Of course. Why?"

"You met some women and they survived and they're happy, so now you think Mariama is alive?" Her voice sounds as tight as the passenger door on the Mercedes.

"Nadia ..."

I hear what sounds like a long sigh. "Oh, I'm sorry. Just feeling a little insecure. Are you safe?"

I'm standing in the dark with strangers camped out around me, in a place that until seven or eight years ago was considered one of the most dangerous on the planet. Atrocities against women and children were a daily occurrence. A Western journalist was killed a few miles up the road.

"I've been here a couple of days and haven't seen a uniform or an AK-47 yet. It's very different than it was during the war, Nadia. Don't worry, I'm fine."

"I'll be here when you get back," she says. "Dr. Conrad tells me to expect the baby to move soon. John, I'm late for work, I have to go. I love you."

"And I love you."

We say goodbye, and the emptiness echoes so loudly the satellite might be an empty drum.

I'm too keyed up to go to bed, and Mohamed, sensing this, finds another jerry can of *poyo*. The truck drivers have long since gotten into their cabs, some with girls that have appeared as if from nowhere. Mohamed stays with me, I think sensing my mood, but I realize he, too, wants to go off somewhere. When I tell him not to wait up, he mumbles something about going to find a country chicken.

Eventually, sleep comes, but my dreams are of cooking fires and eyes to get lost in. Sometime during the night, I get up to pee. Some of the truckers have already driven off. In the darkness I can hear voices, muffled, as if from under a blanket.

For the first time since arriving, I can see stars in the sky. There is no North Star. A satellite tracks from horizon to horizon, and I wonder if Nadia can see it too. No, she's working the night shift—I'm even alone with the sky.

Banging. A metallic scraping sound from just below my head. I open my eyes to light streaming through the car windows—my watch says it's 8:30 in the morning.

"How you sleep?" Mohamed asks, as I climb out of the car.

"Fine, Mohamed, until the earthquake hit." Mohamed waits, his eyes watching me inquisitively. "What?" I ask.

"Last night. I think you were not happy, Mr. John."

"Yes, Mohamed. My wife is not happy that I'm here. I don't have much time, I'm afraid." He nods his head. "How about you, Mohamed. How you sleep, my friend?"

"Ah, Mr. John. Mohamed have a good night," he says, with a leering grin. "And the U-joint arrive while you sleep. Everything good. We de go quick-quick."

The pounding is being done by Mohamed's friend of a friend, getting an early start. With the car still jacked up, we haul the crate out of the trunk and put it back on the rear seat. Mohamed tries to talk me into leaving it in the trunk, but I feel more secure when I can see the thing behind me.

Our departure means the dismantling of the spontaneous roadside stop; the corn sellers and the meat vendors and little kids are already disappearing into the bush. I thank Mohamed's friend and give him some leones for his help. The man smiles appreciatively and waves from his motorbike.

When the Mercedes lurches onto the roadway, I take a look behind me—plastic bags, discarded fruit peels and elephant grass by the side of the road—just as it was before we arrived.

I do not know the date. It is still the dry season.

After the Kamajor attack, the men and boys leave me alone. Commander Abu see I am a nurse and think I am a witch. They make other girls carry the rice—I just carry Jolie's baby on my back and Dr. John's bag with my herbs and roots.

They stop raping Jemi when Commander Abu take her as one of his wives. Jemi be so thankful to Abu for that—now she only need to sex him. She think Abu save her, but I know that is Maskita's plan.

Poor Jemi, now she never goin home. No way.

The number of broken-down vehicles increases the farther north we drive. It's as if the entire countryside is choking to death.

"Mohamed, let's stop before she quits."

"I know a village with an Italian clinic close by, we de go there," he says. He seems distracted, glancing frequently into the cracked rear-view mirror.

"What's the matter," I ask, turning to look behind us.

"A green car sits on us, like a rooster on a hen," he says. "The car is Sierra Leonean for sure."

"We need to clean off that window," I say, wondering about his choice of simile. "I can see a red vehicle, it looks like a bit of a wreck. Cracked windshield."

"How many cars you see without cracks?" asks Mohamed, drawing my attention to the Mercedes' windshield. "Ah, Mr. John, look at that car and pretend you have an American car-washing machine."

"You mean a car wash."

"Yes! A car wash. Now what do you see?"

"Okay, I get it. Under all the dust it's a green car." There is something else. I've seen the car before. "Mohamed, it says In Allah We Trust Taxi Co. on the front. It looks like the Nissan sent by the guy at the airport. The driver, what was his name?"

"Hussein. He say his name was Hussein, Mr. John. He was not happy when you chose Mohamed to drive."

I remember the mysterious phone message: *The mask want to come home.* I glance from the green Nissan to the crate labelled Echo-Diagnostic Equipment and suddenly feel queasy. "Who are they, do you think? It looks like two or three people."

Mohamed's eyes shift from the mirror to me. "Who are they? Mr. John, Mohamed is never followed—not since the war. *Insha'Allah*, who wants a one-armed man in Sierra Leone, eh? What about you? Any enemies you leave behind?"

TWENTY-SIX

"Every curse has a cause! We Africans have been afflicted by curses because of original sin and our dangerous cultural practices! Alleluia!"

Sweat cascades from the preacher's nose and drenches his white shirt. He completes almost every sentence with an alleluia, pausing as the congregation answers his call.

"What curses bring rebels to this village years ago, eh? What curses led to the rapin of our women, or to the cutlasses that cut off so many limbs?" Miraculously, his tie remains stuck over his shoulder, safe from the spittle that propels every word. "Look to your family history! Alleluia!"

"Alleluia!"

"We are a society wrapped in the satanic covenants of the

secret societies. How many in this room have the scars on their back, eh? The scars of Satan! Alleluia!"

"Alleluia!"

I'm squeezed into a pew near the back with Maria, one of the nurses working in the Italian clinic. Her eyes are closed and she is lost in prayer. Around us, the faithful are alive. *Alleluia, alleluia!* Women slap fans against their thighs, men raise their hands in glorious supplication. *Alleluia!*

Taking a moment to let the congregation appreciate his message, the preacher swipes a dripping towel across his face, gathering himself for the climax. "What brings this dark cloud? What makes the day black as the Day of Judgment, eh?"

I look straight ahead, fearing that all eyes will be on me, the white stranger who brought the darkness among the faithful.

The stridency of the message is at odds with the soft glow of candles, one in every window, a scene reminiscent for me of many Christmas Eves, long ago. But this is an African afternoon. And the preacher's sermon isn't about the baby Jesus, it is about curses, secret societies and repentance.

Through an open window I can see the Mercedes, resting her new U-joint in front of the health centre. When we arrived, the two Italian nurses, Maria and Florence, were seated on the verandah. They looked from the cloud to us, as if wondering how we had brought this freak of nature.

Maria is soft, cute, curvy and wide-eyed. Florence has harder edges, a chain-smoker, more curious than welcoming. Yes, of course we could stay the night. No, they hadn't heard of an African nurse named Mariama Lahai or a physician named Momodu Camara. But come in, they had an extra room and saw few visitors.

Maria asked if I would like to join her at a local church service. It was a great way to meet the village, she assured me. There was a visiting preacher, and the sermon was going to be in English. She caught me in a pensive mood—my phone call with Nadia hadn't gone well. A bit of self-reflection couldn't hurt. Along we went, the effervescent Maria taking my arm. She dressed like the local women, a T-shirt, *lappa* and a colourful scarf wrapped around her head of black curly hair.

"There is a reason behind every curse. Generational curses!" the pastor yells. His right hand stretches so far heavenward, his entire body seems to levitate. "If you have divorce for two generations, you have a generational curse! Look at your lives! Alleluia!"

"Alleluia!"

"If you have heart afflictions in two or more generations, you have a generational curse. Look at your lives! Alleluia!"

"Alleluia!"

"If you are a woman and find yourself lusting after another woman's man, look to the past. You may have a water curse!"

"Alleluia!"

"Look to demonic cultural practices! Do not bring masks or carvings into your home, many carry hidden curses! If you bring them into your home, you accommodate the curse! Alleluia!"

"Alleluia!"

Can it be? For years, I've lived with the mask Momodu gave me. I wonder what Bonnie would think of a Christian pastor laying waste to the traditions of the secret societies. And of the irony of First Nations people in North America returning to the traditions the missionaries had "cleansed" them of.

"Rise up and sing praise! Sing to cast out the devil's curse!

Sing so the heavens can hear! Remember Saint Thomas—he who sings well prays twice!"

The hymn is a rapturous delight. Everyone moves, and Maria raises her hands and dances with the rest of the congregation. The harmony is so perfect, and the women's voices so angelic, I sense my own body swaying.

Something magical happens: the gloom outside the windows begins to lift. To the south, the sky clears, the blackness gives way to a ribbon of blue. But the preacher isn't finished.

"Again, I say to you, the root cause of curses are dangerous cultural practices that we Africans inflict upon ourselves! Sleep with the dead! Huh? Poro and Sandei both! Satan's work happens right here!"

He builds on every sentence—screaming louder, imparting more fervency to every alleluia, wringing more sweat with every wipe of his forehead.

"How many times have I seen it during the week of mourning? The Poro and Sandei both, takin the body of the dead for one night. For what purpose, I ask you? They LIE with di body! They LIE with di body, doin devil's works. How many times do di body of an important person return without head for burial? What satanic rituals have been performed?! Curses are the result! Curses are the result!"

When it seems impossible for him to shake any more violently, to shout any louder or to sweat any more profusely, the preacher takes it to a new level—and his physical stature seems to grow. By now, the congregation's chanting, praying, swaying frenzy matches that of the preacher. An elderly woman two rows ahead of us collapses onto her seat. Women on either side fan her vigorously, while everyone else just prays with more fervour.

"If you are going into the pit of darkness, maybe it's tellin you something. Huh? Maybe it's telling you somethin!"

"Alleluia!"

"You can change your course!"

"Alleluia!"

"You can reach for the sky!"

"Reach for the sky! Alleluia!"

"Reach for the sky!"

"Alleluia! Reach for the sky!"

And then it is over.

One towel around his neck and one in his hands, the preacher moves slowly toward the exit. His body is dwarfed by the door frame—the man who seemed to grow with every alleluia is a head shorter than I am. He is a thin man with yellow teeth. He shakes the hand of every congregant as they leave the church. Maria and I fall into line behind women still fanning themselves and men tugging white shirts from wet skin.

The preacher's hand is warm and he offers me a kind smile. His normal speaking voice has no resemblance to his preaching one. Part of me fears that by some holy telepathy he will look into my eyes and see the mask hidden there, a remnant of a demonic cultural practice.

He thinks I'm Italian. *"Buon giorno,"* he says, with a little laugh, then, in Krio, "How di day?"

I mumble something about how inspired his sermon was, and I'm grateful when the next man in line grabs the preacher's hand. As we stroll back to her house, I ask Maria if she attends an evangelical church in Italy. She laughs, her brown eyes wide in mock horror. "My goodness, no. I am a Catholic," she says. "It is the singing that brings me—the African voices. How can I say it? The African voices can transform the most meagre of lives, and bring euphoria to the spirit. Perhaps those with the least in life have the most to gain from prayer, and what is rapturous singing but prayer with a passion, no?"

"Do you believe in curses?" I ask, still unsettled by what I've just witnessed.

She takes my arm comfortably—we are a couple out for a walk. "It is hard to live in Africa and not be open to such things, no? There is so much that happens here—things we do not understand. Ah, we are home now."

Florence is sitting on their verandah, smoking. She wears a T-shirt and khaki pants, her taut nipples pulling at the V of perspiration between her breasts. "Are you saved, Dr. John?" she asks with a wink.

"I will cook now," says Maria. She walks to the outdoor cooking area to join some local women.

Florence remains seated. "I am not good at cooking," she says through a puff of smoke. "No good Italian man would have me."

In no time at all, Maria returns with a bottle of Chianti, uncorks it and pours each of us a glass. How she has kept it in the tropical heat, I don't know, but the first mouthful is delicious. She says she is preparing a pasta primavera paired with salad of fresh tomatoes, basil from her garden and bocconcini cheese that arrived with the recent Italian supply vehicle.

Whereas Maria is all wholesome, sensual curves, Florence has the wiry frame of a distance runner: barely-there breasts, straight lines, zero body fat. She becomes chatty, peppering me with questions about my experience in conflict zones.

"How long were you in Sarajevo? And Freetown? I was in Sarajevo too," she says, her voice wistful, as if remembering a lost lover. She takes such a long drag on her cigarette, I think she might smoke it all in one pull. "I ran the death zone. Many times, I ran the death zone, just to see my boyfriend for twenty minutes." Another long drag. "Don't you miss it?" Puff. "We were exhausted, but so alive." Tilting her head back, she blows the smoke through her nose.

So alive. I wonder if Florence ran the death zone not to be with her boyfriend, but *because* of the Serbian snipers—if the rush was what she lived for, and what she misses.

"Why don't you go back to it?" I ask. "Darfur, the Congo …?"

She draws on her cigarette, holding on to it as long as she can, a tendril of smoke leaking from her nostrils. "I broke down, they wouldn't let me. You were there too. Don't you miss it?"

"Where?" I find myself losing interest.

"Sarajevo. And Freetown during the war."

Off to the side, Maria is stirring a pot of thick, bubbling sauce. She chats easily in Krio with the women around her, no pretention, no wanting to be somewhere else. I feel a sense of sadness—Florence's intensity reminds me of myself. "I did, until recently," I say. For the first time, I feel comfortable looking Florence in the eye. "I don't miss being a medical cowboy. But the people—it's the people I miss."

TWENTY-SEVEN

"Have you ever seen anything like that cloud, Mohamed?"

"No," he grumbles, looking to the north.

We left the two nurses as we found them, waving on the verandah. Maria was smiling, inviting us to return on our way back to Freetown. She was the picture of happiness: content to hand out boxes of condoms, to encourage the women to reduce the starch in their diet, to lose herself in the euphoria of African voices. Florence's smile reminded me of women who've had too much work done—tight skin across unyielding bones, a mask of discontent. I doubt if she'll be here on our return trip.

Mohamed is unsure which way to go. We've stopped at the main road: to the left is the route into the darkness, north toward Kabala; to the right, the way south and the blue sky. Eventually, after the town of Bo, the road will fork toward the east: Buedu. The idling sound of the ancient Mercedes is unlike anything I've ever heard—a cacophony of pops and pings and occasional farts with no particular rhythm at all. The perfect soundtrack for how I'm feeling. I've called Nadia three times since our last conversation, and three times the answering machine has come on, my own voice telling me to leave a message.

The first time I left a message, I apologized for putting Nadia through this. Promised yet again I would be home before the baby kicked. The second time, I mumbled that I missed her. The third time, I hung up.

"Very strange, Mr. John. I grow up in the north and never see a black sky like that. Some call the harmattan the red wind. The sun and sky go red, not black. I never see this black business before."

Something the preacher said comes to mind: *If you are going into the pit of darkness, maybe it's telling you something.* It's something my father would have said. Mohamed waits patiently, his good hand on the steering wheel. His usually expressive face seems reserved, monk-like—even his toothpick is still. *Change your course! Reach for the sky!* Mariama wrote about being on the road to Kabala, but she didn't describe getting there. At some point the rebels must have turned south. I close my eyes. When I open them, the darkness to the north remains. It doesn't feel right.

"I think we should shift gears, Mohamed. Let's go south, toward the blue sky."

He smiles. "You begin to think like an African, Mr. John! Something in your belly tell you it is time to change!" He taps his stump on the wheel—his one-armed version of a high-five.

Even the Mercedes seems to feel better for it—with the blackness behind us, we're soon pushing forty or fifty kilometres an hour with nary a cough. Mohamed is in good spirits, if a little tired. He tells me he found a country chicken for the evening and is feeling healthy again. On that note, he's worried about me. "Mr. John, too long without loving, you will get sick!"

"How did you lose your arm, Mohamed?"

His eyes remain intent on the road, his stump resting on the steering wheel. I wonder if he's heard me. "A rebel bullet," he says, finally. "Mohamed be the only one-armed man in Sierra Leone who lose his arm to a bullet. No axe or cutlass from a boy soldier, no short sleeves or long, just a bullet that smash the bone to pieces."

"I'm sorry," I say. "But you do well with your good arm."

"Some think we will never have another war," he says. "They say we have laws now that stop more wars. Huh! As long as there are snakes in the grass, someone go get bit."

A truck loaded with lumber, Allah Be Praised emblazoned in bold red letters on the back, looms like a pregnant elephant in front of us. Several bags of sand perch precariously on the wood, and on top of it all is the inevitable group of hitchhikers—any transport with a breeze is better than walking in the thirty-eight-degree heat. The beast spews diesel smoke so black it reminds me of the cloud we left behind.

I feel uneasy. On impulse I look to the road behind us. "Shit, Mohamed." A pack of vehicles and, wedged in the middle, a green Nissan.

Mohamed kicks the accelerator to the floor and pulls into the oncoming lane. The Mercedes hesitates. As usual, Mohamed has the car in too high a gear. "Mohamed! I don't think—"

"Not to worry, Mr. John. In Africa, we know the rules of the road—it's like the jungle, small animals make way for big ones."

Speeding toward us in the oncoming lane is a bigger animal—another overloaded truck. "Christ, Mohamed!"

At the last possible second, he swerves, forcing a motorbike with three passengers to slide over to the right, while walkers, hawkers, chickens and a few goats somehow step off the road as one. The oncoming behemoth manages to maintain its lane—a lights-flashing, horn-honking near miss.

"There!" he says. "Mohamed knows how to drive. Only Africans can drive this way." He slaps his stump on the wheel so hard, I think even he must have had his doubts.

"Any sign of the green Nissan?" I ask, afraid to look behind.

"*Insha'Allah*, we leave him in di dust," he says. He doesn't look in the rear-view mirror either.

March, 1999. I do not know the day.

The women suffer bad. Most have women's problems from all the sex. Some have gonorrhea or have trouble holding their water. And many get pregnant. Commander Abu let me treat the women in traditional ways. I pound *kumulie* leaves for infections, and bark and roots from the violet tree for inflammation and headache. Sometimes I give these in a high dose to cause abortion—but I only treat those who ask.

One day Madonna come to me. That woman is a strange one. I have seen her shoot a mammy and her baby, and her face look like she was hoeing the garden. Another time I see her laugh when a rebel cut off the hand of an old man. She is one mean woman.

She come at night, after the men and boys asleep. The moon is full and I see her standin over me. It is the first time I have seen her wear a *lappa*. Wah! She is so beautiful in the moonlight.

"Mariama," she say. "I need you see me."

"I see you," I say.

"I am sick. You must help me."

When she lie down she pull the *lappa* about her hips and I know from the smell what she have. I see bad cases of gonorrhea at Connaught Hospital, but we have western drugs there. In the bush I have only traditional medicine like violet tree bark. But it take a long time to prepare and it is difficult to treat infection like Madonna have. It so bad I do not know how that girl walk and carry a gun.

She is wet with sweat and there is fear in her eyes. With Killerboy dead she knows she must find a new bush husband or she cannot say no to the others. "You must not have sex until the sickness is gone," I say. "When you go for yaya in a town you must find a pharmacy with antibiotics. Or you must get Commander Abu to send you to the MSF clinic in Makeni or Bo. Tomorrow you will help me find *kumulie* leaves to wash the pus."

We hide all next day, so she take me in the evening, under the moon. Madonna have her gun and walk behind. She is so quiet I hear only the bug-bugs singin in my ears. We walk alone in the elephant grass, the baby on my back makin soft sounds like she do. That little girl feel like part of me now.

After a while we come to a stream under good trees. It is so nice I think there is no war on. We sit by the cool water and I think of my mammy. When I was a little girl she would take me to the river near Sumbuya. We just spend time, she washin clothes, telling me stories, then washin my hair. My mammy is so strong the men elect her the mammy queen. All the women come to her. Even the chief come. I remember he bring *poyo* and they sit in the shade talking. Those were good days.

I want to stay in Sumbuya, but my mammy say no. She want me to go to Freetown to learn to be a nurse with western medicine. She say the old ways are good, but she want me learn the new. After I finished school in Sumbuya she come one day with auntie from Freetown. Mammy say, "You go now Mariama, you go live with auntie and learn nursing." She gave me a bag with money for school fees. She never tell me where that money is from, but I think it was money from her whole life, all in a bag. "You go come back when you finish the nursing," she say. That was ten years ago, and I never see my mammy again.

I am pulling roots and Madonna is sitting close by, holdin her gun and watching me. She wears soldier pants tight around her hips and a shirt that show her strong breasts.

"Where you learn to be nurse?" she ask.

"I go nursing school at Connaught Hospital," I say. She nod her head but her mind seems far away. "Madonna, what you do before the rebels catch you?"

"I be a farmer near Makeni," she say. "They shoot mi mammy and pappy and take mi brothers for go fight."

"You have a husband?"

"He a soldier," she say. "He a soldier for the SLA. Maybe one day I see him pointing his rifle at me. But no matter. He nor take me back now."

"What you real nem?" I ask, pickin at some root.

She look at me a long time, like she is makin up her mind about something. "Madonna mi nem now. Anyone else long dead," she say looking away.

I notice something in the bush behind her. I think it is moonlight playing tricks, but it move and I know what it is—a man standin still as a tree with no wind. He is wearing a strange hat and a ronko shirt and no pants. He holds a rifle that looks very old, like you see in pictures of times gone by. Then I smell it—the same stink like I smell the day Killerboy was shot. It is the smell of rotting flesh. Kamajor. He nod his head like he is my friend, but his eyes stay on Madonna.

Madonna start looking at me strange like she is having a feelin for to make her scared. She sniffs the air and I see she smells it too. That is when she knows. Everything is standin still, quiet all around us. I feel sweat fall between my breasts. All of a sudden Madonna turn and starts shooting at the Kamajor.

I fall to the ground and hold the baby under me, our faces are close and I can feel her nose on mine. Madonna's rifle is so loud I cover her ears with my hands. That baby give me such strength. The firin stop and I see Madonna, bent over, walkin slow through the smoke from her gun. She move like a cat in the moonlight to the spot the Kamajor hunter was standing.

I think for sure that man is dead. Only a rifle from olden times, and Madonna so good with her weapon. She call me then, looking at the ground. I feel like turning and running away, but I know Madonna catch me, so I take the baby and go and stand beside her. On the ground there is nothing—no blood, no body, no footprints. "Them Kamajors have special medicine make them disappear," she whispers. She look at me strange, like she want to say something, but she stays quiet.

I do not tell her I have seen that man before, when Killerboy was shot. I do not tell her that man nod his head at me like he know me. When we go back Madonna tell me to walk in front. I feel her eyes and know she is staring at me from behind as we walk. My mind is racing along, trying to understand. That man was so strange. I do not know what he want or why he do not shoot me with his gun. To him I look like a rebel woman but still he just wag his head, like he say, "Kushe, ow di bodi?"

Everyone speak of the Kamajors like they all have magic stronger than the rebel guns. Kamajors disappear they say, or stand up to bullets, or make your monthly blood come. And the things they do! We see bodies with organs cut out, or eyes gone. It makes me wonder who is good in this world.

As we go back to camp I notice something strange. That bad smell is gone. Now I know what they say must be true. The Kamajors keep organs of their enemies, that is what makes them smell so bad.

Oh dear Jesus, what can I do? Where can I go? The evil is everywhere.

"Mr. John, it nor my business, but what is in di box?"

For several miles, Mohamed has been unusually quiet. I know he's skeptical about the "echo-diagnostic equipment." I know, too, that he's Poro, the distinctive scars along his spine are there for all to see. But then, most men in the country are either Poro or ex-Poro, the latter usually born-again Christians. And Mohamed is a Kuranko man. I remind myself of Momodu's words: *Trust the Kuranko*. This is a country where mystery and intrigue are as thick as the humid air—if I can't trust Mohamed, what am I doing, driving with him into the most isolated parts of the country?

"It's a mask, given to me during the war by my friend, Dr. Momodu Camara. I really don't know much about it. The rebels were entering the city and Momodu felt threatened. He brought it to me in the middle of the night and asked me to keep it for him. I promised I would return it if I could."

Slowly, Mohamed's head swivels toward me. His stare is so intense, I reach out to grab the wheel.

"May Allah help us! Your Momodu Camara was the son

of Ibrahim Camara! But Mr. John, you said he was born in Freetown."

"Well, I assumed he was. He seemed pretty worldly, and he was educated in London. He had a British accent."

Mohamed is so incredulous, he does something remarkable—he slows down and pulls the Mercedes off the road. When he finally speaks, he takes pains to punctuate each word, as if making sure the imbecile seated beside him will understand. "Your friend's father, Ibrahim Camara, was the greatest living Kuranko, a high priest in the Kamajor hunter society. It is a Mende word, it mean "to disappear." Ibrahim Camara was from the northeast, near Guinea. Uh! The RUF dogs murdered him during the war. They say his medicine was so strong, he himself had to tell the rebels how to kill him." Mohamed pauses, his eyes burning into mine. "The mask give power to the medicines that make Kamajors invisible to bullets. You have in the box the most powerful mask in Sierra Leone!"

TWENTY-EIGHT

We've attracted a small crowd of young roadside hawkers, who surround the car with the usual head-borne platters of fruits and vegetables. Inquisitive eyes and snotty noses are framed by the open windows.

"Oh, my friend. You had that mask on your wall in Canada? And you brought it through Lungi Airport in a box you call medical equipment? Allah be praised, you are a wonder."

Oblivious to the seriousness of our discussion, the young merchants reach into the car, a moving bouquet of unwashed hands holding pieces of ripe fruit of every description. "You de buy from me? You de buy from me?" The eyes are hopeful— selling a few bananas would make their day.

Mohamed's revelation about the mask is like being told an

asteroid is coming—no one knows where the thing is going to hit, but when it does, everything, everywhere, will be different. In the back seat, in a battered wooden crate, rests a mask that was somehow important to the Kamajors, the secret hunter society that many Sierra Leoneans feel was instrumental in winning the long civil war.

"Do you believe it, Mohamed? About the powers of the Kamajors?"

Mohamed's eyes look straight ahead, as if staring at something only he can see. When he answers me, his voice has an authority to it—the kind of voice doctors use, or try to use, when confirming a diagnosis to a disbelieving patient. "It is true, Mr. John. It is all true."

I hesitate to ask my next question. "How do you know?"

Slowly, his head turns toward me. I can no longer hear the children—it's as if all sound has been absorbed into the bush around us. "I am Kamajor." The words come from his lips, but I have difficulty understanding. Or maybe I'm too afraid.

Slowly, the pieces begin to fit. Ibrahim Camara was Momodu Camara's father, and the man sitting beside me was a member of the same mysterious hunter society. The excitement in my gut is like water gushing from a spring—what else can Mohamed tell me? "Alright. So, now that you know who my friend Momodu Camara is, where should we be looking for him?"

Mohamed's expression changes and his eyes tell another story, something I'm slow to register. "I am sorry, Mr. John. I never guess your Momodu be the son of Ibrahim Camara. There are many Camaras in Sierra Leone, and you say Momodu was from Freetown. He would have been a great man like his father."

"Would have been?" No. Suddenly I want Mohamed to stop talking.

"Mr. John, your friend Momodu is dead." Mohamed looks off into the distance. "He was a member of the Civil Defence Forces. I, too, was with the CDF. Most of us were from the Tamaboro or Kamajor hunter societies. The rebels fear us bad, even more than the Nigerians. The rebels have a long list of enemies: people with the government, chiefs, *sowas* and their families. Momodu Camara was caught in January 1999, in Freetown, at his sister's house. The rebels lock the whole family in the house and burn it to the ground."

"Jesus, Mohamed ..." The air is too heavy to breathe. I've assumed I wouldn't find Momodu alive, but I've never contemplated him being murdered in such a way—one of Sierra Leone's brightest and most compassionate sons, butchered by a motley gang of boys and teenagers wearing rags on their heads. *January 1999.* The excitement I felt a moment ago turns to nausea— Momodu may have been killed on the very night he left the mask with me.

Even the child hawkers sense the gravity of our conversation. As one, the many pairs of hands withdraw through the windows. The eyes of the children are fixed on Mohamed.

"And the green Nissan?" I ask, afraid of what else Mohamed might know.

Grinding on a new toothpick, he hesitates, gives his shoulders a shrug. "Unless they are following us for electro-what-do-you-call equipment," he says, "Mohamed thinks we are not the only people in Sierra Leone who know that the mask has returned."

Nadia picks up on the first ring. "John?"

"Hi, it's me."

"You sound far away today."

I feel far away. We've stopped at another roadside market. It's very hot. I have a bag of groundnuts on my lap and a Coke as hot as soup on the dash in front of me. A throng of kids with trays on their heads waits patiently beside my window—in Sierra Leone, the store always comes to you. Mohamed has decided I need some time alone. He is off to the side, talking with a man who sells bush-meat along the side of the road.

"I tried calling a few times."

"I'm sorry, John. I'm better now."

"Were you sick?"

She laughs. "Let's just say, even Finnegan is getting tired of all the long walks I've been taking. How is it going?"

"I have some bad news, I'm afraid. Momodu is dead. He was murdered in the same month I left the country."

The line is silent. I was going to tell her about the mask and Mohamed and how I'm beginning to think that every- thing is strangely connected—that I don't know how, but even Mariama's disappearance may be linked to everything else, but the words remain formless deep in my throat. I imagine Nadia sitting in her chair, one hand on her mouth, trying to compre- hend what I've said about Momodu. Or maybe she has one hand on her belly and she's shaking her head at the futility of it all.

Finally, she says, "I'm so sorry about your friend."

Mohamed and the bush-meat seller are standing apart from everyone else in the market. Some children approach them and Mohamed waves them away. There is something unusual about the man. Sierra Leoneans, regardless of how poor they are, take pride in being clean. This man is dishevelled and filthy.

"Well, I guess half my journey is over," I say.

"Half your journey?"

"There's still Mariama."

The only thing I can hear is her breathing. I wonder if she can hear mine. I should tell her I'm on my way, that I will leave this place of mysticism and myth and women bent over hot stones. I will cut off the part of myself that brought me here and move forward, for isn't that what Nadia and I have always done—thought not of what was behind us, but where we were going?

"Nadia, do you remember the day you came home from your long walk? You told me to come here. You said you might even change your mind, but you knew it was the right thing to do."

"I remember. I suppose I still believe that, although the longer you're away, the easier it is to worry and second-guess everything. You can come home, you know."

"I know, it's—"

"But if you don't, there's something you need to do."

"Yes?"

"Prepare yourself for whatever it is you find there, okay?"

The silence is as long as the miles between us. When we say goodbye and I love you, it feels forced. For the first time since returning to Sierra Leone, I feel a loss of sensation in my hand, a numbness that starts in my palm and seeps, pore by pore, into my fingers. And there's something else—an overwhelming sadness that grows like a tumour in my gut. I wasn't prepared for the news about Momodu. And I have no idea how to prepare for Mariama, alive or dead.

Mohamed returns with the bloody leg of a duiker and throws it in the trunk.

"You like bush-meat, Mr. John?"

"Will it keep in the trunk? It's thirty-five degrees, Mohamed."

"Ah, no problem. When we stop tonight I will have a woman cook it." He puts the key in the ignition, pauses and turns toward me. "You look bad, Mr. John."

"I was just talking with my wife. Being here is not easy on us."

"Okeh, okeh," he says, as he starts the Mercedes and pulls onto the roadway. He and the bush-meat seller exchange waves. Mohamed pops a new toothpick in his mouth and bounces his stump on the wheel. "We have a Krio proverb, Mr. John. It say, 'As the drum beats, so the dance goes.'"

Everyone is jumpy when Madonna and I come back. We stay in a village the rebels raid that day. The new girls are placed in one house, the new boys in another. Madonna and Commander Abu talk for a long time. They look my way, shakin their heads. I know I got to go run away soon. Fear fills my belly like a bowl of rottin chop. Those rebels kill anyone, old men, old women, young babies, everyone who gets in their way. They need me for nursing now, but what will happen when we get to Buedu? I see the things they do if you get caught tryin to escape. It is too bad to talk about.

The baby is uneasy and fuss. I feed her rice mush with ripe banana but she still fuss, like she is in pain. Even she know Abu is watching me, thinking I am a witch. At night he puts more guards around the camp and sends a boy to sit in the sick house with the wounded and me. For sure Abu nor trust me anymore, but those young boys make bad soldiers. In the morning the boy is sleepin, his rifle in his arms. If those Kamajors want to kill us they be smart to come at night when the young boys guard us.

Commander Abu move camp every day. The women and girls do all the carrying, the boys and men just carry their guns. Everyone is so tired. The pregnant girls struggle to keep up. Many girls get pregnant and hope it will lead to less sexing. It is taboo to have sex with women feeding babies. But the rebels forget their culture. Those girls get old quick. They only sleep when the men and boys sleep, not before.

We are all afraid. Afraid each morning of what the day bring. We are even afraid the war will end soon. Everyone know rebel women are damaged goods. I don shame to my family to be with the rebels. Everyone say a rebel woman is worse than a rebel man. I feel shame for this, shame every day. Some girls run away, knowin they will be shot or cut like a mango when the rebels find them. They know if they go home they will bring shame to their family. Some try for go to Freetown or Bo, any big place for to get lost.

Some, like Madonna, enjoy the life. Before the war they are nobody, just a poor farmer or fruit seller. They are lucky if they have enough rice to eat and two *lappas* and an outfit for Sunday. Now some rebel girls have more power than a mammy queen. They never have such clothes before. They have others who carry for them, cook for them, get firewood for them. The strongest with the gun, the meanest in camp—they are the ones who become big.

Everything is so upside down. Boy soldiers like to make the older men beg. Beg them not to rape their wife in front of them. Beg them not to cut off their arms or the arms of their children. The strong ones, like Maskita or Madonna or Abu, like to hear those sounds too. The sound of people beggin is sweet to their ears.

Some choose to die. I wake up one day and see a girl named Amy, sixteen and very pretty. Amy is hangin by her neck from a tree. They capture her near Makeni and all the boys say, "Look at the pretty one." They make sure they spoil her. She know she will never bring a bride price now. They spoil her every night then make her carry a bag of rice on her head in the day.

I see that body and I think maybe Amy is better off than me swinging like that. She does not feel shame no more. I look in my arms and Jolie's baby look back at me. Those little eyes on mine, telling me something. I know what she say—Amy is someone's baby.

So I take a knife and go cut Amy down from the tree. I wash her young body and wrap her in white cloth. Somethin strange come over me then, like I do not care what anyone think. I am alone with that girl's body and I feel my belly warm with a love I have not felt for a long time. From somewhere long ago a voice come up in me, a Mende mournin song my mammy used to sing when she prepared the dead. I sing,

> E yala yala e yalao
> E yala yala e yalao
> E yala yala nunga e yalao

I look up and see other women putting on something white, our mourning cloth. They hum the tune from deep in their throats. As I wash Amy's body she look young again, like a girl who has not been damaged by this life.

I feel a darkness cover me—Commander Abu, he stand so close his shadow cool me from the sun. I can feel his anger. Commander Abu does not speak Mende and has ordered us not to speak it when he is in the camp.

"Mariama," he say, "there is no time. Put her in di hole and we de go quick-quick."

Behind me a few women continue to sing, *"E yala yala e yalao."* Maybe this gives me strength, for I do not feel afraid. "Thank you commander for you bring me cool shade," I say. "I will not go before I finish wrappin her body and we eat a mournin meal of rice and *plassas*. And then we will put some in the hole with her to help her on her way. Only then will I go."

I can feel the feet of Jolie's baby on my back as I say this. I have seen Abu put a bullet in a boy's head when he move too slow getting him some *poyo*, why would I speak to him this way? My hands keep washin Amy's cold body and I do not catch his eye.

"You defy me Mariama! What was that you was singin?"

Slowly my eyes raise to his. There is fire there, and something else I see but do not understand. Abu look like he has a big talk goin on in his head. So I sing in English,

> He has taken away,
> He has taken away.
> What God give to us
> He has taken away.

His breath come out like the hiss of a snake. "You stand now Mariama," he says.

"I will not stand," I say. My voice sound stronger than I feel inside. "Not until she is ready."

There is something in the commander's eyes that I see before when I fixed his wound—it is the look of one who has come to a fork in the path, not sure which way to go. "Mariama you a witch for sure. We de go in thirty minutes. If you not ready, then you body will lie on the girl in that grave."

He walk away and all the men and boys look down at the ground—everyone interested in their shoes or have a sliver in their toes. I know then if I do not escape soon I am goin to die or lose my soul to the devil.

The baby on my back kick me again. "If we escape I go give you a name," I say. "I go give you a special name."

TWENTY-NINE

Mohamed isn't himself. He seems preoccupied, and the deeper into the country we go, the more distracted he becomes—staring ahead, checking his rear-view mirror and mumbling to himself. My driver-detective with a manic tendency to chuckle and to sing along with Dolly has lost his considerable joie de vivre. My revelation about what is in the box has rattled him. I welcome the silence.

We stop in a village for the night and Mohamed finds a family that agrees to take me in. He hauls out the bloody duiker leg and offers it to the woman of the house. She accepts the leg with the smile of someone receiving a Christmas turkey. Before long, the smells from her cooking fire make me forget my misgivings about bush-meat stored in the tropical heat.

They have two rooms—one for storage and one that serves as the parlour-bedroom for the couple and their two children. The man places my pack on the bed and nods his head in a welcoming way. The bed is ancient: a filthy mattress on a rusted spring frame. When I protest about taking the family's only bed, he laughs as if I've told an outrageous joke. Of course I will have the bed, am I not their guest?

Mohamed insists on sleeping in the car. I worry out loud about him getting malaria, to which he dismissively waves his hand. "No problem," he says. "I am African, Mr. John, I get malaria every year. *Insha'Allah*, I am still alive."

I sling my net over the bed and lie with my head on my duffle bag—the yellow light of my headlamp illuminating the words in Mariama's diary. It doesn't matter how many times I read it, I just start where I left off and read it again. The beam of light shines on the faded handwriting: Mariama recounts sitting in the shadow of a thug named Abu, defying him. Abu thought she was a witch. Witches don't do well in Africa.

It is only when I turn off the lamp, put the book down and stare into the darkness that I let myself think of Nadia. I know she won't plead with me, and she shouldn't have to. She needs me, and I should be with her, but I have a sense that the couple we used to be, the couple with enough love to look forward but never the strength to look back, won't last.

Nadia had it right the first time—this journey is the right thing to do.

"What you do with the mask now?" Mohamed asks, out of the blue. We've been driving for two hours and have barely said a word to each other.

Mohamed seems to think the men in the green Nissan are following us because of the mask. But why? The war has been over for seven years, and the country is peaceful. If it's the mask they want, why haven't they tried to take it? We've covered miles of roads with nothing but bush on either side—plenty of opportunity to run down a slow-moving 1966 Mercedes.

"My priority is to find Mariama now," I say. "I've only got another week or so. If we don't find her, I've got to go home." I glance at Mohamed. He's chewing on his toothpick so furiously he could get slivers. "Okay, what?"

He takes his eyes off the road and glares at me. "You are the keeper, Mr. John."

"In that case, the mask is in trouble. I'm clearly not up to the task."

We spend a night in a small market village with a health clinic run by a Dutch NGO. The nurses recommend the Happy Guest House: two rooms, separate flush toilet and a verandah facing the setting sun. The village chief, a gregarious, heavy-set fellow, joins us for *poyo*. Women and children gather on the baked clay while men sit or lean on the verandah. It is always the same—the presence of the chief seems to turn the gathering into a public meeting.

One jerry can of *poyo* leads to another. As the sun sets, platters of rice and *grin-grin* and potato leaves are laid out. We eat using flashlights and a lantern. People come and go, and I'm surprised that so many drift in and out of the darkness.

No one has heard of a midwife matching Mariama's description. I notice, or perhaps imagine, a few women standing back, looking from me to Mohamed, whispering among themselves. Mohamed tells me they are traditional birth attendants—women trained through word of mouth and experience to deliver babies. They are also *soweis*, the women who perform the Bundu initiation. The birth attendants are curious and polite, but the message is clear—childbirth is women's business. I'm struck with the impression that either we're asking the wrong questions or we're the wrong people to be asking after a midwife in the first place.

Finally, the last of the *poyo* is drunk and our visitors disappear into the night.

"I'm exhausted, I have to go to bed," I tell Mohamed.

"We will leave early," he says, making no effort to move. There is an edge to him now, and it is easy to imagine Mohamed as a Kamajor. As I walk away, I look back to the verandah—he sits against the door frame, staring into the distance, as if expecting something or someone to come out of the darkness.

"Bonnie! How are you?"

"John? Are you back?"

"Still here. I guess the place is growing on me. I'm under my mosquito net, wearing a headlamp and enjoying the jungle sounds. I thought I should check in and make sure you're still campaigning for me to become the new department head."

"It's so nice to hear from you—Nadia told me your cell phone worked great. The two of us had a wonderful lunch. I love her, she's quite a lady."

This is a surprise. Bonnie and Nadia have only met at Psychiatry department Christmas parties. I wonder if Nadia initiated the get-together, and if she told Bonnie about the tension between us. "My two favourite women having lunch. Should I be freaked out?"

"Yes, for sure. It's all the more reason for you to come home soon. I might just take her to the Mirror Image."

"I'm on the next plane," I say.

Bonnie's chuckle is mischievous, and I smile at the thought of the two of them in the bar with all the mirrors.

"Nadia told me about your friend Momodu. I'm sorry for your loss."

"Thanks, Bonnie. I have a tough time accepting it. Momodu always seemed larger than life—the kind of person who would survive any calamity. The Sierra Leoneans loved him …"

My voice fails me. Bonnie, always comfortable with silence, waits on the other end of the line. The phone beeps a warning that the battery is low. Finally, she says, "John, I have some good news. It's about Art McLeod, your Mr. Neat 'n' Tidy. He's stayed on the antipsychotics and is doing so well he checked himself into rehab. One day at a time, but doing well so far."

"Hmm. Great news. Tell him I'm happy for him." I have a vision of the man in camouflage clothing pushing his buggy. "Did you know he was a teacher in an earlier life?"

"Images are deceiving, aren't they?"

"Well, as you said, one step at a time."

"John?"

"Yes, Bonnie?"

My headlamp picks up a spider on the ceiling the size of my hand.

"Where is the mask?"

"It's here by my bed, just as you recommended, safe and sound in a poorly disguised crate. Why?"

I shine my headlamp toward the crate in the corner of the room, half expecting the mask to open the lid and climb out. The crate remains closed.

"Your friend Momodu trusted you with it. What are you going to do with it now?"

I stare at the spider, trying to remember what Mohamed had said, something like *you are the keeper*. "My driver, Mohamed, is kind of uptight about the whole mask thing. I would give it to him, but he doesn't seem to want it either. You were right—the mask is a big deal here." More beeps in my ear. "Bonnie, this phone is just about done."

"I'll call Nadia for lunch again. Look in on her."

"Thanks. That would be great. She said I needed to come here, to figure my life out. Since I've arrived, well, it hasn't been good between us. She's back and forth, and we're both a little insecure—always skating around things."

The beeps are constant—the battery is about to die. "You know, Bonnie, I'm lying on a straw bed with only a net between me and the biggest spider I've ever seen. I don't even know the name of the village I'm in. I'm feeling pretty far away from the world I'm used to. I'm way over my head. It's getting freaky, like the women in my life have this prescience or something. It's like you're always a step or two ahead of me."

"Well, never underestimate strong women," she says. "And John …"

"I'm about to lose you, Bonnie."

I don't think she hears me. She says, "Nadia told me she feels guilty that she asked you to go on this trip. She's worried about you. How are you, really?"

How am I? Frightened. Leaving Nadia on her own frightens me. The people in the green Nissan frighten me. Admitting that Mariama may have met the same fate as Momodu frightens me. Knowing Mohamed was, or still is, one of these Kamajors frightens me.

"I'm fine, Bonnie. For the first part of this trip, I spent most of my time anticipating what I would say to my friends if I found them. Now I'm kind of numb. I'd always thought Momodu had a better chance than Mariama of making it, so, well, I'm kinda wearing down, I guess."

The line goes dead. I turn off the headlamp, wondering if the spider will be there in the morning. I hope it is.

THIRTY

It's as if there's a hole in the Mercedes and my driver's significant presence is slowly leaking away. Occasionally, I try to pull him back. I play the tape I'd begun to loathe just a few days before: Dolly, Shania and the nameless choir. He doesn't sing along and offers monosyllabic replies to my questions. He drives, checks the rear-view mirror, stares ahead.

Mohamed doesn't say it in so many words, but he's become obsessed with the mask. The more he withdraws, the more I'm tempted to drop the crate at the next petrol station. My concern is finding Mariama, but we're running out of time and places to look.

Just before the city of Bo, we pull in to Taiama, a small village on a rock-strewn river bend. The women in the clinic there don't know of anyone matching Mariama's description, but they offer us a lunch of leftover groundnut stew and some *poyo* and leave us to eat in the shade of their house.

I notice a woman being led along by a young boy, possibly her son. She's in her thirties and is totally blind. "River blindness," I say. "It must be common here, with the blackflies by the river."

"Ah, yes, blackfly fever. I have heard the blindness is from the eggs hatching worms in the eyes," says Mohamed. "But our people believe in juju. Many believe the worms in their eyes are not from the fly eggs, but from curses—everyone gets bitten by the flies, but not everyone goes blind."

"Everyone gets bitten, but not everyone goes blind," I say, watching the young mother and her son. She carries a platter of laundry on her head. Her balance is perfect. She reminds me of Mariama in that hallway years before—a picture of elegance amidst all of the suffering. "Mohamed, I have to go back to Canada."

He seems not to have heard me. "Have you ever put it on?" he asks.

"You mean the mask? On my head?"

He's looking at me intently. "The mask is powerful for the wearer, Mr. John. When a mask is used, the identity of the wearer is hidden. This will protect the wearer from others and keep the power of the mask strong. I think this mask would have magic squares on the inside, and in these are secret words—words that tell the wearer how to use the mask. But it is the mask that choose the wearer, you see." He fills my mug, his eyes not straying from mine. *It is the mask that choose the wearer.* "Mr. John, are you sick?"

"This *poyo* is strong stuff. I feel drunk." I like having him back. Engaged. I've put my trust in him—what do I have to lose? "*Secret words?*" I say, recalling the night in my office when I put the mask on my head. "Mohamed, when I put it on I saw some kind of symbols. I have no idea what they were." I feel dizzy and wait for it to pass. "But there was something else …"

Mohamed stares at me, his body is completely still. "I had a dream the night Momodu left the mask with me. I saw some sort of clearing at the foot of a mountain. It had a fence, like a fence of leaves and sticks, and in front were some strange figures. They seemed part animal, part human, made of sticks and some kind of grass or dried plant." I close my eyes for a moment, catching my breath. "Behind the clearing, rising out of the trees, the mountain cast a huge shadow. It was as if the place never had any sunshine."

Mohamed's jaw unhinges, leaving a bubble of palm wine suspended from his lip. "The mask of Ibrahim Camara has revealed its sacred grove to you? Mr. John, this is very strange. A mask speaking to you, and you are not a Kuranko man, not even a black man! We must go and find your Mariama, and then return this mask. And we must be very careful."

"But where will we take it?" I regret even asking the question—I don't want to encourage him.

He's already walking to the car. "Ah, I do not know. We must find out. But first your friend. You hire Mohamed to bring you to two friends. One is dead. If the nurse is alive, we will find her."

We settle into the Mercedes and Mohamed revs the engine. "We're running out of places to look, aren't we, Mohamed?"

"The rainy season will start soon," he says, looking toward some monstrous clouds on the horizon. "When the rainy season come, we go nowhere."

Day after day we walk. It is so long since we leave Freetown. The rainy season come soon. In the dark of night we pass Taiama and join some more rebels. They all talk about making a big attack on Bo. I see no sign of Maskita. That man have all the girls he want so maybe he forget about the nurse named Mariama Lahai.

We meet another rebel group today. With them is a doctor I know from the Military Hospital in Wilberforce. He tell me Maskita capture his whole family and keep them near Buedu. If he leave the rebels, Maskita say he will kill the whole family. I ask him if he know if the foreign doctors come back to Freetown. Some come back he says, but he does not know who.

Before he go he give me some morphine. Do not let the commanders know what it is, he say. If they ask, you go tell them it is a drug for women's problems. I am happy with this. Maybe if I help our wounded with their pain we will get some sleep.

At night I stay with the sick and I am left alone. The rebels are all afraid of catching a curse from the unlucky ones, and now maybe they think I am a witch. So I sleep with the baby and listen to the moaning of boys and girls askin for their mammys and wanting to go home. Funny thing how they cut off the arms and legs of someone's ma or pa, but when they are sick they ask for their own mammys.

Now Jemi is hangin around Abu all of the time. He teach her to use guns and she has become his favourite wife. She go on raids and come back with new girls, pushing them with her gun. When she take drugs and go on yaya raids she looks crazy like the rest. At first I say, Jemi your mammy is waitin for you. After this war your mammy need you. But Jemi just look at me, her eyes far away. I have no mammy, she say. Abu look after me now.

I know Jemi speak the truth. She will have no family after the war. Even if her mammy survives and Jemi returns to her village, those people will know. Even if the government say forgive and forget we all know there be no forgetting this.

She have no family now, just Abu.

The closer we get to Bo the more vexed the rebels become. The town is defended by local people, Kamajors and some SLA. They say it is the only town that never fall to the rebels. We are camped by the river and Commander Abu come back from a raid with a prisoner, an SLA officer. His face is swollen from beatings and they pull him with a rope around his neck. Abu tell some boys to tie him to a stick and leave him in the sun. Abu and his men are so happy to have a Big Man to play with.

"Mariama, you go give him water but no nursin," Abu say.

"Commander, let me wash his cuts and give him shade," I say. I try to make my voice soft so he take pity.

"Water but no nursin, I tell you." Abu is so fierce I look down at the ground. It is the look you see in some boys before they have sex, like he is wound up too tight.

I bring water and feed the soldier with a cup. "What you nem?" I ask.

"I will die tonight," he say. He has a major's rank, but his eyes are the eyes of a young boy who is afraid. I have seen those eyes so many times I think it will leave a stain on my soul. "It is bitter," he say too loud, handing me back the cup.

"Stay quiet and drink, I put some powder for to kill di pain."

"I think you do not have enough powder," he say. His accent is Freetown. He has an education, which will make it go bad for him—the rebels hate anyone who can read.

"Later I will bring some more. It will help you tonight. I am sorry."

His eyes are wet and we both know without saying what will happen tonight.

"God will bless you," he say.

That night they all take drugs. Ganja. Cocaine. Brown-brown. None of those boys and girls take drugs before the war. Now they take it before every raid, and before sex. It make them so crazy. I see Jemi and Madonna dancin like she-devils they are so high. Their shadows dance on the prisoner—he is the only thing that does not move.

The moon is up when I bring him water again. "It taste worse than before," he say. Even then that soldier give me a little smile, the last he will give.

"It will help," I say. "Do you believe in Jesus?"

"I am saved," he say and then he start to cry. I give him more water and hope the paracetamol and morphine powder make his way easier.

All night long I hear that officer scream. "Kill me! Kill me!" he scream. I pray to Jesus to let that man go. In the sick house even the wounded fighters look scared. We all pray for that man. Finally the screaming stop, but the laughter and dancin go for a long time that night.

When Madonna go to her bed she have blood on her mouth. I learn that Madonna and some others eat the heart and liver of that man. She is the only girl I ever meet who do such things. After that night I know a curse be on that group for sure. I have a bad feelin that curse going to punish us all.

Commander Abu say I de go see Maskita in the next few days. He have a smile more nasty than the blood on Madonna's face. I know I need to go soon, but they watch me so close. Soon I must take a chance.

Since they kill the SLA officer I have been sick with malaria. I
have some drugs from a clinic the rebels raid, thank you God for
looking out for me. The fever help me not to think what they do to
that man. Instead I think of Dr. John. I see his face like he is there
beside me. One time I go to where the white folks live, the expat
compound they call it. People from America and Europe. Dr. John
ask me if I ever drink red wine. No, I have only tried *poyo*. So he
give me some. It is much stronger than the palm wine. One glass
make me feel like dancin, even with the white folks.

  Momodu Camara was sittin beside us drinking whisky.
Momodu have a way with the foreign doctors and nurses, they
all like him. He and Dr. John were good friends, but Dr. John never
really know the man sittin beside him. Those white folks think
Momodu was a doctor just like them. He was a good doctor, sure,
but that is not all he was—not in Sierra Leone.

THIRTY-ONE

I'm awakened by a thumping sound. My first thought is, not another U-joint. My eyes open to a sign welcoming us to Bo. Mohamed is bumping his stump on the steering wheel. "How you sleep?" he asks.

Through the dirty windshield, I take in the dusty streets. "I sleep fine," I say.

"Good. We have been going about our search, how do you say, butt-backward!"

"Ass-backward. Mohamed, watch the road, please."

He honks the horn randomly. "Yes, *tenki*, ass-backward. We ask simple aid workers and Sierra Leoneans about your nurse. Why? They know nothing—only their own little worlds!"

"Go on ..." I'm intrigued by the sudden enthusiasm.

"What do they know about this country, eh?" He grins and shakes his head. "We de go ask the Lebanese! The Lebanese run this country. Forget what Sierra Leoneans say—what do they know? The Lebanese know what is going on!"

I'm having difficulty following, but he has my attention. For miles, my driver has been completely withdrawn—so much so that I've been thinking about asking him to turn around and take me back to Freetown. But this is more like the old Mohamed A. Lee.

"I thought the Lebanese specialized in business. How will they know about a Sierra Leonean midwife?"

"Ah, my friend, you are part right. The Lebanese know about money. They are, how do you say, connected! I never meet one with less than three cell phones, and they keep backups in their four-wheel drives. They are like Arabs—they nor know anything about women or midwives! But they know people who know women, and doctors. God willing, they will know!"

I laugh, thinking he may have a point. I remember many weekends spent at River 2 Beach, a stunning stretch of sand and surf south of Freetown that goes on for miles. The beach was a weekend party hub for Lebanese men, who came to drink, suck on water pipes and sing cheesy karaoke songs. For the most part, they seemed to prefer a stag atmosphere—men dancing and singing with other men. That is, until late at night, when carloads of African women from nearby Lumley were brought in for sex in the beachside bungalows. The women were gone at the crack of dawn, leaving the men together again, sleeping on the beach until their wives and girlfriends joined them later in the afternoon.

As we drive into the centre of Bo, it's clear that commerce, notably the trade in diamonds, is the domain of the Lebanese here. Mansour Diamonds, Abbas Diamond Enterprises, Salim Trader in Diamonds. The town has the feel of the American Old West: clapboard two-storey buildings, many with the Lebanese owners or their wives sitting behind a railing on the upper floor, surveying the action in the street below.

There is something else about the town. "Mohamed, what's with all the motorbikes and young men?"

"Ah, they are all ex–rebel boys. The government give motorbikes for guns. Forgive and forget, and get a motorbike!" he laughs, bouncing his stump on the wheel. "You turn you back, they steal you mother!"

Despite Mohamed's warning, Bo has an easygoing feel. The streets are crowded, dusty and cluttered with merchandise.

"Mohamed, each store advertises diamonds, but they're filled with televisions or fans or building supplies."

"Ah, what did I tell you? The Lebanese are, how do you say, opportunists. If a man can afford to buy diamonds, why not sell him a new television or toilet at the same time?"

"Good point," I say.

Mohamed parks at the shop of Salim Assad—Purveyor of Quality Diamonds. The street bustles with enterprises large and small: money-changers, diamond traders, orange sellers and beggars. We step over a ditch full of plastic bags, discarded Coke cans, rotting fruit. The blue-grey water smells of diesel fuel.

"Money! Leones, four thousand to di dollar, you exchange wit me?" Surrounding me like mosquitoes are three money-changers, each in his twenties, each one holding a wad of folded leones arranged like a fan. One holds his stack so close to my nose I can smell his cigarette-stained fingers. I start to back away when a tall, threatening presence appears between us. It takes me a moment to recognize the man with the ferocious expression is Mohamed.

"Where you manners! Lef him be now!" he shouts. He raises his hand to cuff the man closest to me. The young men slink away, as if fearful that more than a swat is coming their way. I stare at my one-armed driver—it's as if he suddenly became three times his actual size. "Ex–rebel boys," he explains with a shrug. "They have no manners."

The shop of Salim Assad is like a mini–department store. Refrigerators, cases of Coca-Cola and Fanta, toilets in several colours. The dust-covered soft drinks are perched on filthy televisions, giving the impression that the inventory isn't flying out of the store.

I follow Mohamed into the dark interior. Along the back is an ancient wooden counter. Behind this sits a Lebanese man sporting a two-day-old growth of beard. Beside him is an attractive woman wearing a white lace hijab. He looks to be in his mid-fifties—she a decade and a half younger. Off to the side, a young African woman is listlessly dusting the televisions.

"Ah, my brother Salim! It bin too long!" exclaims Mohamed.

The man with the five o'clock shadow lifts his head, his eyes shifting from Mohamed to me. His expression softens into a guarded smile. Mohamed, I think, isn't one of this man's closest brothers. "Mohamed, we never see you in Bo. *Ow di bodi?*" Salim asks.

"*Di bodi fine,*" says Mohamed. "And you?"

"Fine," says Salim. He turns to me. "You have brought a friend. Aminata! Bring tea." The young African woman abandons her dusting and disappears into a back room.

"This is Mr. John. He is a friend of Sierra Leone," says Mohamed.

Mohamed and Salim banter in Krio until Aminata returns carrying a silver tray with boiled water, silver teapot and glasses. She drops a handful of fresh mint, a half-cup of sugar and some cardamom into the pot. As she pours the water, the stale, dusty atmosphere is transformed by the aromatics of mint and cardamom.

Aminata smiles and offers me, then Mohamed, a steaming glass. Mohamed favours her with a look that is unabashedly lecherous. She holds his gaze with a coy smile. I've seen this before.

"My friend is interested in buying a coloured diamond," says Mohamed, shifting his gaze from Aminata to me.

I swallow, scalding my tongue and throat. Mohamed subtly shakes his head and his eyes darken.

"Ah, then you have brought him to the right place," says Salim, smiling warmly. "I specialize in coloured diamonds—we have pinks, purples and yellows. Every day, I receive more. Of course, because you are a referral from a brother in Islam, I will offer you the best price in Bo. There is no need to look elsewhere."

The Lebanese woman, who I assume is Salim's wife, stands and dips her head toward me. She turns and retreats to a back room. Complementing her hijab is a pair of tight designer jeans and a backside replete with glittering sequins in the shape of two hearts, one on each cheek.

"Really, I am here for other purposes," I stammer. Mohamed

glares at me. "Well, perhaps something small for my wife ... I would be happy to see what you have to offer."

The door to the back opens, and the attractive Lebanese woman, still not introduced, returns carrying a simple wooden box. She smiles, opens the box and withdraws a small velvet pouch. She sits across from me and waits. Aminata brings a chair and gestures for me to sit. Switching on a reading light, the woman in the hijab places a square of black velvet on the desk before me. Her kohl-blackened eyes find mine. I glance toward Mohamed and almost imperceptibly he nods. The stillness is broken by the clackety-clack of raw, uncut diamonds cascading onto velvet. She brushes the diamonds back and forth with her long-nailed fingertips. *Clackety-clack. Clackety-clack.* My eyes follow the stones—they are unpolished but beautiful. She rests a finger on one, moves it toward me with a nail, draws it back. Her eyes return to mine.

She takes a pair of tweezers and moves each gem, one at a time, toward me, pausing to give each its due. Pinks. Yellows. Purples. Browns. It's a dance, her hijab adding to the intimacy, as she moves one stone to the front, pauses, catches my eye, then moves on to the next, the two of us alone with the diamonds. Dust motes float lazily through the light under the lamp, sparkling like angel dust in a teasing rhythm—*see this, see what I have for you.*

"As Mohamed's friend, of course, I will offer you a price unmatched by competitors. You need not look elsewhere," Salim says again, breaking the spell.

I feel dazed, vaguely aware of the voices of others: Mohamed haggling over the price of a pink one, Salim offering to throw in the television of my choice with any purchase. A pink diamond and a Panasonic for only three thousand American dollars. Did he say that? It's all too much. Is anywhere on the planet farther from home than this little shop of a diamond seller? *Clackety-clack.*

"Perhaps we will come back another day, my friend is looking ill," intones Mohamed in the background.

They're staring at me—Salim, his nameless wife, Mohamed and Aminata, her dusting rag suspended over a television.

"The heat," I mumble.

"Mr. John was here during the war," Mohamed says. "He fought bravely to save the maimed and dying. He stayed even after our own politicians left the country—perhaps even after you and many of your brothers retreated to Lebanon." The diamond seller shrugs. Mohamed, feeling this is his moment, makes his pitch. "He now seeks a Sierra Leonean nurse, good with the women things, maybe a midwife, taken by the RUF during the war."

Salim seems genuinely curious. "What do you hope to gain by meeting this woman, who may be long dead?" he asks.

"To be honest, she was a good friend and colleague," I tell him. "I made a vow to return, and that is why I'm here. It's hard to explain."

A vow to return? Had I?

"Um, I see," says Salim, "a nurse who was a good friend." He looks pointedly at Aminata, smiling. "Medical people are not my specialty. I can tell you where to buy a cell phone and how much money the politicians really make, but nurses and midwives? I know only my doctor."

"Ah, my brother," says Mohamed, "you have people throughout the country, contacts who know what goes on, eh?

You know the people who can find out these things. Mr. John has only small-small time. Can you help us, then?"

Salim takes a long sip of his now-cold tea. The room is quiet; the diamonds are safely back in their little bag.

"Tell me her name," he says. "If I help you find her, you come back to Salim, maybe you buy your wife a purple diamond."

It's my turn to smile. "I might just do that."

Salim's wife returns the bag to the wooden box, smiles and walks to the back room. Aminata resumes her dusting.

As we step out of the shop, the light blinds me. I feel buoyed; perhaps Salim can help us after all. "What do you think, Mohamed?" I ask.

"I don't like what I see," he says.

"What?"

Mohamed touches my elbow with his stump, his good arm pointing down the street. I squint into the light, wondering what amongst the motorbikes, fruit vendors, diamond sellers and money-changers he wants me to see.

A filthy green Nissan with a broken windshield, the words *Allah* and *Trust* barely visible through the grime, pulls out from a side road and drives away.

THIRTY-TWO

An old woman, sitting sidesaddle on the back of the motor-cycle, slips effortlessly down to stand on the ground. She wears a traditional orange print dress, head tie and matching top, or *docket*. Her driver is in his mid-twenties, bold eyes, wraparound sunglasses propped on his forehead and an open shirt revealing a gold chain and cross. The old and the new Sierra Leone.

They study the sign hammered onto the trunk of a mango tree: Freedom Guest House, Abu Said, Prop. Abu is one of the many "cousins" Mohamed has in Bo. We've been whiling away the hot afternoon in the shade of the verandah, drinking cold Star beers and Fantas. I've been taking photos of Abu's wife, Yeamah, who poses with her baby, and Yeamah's younger friend Jameela. They giggle and point at the camera with every photo

I show them. Jameela, who has been brazenly flirting with me, looks miffed by the intrusion of the strangers.

The old woman lingers, unsure, as if afraid to venture out. My telephoto lens captures her and the vain driver in a single frame. She spots me and waves. Leaning on a walking stick, she walks unsteadily toward us, favouring her right leg. The driver stays where he is, wiping his shades and leaning on the bike—a study in cool.

The old woman greets everyone in Mende, and everyone greets her in the same way: *"A wua naa?"* Are you there? *"Bi siε."* Thank you. *"Kahui ii yee na?"* How are you? *"Kaye gbi ii Ngew ma."* I am well, by the grace of God.

Mohamed exchanges a few words in Krio with her and breaks into a big smile. "She was sent by my friend Salim," he says. "She has news."

News? I haven't got over the news about Momodu. This is Sierra Leone, after all—when is the news ever good? "Would you like a beer, or Fanta?" I offer, trying to remain calm.

"A Fanta, please," the old woman says in a soft voice, wiping her face with a handkerchief of the same print as her outfit. She says something to Yeamah, her head nodding toward the baby with a grandmotherly smile. Everyone is so patient. Jameela runs into the house to get the Fanta and we wait—the protocol for visitors seems to be that no news is more important than a relaxed welcome. I switch from feeling unprepared for whatever news she has, to wanting to scream at everyone to get on with it.

Jameela returns with the orange soda, and the old woman says, *"Bi siε,"* and takes a long drink. Facing me directly, she wipes her lips with her handkerchief and says, "You look for a midwife."

She phrases this not as a question, but as a statement of fact, as if saying, "The earth is round."

"She is a nurse, last seen in Freetown in 1999, during the war. She may be a midwife. Her name is Mariama Lahai," I say.

The old woman nods her head slowly, the behaviour of one who has lived long and seen much. The two friends Yeamah and Jameela are attentive and openly curious about the business involving their white guest and the old woman.

"I hear of such a woman, but I nor know her name. A Mende woman, way in the diamond fields to di south and east. Women walk or beg rides for go there. Many say no to help from foreign clinics, they like better to see this woman. Some say she a *sowei* in the Sandei society."

If Mariama is alive and is a *sowei*, a senior woman in the Sandei secret society, why would this woman tell me?

Reading my thoughts, the old woman smiles. "I bin born again, I nor mind talkin about the secret societies," she says.

Jameela stares out onto the street, alone in her thoughts, as if no longer interested in our visitor. Yeamah is expressionless, but her eyes remain fixed on the old woman. I suspect that Yeamah and Jameela are both Sandei women. If so, they would loathe such open talk about a *sowei* with an outsider.

"Why do you think this might be Mariama?" I ask.

She shrugs. "It may not be the one you seek. After the war, before I bin saved, I de go Kenema and hear of a new midwife, a woman who live somewhere in a small village near di border, one who all di Sandei women go to. She had no man 'cause she been with the rebels. But she is good with the knife for initiating the girls. Some say she a witch."

"How do we find her?" I struggle to keep the urgency out of my voice.

She looks at Mohamed. "You de go far-far, past Kenema, in the diamond fields to the east. Maybe you go the border with Liberia. Ask di women, they will know."

She stands to go, patting the sweat from her forehead. She waves to her driver, hesitates and turns toward me.

"If she the one you seek, be careful. Witches have power you nor understand. It is the price of sin. Satan himself works through her."

The old woman waits, unmoving, while her driver revs clouds of blue smoke from his motorbike.

"Mr. John, you have some leones?" asks Mohamed.

"Oh, sorry," I say, reaching into my pocket. I give her eighty thousand leones, a little more than twenty dollars. She takes the money and nods her head.

"*Tenki,*" she says.

As she shuffles toward the motorcycle, Yeamah and Jameela glare after her. When they look back at me, their faces are wooden.

"Mariama Lahai is my good friend," I say. "I respect the traditional ways—if she is a Sandei woman, she is still my friend."

Not a word passes between them. Finally, Jameela turns to me. She seems different—the flirtatiousness gone. "What is it?" I ask. "What's the matter, Jameela?"

She shakes her head dismissively. Cautiously, as if lifting a dead snake, she carries the empty Fanta bottle into the house.

Nadia picks up on the first ring. She sounds excited—by her tone, I think she's smiling. We talk about her work, and lunch with Bonnie, and the food in Sierra Leone, and rain on the skylight, and mysterious old women and enigmatic young ones wearing hijabs. Nadia has an ability to find her smile—she can go for days without it and then, for reasons that often escape me, find it again. Early in our relationship, I would take notice and ask her what had changed. Invariably, she would shrug and say something like, "Nothing has changed. Do you want me to stay unhappy?"

"Has the baby kicked?" I ask.

"No, nothing dramatic yet," she says. "But I think there's something, a flutter, like little bubbles."

"I love you, Nadia. And I'm sorry for all this."

"I know, John, and I love you. You are there—you must make the most of it. The old woman, do you trust her?"

"She said Mariama is a *sowei*," I say. Before I left Vancouver, Nadia and I had talked for hours about the men's and women's secret societies in Sierra Leone.

"John, I would be surprised if she wasn't." She sounds tired. "You're near the place where the diary ends," she says, as if she's been following along, retracing the route with me.

"Yes, that last awful chapter."

"When I read it, I knew you would want to go, and I was afraid. I still am. But I miss it …"

"You miss what?"

A pause. "Her diary. The poetry of it. She's a woman I would like to have known."

THIRTY-THREE

April, 1999

Buedu feel like the pit of hell.
Smoke from the fires
Hang like a blanket over the air.
There is no happiness in this place,
No young girls, with plaits in their hair,
No young boys, with smiles on their faces,
Buedu feel like the pit of hell.

I do not have to see the sickness here,
I can smell it everywhere.
Dead eyes watchin through the black of night,
Sick bodies with grey souls,

Waitin for death.

Buedu feel like the pit of hell.

Comin into the town we see a body on a stick. A girl. That is what the rebels do when someone try to escape. They leave the body for days. If you do not see what they do, they know you smell what go happen to you.

Jesus, I pray! Lord baby Jesus help me from this wicked place! Even Madonna and Terminator look scared, like they want go back to the bush. I am so angry, angry with my own self. I have had chances to run away but I have waited too long. These rebels trust me now, why do I wait so long? Maybe I too have a curse on me.

The people are dirty, like they do not care. The smell is so bad I put my head tie about my nose. RUF slogans paint the sides of houses. "Long live Foday Sankoh," "Long live Maskita" and "Charles Taylor, friend of Salone," they say. Hollow eyes follow us from dark windows and verandahs. No hellos greet us, no smiles, no thanks to God. All those eyes are watchin us and no one say a nice word.

Commander Abu take us to the middle of town. There is a Catholic church and beside that the mission house. It is the largest house on the street. In front is a motorcycle, fancy and clean like I have never seen before. Standing there like a politician is a man wearing a western suit, clean and brand new. Some white men are taking the man's photo. He look like a fancy Freetown man dressed in wedding clothes.

The white men are recording everything he say and taking his photo like he is a star in the movies. He is happy and laughin like a Big Man do, no care in the world, no war, no rape of someone's daughters and sisters and mothers, no *pikins* with their arms chopped off. I hear him saying the RUF will stamp out corruption and make all the children go to school.

Commander Abu seem like a child, waitin in line for bananas

at the market. The man keep talkin to the journalists about the revolution and how bad the government is, and how he de go change things when the war is over.

When he run out of things to say he sees Abu. He give a big smile, like he is Abu's pappy. "One of my commanders has returned from our war against the corrupt politicians who beggar this country," he say, shakin Abu's hand and lookin around, posin and smiling some more.

When he turn our eyes meet. I have seen those empty eyes before—it is Maskita.

Three girls, all younger than me, all wearin jeans so tight I wonder how they can breathe. They have makeup on their eyes and lipstick on their mouths—even the Aberdeen women do not look like this! They say their names are Baby, Veronica and Fatmata—Maskita's bush wives.

"So you the nurse he be waitin for," says the girl named Fatmata. She is standing with her hands on her hips, but she smiles in a friendly way.

They stand around me in a circle, so close I can smell their gum and perfumes. If you close your eyes you could find them just by the sweet smell. I know they can find me too—I have been bathing in rice ponds and pits from diamond mines along the road and I wear the same clothes every day.

I hold on to the baby and she stay quiet. She always quiet when I am afraid.

"Your breasts nice but too small to feed that *pikin*," Veronica say.

"I adopt this baby," I say. "I feed her rice porridge and ask sucking mothers to help me. She is a good baby."

"Maskita like em young, but maybe she too young even for him," the one called Baby say. They all laugh like they know something secret. She put her hand on my waist. "You got good bodi, I see why Maskita waitin for you, but you clothes no good."

Those girls have a room full of stolen clothes. They say Maskita only like western clothes, so they throw fancy jeans and shirts and little underwear on the bed in front of me.

"Maskita say he take us to France after the war," say Fatmata. She say this but she do not believe it is true. Her voice is like we use when we are tired of the rainy season but still it rains every day.

"My baby hungry," I say. "Maybe I de go get some food."

Wah! They look at me like I am something they have never seen before. Baby calls through the door and a small girl, maybe twelve years old, come in from the next room. She is dirty and scared. "Take di baby and find a sucking mammy to feed it," Baby say.

I do not want to hand the baby to this child, but Baby looks me straight in the eye and say, "When Maskita say he want you dressed and ready, you nor feed no baby then. You get dressed or you have no baby to feed. Jus' do like Fatmata do, she Maskita's favourite."

Fatmata stand by the bed, her hips swung to one side. She hold up some little panties like I have only seen in books. Then a shirt so small I think she is takin it for herself. "Put these on, maybe Maskita take you to France some day."

They laugh again, but their eyes, they tell a different story. Maskita's bush wives dress me in clothes like they wear. Clothes Maskita like. They give me a bra that push me up but do not hold me in. I look in the mirror and I cry. He want a girl like the girls in Aberdeen who go for the foreign men, soldiers and aid workers and politicians. None of those girls are happy, but the men give them money and they all pretend to be.

I hear the door behind me. The other girls go quiet then—I know who come in. Maskita smile like the devil must do when he steal a soul from Jesus. He go lie on the bed and call Fatmata over. She is wearin a short skirt and bra that push her breasts up so high she could lick them if she want to.

"It bin long time," he say.

I stay quiet, tryin not to shake.

"You know who I am?" he say, still lookin my way. Fatmata lie down behind him and they both watch me, two cats waitin to be fed.

"You Maskita," I say.

"Abu say you a witch."

"I am no witch."

His smile does not change—it is like the mask the Poro wear, a devil for sure. "Why they call me Maskita, you think?"

I look at him and just shake my head. He wag his finger like he teaching a student who has not been listenin. "They call me Maskita cause I sneak at my enemy when they do not expect me and I sting—I sting so bad they don't forget. You have lot to learn nurse, lot to learn. An I tell you, you better learn quick or you de vex me. If you de go vex me I give you back to my boys for some teachin you will not forget." Still smiling he starts playin with himself and says, "Show me what my boys teach you already. You do me now."

I feel such shame, standin in clothes that are too small and are not my own. I feel my body unwilling to move. I want to pass water but I cannot hide it like before, so I hold on and feel the pain twist my belly in a knot. I say to myself, "One night, just get through one night." I know if I do not please him I will die and they will throw Jolie's baby away.

Fatmata dip her eyes to me—do this, she seem to say, do this! Maskita's eyes do not move. He continues to stroke himself, makin himself big. Fatmata says nothing but her eyes are screaming at me, Do this! Do this!

> My body stop feelin then.
> I cannot feel my legs,
> I cannot feel my arms.
> My heart is beating,
> But it is not my own.

> I am watching a video in the parlour,
> A woman in clothes that are too tight,
> Movin slowly toward the bed.
> Into the pit of hell I go,
> With the devil himself.
> My heart is not my own.

THIRTY-FOUR

"Diamonds," says Mohamed. "Everywhere diamonds. Sometimes in the rainy season you see them sparkle on the ground beneath your feet. You see why the war start here—Taylor's thugs from Liberia and our own. They want the diamonds and they call it a revolution."

The birthplace of the RUF is a landscape of craters. Many are overgrown with grasses, scrub and feral rice. In the newer holes, young men stripped to their underwear toil with pickaxes and shovels, their mud-smeared bodies rippling with the muscles of prizefighters. All day, every day, they dig, scrape and sift through the mud for the little stones that go *clackety-clack* on velvet.

Women and children hang out around abandoned holes that hold water from the last rainy season. The women stand bare-breasted, doing laundry and working large circular fishnets. Like women everywhere, they are practical—a hole after a rain is much more likely to yield a fish than a diamond.

There are very few vehicles, and none carrying white expats. We've passed a few soldiers walking along the roadside but haven't encountered any checkpoints. Instead, it is mile after mile of fresh and overgrown craters, the terrain as desperate as the people that live here. Houses and schools with blown-out walls, bullet holes, collapsed roofs and tired graffiti. It is easy to imagine the atrocities that started here and spread throughout the country—a plague that lasted more than a decade.

As we approach the border with Liberia, we run out of health clinics. We show Mariama's photo to women at the roadside and in the markets and receive the usual blank stares; they don't know, they haven't heard of the midwife we ask about. I begin to doubt the veracity of Salim's messenger. Could the old woman have made up the story about a mysterious midwife? Perhaps just for money, or maybe Salim coached her, feeling he owed Mohamed something. Asking about a woman who is trusted by other women and who may be a midwife is stepping into the world of the secret societies.

Trusted. A woman who is trusted.

"Mohamed! We've been missing something! Shit! How stupid."

Mohamed's toothpick pops out of his mouth and onto the filthy dashboard. He favours me with an expression that suggests I'm suffering from the heat. "Mr. John?" he says. "You okay?"

"Mohamed, remember what you said about the Lebanese not knowing women?"

"Ah, yes, they are hopeless. African men have a way, how do

you say, a way with the women. But the Lebanese, it's a wonder they have children."

"We're just as bad! We're still going about this all wrong. Mohamed, what do you know about the Sandei or Bondo society?"

"Mr. John, the Sandei is women business. It nor be good to interfere with the women's society. And they nor know about the Poro. What we do in the sacred bush, we do not say. It is our way."

"Precisely. So why would any of these women tell us about the whereabouts of a *sowei*?"

Mohamed holds the steering wheel with his stump, freeing his hand to reach for another toothpick. "But Mr. John, if we do not ask di women, how will we know?"

"The problem isn't that we've been asking, but who has been *doing* the asking. Women talk with other women—around the cooking fire, bathing in the streams, washing clothes—it's the same in my country, but they call it 'doing lunch.' It's always outside the hearing of men. Right?"

"Yes, we are not interested in such things."

"Exactly. We need a woman to do our talking for us, someone who would be credible with other women. But who?"

Mohamed doesn't hesitate. "Jameela."

"Jameela. She didn't like the old woman, did she?"

"No, Mr. John. Jameela is a Sandei woman. And she like you, Mr. John—that girl be your country chicken, no problem."

"Okay, Mohamed, stay focused. Jameela is a big flirt, but she seemed strange when the old woman left. Will she trust me?"

"You ask her anything, Mr. John. That girl do what you want, no problem."

We could drive all the way back to Bo and hire Jameela to be our spokeswoman, but that seems impractical. I have no time to waste, nor do I wish to tempt fate with Yeamah's alluring younger friend. We decide to take advantage of one of the great anomalies of Sierra Leone—few people have running, potable water, but cell phones work just about everywhere.

The plan is simple: if Jameela agrees, we'll select young women with babies, hand them Mohamed's phone with Jameela on the line, and have her explain that she is in urgent need of a midwife. She will fib that she's having a difficult labour and is hoping to have her husband, played by Mohamed, bring the midwife to her in Pendembu, a small town not far behind us.

Mohamed calls Jameela and speaks with her in Krio. My friend uses a tone that I've heard before, but only when he is in the presence of a beautiful woman. He lowers his voice and softens the vowels, and it is as sensuous as a tongue on skin.

"Well?" I say.

"Mr. John, what did I tell you? I tell her if she do this, you de come back to Bo and treat her nice. She say she wait for you."

"Mohamed!"

We haven't driven very far before Mohamed points to the side of the road. "Ah, Sierra Leone full of pregnant girls," he says.

Standing under a *palapa* lean-to is a young woman, obviously pregnant, selling charcoal. Mohamed pulls over, speaks briefly with her and dials his cell phone. As the young woman talks to Jameela she becomes animated, giggling and waving her hands. I wonder if Jameela has deviated from the plan. Finally, she returns the phone to Mohamed and points in the direction we're going—toward the Liberian border.

As we depart, Mohamed hands the phone to me. "Jameela want to say hello," he says.

"Hello, Jameela. How are you, my friend?"

"Oh, Mr. John, I am good. I hope you come back to Bo." She sounds a little breathless.

"Jameela, what did the young woman say?"

"She says she does not know one Mariama Lahai, she knows many Mariama Lahais—it is a common name." She pauses. Her voice sounds different again—wary. "But she say there is a woman who many go to for birthing help, somewhere near Buedu."

Buedu. Just the name makes me feel sick. It is the place Mariama's diary comes to a horrifying, and abrupt, end.

That man is the worst thing on two legs. All night he have me and Fatmata sex him. I see why she is his favourite, she do anything he want. He smoke the ganja weed and take cocaine. He go crazy with the cocaine and just want more sexin. He keep sayin he goin to make a movie, show the world how Maskita go all night and sting the girls too.

He keep a pistol by his bed. Between the sexing he like to stroke the metal with his hand like it is part of himself. One time he take the gun and touch it to my lips. I feel the coldness on my tongue.

"Pull the trigger if you like. Shoot me now," I say.

His eyes go to the grey metal on my lips and I am sure he will do it. I look at him with no fear. "Pull it now," my eyes tell him.

He slap me with the steel, right across my head. But I do not cry—I am in hell and tears put out no fires there. The pain even feel good to me now—it give me something else to feel than that man on my skin. As my blood drip down onto my breast I am surprised to see the colour is still red. Tonight I have been changed forever, but my blood is still mine.

Maskita tell me to go and clean my face! I get up but something make me stop. I do not cry. I stand there for such a long time and he do not even see me. Fatmata move her head from side to side like she know what I am thinking. She try to give him more ganja to slow him some but he slap her and say, "That not what I want, don vex me woman!" It would be so easy now. I should take his gun and go shoot him dead.

I go to the rice pond and wash. I wash the blood from my head and when I am clean I put on my own clothes—the *lappa* and shirt I found in Waterloo. I will not, ever again, wear the clothes Maskita want me to wear.

When I am clean, I take Jolie's baby, my baby, and go sit in the Catholic church and pray. The rebels have made the church ugly with their writin on the wall, but I am alone there. Even they are smart enough to know they bring curses upon them for spoilin a church.

I will not write any more of this. Who am I writing to? I do not even know why I write. I am an African woman and Maskita is not the only one who do not see me.

If I do not get away today, I will surely die.

"Mr. John, you are far away."

"Mariama's diary," I say. "It ends near here. I think we've struck out, Mohamed. The last two women didn't seem to know anything about her."

"The diary, how does it stop?"

My one-armed friend manoeuvres the car around another pothole. His optimistic side has returned. Does he really think someone is going to say, "Go to the third house on the right, she lives there"?

"She was raped again," I say. "In a house that must have belonged to a priest, beside the church."

"And that is all she writes about, the bad things the rebels do to her?" Mohamed slows the car—he's spotted another pregnant girl with a platter of freshly washed clothes on her head.

"No. She writes about good things too," I say. "I think the thing she liked most was the way it felt to be with other women, like plaiting each other's hair. Why?"

He pulls up beside the girl, who stops and regards us warily. "Good," he says. "This Mariama Lahai is a real Sierra Leonean woman. Even after something so bad, she remembers why she want to live."

Mohamed gets out of the car, speaks with the young woman briefly and hands her his cell phone. She can't be more than fifteen. She holds the phone away from her ear, as if afraid of it. When she hands it back to Mohamed, he speaks briefly with Jameela. I offer the girl a few leones and she smiles. She turns and resumes her walk along the road, the platter of laundry still balanced effortlessly on her head.

"Okeh, okeh," says Mohamed. "In a few kilometres, look for a small road at a junction before Buedu. There is an old building destroyed in the war. That is where we turn."

"Turn? She knows Mariama?"

"No. But she know of a midwife the women go to. Look for the old building …"

The junction is little more than a track intersecting the main road. It isn't on our map. The building is roofless and the walls are covered in graffiti and something that looks like green mould. Mohamed stops the car—the old Mercedes' star pointing toward a break in the bush, a track wide enough for a single vehicle.

"What now?" I ask. My skin crawls with images of snakes and furry insects. The idling engine sounds even more unsure than usual. If we proceed, there will be no service stations, no medical clinics. If Mariama is here, I cannot imagine why.

"The girl say we take this road," Mohamed says.

"It's not really a road …"

Mohamed shoves the Mercedes into gear and we lurch forward. He thumps his stump a couple of times, as if trying to reaffirm his own commitment to taking on whatever lies ahead. I find myself gripping the door, perhaps an unconscious response to a voice in my head, a voice that is droning the obvious: this is not a good idea. After a journey spanning the breadth of Sierra Leone, Mohamed has us on a track to nowhere. No one has any idea where we are.

I think of calling Bonnie—I don't want to scare Nadia—but what would I say? Bonnie, we're heading into the bush, don't know where we are, just thought you should know.

I wonder if the first of Charles Taylor's Liberian thugs might have come through here at the beginning of the war, more than two decades ago.

"Where do you think the green Nissan went?" I ask, as we crash through a series of potholes.

Mohamed checks his rear-view mirror and looks yet again at the crate in the back seat. He shrugs. "The last time I saw, it was in front of Salim's shop."

"We're on our own here, aren't we?" I say, taking in the impenetrable wall of greens and browns on either side.

"In English you have a good sayin, Mr. John. You say, 'What good for the goose, also good for the male goose.'"

"You mean the gander."

"Ah, yes, the male goose."

He doesn't elaborate. I feel angry with myself. I've been in denial about the Nissan, hoping it would just disappear. Now we're alone, heading deeper into the bush that sheltered rebels for a ten-year civil war.

We come to a bridge: four logs set together like chopsticks over a slow-moving stream. Meant more for motorbikes than cars or trucks, the bridge causes even Mohamed to stop. In the distance, billowing clouds foretell the end of the dry season—in a few days, the bridge could be gone.

Women and girls stripped to their panties stand about in the brackish water—beating laundry, hanging clothes on nearby bushes or just splashing about. No men. They stare at us. A few children approach the car, their hands raised shyly to the *pumui*, the white man. I smile, and their faces brighten, wide-eyed and giddy. They are even more curious than the scores of children we've passed along the way—*pumui* here are a rarity.

"So, what about the people in the green Nissan?" I persist, glancing in the rear-view mirror. "I'm not sure I get what you mean about the goose and gander business."

Mohamed contemplates the bridge, his stump and hand resting on the wheel. He turns, and I notice something—a scar, like a squid tentacle, running from his neck to his ear. I've driven across Sierra Leone with the man and never noticed it. What else don't I know about Mohamed?

"Okeh, okeh, I make it simple. We have a proverb, it say, 'If you eat a rat, you must also eat the head.'"

"Yes?"

"That mean, finish the business you start. Some snakes from the war still lurk in the grass."

I've heard that tone once before: when Mohamed chased away the money-changers in Bo. It's the kind of tone you don't want to hear in a darkened alleyway with your back against the wall—or on a track in the middle of the bush bordering Liberia. Mysterious as ever, he shoves the Mercedes into gear and rolls us across the chopsticks.

The road is little more than twin ruts of red clay winding around ponds choked with lilies and rice. The jungle is a thick wall of green, cut occasionally by narrow footpaths that disappear within feet of the track. We haven't seen another vehicle for hours. If the Mercedes fails us now, we're in for a long walk. It's so humid, our clothes suck into the seats like feet into mud. Mohamed warns me the rainy season is about to start—a warning he emphasizes hourly, as he seems more focused on the sky than the road ahead.

Still, he takes the Mercedes deeper into the bush—no villages, few people, nothing on a Google map—just a track of red earth snaking ever farther into the abyss of green. Despite the dry-season dust, the feeling here is of damp humus and decay. Rounding a turn, we come upon another pond—more women and naked kids splashing, clothing laid out on grass and bushes to dry. Every set of eyes turns toward us.

Ahead is a young woman, pregnant—to my eye, close to full term. Barefoot, she walks alone under the searing African sun. "Ask her if she would like a ride," I say.

Mohamed exchanges a greeting. She hesitates, her eyes bouncing from him to the car, to me, and back to the car again. "Is she afraid of us?"

"No. It is the car. She has never been in one like this," Mohamed says.

Like this? Does he mean this nice? I get out, smile as warmly as I can, and open the back door. Mohamed moves the crate into the trunk to give her room. As she moves to get in, I'm tempted to put my hand on her head, like police officers do, to protect her.

She strikes a pose universal among expectant mothers— hands on her lower abdomen, eyes distant. But she is not, I am sure, thinking about the sex of her baby. Every woman in Sierra Leone knows women who died giving birth. When she goes into labour, she will have no man to hold her hand, no fetal heart rate monitor, no scalp clip connecting baby to machine, no forceps, no drip to keep her fluids up, no high-risk team to come running if the baby's heart rate plunges, or speeds up, or becomes erratic. Afterward, there will be no incubator to warm a preterm baby, no blue hat for a boy, no pink one for a girl, just herself and that sun, walking back to wherever she has come from.

Curious, I glance back at her. She catches my eye in the way of African women: assured, polite, a smile that is at once confident and shy. She gazes out the window. She seems small. Vulnerable.

"Ask her the name of the village she is going to," I say.

Mohamed chuckles when she tells him. "Lileima. It is a good name for around here."

"Why?"

"She say in Mende the name means 'peaceful place.'"

I smile at the irony. "Go slower, please, Mohamed, especially over the bumps. Ask her how far she has come."

When he speaks with her, he sounds gentle, almost fatherly. "Four villages back," he says.

She has walked roughly fifteen kilometres in the heat. I offer her my water bottle, but she doesn't take it right away. She would have drunk water from any of the ponds, water that was cloudy, swimming with flecks of dirt, plants and bugs. Finally, she smiles, takes the bottle and knocks back a long swig. She hands it back to me. "*Bi siɛ*," she says. Thank you.

"What's her name?" I ask.

"Najwa, her name is Najwa," he says.

She smiles again, knowing we're talking about her.

"Ask her the name of the midwife she's looking for." I regret being so impulsive—I'm not ready, afraid to hear her say the name I'm hoping for.

Mohamed does as I ask, glancing at her reflection in the rear-view mirror. At first she doesn't say anything. Perhaps she's confused—men don't usually concern themselves with such things as midwives.

She says it then, in a strong, lilting, Mende accent: "Mariama Lahai."

I can't look at Mohamed. It's as if my neck has seized, and I'm afraid he'll say Najwa was just kidding. I stare at the narrow track ahead of us, thinking back to an earlier time.

I didn't know it then, but the evening would be my last in Freetown. In defiance of the rumours that we were about to be evacuated, we decided to have a party. We hadn't slept in days. I was surprised to see Mariama arrive, accompanied by Momodu Camara and three or four of the local staff. She had always avoided the expat social gatherings, a little aloof, or perhaps just shy. I gave her a hug and she hugged me back. The feeling of her breasts against my chest was thrilling. "You will be gone soon, Dr. John," she whispered. When I mumbled that I would return, she hugged me a second time. "You will be gone," she said again.

We drank wine from stained coffee mugs on the verandah, trying to ignore the occasional sounds of gunfire from somewhere on the outskirts of the city. It was the first time I'd seen her wear a Western skirt, short, to just above her knees, the white of the fabric contrasting with the rich chocolate of her skin. Triangles of sweat darkened the T-shirt below her arms and between her breasts.

Her first taste of red wine brought a pucker to her lips. "I have not tried this before," she said.

"It's not very good, really," I apologized. "Wine doesn't keep well in the tropics. Try little sips." I felt foolish; the wine was awful. But Mariama smiled and sipped. She giggled a "yes" when I offered to refill her mug.

When the others went into the parlour, we stayed out on the verandah. Our view was of the compound wall topped with rusted razor wire, and the white minaret of the small mosque next door. We sat close on the bench and listened to the sounds of partying from inside the house and gunfire popping in the distance.

"Thank you for your help today, Mariama," I said. "You have a gift, you know."

"No, Dr. John," she said, putting her hand on mine. "I am just a nurse. But I think you do not mind what I say, so I speak up."

We had been working on a double amputee, a young woman who had lost so much blood I was sure she would die. Mariama stood across the stretcher from me. I was struggling to insert a central line through the woman's groin; there wasn't much else to work with. Mariama did something I had never seen before: she touched my hand, guided it down a few centimetres and said, "There, now, Dr. John, I think if you try this way you will get it in." Nurses don't do that with doctors. But Mariama did.

Momodu and the others came out on the verandah saying they were walking over to the Irish compound—the largest living room available. Momodu's eyes twinkled as he looked from me to Mariama and back again, as if to say, "I don't expect you to join us." When I asked Mariama if she wanted to stay behind, she looked over the rim of her glass and said, "I do not mind." The sounds of distant chaos and the flashes in the eastern sky added an edge to the moment; my skin prickled, and I wanted it to last forever. As the others walked away, her leg touched mine. It felt electric.

I went inside for another bottle of wine. When I turned, she was standing there, barefoot, her body framed by the doorway. It's an image seared into my memory, a moment lush with longing and anxiety and a question I tried to ask with my eyes. She stood perfectly still, as if to give me a moment to take in what was before me. The light from the verandah etched her body in silhouette—her breasts taut against the T-shirt, her legs apart. Mariama, at that moment, was the most sexually provocative woman I had ever seen.

She walked toward me and took my hand. She was like a dancer, light on her feet, leading me and lifting the net above the bed, her skirt and top falling away. The silky cocoon of gauze enveloped us, like an ephemeral boundary keeping the outside world from our skin. Mariama's kisses were wet, her lips sensuous pillows, opening hungrily. She smelled of almonds. I put my tongue in her ear and she closed her eyes, groaning, pulling me deep within her. She wrapped her legs tightly and held me there, squeezing, not letting me move. "Stay," she whispered, and I did, the length of my hardness deep and still and locked within her.

Her pelvis arched, holding and squeezing until she gave a little shudder, a letting go of breath, and she whispered, "Okeh." It was like she wanted me to move, and so I did. She opened her eyes, watching me, and when I came, she released a long sigh.

Afterward, she lay quietly, the mosquito net bunched under her head. Open as a split peach, one knee up, exposing her vaginal lips and showing nothing in between. A scar where her clitoris should have been. A beautiful, sexual woman.

It was the night before the rebels came.

THIRTY-FIVE

My excitement seems out of place with the slow rhythm of the village. A rundown Catholic mission marks the entrance to a collection of one- and two-room houses nestled into the bend of a slow-moving river. Everyone stares—women around their cooking fires, men with pickaxes balanced on their shoulders, boys and girls in school uniforms. A mob of young children run beside us, the braver ones touching the car, others holding back. When I greet them in Mende, the grins turn to laughter. Better than the last day of school.

Resting on a stump beside the track is an old woman. She balances a weathered walking stick across her knees. She doesn't get up—her expression remains as neutral as the wood she is sitting on. When we pull up beside her, the children become quiet, the Mende way in the presence of elders.

Mohamed, I have learned, is blessed with social skills that go well beyond those needed to disarm a willing country chicken. He greets the woman through the open window and in a moment brings her to such a fit of laughter she has to catch her breath. She stands and points her stick toward the end of the track. Wiping her wrinkled forehead, she resumes her seat and waits for us to go.

"She say we will find two huts at the end of the road, one under a big cotton tree," Mohamed says.

"Perhaps we should leave the Mercedes here. The track is bumpy, and it'll be easier for Najwa if we walk." Everything is happening too quickly—a few days ago, I despaired that I would never find her, now I feel unprepared.

Mohamed is having none of it. "She take you this far, Mr. John, now she take you the rest of the way. Najwa is an African woman, she can handle some bumps in the road."

We bump and weave by a few more houses, a one-room mosque and a burned-out school. By now it seems we've attracted every child between four and ten years old in the village, each one waving and yelling, "*Pumui! Pumui!*" After a few moments, the track comes to an end.

Standing like a protective mother over two small houses is a magnificent cotton tree on a hill. The lower building is mud and wattle with a small verandah and a thatched roof. The upper building has a rusted metal roof and plastered walls that reveal faint patches of blue paint. It has a larger verandah and a covered cooking area close by, suggesting it is the main house. Separating the two buildings is a well-tended garden of cucumber, squash and cassava.

A small goat, black with a white head, lies like a dog on the top step of the upper house. He chews his cud, observing us lazily. On the verandah above the goat is a girl, sitting at a desk, her back to the wall. As I get out of the car, the crowd of children backs off—seeing a *pumui* in a car is one thing, having him get out among you is quite another. They become silent, wide-eyed, as if wondering what other miracles are in store.

"*A wua naa, a wua siɛ*," I say.

"*Bu wua, bi siɛ*," they whisper in unison.

Mohamed leans against the Mercedes, watching me, a smile softening his eyes. He says something in Krio to the kids, causing them to giggle.

"I will walk back to greet the chief," he says. "Remember, it is something you must do before the end of the day."

"I will. Tell him I'll be there shortly," I say.

I look back to the upper building to see the girl, perhaps ten years old, still sitting there. She's in a green-and-blue school uniform. Her hair, done in perfect plaits, is accented with a pink ribbon over her left ear. Lying at her feet is a little terrier, a clone of every other dog in the country—filthy, spotted cream and brown.

The dog stiffens as I approach. The little girl says something to him and he seems to relax—at least he wags his tail. She smiles.

"*Bu wua, bi siɛ*," I say. "*Kahui ii yee na?*" How are you?

"*Kaye gbi ii Ngew ma*," she says, giggling. I am well, by the grace of God. Then, in English, she adds, "A *pumui* who speaks Mende?"

"No, but I've got '*Bu wua*' and '*Kaye gbi ii Ngew ma*' down pretty good. And you speak English very well."

"Yes, of course," she says.

"Is this the home of Mariama Lahai?"

She points to the lower building. "Yes, she is down there, delivering a baby."

"Oh." I keep my eyes on the dog, who looks like he'll spring if I take another step. "Will she be long?"

"No, it will not be long now." The girl is mature and confident for her age. She gives her name, which sounds like *Ka-bon-dee*.

Najwa is waiting shyly beside the Mercedes. "Oh, I'm sorry, this is Najwa," I say. "She has also come to see Mariama."

The girl smiles at Najwa and speaks to her in Mende. The young mother-to-be answers respectfully, patting her belly with both hands. She uses the Krio phrase *small-small*. The girl nods her head as if she understands perfectly—such an old soul, perceptive, and already confident in her own skin. She invites me to wait in the shade and, taking Najwa's hand in hers, leads the young woman down the hill to the other building. The little mutt trots alongside, his head moving back and forth, as if keeping a protective eye out for his small charge.

Until this moment I've never been sure if Mariama was alive. She has probably married, or has a man. It has been so long, and I've come so far. Why? To heal myself? Say I'm sorry? I'm gripped with a sudden sense of panic—she could be someone's second or third wife, and my arrival could be a terrible threat to her. Even if she is single, how will she respond? It's been ten years.

I look around me, and what I see is not a home with skylights and a garden with maples and an outdoor shower. The outside of her home has the usual cooking pots, a smoking fire, a desk on the verandah and a long bench against the wall to take in the view of the river. Off to the side is something like a lean-to, with plants hanging to dry and a table with a mortar and pestle. She lives in a place of chickens and goats and dogs left to heal their own wounds. Mariama's world.

This is not the home of the woman I'd known, or thought I knew—a westernized nurse in her uniform and cap, a woman trained to draw a syringe, start an IV. I look up at the beautiful cotton tree, and I'm struck with my naïveté—the vastness of it. We are of different worlds, Mariama and I.

If she's delivering a baby, she could be a while, so I set out to find Mohamed and greet the chief.

He isn't difficult to find. Near the mosque is a large house with a group of people milling about on the verandah. The chairs and benches are taken up with men, undoubtedly chiefs and elders—younger men and several women stand casually in the background. As I approach, I notice three beautiful women off to one side, undoubtedly the paramount chief's wives. At the end of the verandah stands a man with a rifle, the first I've seen since my return. The battered weapon is easy to recognize: an AK-47.

Mohamed sees me and lightly taps his wristwatch. This is our code, telling me that the man he is sitting beside is indeed the paramount chief. I am to be deferential and offer a gift of money and the gold-coloured watch I have in my pack for just such an occasion.

His name is Mussa. Befitting a chief of his stature, he is corpulent and relaxed. Everything about him is big—his sequined, white-framed sunglasses are so enormous they extend halfway up his forehead and down to the bottom of his nose. A carved aluminum cane, the badge of a chief, rests in the crook of his arm. On his feet is a pair of black Western cowboy boots with pointed toes. This is a man who spends some time in front of a mirror.

A dog is fast asleep at his feet. Mussa smiles appreciatively when I greet him in Mende, and he gestures for me to take a seat beside him. The chief introduces three other men—two are section chiefs and the third is the "speaker" for the chiefdom. Through Mohamed, I say that the people in Lileima are among the friendliest and most welcoming I have met. Smiles all around. I add that the children look healthy and the women seem happy. More smiles. Mohamed nods his head, and I reach into my pocket for some leones. I shake each chief's hand and simultaneously pass some money to each one. I give the largest amount to the paramount chief.

Mussa thanks me and turns to Mohamed, his expression grave. After exchanging words, Mohamed looks to me and says, "Mussa asks what your business is with the rebel woman."

I hesitate, feeling the eyes of Mussa, Mohamed and the villagers fixed on me. *Rebel woman?*

"You mean Mariama?" I ask. Mussa answers with a barely perceptible nod.

Mohamed had instructed me to take my time when speaking with a chief. "You make di Big Man feel like di Big Man," he told me, by which I assumed he meant I should be deferential and agreeable. I avert my gaze toward Mussa's wives. Each one would have been promised to him at an early age, after their initiations. One of the women, the youngest, is pregnant. The other two have young children on their hips. Had Mariama delivered the babies of these women, the children of the paramount chief?

"Mariama was a nurse I worked with during the war," I say. "A particularly good nurse, very good with women. She was not a rebel."

Mussa stares over my shoulder in the direction of the cotton tree. He speaks sharply to Mohamed. To my surprise, Mohamed replies in an equally sharp tone. The only word I understand is Mariama's name, which is repeated by both men. The villagers, male and female, lean in, their heads moving back and forth between Mussa and Mohamed as each one speaks. The argument, if that is what it is, ends abruptly. Mohamed nods to me again—his cue that we should wrap up the meeting. Once again, I thank the chief for his hospitality.

"What was that all about?" I ask, as we walk away.

Mohamed sucks on his toothpick and spits. "He say we are not the only strangers in the area. He want to know our real business—strangers bring *palava*, trouble. And he nor trust the rebel woman. She be cursed, he say."

"But Mariama was a nurse working for the hospital during the war. She was no more a rebel than I was."

"My friend, none of the women, how you say, just wake up in the mornin wantin to be a rebel. But many were captured. Some took to bein rebels—they had much power and plenty more nice things than before they become rebel women. But most hate the life and suffer so bad by the men. The government say forgive and forget, but this nor easy to do, no way."

"Yes, Mariama said as much in her diary. But why does Mussa allow her to stay if he doesn't trust her?

Mohamed chuckles—a mirthful laugh that brings a sparkle

to his eyes. "Ah, Mussa don't become chief for bein stupid. He say she good with the women, and his wives like her." He pauses as we approach the two houses under the cotton tree. A woman is standing with the little girl on the verandah of the upper house. My breath catches and my legs feel heavy, like I'm walking in mud.

"Mussa say your friend is *kpako nyaha*, a Big Woman, with no man to protect her," says Mohamed. "Your friend Mariama is the most powerful woman in Lileima. Huh! Mussa not stupid, but Mariama, she a smart woman for sure."

Mohamed puts a new toothpick in his mouth and sucks loudly. He stares at the house below the cotton tree, his eyes reduced to slits.

"What is it, Mohamed?"

"Your friend Mariama is smart, but Mohamed thinks she must be very careful. Mussa nor trust her, and no one more powerful than the paramount chief."

THIRTY-SIX

On the verandah of the upper house, the woman stands motion-less. Her bare feet are rooted to the weathered boards—one hand on a wooden post, one limp at her side. She stands like a sentinel in front of the little girl—watchful and protective. I feel her presence above me, but my eyes refuse to focus. I look about, expecting a man to step out through the door. My mind whirls, and I wonder if this is all a mistake.

I draw closer, aware of her bare feet, her *lappa* and T-shirt. And then I can see again—the woman who stands above me. It is Mariama Lahai, and her smile is warmer than the African sun.

"Dr. John," she says quietly, "you have come. It has been a long time, and I have been expecting you." She pronounces the words so clearly it's as if she has practised them over many years.

My arms go out to her and Mariama presses her face so deep into me it hurts. She quivers—a tremor that builds until a long, anguished sob wracks her body. My tears flow onto her hair and her tears drench my shirt. I can feel the beating of her heart and smell her, and the almonds and fresh earth take me back to an earlier time. She takes a breath and sighs into my chest, letting go and moulding her body into mine. It's as if the power and protectiveness drain out of her and I can feel the young woman again—vulnerable, supple, giving.

Finally, my eyes open to the little girl and the goat and the dog. Mariama tilts her head back, and her smile squeezes more tears from her eyes. I put my hands behind her head and look at her. The last time was so many years ago, under a net as we lay on my bed. Her eyes then were mischievous and playful—today, they tell of events more tragic than anything I could ever imagine.

"There, now," she says, "I'm happy you have come, Dr. John, so happy."

"Mariama, it is so good to see you."

The little dog growls a throaty warning. "Poco!" Mariama scolds without looking at him. "Poco watches for me and Kabande, Dr. John. He will get used to you soon."

A scar traces her left temple—she notices me looking at it and two more tears flow down her cheeks.

"Mariama, I …"

I've forgotten all about Mohamed. When I turn toward him, he is motionless, his head bent respectfully toward the ground. Mohamed is a Sierra Leonean, he doesn't need to read a diary to understand.

"Mariama, this is Mohamed A. Lee, my friend and guide from Freetown."

They greet each other in Krio. Mariama asks Mohamed some questions, and he answers quickly, waving his hand toward the Mercedes and the track through the village. "Okeh, okeh," she repeats several times, still wiping her eyes with the back of her hand. She asks more questions, often looking toward me, and with every "okeh" the look of wonder spreads across her face.

"How was your delivery today?" I ask, as she points to the bench against the wall.

"It was long, her first, but it go fine. Kabande, Dr. John and Mr. Mohamed are friends. They will stay with us. Go to Sarah for groundnuts, then choose two of the chickens for us."

"We brought some food with us," I say.

A chicken pecks at her feet and Mariama waves it away. "Dr. John, do not worry. Most women pay me with chickens. As you can see, we have plenty to eat. But if you have a bag of rice, that will be nice—a bag is a hundred thousand leones!"

We both watch as the little girl skips away, the dog Poco trotting beside her. "Kabande is a bright little girl," I say. "I'm amazed at how well she speaks English."

"My daughter has a special gift," Mariama says, using a stick to swat some chicks off the verandah. "She reads books in English. We have a Catholic mission in Lileima, and two nuns from Ireland. Kabande goes every day to learn English. Then we read together—it is our time, lying on our bed, reading stories about faraway places."

"Kabande," I say. "Is it a common name?"

She graces me with another smile. "It is not a common name.

It is the Mende word for 'miracle,' the word her mother had on her lips when she died."

"Her mother died in childbirth?" My breath catches in my throat as we watch Kabande's pink ribbon bobbing among the cassava plants. Mariama takes my hand and gives it a squeeze, perhaps sensing I need a little more time. "You remember that day at Connaught Hospital, Dr. John? Jolie was Kabande's mother. Together we delivered Kabande into the world on that bad, bad day."

Finally, I understand. The nameless baby I pulled from Jolie's womb, and who Mariama carried across the breadth of Sierra Leone, is here before me. "Kabande," I say. "Miracle."

The downy under-feathers of two chickens cover Mariama's and Kabande's arms and waft about our feet. Poco lies stretched out between them, his muzzle against Kabande's toes. In the distance, the river carves a half-moon bend in the forest to the west. On the porch of the building below us, Najwa and Sarah, Mariama's young apprentice, chat like sisters catching up on each other's news.

"Dr. John, how did you find me here?" Mariama asks suddenly. "What? What is wrong?"

"Your diary. It was found in Buedu. I have it. It is what Mohamed and I used to find our way." Having looked at what I had no permission to see, I feel like a voyeur. "I'm sorry."

She looks toward the river, and then, slowly, turns toward me. "So you know, Dr. John? You know what happened to me?"

"Yes, Mariama, I know everything up to Buedu, when your writing stopped."

She nods her head slowly, and absently runs the back of her fingers along the scar on her temple. She drops a chicken into a plastic tub and picks the feathers off her arms. Occasionally, a bit of down floats off her fingers, coming to rest again on her lap as if refusing to part with her.

"You're a long way from Freetown," I say, watching Sarah and Najwa.

Mariama smiles. "This is my home now, Dr. John."

"Mariama, I'm sorry. I'm sorry for leaving you that day. I'm sorry for losing my nerve. What I did was unthinkable—it's haunted me all these years."

Her eyes focus beyond the river. "It was a bad, bad time. The rebels, AFRC, Kamajors, the Nigerians—they all committed atrocities, but the rebels were the worst."

We take our time, peeling off the layers, slowly looking into each other's world. With each step, I need to resurface, like a diver coming up for air. "You've found such a beautiful place to settle," I say, enjoying the river, now bathed in the oranges and greens of early sunset.

"It is where the war took me. It was like being on a slave ship from long ago—you get on, and it takes you, and if you are very lucky, you survive and it lets you off." Her fingers work through the entrails of the chickens, dropping hearts and livers into a separate bowl. "Kabande, go down and see how Sarah doin," she says.

The little girl rinses her hands in a tub of water and with Poco beside her sets off down the hill.

"Poco seems like a loyal little dog," I say.

Her eyes follow mine. "He is good with snakes. He have no fear."

Our attention shifts to Mohamed and Mussa, who are walking toward us, engrossed in a heated discussion. They stop at the edge of the garden, find an old log for a seat and stare off toward the road.

"Mariama, the night before we left, I think of it often."

"Hmm. That is so long ago." She smiles, rinsing her hands in a bowl of soapy water. "You have a woman now, Dr. John? A wife?"

"Yes, her name is Nadia. We're expecting our first baby."

"Ah, God is good to you, Dr. John. Then you must return to her soon."

"And you, Mariama?"

"There are no men in my bed," she says. "The rebels catch me three days after you go. I was with them four months. It is hard for many, especially the older ones, to forget what the rebels do. Even women and girls do bad things."

"But you were captured, Mariama, you and the others were victims."

"Do you know what a bride price is, Dr. John?"

"Isn't that what a man pays for a girl who has been promised to him?"

"Traditionally, he often pays in kola nut to the father of the girl. The girls are expected to be unspoiled. When the rebels come, they took many of the girls. All of them raped many times. The girls took bush husbands to survive the war, but they knew when they go back to their villages they would not be trusted. Many did not return."

"And if they did return—what happened to them?"

"No one want to pay for damaged goods. Many ask for their bride price back. Some men take them back, maybe as a second or third wife. Some girls go to Freetown where no one know them, and some girls go back to their bush husbands. Do not worry for me, Dr. John," she says, placing a reassuring hand on mine. "God has been good to me."

I pull up a chair to her cooking fire. Mariama places a wooden mortar between her feet and uses a bottle as a pestle to crush chili peppers, which she mixes with onions and tomatoes. She adds peanut oil to a pot and places it on the stones. When it's hot, she throws in the paste, and the oil explodes with spitting aromatics. She swivels from the pot to the tub of chicken pieces, seasons the meat with salt and pepper and crushed Maggi cubes and adds this to the sizzling sauce.

Mariama glances toward me a few times and looks away quickly, as if suddenly shy. The expression reminds me of the day we met, when she was eating a mango. "Dr. John, our men do not watch us cook. They only eat."

I laugh and say, "In my home, my wife likes to watch *me* cook."

"You cook for her! Hmm. Do you cook groundnut stew for your wife?"

"No, but after today I will. It smells wonderful."

She stands and uses a stick to shove some of the coals aside—her way of turning down the heat. "It must cook slowly," she says. "When the smell goes, then it is ready."

We watch Kabande come back up the trail through the garden, Poco walking in front of her. There is a lightness to the way she walks, and her head seems to float above the cassava plants. When she steps onto the verandah, she rests her hand briefly on Mariama's shoulder. Quietly, she says, "Sarah say the baby has not turned."

"Okeh, okeh," Mariama says. She looks toward the lower building with an expression I've seen countless times with clinicians—Kabande's news is not what she wanted to hear.

I fetch Mariama's diary from my pack and place it on the porch step. I feel relieved, lighter. Mariama sighs, her eyes fixed on the book with the worn leather cover. "Thank you, Dr. John. God send this book to you. He want you to read it, so I do not mind. Later, I will show you the ending. But first, we will eat."

In the failing light, she takes a bowl and fills it with the red, nutty rice. On top of this, she ladles the groundnut stew, which is now a thick, fragrant peanut sauce filled with the chunks of chicken. She hands this to me and fills another two bowls. Kabande takes one to Mussa and Mohamed and another to Sarah and Najwa. Mariama and Kabande sit with the cooking pot between them and eat what is left.

I find the demeanour of the men odd. They eat wordlessly, heads hunched over their bowl, washing everything down with long drafts of palm wine. Mohamed has placed a lantern on the Mercedes and they remain close by, like two sentinels standing guard over Mariama's compound. Occasionally, they become embroiled in an argument, raising their voices and waving their greasy hands like symphony conductors.

"Mohamed should be careful, arguing with the chief like that," I say.

Mariama pulls apart a chicken neck, teasing the bits of meat from the vertebrae with her tongue. "Mohamed is an elder in the hunter society," she says. "He tell me he was a Kamajor officer in the CDF during the war. Mohamed is his own man, Dr. John."

"I couldn't possibly have found you without him," I say. "I often doubted him—he can drive me crazy at times—but he kept that old car on the road. At first we headed north toward Kabala. The winds brought in a big black cloud—it seemed to be following us, and yet it stayed in front of us as we headed north. It even had Mohamed rattled. When we changed direction and came southeast, it went away. It was weird."

Mariama listens intently. "I do not think it was the harmattan wind," she says, finally. "That wind is dust and will look orange or red in the evening sky."

I find her expression curious, like she's holding on to something. "If it wasn't the harmattan, what do you think it was, Mariama?"

She stares into her cup, her head tilted, as if she is watching Mohamed and me drive through the black cloud. "I do not know," she says. "It is a mystery to me."

THIRTY-SEVEN

Morning sounds—someone drawing water from a nearby well, another chopping wood, pots and pans scraping on the rocks of a fire, and from the mosque the muezzin's dawn call to prayer. I drift off, dreaming of Nadia calling as my phone runs out of power. I open my eyes to daylight and an empty room. There is a book on Mariama's desk—her current diary. Beside this is a stack of medical books and a small teddy bear, perfectly clean, as if it has never been cuddled. Along the far wall, Kabande has her own space, a rickety wooden table, a lantern and a shelf with an assortment of books.

Mariama's home is a simple room. It smells of mould and woodsmoke. The walls may have been painted at one time, but it has been so many years they seem to have forgotten. They are the colour of walls in most Sierra Leonean houses: mottled grey. There are no photos on the wall, no evidence of an earlier life of family and school and friends from years gone by. The only thing hanging, other than some clothing from nails, is a calendar with a photo of Tower Bridge in London. It is dated 1995. The ceiling is a patchwork of palm woven together below the metal roof.

In one corner is the rusted-spring bed which Mariama and Kabande share. At the foot of the bed are two rice bags in which they keep their clothes. Across from this is a storage area—a large bag of rice, plastic pails and basins and some used plastic bags. A ratty couch, my bed for the night, takes up the centre of the room, along with a chair and the crate labelled Echo-Diagnostic Equipment for the People of Sierra Leone.

I throw on some clothes and step out onto the verandah. There, I find a bowl of rice and leftover groundnut stew wrapped in a towel and a pail of water for my bucket shower.

"How you sleep, Dr. John?" asks Kabande. Dressed in her school uniform, she bends over a larger pail of dishes and soapy water.

"Kabande, your smile is as beautiful as your mom's," I say between mouthfuls. The stew is better on the second day, and I'm ravenous. "I sleep just fine. How you sleep?"

She shrugs. "I have good sleep. I am glad you have come to visit us, Dr. John. Do you have some books?"

"Books?" I wonder if I have a notebook in my bag.

"To read," she says. "I would like new books to read."

"Uh, yes, I have something I found on the helicopter. It is, well, about a boy who, well, goes on a trip in a fruit called a peach. It is a popular children's book."

Kabande remains bent at the hips, arms covered in soapsuds,

her eyes wide. I'm not sure what books the nuns are using, but I suspect *James and the Giant Peach* is a stretch. I get the book and hand it to her. "What is a peach?" she asks. She opens it and leafs through the pages. Her eyes sparkle. Answering her own question, she says, "Oh, it is big like a mango. Like a mango that is not smooth."

"Yes," I say, relieved. "It is just like a mango that is not smooth."

As she flips through the pages, I feel an emotion so strong I have to turn away. I mumble something about going to wash. I can't know the love Mariama feels for Kabande, but I get it. The little girl with the big eyes and precocious nature is easy to love.

As Kabande heads off to school, James and friends in hand, I take the bucket behind the house. The cool water feels soothing in the early morning heat. I'm towelling off when I sense that I'm not alone. On the hill above me, someone is leaning against the cotton tree, holding a rifle. I recognize him from yesterday—the man standing at the end of Mussa's verandah. He stretches his back, the gesture of someone who has spent a boring night.

"Are you ready, Dr. John? I will take you to the river." Mariama is standing beside me, holding an empty platter. Her eyes follow mine to the cotton tree.

"Who is he?" I ask.

"Someone I do not know," she says dismissively. "Now, let us go."

She places the platter on her head and leads me down the hill and through the garden. As we slip by the Mercedes,

I notice the windows are open, revealing Mohamed's sleeping form in the back seat. There is no sign of Mussa. I look behind us toward the cotton tree; the man with the rifle is gone. "I saw that man yesterday, at Mussa's."

"Men's business," she says, as if that explains everything. She glances up at the sky. Cumulus clouds thicken above us. Thunder rumbles in the distance—the rains can't be far away.

We follow Poco past the birthing hut. Najwa and Sarah are on the verandah. Najwa is lying on her back, head down, on a plank of wood that has been tilted about thirty degrees. Sarah squats beside her, speaking quietly, supporting a pillow that keeps Najwa from sliding down the plank.

"Why is she doing that, lying with her hips up?" I ask.

"Ah," Mariama sighs, "the baby is breech. Sometimes they turn by themself if you put the mammy so the pelvic bones are higher than the baby's head. If the baby do not turn by itself today, we will try to help it. You remember who taught me that, Dr. John?"

"Taught you what?" I find myself considering the risks of breech deliveries. I've never seen a woman inverted in an effort to help the baby turn. If Najwa were in a North American hospital, the plan would more likely include a scheduled Caesarean section.

"Dr. John, you show me how to turn a breech," she says, maintaining her pace ahead of me. "I watch you do two at Connaught Hospital! Maybe you helped me to become a midwife. Wah! Imagine that! A man helpin a woman to become a midwife!" She laughs joyously.

"To be honest, Mariama, when I left Sierra Leone, any confidence I had in my hands must have stayed on the ground. Things changed. Maybe I was cursed too."

"What you mean, cursed too?" She turns, holding a sharpened stick in her mouth, cleaning her teeth.

"Don't you remember? You told me the old woman who pointed her finger at me in the hallway said Jolie was cursed."

She offers me a weak smile and turns onto a narrow path toward the river. I follow closely behind, watching for snakes, through stands of bamboo, elephant grass, cassava plantings. She maintains a steady pace, her movements still those of a dancer, light on her feet, *lappa* swaying with her hips, the platter steady on her head. Poco stays in front of us, his head moving from side to side. Mariama stops occasionally, smiling with delight when she sees a plant that she wants. From some species, she takes the roots; from others, the leaves or a slip of bark.

We come around a bend and the river opens up before us. Rays of early morning light reflect through swirls of mist rising from the water. I hear giggling. A group of five women stand before us. They've been bathing and fishing with nets in some abandoned mine holes. Some turn to put on bras, others remain as they are, wearing only panties and amused expressions on their faces. As they banter with Mariama, I catch the word *pumui.*

"What did they say?" I ask.

She doesn't break her stride. "They want to know what it is like having a white man for a husband."

"Okay, now I'm interested. What did you say?"

She chuckles. "I say the white man like his sleep."

Just before the river, we come upon a gnarled, axe-scarred tree. She squats, removing the platter from her head with one hand and bunching her *lappa* between her legs with the other. She picks a bunch of leafy shoots and ties them into bundles, which she arranges on the platter. A cloud darkens the sky above us and Mariama works quickly.

She catches me staring. "What is it, Dr. John?"

"Mariama, will you ever just call me John?"

"No, Dr. John, I want to remember you as you were. You will go soon, and you will be Dr. John when you go."

She puts a piece of leaf in her mouth. Tasting. A slow, lingering smile that is so pretty I feel light-headed. It is an image of Mariama I would like to make last forever. Mariama, I realize, is happy.

It is a day that almost makes me forget about the black cloud and the mysterious green Nissan and the news about Momodu. As the sun dips across the river, I sit back on the verandah, enjoying the company of the temperamental goat and the ever-watchful Poco. Mariama is bent over her fire and Kabande sits at her outdoor desk, peppering me with questions about the differences between America and Canada, and what Freetown is like, and what it is like to fly in a jet plane.

I'm thinking about how this bright young girl is already aching to leave Lileima when Sarah comes running up the hill from the birthing hut. Mariama listens calmly, then turns to me and says, "Dr. John, will you come?"

"Sorry?"

"The baby has not turned," she says calmly. "She is having small pains, but she is not in labour. We must turn the baby now. We can show Sarah how to do it."

"But Mariama, I thought birthing was women's business.

Won't my presence be frightening to Najwa?" I haven't done any obstetrics in years; it's not something to be taken lightly.

"It *is* women business, Dr. John, but I tell her you be a good doctor—if Mariama say so, the others listen. We must go now." She smiles and takes my hand, leading me down the hill after Sarah. As we follow, Mariama's apprentice keeps glancing back at me. She wears an expression that seems to say, "Now this I have to see."

At the birthing hut, Sarah steps aside, shyly letting me into a room I suspect has never received a man. The room is simple, and much smaller than Mariama's house. The only light is from kerosene lanterns. Najwa lies on one of two beds placed in an L shape. A small wooden table in one corner holds a metal basin and some string, some gauze, a pair of scissors and a scalpel. Beside the bed is a plastic Coke bottle containing something that looks like palm oil. Along one wall are some shelves with bottles of what appears to be powdered herbs.

It is quiet but for the gentle sound of Najwa's breathing. She is naked from the waist up, wearing only a short *lappa* around her hips. Her abdomen glistens with palm oil.

Mariama washes her hands in a bowl of soapy water and sits beside the young woman's waist. She gestures for me to do the same. She dips her hands in some oil and places them over Najwa's belly. Mariama says something in Mende, her tone calm and reassuring. Sarah sits on the edge of the other bed, relaxed, watching silently. I feel like an interloper—it has been a decade since I was last in a room with a woman about to go into labour.

Beside the bed is a battered black leather bag—or it had been black, at one time. She says, "Your bag, Dr. John. Do you remember leaving me your bag? It was a wonderful gift, a gift that saved my life and the lives of many others." She pulls out a time-worn stethoscope and listens to the fetal heart, moving her hands easily about Najwa's abdomen. "Good, the baby's heart is strong." She places her left hand at the top of the uterus; the shape she palpates there is clearly the fetal head. But the head is low, and the buttocks and legs are set lower, between the pelvic bones. We exchange glances, and I see the concern in Mariama's eyes—this will be difficult and painful.

I can feel the rhythm of Najwa's breathing, warm against my thigh. I find myself giving way to it all, the wavy glow of the kerosene lamps, the simplicity of the bits of string and the raw smells, women smells—a collective perspiration that I find strangely erotic. It is as if I am sitting with one woman, one set of thoughts, one set of lungs, one vagina, alone. I remember something from long ago, something a younger Mariama said to me in the midst of an obstetrical crisis: "You be in Africa now."

"Dr. John, the buttocks sit between Najwa's pelvic bones. Can you try? It is easier to push up from your side." Mariama's voice seems far away, but the flames in the lamps flicker as if even they respond to her words.

"It's been years, let's switch places and you ..."

The scar on Mariama's temple throbs angrily. "Ah de wit you!" she says in Krio. I am with you. "This is not something you lose, Dr. John. Najwa is watching now. Waitin. Put your hands there and feel di baby now."

Najwa remains perfectly still, her eyes like two full moons in the dim light. I dip my hands in the palm oil. An aromatic smell wafts through the room. I crouch, one knee on the bed, my weight over Najwa's body. My hands glide over the slick round-ness of her, massaging, feeling the bump of the fetal head, the points of the feet, the tiny butt. The oil warms quickly, allowing me to add pressure with one hand while easing off with the other. Her womb is as soft and malleable as warm putty. It is easy to feel the fetal buttocks, the legs angled up in a frank breech. The baby could be delivered this way, I think, but it would be risky to the child and extremely painful to the mother.

When she goes into labour, the forces will be downward. I need to move the baby back up and into the uterus, then manoeuvre a gentle flip and guide the head back down. I can feel the little body rock slightly, yielding to the pressure of my palms, but not giving way. I push gently, trying to move the butt with my right hand while guiding the head with my left. Najwa's pelvic bones draw down, resisting, and causing my wrists to tire. She begins to struggle, a faint moan coming from deep within her.

"I'm not getting it, Mariama. Let's switch; you try from this side." I hear the tension in my voice. It has been so long—why is she making me do this?

"Feel the womb in your hands, I can see it givin way," she whispers, her tone gently hypnotic. Her eyes are on my hands as if willing them to move the baby. "She's not in labour yet, you have the time, the baby wants to go head down, you're just helpin it along the way, helpin it come around, then down, nice 'n' slow."

Down. "Mariama, have you ever tried it in that head-down position, the momma's head down, like when she was on that board outside? Maybe we can use gravity to help us."

"I am by myself most times." A hint of a smile tweaks the corner of her eyes. "But we have the help, let us try."

Mariama exchanges a few words in Mende with Sarah and Najwa. Sarah helps Najwa off the bed and they move out to the verandah. It is dark now, and Kabande, who has been waiting there, reading with my headlamp, quickly fetches another lantern. Najwa is up and onto the board in a moment, hips high, head well below her pelvis.

A flash of lightning brightens the sky, revealing the silhouettes of Mohamed and Mussa, back sitting on their log by the Mercedes. There is something else, a metallic reflection under the cotton tree, suddenly lost in the darkness.

Mariama and Sarah take up positions on either side of Najwa's head, their bodies wedged against her shoulders, keeping her from sliding down the board to the floor. Mariama's eyes are closed, as if she is deep in thought, or prayer.

Sarah and Najwa look to me, waiting. Again I move my hands back onto Najwa's abdomen, massaging, trying to use my body weight to move the fetus downward, out of the pelvis, toward Najwa's head. I breathe deeply, visualize the fetus moving, the pelvis easing off. As I slowly increase the pressure, my wrists begin to burn. Nothing moves.

"I can't get it to go!"

Mariama slowly lifts her head, opening her eyes and staring at me. She has that now-familiar, slow-burning fire in her eyes. "Yes, you will, you will do this," she says. She might just as well say the sun will rise tomorrow, or that it will be wet this rainy season—she is as committed to her words as she is to breathing. Years ago, I handed a baby to her, and she had the same look in her eyes.

With my greasy hands still on Najwa's belly, I brace my legs farther behind me and let my breath escape in a long, grunting push. Nothing. I feel something, deep within me, that causes my gut to tighten. A sudden memory flash, like graffiti on a passing train, a lifeless baby, limp in my hands. *What if I can't do it?*

Najwa is no longer looking at Mariama—she is staring at me. Two round, tear-filled pools, unblinking, the wetness spilling back onto her temples. Still she remains quiet, stoically sucking the hot, humid air, letting go, waiting for me to continue. Najwa trusts Mariama so completely she has given her trust to me.

Again I lean in to her, my right palm low in her pelvis, my left on the fetal head, drawing around and down, keeping the forces in unison. Suddenly, as if the fetus has changed its mind, the buttocks slip out from the pelvis, causing Najwa to gasp. The baby flips, a watery in-utero somersault that finally comes to rest with the head down in the pelvis. My hands remain fixed where they were, then slowly move as if by their own volition, a kind of muscle memory that comes from no conscious thought. *Check the presentation. Make sure.* The buttocks are up in the uterus. The head is engaged, presenting firmly in the pelvis. A vertex presentation.

"Sweet Jesus! It turned!"

They stare at me—Mariama and Sarah, sweat-drenched T-shirts and *lappas* plastered to their bodies, and Najwa, glistening breasts rising and falling—three women and a little girl, frozen. Another flash lights the sky, followed by a rumbling boom. Still they watch me, eyebrows arched, lips slightly open.

"Haven't any of you seen a man turn a baby before?" I ask, shrugging my shoulders. I can feel the adrenaline, my heart pumping. It is so sweet. "Najwa, let's get you up so gravity can keep your baby's head down." I try a high-five with Sarah, but she jumps backward, startled. Mariama giggles. Najwa smiles, tentatively, and the damn breaks—they laugh hysterically. Kabande, when it is her turn, does a little jump to meet my hand with a big smack.

"Sarah can watch Najwa now," says Mariama. "I think she

go into labour soon. Let us go up to the house." Smiling broadly, Mariama starts up the hill.

"Good idea. I could do with a little celebration," I say to her back.

Mariama's clinging T-shirt and swaying *lappa* shimmer before me, the garden plants brushing against her legs. The clouds open, allowing the stars and a half-moon to cast their soft light upon us.

"The cotton tree is so beautiful against the moonlight."

"She is the mother tree," she answers.

"Hi, it's me. How are you?"

"John, I have some news."

The line is silent, or maybe my heart is beating too loud. I've been sitting on Mariama's verandah, my back tight to the mud wall, mesmerized by the dancing shadows of moths and mosquitoes in the lantern light. "Are you still there, Nadia? What's your news?"

"I felt butterflies today, something like little butterflies floating inside me. I think she will kick soon."

"Nadia, that's wonderful." I hear another voice in my ear, from years ago, my father, something about swearing an oath to keep my promises. *Before the baby kicks.*

Mariama steps out of the house and hands me a mug of *poyo*. She notices the cell phone in my hand and hesitates—the first time all evening she has seemed unsure of herself.

"Where are you now? John?" Nadia asks, sounding so far away.

"I've found Mariama." My own voice is so weak, I'm not sure she's heard me. "She's alive. She's here with me now."

"Oh." A pause. An audible sigh.

The moths dance about Mariama's head as if they, too, are drawn to her. She places the jug beside me, turns and walks back into her house.

"She seems fine," I say.

"And you? How are you, John?"

"I turned a baby today." I regret the words—another woman's womb, someone else's baby.

"You what?" She sounds like she's falling.

"Oh, it was nothing. Mariama asked me to help turn a baby." I feel like I've stuck a knife in Nadia—I've found my cliff-edge.

"Nothing! Oh, John, how can you say that? You told me you lost your confidence after that day when Mariama made the cuts for you, the day you were separated. I know what turning a baby is like; you can only do it if you feel with your hands. I'm so happy for you."

"Nadia, you're not upset?"

"Upset? Why would I be upset?"

My head is spinning. Am I imagining this? "Nadia, I promised you. I feel so guilty. I'm letting you down."

"Yes, you promised, and she hasn't kicked yet. I knew there was a reason for you to go. Maybe this is it?" She sounds like the old Nadia—smiling again.

"How did I ever find you?" I say.

A pause. "You didn't, John. I found you, as you were falling. Remember?"

I tell her I love her and say good night and sit with my back to the wall, a white man drinking *poyo* alone. Or am I? Occasionally,

I catch the reflection of light on steel under the cotton tree. And across the garden, in the Mercedes, I can see the firefly glow of a cigarette.

One of Mohamed's proverbs plays on my mind—something about snakes in the grass and eating the head of the rat.

THIRTY-EIGHT

"What is really in that case?" Mariama asks, so softly I can barely hear her. We are sitting on the couch, our feet and a kerosene lantern resting on the filthy crate marked Echo-Diagnostic Equipment.

"Why do you ask?" I feel protective of the crate's contents even here, with Mariama.

"There is a presence in this room that has never been here before, a presence that is more than you or me or Kabande. It is a powerful presence, Dr. John."

Everything has gone quiet. No nighttime insects, no voices from the village—even the sound of Kabande turning the pages of her book has ceased. It is so humid, the shadows seem to stick to the earthen walls. Mariama waits, mug to her lips, eyes over the rim, watching me. Nadia had done the same with her cocoa—the posture of women who *know* they won't be denied.

A hammering on the door breaks the silence. The door opens and in walks Mohamed. He grabs a chair and moves it opposite the crate, facing us.

"I see the light on," he says, filling his mug and mine.

"You see Poco outside?" Mariama asks.

"I hear dogs barking but see none," says Mohamed.

"Mariama was just asking me what is in the box," I say. I'm beginning to wonder if I'm the only person I know who isn't semi-clairvoyant.

"Okeh, okeh," he says, his expression suddenly grave.

Mariama nods her head. "Kabande?"

"Yes, Mammy?" Kabande turns from her desk, facing us.

"If you wish to listen to us, then you come to this side."

Kabande doesn't hesitate. *James and the Giant Peach* in hand, she joins us, squeezing between Mariama and me on the couch. The little girl doesn't seem out of place between us.

My three African friends stare at the crate.

"It is a judgment mask," Mohamed says, "the medicine used by Ibrahim Camara, Momodu Camara's father, to initiate the Kamajors in the fight against the rebels."

Mariama's eyes shift from the crate to Mohamed, then to me, before resting again on the wooden box below our feet. Slowly she nods her head and whispers something that sounds like *"wah!"* The expression on Mariama's face suggests the entire world now makes perfect sense.

Kabande, wide-eyed, watches her mother as if hearing something in Mariama's thoughts that I cannot. I'm struck with a realization: Kabande is learning *to be* her mother. Mariama keeps nothing from her, and the girl seems eager to soak up everything she can.

"Mr. John tell me he put the mask on the wall," Mohamed says.

Mariama and Kabande turn to me, speechless. It's as if he had said, "Mr. John hung the Sacred Host on the side of a train," or, "Mr. John is thinking of publishing a caricature of the Prophet in a magazine."

"I hung it as a souvenir. People found it curious," I mumble defensively. Still, they say nothing. "Well, some people responded more strongly than that, I suppose. A nurse colleague, Bonnie, seemed taken by it. Sometimes I thought Bonnie was, well, listening to the mask. She once said I shouldn't underestimate it."

"What is this woman like?" asks Mariama.

"Powerful. She is of two spirits, male and female—a natural healer. I think her grandfather was some kind of medicine person."

"Powerful," she repeats softly. "And a healer. Masks do not speak to everyone, Dr. John. And this is a Poro mask—it is not for women. But this woman is of two spirits?"

The question evokes an image of Bonnie—looking toward me, the mask over her shoulder. "Yes, she is female, but it is like she has both male and female identities."

"Mr. John, that mask not for di wall," Mohamed says. "Such a mask can make you sick. When Momodu Camara give you the mask, he know it want to come back to the sacred bush where it belong. He give it to you knowin it would want to come back and guide you."

"If this mask is for good, why would it make me sick? Over the years, Mariama, I've felt like I've been afflicted with something. I had this sensation of losing all feeling in my hand, something that would happen when I let myself think of that last day at Connaught, when Kabande was born. I've always feared it was some kind of conversion reaction—something psychological. You put your hand on mine when I couldn't move the scalpel, you made the cuts for Jolie's C-section—all I did was lift Kabande out of her mother. I remember you told me that strange old woman sitting in the darkness said Kabande's mother, Jolie, was cursed—I never knew why she would say that."

Mariama smiles a sad smile. "Yes, I told you that. Dr. John, I lied to you that day. I am sorry. But I must tell you now. The old woman, she said something else."

My throat feels like dust. "Something else?"

"She say, 'The white man have a curse. He have a curse that others can see, but he cannot.'"

THIRTY-NINE

"A curse? She said *I* had a curse?" The dancing shadows make it easy to remember the woman with the sunken eyes, her back against the wall of the hospital corridor, pointing her finger at me. "A curse that others can see," I repeat in a feeble voice. "On our way here, I went to a church service with an Italian nurse. The minister was preaching about curses—he said that for every curse there is a cause."

"Ah, everyone here believe in curses: Catholics, Muslims, everyone. But they are only as strong as you believe they are. That minister should say the biggest cause is *believing* in curses. Dr. John, you did not abandon me or Jolie or Kabande. Many times you showed me how to make those cuts—you taught me!

You did not leave Jolie to die. She could not have survived. I had only Kabande to take care of."

I can feel her eyes burning into me. Slowly, she tilts her head, shifting her gaze from me to the crate. She squints her eyes as if trying to see through the battered wood and layers of dust.

"Dr. John, that old woman saw a curse around you soon after Momodu left you the mask. Already the mask was trying to return to its sacred bush, but I think when you go to North America, it make you anxious, wantin to return."

Mohamed takes a long draft of *poyo*, smacks his lips and pours himself some more. I hold my own mug toward him for a refill—my hand is trembling. The hectoring voice of the preacher railing against the secret societies echoes yet again: *Do not bring masks or carvings into your home, many carry hidden curses.*

I had the mask with me in Ghana for a year and then hung it on my wall for close to a decade. I think of all the symptoms I had: my hand, my sleepless nights, my compulsion to numb myself in the outdoor shower. Since returning to Sierra Leone, I've taken a bucket shower daily, but I've never felt anything other than a need to wash or cool off.

I feel Kabande's hand on mine. She looks up at me and asks, "Are you okay, Dr. John?"

"Yes, Kabande, I am fine." I look to Mariama and say, "But someone far from here has stood by me. She needs me now, and I need her. It is time for me to go."

"The mask must be returned," mutters Mohamed.

"Momodu is dead," I say, "and I've kept my promise to him. Mariama, I'm happy I've found you and that you are happy here. And it is such a wonderful surprise to meet Kabande, but I really must go now."

A boom of thunder and flash of lightning rock the tiny house. Mariama stares at the crate at our feet. "Momodu is not dead," she whispers.

Mohamed's jaw drops and the toothpick falls from his lip.

"What? Mariama, what did you say?"

"Momodu Camara is alive. I am the only person outside of his bush who knows who he is, and where he is. It was Momodu Camara who saved me and Kabande from the rebels."

"But Momodu die in his home, with his family in Freetown," says Mohamed.

Mariama sits quietly for a moment, weighing what she is about to say. "Momodu is alive. He did not die in Freetown. After Najwa births her baby, I will take you to him. He lives in the north, on the border with Guinea."

Momodu is alive. But over the years I'd checked many times—my friend's name has never shown up on any official refugee document. My confusion turns to panic—I promised Nadia—I need to get home.

"Mariama, can't I just give the mask to you and Mohamed? As much as I'd like to see Momodu again, I'm afraid I'm out of time. I've promised Nadia."

Mohamed bangs his cup on the crate. "You are not Poro!" he spits, his voice rising. "You belong to no rival society. To the mask, you are, how should I say, like any stick in the forest. You are no threat. It is not my mask to take, Mr. John, and a woman cannot take it."

"Threat? What threat is there?" I ask, frustrated.

"There are still those who would like to return our country to darkness," Mohamed says. "The mask is a threat to them, but only if it is returned to its home. They would destroy the mask if they could find it. And they would destroy Momodu Camara."

"The green Nissan? Mohamed, if the men in that car want the mask so much, why haven't they tried to take it already?"

"I have wondered myself. All across Sierra Leone, I ask myself that question," says Mohamed. "Momodu Camara knows he and his sacred bush are still hunted. Huh! That is why he has kept the secret even from the Kamajors. The men in the green car think you will lead di way to Camara. Then they have the mask, the *sowa* and the bush."

There is a knock on the door. Unlike Mohamed's assertive banging earlier, this sounds like the faint tap of someone who wouldn't come in even if asked. Neither Mohamed nor Mariama move.

"Shall I get it?" I ask, starting to get up.

"Stay!" commands Mohamed. He strides to the door and opens it. I can see Mussa and another man, both holding rifles, standing off the verandah. After a short exchange in Krio, Mohamed turns, his face grim. "Mr. John, please stay in di house tonight. I de go now. When Mariama is ready, we leave for the sacred bush of Ibrahim Camara." Without saying another word, he steps into the night.

Mariama rises, taking Kabande's hand. "We go to bed now," she says to the little girl. "I think Najwa will have her baby tonight."

As Kabande walks to their bed, Mariama turns. She has a book in her hand, a dog-eared scribbler. "You have questions about what happened after my old diary stopped, Dr. John. This will have what you need to know. It is the only paper I could find after my escape from the rebels. Good night. Tomorrow will be a long day."

I lie on the old couch and stand a lantern on the crate beside me. The book is the kind I remember from primary school—lots of space between the blue lines. There is no leather cover, but the telltale smell of mould and dampness feels familiar. Across the room, Mariama and Kabande lie in the darkness under their net, speaking in low tones. The only other sounds are the echoing booms of thunder.

I miss my own bed, and the skylight, and Nadia beside me. I don't know why this is the moment I long for home—maybe I'm tired of who I've become, tired of not giving Nadia what she deserves. She hasn't wavered, but I have. I've become a man with two faces, two personas—I want only one.

I open the scribbler and look at the familiar script. As I begin to read, it starts to rain.

June, 1999

I have lost my diary. Maybe Jesus want me to lose it, I do not know. It is more than a month since I have a book to write in. This is my new book and I pray I will have some good news to write.

After the night with Maskita I go wash in a pond. The blood from my head turn the water pink but the bleeding has stopped. I am so dirty I think I will never clean away the smell of that man. My skin is bruised and I hurt but I do not care. I just wash and I wash and I wash. So many times I think of taking a gun and shooting myself, but every time it is the same—Jolie's baby look at me with eyes like a woman's eyes, and she keep me alive.

I was sitting in the Catholic church with the baby when the Kamajors attacked. Wah! It was like the end of the world. Bombs and bullets and whistles blowin and people runnin every which way. Again the baby did not cry, but she look at me with soft eyes like she is tellin me to calm down. So many times this baby make me want to take her to a nicer place.

"Today we will escape and I go give you a name," I say to her. I tie her in a *lappa* around my back and we go sneaking between some houses. The rebels were in front, between us and the Kamajors. I see Commander Abu and Madonna, their backs to me, shootin and yellin to the others. They fight like they have nothing to lose—they have done such bad things to their enemies they will never be taken prisoner.

I try to go the other way, thinking maybe I can just walk into the bush away from the shooting. But the fightin is everywhere and does not stop. I am near a mosque when a bomb explode so close the mud drops like rain around me. It blow the breath out of my lungs. I sit with the baby in front and my back to the wall. Over and over I tell myself this day I will escape or I will die. I pray to Jesus but I am afraid he no longer hears me, I think I am too far from his world.

I am just about to run when I see three Kamajors draggin someone who is still alive. It is Terminator. He is bleeding from his chest and cryin like a baby. The Kamajors are teasing him with their knives—one has a knife to his throat and another pulls Terminator's pants off his body. He knows what they go do to him.

What I see I will not forget, I do not want to write the words— but even Terminator, for all the bad things he do, should not die like that.

After what I see I do not want to run to the Kamajors—I think maybe I will try to go hide alone in the bush. But how? I am standin in one spot, afraid.

Madonna see me then. Her eyes have the look of death. "Why you nor fightin?" she scream. "You a rebel woman, you think those Kamajors help a rebel woman like you?" She pick up a rifle and put it in my hands, then she push me ahead with hers. "You fight or I shoot you both," she screams.

She push me toward the fighting. I am so afraid. I have the baby on my back and I think Madonna will make me put it down and walk away. By burnin houses we go, stepping over bodies along the way. Everywhere there is so much noise and smoke and screamin, it is like being in hell.

We come to a rice pond between some houses and the trees. That is when I see the man, the same one I see before. He is wearing women's hair, and beads, and a medicine bag from his neck. He stand still like a tree on the other side of the rice pond, just standing quiet, nor bothered by the bullets.

Lord Jesus, what a smell, like long-dead bodies. He give me a little wave, just like before. I am afraid of what I see the Kamajors do, but I am more afraid of one more night with Maskita. I do not stop to think, I throw that rifle down and run. I go fast as I can, runnin across the water, sinking in mud, getting up and running some more. The bullets go by my head with a zippin sound, zip, zip, zip. I know Madonna is behind me. Zip, zip. The mud at my feet explodes with bullets, but still I go, feeling the baby on my back. Even then her warmth give me strength.

When I fall again I look back and Madonna is standing there, gun on her hip, shooting toward the bush. She look down at me and move her rifle to my face. "You a rebel, no one take you back!" she scream. She is breathin so hard her nipples look like they going to burst her shirt.

"Shoot me then!" I say. "Shoot me cause I nor goin back. Shoot us both!"

Madonna stand a long time, blue smoke from her gun so close

it burn my throat. I am sure she want to go shoot me, but I stay still. That is when Jolie's baby start to cry. Funny how that *pikin* always stay quiet when other babies cry. But now she cry so loud I think Madonna go shoot us just to shut her up. I take the baby off my back and hold her to me. She make little noises, noises like a little goat calling its mammy.

I think both Madonna and me hear nothing else then, just the calls of the baby in my arms. I see Madonna's eyes change. Sad eyes. I do not see the mean rebel woman in front of me. No, all I see is a farmer from Makeni. The baby in my arms break her heart, right there, on that field of blood.

"I wish I be you Mariama," she say. "I hope they treat you good." Madonna turn and walk away, so slow I am sure she is going to catch a bullet. Maybe she want to die, I do not know. My heart says, "Run Madonna, run!" But she walks through that rice pond so slow, like a young girl alone on a Sunday stroll.

The Kamajor man lifts his rifle up like he is going to shoot her dead. But he wait. And he wait. Then he look to me and nod his head and let the rifle down.

I run to the strange man. The closer I get, the stronger is that awful smell. The man turn his back and walk into the bush like he already forget I am there. He is so easy to follow. I just use my nose.

Oh, Papa God, I pray, make this be the right thing to do.

All day we walk and not once does that man look behind. I think maybe I will just stop and go another way, but then I think, "Where can I go?" I am not from this place, I do not know who is bad or who is good. So I just follow the smell.

After some time we come to a camp on the side of a hill. Many people are living there. I see women cooking and a medical tent for the wounded. In front of that tent the Kamajor finally turn his body to face me.

"Hello Mariama," he say. "It's so good to see you again. We can do with a good nurse."

He wear the *jiggae* of cowrie shells and dirty ronko shirt. On his head is a wig just like a woman, but I see by his arms that he is a man. He see me. I see him, but I do not believe what my eyes are telling me. My legs feel so weak I do not think I can take another step. Please, Papa God, let my mind not be playing tricks.

It is Dr. Momodu Camara.

FORTY

Gunfire shatters the night. I reach for my headlamp and point it toward the bed in the corner. The fear in Kabande's eyes tells me it's no dream—what I heard was real. "Let's find your mammy. She's gone to the birthing hut to deliver Najwa's baby."

Sometime in the middle of the night, Sarah had come. Mariama rose soundlessly and was dressed and ready to deliver a baby in ten seconds. Without even looking toward me, she said, "Get some sleep, Dr. John. Najwa is in labour now, I think it will not be long." She was out the door so quickly, I didn't say a word.

I slept fitfully, occasionally hearing voices in the distance. I'd thought of calling Nadia, it would have been mid-evening her time. But she would detect something in my voice, ask me what was wrong. How would I tell her I'm going to hop back into the Mercedes with Mariama and the mask and, oh, by the way, Momodu is alive and I'm not coming home quite yet?

I didn't call.

I take Kabande into my arms and we leave the house. "Poco?" Kabande asks, looking for the little dog. "Where is Poco?"

"Maybe he's with your mammy," I say.

Flashes of lightning explode on the horizon. I think about the track we followed to Lileima—if the rains settle in, it will be flooded. We'll have to wait it out.

"Poco. Where's Poco?"

We're almost through the garden and my clothing is already soaking wet.

"It's okay," I say. "Everything's fine." I realize how silly I must sound, even to a little girl. Why am I running if everything is fine?

Yellow light flickers through the window of the birthing hut, the feminine softness of it in stark contrast to the violence of the distant sky. I open the door without knocking. The little kerosene lamps are turned low, and it takes my eyes a moment to adjust. I sense something burning, the smell reminiscent of the sweetgrass North American Indians use.

Mariama and Sarah sit on the bed on either side of Najwa. The young mother lies quietly, a baby sucking at her breast. Something at the foot of the bed catches my eye—it is carved like a human head, with eyes, a nose and stylized rings around the neck. A vagina is carved into the forehead, and above that is the form of an erect penis. The head is black and inlaid with several white cowrie shells. It is a helmet mask of the Sandei, the women's secret society.

The women are expressionless, unmoving, unblinking,

staring at me. The sucking of the tiny mouth on Najwa's nipple is the only movement in the room. I know from the stillness of Kabande in my arms that her eyes, too, are fixed on me. I feel a wall between us—the openness of the day before, when we were turning Najwa's baby, when Mariama *asked* me into her space, is gone. This is a woman's place, women's business.

"Mariama, I'm sorry, we heard gunshots ..." Kabande squirms out of my arms and runs to Mariama.

Mariama calmly nods her head as if coming out of a meditation. "Dr. John, we are okay. Najwa's baby come and everything is fine. Please wait in the house. Go there now and wait for me."

I start toward the house, wishing I were dreaming. But the explosions of thunder and the dripping cassava plants against my leg are real enough—too real. A flash of lightning turns the night into day, revealing the Mercedes in front of me. Empty. I look up the hill toward the base of the cotton tree. It's too dark to see if the man with the rifle is still there, but I sense that he, too, is gone.

The raindrops feel like frozen grapes smacking my head. Within seconds, the din of hail hitting the roof of the Mercedes is deafening. I'm tempted to strip and stand naked to it all, maybe yell "I surrender" and let my skin be scoured by whatever the African sky wants to throw at me. But this is no cold shower—it hurts like hell.

I climb into the back seat of the Mercedes, lay my dripping head on Mohamed's filthy duffle bag and listen to the pounding. I'm cramped, and wet, and my back aches. It shouldn't have been a surprise, really, that everything would be so different now.

Strangely, it is not Nadia's or Mariama's face I keep seeing, but Bonnie's—my two-spirit friend. If Bonnie were to see me squeezed into this car, she would probably say I am right where I'm supposed to be.

Gradually, the storm plays itself out—the violence easing into a rhythmic patter that feels gentle and soothing. Soon, despite myself, I fall asleep.

FORTY-ONE

The rain has stopped and it is completely quiet—no chickens, no bleating goats, no sound of any kind. It is light.

Suddenly there is a scream, long and heart-rending and helpless. I struggle with the car door and get out. My first feeling is relief—Mariama and Kabande are standing on the verandah of the house. Mariama is rigid, her arms wrapped tightly around her daughter. Kabande is sobbing hysterically—something is very wrong.

I run up the path. All I can think of is the man with the rifle. I reach the verandah and my eyes follow Kabande's. What I see stops me: Poco, the faithful mongrel protector of Mariama and Kabande, is hanging by his back feet from the roof of the verandah. The dog's throat has been cut.

Mariama is comforting her daughter, but there is something she can't hide—fear. "They say I bring *palava*," she says, staring at the pool of blood at her feet.

"Who?" I whisper, putting an arm around the two of them. "Who did this?"

"Something happen in the night, Dr. John. You hear the guns. No one wants trouble." She rubs Kabande's back with her hand and her gaze slowly shifts down the hill toward the birthing hut. She sighs so deeply, it reminds me of something I've seen many times—a person releasing their last living breath. "Now we must go, Dr. John."

I assume she means she is ready to show us the way to Momodu Camara. "Will Sarah look after things while you're gone?"

We stare at the pool of drying blood at our feet. "No," she says. "Lileima is no longer our home. Sarah will be the new birth attendant here. We will not return."

I must have heard wrong. "Mariama, are you sure? I can talk with Mussa, or maybe you can have a meeting with the women— I'm sure they'll support you."

She sighs and takes my hand. "Dr. John, I have been given a warning. Now we must go."

"But Mariama, you're a threat to no one! You deliver their babies. Christ, you live a celibate life—you're like a nun, a model citizen! It's me who brought this trouble. It's me, for Christ's sake."

Mariama continues to hold Kabande, letting the girl sob into her body. She offers me a weak smile, wordlessly trying to tell me something. Slowly, I begin to understand. The old woman in Bo had said the midwife who lived somewhere near the Liberian border was rumoured to be a witch. I know of camps in Ghana that exist for one reason only: to be safe havens for women summarily accused of being witches. They are for the women's protection from society, and for society's protection from the witches.

"I'm sorry, Mariama."

I find a shovel, then cut Poco down and carry him into the clearing behind the house. Mariama and Kabande follow, the little girl now weeping quietly. I realize, as I dig a grave for Poco, that Mariama is right. She has lived with the rebels and she is well educated. She has a powerful presence. Women her age who have never married are almost unheard of in rural Sierra Leone. Mohamed had said there was a Mende term for powerful women who depended on no one: *kpako nyaha.* Such power is considered trouble, *palava.*

I lower Poco into the hole and ask if either of them wants to shovel in some earth. Kabande shakes her head and Mariama says, "You do it, please." Kabande's eyes are dry now. Mother and daughter, hand in hand, wait and say nothing. Finally, there is a little mound of red earth among the greens of the cassava plants.

Mariama says, "Okay, it is time to go." Just as she'd been dressed and ready to deliver Najwa's baby in ten seconds, she is somehow capable of picking up immediately and leaving her home. It is the only place she has lived in since the war, a place where she is somebody, a *kpako nyaha.*

Bury the dog and go.

The crate is strapped to the roof of the Mercedes. Najwa and Sarah wait on the verandah as Mariama brings out the things she will be taking—a few pots, a couple of rice bags stuffed with clothing, some bottles of herbs and little else. As Mohamed places them in the trunk of the car, Sarah and Mariama embrace, speaking softly, gently touching each other's cheeks with their fingertips.

Najwa joins us, carrying nothing but a small basket of provisions and the baby she gave birth to four hours earlier. I stand in amazement as Mariama, Kabande and Najwa pile into the back seat of the Mercedes. There is room to spare. Mohamed opens my door and says, "We de go now, Mr. John."

I take in the life Mariama is leaving behind—two huts, a well-tended garden and a cotton tree. And Sarah, who is on her knees, her face in her hands.

No flock of running schoolchildren follows the car. There are no men anywhere, but there are women. It seems that every woman and girl in Lileima is outside—women sitting by their fires, women standing by the roadway, women with babies, young women and old women. They have come out to say goodbye. No waving. No calling out. The women watching Mariama Lahai leave are as stoic and restrained as the woman they are saying goodbye to. As Mohamed slowly drives us along the track, they all stand, lifting babies to hips, facing Mariama and nodding their heads.

I have no idea how Mariama responds—I cannot bear to look behind me.

The old woman with the walking stick waits at the place we had first seen her. She stands and waves her stick, gesturing at Mohamed to stop the car. She reaches her gnarled hand through the back window and places something that looks like a leather pouch in Mariama's hand. She cups Mariama's hand in both of hers and says a few words. "*Mua lɔɔ, gboma,*" they say to each other. We shall see, okay?

It is the Mende way of saying goodbye to someone you don't wish to say goodbye to.

My last memory of Lileima, *peaceful place*, isn't the old woman— it is the green Nissan that had followed us for so many miles. At the entrance to the village, the car sits abandoned by the side of the road. The doors are wide open and the windows have been shot out. Shards of glass are everywhere. Blood covers the interior, an abstract of red and brown turning the dust and glass fragments to a macabre paste. Strangely, there is no crowd, no gaggle of curious children, just the bloodied, shot-out Nissan, alone, as if invisible to everyone but me.

Mohamed stays focused on the track ahead of us—the broken and bloodied car is of no interest to him. In the back seat, Kabande gawks at the wreck, but Mariama seems as uninterested as Mohamed.

"Mohamed, what happened?" I say.

His eyes stay on the road. "Remember Mohamed tell you, never eat a rat without eating the head. Those two rats are dead now."

"But who were they, Mohamed? And who did this?"

"Snakes in di grass," he says, pronouncing it *sneks*. "You see a snake, you cut his head before he bite you."

"I'm sorry, Mariama," I say. "I brought this trouble, not you."

"Dr. John, you did not do this. Jesus is good to me."

Jesus is good to her. My friend is a refugee again, more than a decade after the end of the war. A woman somehow strength-ened by her Catholic and Sandei worlds. The body and the blood—this country is a host of long-suffering women.

Mohamed decides some music therapy is in order. He puts the battered tape into the cassette player and sings along with the tune about being rich despite having no money. Rain starts beating on the roof of the Mercedes and the strangest thing happens: Mariama and I join Mohamed and Dolly. We all sing along.

FORTY-TWO

Only two days of rain and the dust of the dry season is a long-ago memory. Around us, the new greens of the jungle choke the track of slick, red mud. Mohamed's response to the thunderheads, and my own urgency, is to drive with the vigour of a much younger man, sliding around corners and hitting overflowing streams at full throttle. The ancient Mercedes hasn't felt a soothing squirt of windshield washer fluid in years, but this doesn't stop Mohamed from using the wipers. The effect is a back-and-forth, back-and-forth goo the colour of rich mocha.

Najwa perches uncomplainingly on a clothing pillow Mariama has fashioned in the shape of a doughnut. Despite my requests that Mohamed drive with more attention to Najwa's comfort, he seems incapable of doing so. To Mohamed, childbirth is women's business and Sierra Leonean women have bottoms of steel. The stoicism of the women in the back seat does nothing to disprove his belief—they watch the countryside pass by the chocolate windows without complaint. Najwa holds her baby to her breast and looks like she's been at it for years.

We drop Najwa and her baby somewhere before the main road. There is no sign, no intersection, just a narrow footpath leading into the bush. But Najwa knows where we are. She stands beside the trail, basket of provisions on her head, new baby tied to her back, waiting for us to go.

I hand my camera to Mohamed and we pose beside the car. Mohamed needs several tries—too much sky and not enough people, or too much foreground and headless torsos. When he gets it right, the photo is perfect: my arm around Mariama, Najwa holding her baby and a brightly smiling Kabande in front of us all. The women stand tall, barefoot, oblivious to the mud.

Mohamed drives hard, retracing the route toward Bo. After a couple of hours, we stop at a market along the road. Mariama and Kabande mingle easily among the traders, bartering for fruit with one, complimenting another on her plaited hair. I wonder if Mariama recognizes anyone—women with stories similar to hers, or men who once called themselves Dr. Death, or Rambo, or Colonel Bloodshed.

Occasionally I see, or imagine I see, Mariama hesitate in front of a woman selling potato leaves or oranges, offering a nod of her head, a subtle smile or a few words, as one might to someone you once knew but didn't want to recognize. The trader responds with a similar gesture, a covert acknowledgment, perhaps, of something shared.

Back in the car, Kabande reads *James and the Giant Peach* aloud, mesmerized by the world of an orphan boy who is transported with a cadre of insects, in a peach, carried by seagulls up and away from ravenous sharks, and ending up, of course, in Manhattan. The nuns of Lileima have done their job well: Kabande reads passionately and fluently. Mariama, her arm tight around her daughter, follows along, as enraptured with the story as Kabande.

Perhaps it is more resilience than acceptance—Mariama has such an ability to adapt and absorb pain. I wonder about the similarity between her and Nadia. In the years we've been together, Nadia has talked of her experience in Bosnia only once. She left Croatia and has no interest in ever going back. She is already as protective of our baby as Mariama is of Kabande. Nadia said she would like to have known Mariama, and it is easy to see why.

Somewhere along the way, I ask Mariama if she took part in the Truth and Reconciliation Commission—a process where rapists and their victims were often in the same room together. I've been trained to equate talking with therapy—"getting it out" is considered a precursor to exorcizing one's demons. She takes a moment, searching for the words. "Once you damaged," she says, looking out the window, "it is always so."

Mariama thinks I'm damaged too. She feels I've suffered in ways I don't understand. Of course, she's right—it may have taken a trip to Sierra Leone, but I'm starting to see. She seems to think my case isn't hopeless, that Momodu will know what to do. As for her, it is always the same—God will decide.

I've always believed in free will—we live by the choices we make. Or do we? I'm not sure I've chosen to be taken to the sacred bush of Momodu Camara. As the hours pass and we retrace our route toward Bo, I feel like my friends are choosing for me.

Mohamed has a Kuranko adage, "*latege saraka saa*," which describes how fate is something that just *is*, something that can't be altered, no matter what. He couldn't have done anything about his arm getting in the way of a bullet. No matter what, he was destined to be a one-armed man.

I want Mariama to find whoever cut Poco's throat and tell him that he's not put any curse on her—that he won't scare her out of her home. I want to ask my friend why she gave up so easily. She had respect. The women came to her.

Accept the good, for they are God's blessings.

Accept the bad, for God works in mysterious ways.

Accept.

This is how she sustains herself—her secret to life. It is something I envy.

I turn in my seat and Mariama smiles at me. Unbelievably, it is the smile of someone who is at peace.

In Bo, we stay at the Freedom Guest House. Abu, Mohamed and I sit on the verandah, drinking Star beers while the women cook under a roof out of the rain. Mariama squats beside Yeamah and Jameela, easily assuming a place at the cooking fire with the other women. They chat continuously as they prepare a meal of rice and spicy goat soup.

Kabande has been adopted by the local dog, another brown-and-cream mongrel. The little girl sits to the side, the dog at her feet, showing the mutt pictures of a peach and a pack of centipedes on their way to Manhattan.

I had worried about Jameela, but I needn't have. When we arrived, she stood on the verandah with her friend Yeamah, but her eyes weren't on me—they were on Mariama and Kabande. At first, Mariama seemed familiar with Jameela but unsure of her, speaking quietly to her as if not wanting to be overheard.

"You know each other?" I asked.

"Jameela was captured by the rebels," Mariama said. "This family knows everything that happen to her. They are good, Dr. John, they have accepted her."

"I don't understand. She knew we were looking for you—she didn't let on."

Mariama smiled. "Dr. John, she thought I was dead. It is not our way to talk about sad things with strangers. But she prayed for you to find me."

Now, as they go about their cooking, I'm struck by their ease in each other's company. Jameela occasionally glances my way, but like the dry-season dust, her flirtatiousness is gone. When the goat and rice are ready, the women serve the men with one platter and then sit together sharing another.

Afterward, we hang out on the verandah, drinking *poyo* and looking out at the rain. Mariama sits with her feet stretched out, legs crossed at the ankles, the pose of a woman enjoying the summer holidays at the lake.

"You are thinking, Dr. John," she says.

We are within hearing of everyone, but it is, I've learned, the way of the open verandah.

"Momodu went to fight …" I say, thinking back to the night he came to my room in Freetown. "The night he left me the mask—he was actually going to fight with the CDF?"

She says something in Krio to Mohamed, who listens intently. In English, she says, "Momodu hid his identity even from the CDF leadership. There were too many traitors, people changing sides. He made it to the provinces and met with some Kuranko men who formed their own CDF unit. To outsiders, Momodu pretended he was a Guinean physician volunteering in the fight. Momodu was not with his family when the rebels burned their house in Freetown. But no one knew that, Dr. John—this is why Mohamed thought Momodu died."

My friend liked to read *The Lancet* and *Science*—hardly the sort of fellow who maintained a secret life, let alone one involving magic fetishes. "Mariama, do you really believe he has some kind of magic?"

"I know it all seem strange, Dr. John, but Momodu is a *sowa*."

Mariama retells her story of being led by the Kamajor away from the rebels in Buedu—how that man was Momodu Camara. She pauses, using her finger to fish out bits of husk floating in her wine.

Jameela, sitting sideways on the railing, remains completely still. She is younger than Mariama, in her early to mid-twenties. She would be pretty but for a fatigue that colours her—the expression of someone wanting sleep. She seems so different from the flirtatious and overly sexualized young woman of a week ago.

"Mariama, in your diary I read up to the part where Momodu rescued you, but I didn't read anything after that."

She takes a long draft of the palm wine. I think I know what is coming, but I need her to say the words. "Dr. John, I spent the next year nursing with Momodu. His wife was at his home in the north."

A year working together—a beautiful, intelligent woman and a charming man. Momodu had never suffered from a cold bed in Freetown. "I'm sorry, it's none of my business," I say.

A playful smile transforms her. Even Mohamed wears a grin from ear to ear. "What? What is so funny?" I say.

"Dr. John, the Kamajors have strong medicines, but only if they follow the Kamajor way," says Mariama. "During the war, they were not allowed to do man and woman business, because it would reduce their power. Momodu had no women in his bed while I was in the CDF camp."

It's my turn to smile. Man and woman business, I am coming to believe, is complicated.

"I went to Lileima after the war," Mariama continues, "and Momodu went home to the north. He is a Muslim man—he can have many wives. I could have gone with him …" She shrugs her shoulders, not finishing the sentence—the look in her eyes says enough.

There is a flash of lightning and the rain pounds the zinc roof above our heads. Jameela continues to sit on the railing— she hasn't said a word since dinner. Splashes of water soak her head and clothing, but still she remains exposed, the heat of her body sending tendrils of steam from her T-shirt.

"Jameela," Mariama says, "come and sit out of the rain."

Mariama and I move apart and Jameela sits between us, so close I can feel the heat of her.

"Jameela, you met Mariama during the war?" I ask, as the rain subsides.

Jameela's eyes stare into the blackness. "Mi real name Jemi," she says.

FORTY-THREE

"You think I should stay in Lileima," Mariama says, out of the blue.

"Mariama, you just look at me and you know what I'm thinking. How do you do that?"

We're in Makeni, stretching our legs and sucking on oranges while Mohamed refuels the Mercedes. Somehow Kabande has found another mutt. She skips ahead of us, throwing sticks. African dogs aren't retrievers, but they don't seem to know that around Kabande.

"I have no man, Dr. John," she says. "Your thoughts are fresh to me."

"Well, okay. I was wondering why you seemed to give up so easily. In Lileima you were somebody. They needed you." As we stroll through a market, eyes stare at us from every direction; we're a curiosity among the monotony of groundnuts, plantains and sweet potatoes.

"We have a saying," she says. "You nor know the value of a cow until you lose it."

"You're not a cow!"

She laughs and shakes her head. "Dr. John, sometimes you do not listen. We have another saying: You nor know the value of shade until you chop down di tree. The men who killed Poco knew that dog was not like most dogs to Kabande and me. In Africa, dogs are for killin rats. They belong to the village. Everyone knew Poco was different to us. When they killed Poco, it was a warning. It was no choice for us to go or stay. Kabande's life and mine are more important."

Around us, shirtless young men wearing gold chains and garish watches cruise about on motorbikes. Makeni was a rebel stronghold during the war. The ex–child soldiers remind me of that young man driving down Commercial Drive in his black BMW. Their message to the world is the same: "Look at me."

"Doesn't it make you angry?" I give a few leones to a girl and pick out some gum off the platter on her head for Kabande.

"Anger is okay for God," she says. "It do no good for me."

"Sometimes anger gives us the energy to do what we need to do."

She taps my fingers with hers, the way she did in the hallway in Connaught Hospital so long ago. "Dr. John, Mussa is protectin his village like I am protectin Kabande. They know about trouble. Now they know about peace. No one trusts an unmarried woman. Even the women I help with babies. To them, I am still an unmarried woman."

Kabande and the dog join us as we meander back to the petrol station. A couple of fellows sporting knockoff designer shades and plenty of gold bling are hanging out with Mohamed. One has a cigarette in his mouth. The ground around the Mercedes is black from oil and fresh petrol spills. No one notices the cigarette. Unmarried women are *palava*, but cigarettes in filthy petrol stations threaten no one.

The road from Makeni to Kabala is paved, and Mohamed has the Mercedes in fourth gear. There is the usual parade of white SUVs, motorbikes and sketchy trucks, pedestrians carrying loads of brush on their heads and men holding pieces of fresh bush-meat on the side of the road. The farther north we go, the hillier and cooler it becomes. We come across Fula, Limba and Kuranko people, boys tending cattle and women traders, in a landscape bursting with the new life of recent rains.

I try calling Nadia but get the recording, so I call Bonnie. She sounds excited. "John, I was just talking to Nadia. She told me you're on your last leg. Sounds like quite a trip."

"We're passing through Kabala. Do you remember? I told you a story about spending a night here when the local Poro came through on a parade and scared the heck out of me and our French nurse."

"I remember, and it freaked me out, John."

"How are things?"

"Quiet lately, and Dr. Smith-Charles says hello." A pause. "Do you still have the mask?"

Ahead of us, a little boy with a long stick is herding cattle across the road. Mohamed slows the Mercedes and honks his horn. I don't answer Bonnie's question right away and she, true to form, waits quietly on the other end of the line.

"Yes, the echo-diagnostic equipment is now tied to the roof of the car. Apparently the mask was some kind of medicine used by one of the secret societies to make them impervious to bullets. I guess the bad guys wanted to destroy it."

She is silent, but I can sense her presence over the line. Finally, she says, "That may be what the mask was about to the Sierra Leoneans, but I've always been more concerned about what it means to you. What's that banging noise?"

"It's the sound of rain on the car roof. The rainy season has started.... Are you there?"

The line has gone dead. I feel a sudden queasiness—for the first time in the entire trip, my phone has dropped a call.

FORTY-FOUR

We're back to slick, rutted tracks and chopsticks for bridges—like the road to Lileima, only cooler and darker. Kabala is hours behind us, and we haven't passed a village of more than a few houses in some time. The door handle on my side has seized—only Mohamed seems able to open it.

Visitors here are rare, and the few Kuranko and Fula people we pass stare unselfconsciously. Occasionally, Mohamed will ask for directions or Mariama will buy some fruit from the women walking along the road. The road is so narrow, the sun is lost in the forest canopy. The tires on the Mercedes, already bald, slither snakelike along the greasy ruts. Mohamed steers like a rally driver, speeding up through streams that flow over the track, and gently manoeuvring around flows of red mud that ooze off the hillsides.

Incredibly, Mariama says she's never been here. Neither has Mohamed, who follows her directions unquestioningly. Mohamed seems to have surrendered entirely to Mariama's leadership.

We stop at a fork in the road. The way to the right has recent tire tracks and is relatively well used. The left is partially overgrown, more appropriate for foot traffic than for vehicles. Mariama doesn't hesitate. She points to the path less travelled.

Slowly, we switchback our way up a mountain, occasionally catching views of what I think is the Guinean frontier. The sky darkens as a series of thunderheads block out the sun. Mariama leans forward in her seat, studying the trees as one might road signs. Kabande has put her book down, her eyes glued to the terrain. It is uncharacteristically quiet; no one speaks. Even the diesel noise of the Mercedes is absorbed into the trees around us.

We round a bend and Mohamed breaks hard. Looming through a gap in the forest canopy stands the mountain, her sides wet with recent rains. A tree has fallen, or has been felled, across the track in front of us.

Before us is a phantasmagorical world. An unearthly landscape of ghoulish creatures, part human, part animal, made of sticks, dried grasses and raffia. Throughout the space are winged animals with long necks and protruding teeth. There are humanoid figures carrying smaller ones on their backs, and others with large heads and gaping mouths. The raffia creates an impression of movement, causing me to check and double-check that the ghastly creatures aren't alive.

There is something else, grass-covered sticks shaped into symbols—like an ancient script consisting of circles, crosses and squares.

"I've ... seen this before," I say, struggling to breathe.

"You have seen *this*?" asks an incredulous Mohamed.

"The night Momodu left the mask with me in Freetown. I saw this in a dream—it was this mountain, this grove ... Mohamed, this is the place I told you about. And there's something familiar about the symbols—I saw them when I put the mask on my head in my office. On the inside of the mask there are symbols like an alphabet; I think they're the same as the ones here."

Thunder echoes off the mountain. Above us, a cloud shuts out the afternoon sun and sucks the colour from the world around us. A sudden wind animates everything, making the grove and forest come alive.

"Okeh, okeh, okeh," Mohamed says, staring at me. "The symbols are meant to touch the face of the wearer. When the mask is put on, the *nyene*, the spirit, and wearer are one."

I turn to Mariama in the back seat. She and Kabande are holding each other's hand. They appear completely calm. "We are here, Dr. John," Mariama says, smiling. "This is the sacred grove of Momodu's father, Ibrahim Camara."

A clattering sound draws my attention back to the grove. Toward the back of the clearing is a barricade of sticks and raffia, and at the centre of this is a low, box-shaped passageway. Bits of something reflective, like tinfoil, flutter in the breeze. Voices come from the other side of the barricade and men suddenly emerge strolling through the passageway. I feel like an intruder caught in the light, exposed.

"Shit, Mohamed, maybe we should move on ..."

"Too late," he says, opening his door. "Mariama and Kabande, you stay in di car. Mr. John, we get out now and say hello."

I look at my window that won't roll down and the door handle that never works. I give it a pull. The door opens soundlessly.

The men emerge, bent at the hips, some holding sticks, like ants streaming out of a dark hole. They stop when they see us, a dozen men as surprised as we are. They're dressed casually—jeans, ball caps, T-shirts—except for the last man. Tall and well-muscled, he is shirtless, his torso glistening with sweat. His expression is so ferocious, he could be one of the ghoulish creatures suddenly come alive.

We stand twenty feet apart. His startled gaze shifts from me to the mud-caked crate tied to the roof of the Mercedes. My stomach churns, my mouth is dry.

The man smiles. "John Rourke, it is you! You look so frightened I didn't recognize you."

It takes me a moment to recognize him without a white coat, pens in the breast pocket, a nametag and a gentle smile.

My friend, Dr. Momodu Camara.

FORTY-FIVE

"Remove all of your clothes," Momodu says. Without waiting, he strips himself naked. His back and chest are heavily scarified, the result of ritualistic cuts from his Poro initiation as a boy. "It is okay, John. You have been weakened. I will cleanse you now, before the bush-devils come for the mask. After tonight, it will be over."

We're in a hut set apart from the village. The roof is thatched and the walls are of mud and wattle. A long plinth of sticks lashed together with rope stands alone in the centre of the room. On either side of the plinth are two huge metal pots, each full of steaming water, each resting on three stones around a bed of glowing coals.

Momodu drops bunches of herbs into the water and the hut

is filled with a pungent scent reminiscent of eucalyptus. The evening is already hot and humid, and the vapour from the two pots transforms the hut into a steaming sauna.

It will be over. I'm not sure what he means. I want to speak out, tell Momodu this is all going too far, but my exhaustion consumes me. I'm aware of removing my clothes. Momodu has me sit on the plinth facing him. He places his hand in a bowl of rice and rolls some between his fingers, forming it into a ball. He rolls the ball in a bowl of palm oil and offers it to me.

"The rice is for new life, John," he says gravely.

The heat and humidity have leached away my appetite, but I force the ball into my mouth and the palm oil helps it slide down my throat. Using both hands, he offers me a cup of tea-coloured liquid. I have no idea what it is, but I'm so hot I would drink anything. I swallow it. My throat burns and I feel dizzy.

Momodu gestures for me to lie face down on the plinth. The wooden platform is uncomfortable but strangely energizing against my skin. I let the steam and the herb smells and the heat draw me inward, my mind and body letting go. I'm aware of him taking a bundle of branches, dipping it into the steaming water. Momodu switches the dripping branches against my skin. Over and over, he whips my back, buttocks and legs. The fragrant liquid is scalding, but I'm in another place, and the pores of my skin are receptive to the heat.

My senses sharpen, and I feel years of sights and sounds and smells burning out of me. Images flood my consciousness: a little girl, lying on the pavement with pink bubbles coming out of her chest; a mother with pleading eyes; another girl, Kabande's mother, Jolie, her arms in rotting bandages, staring into the blackness behind me.

I feel sick, my head spins and I want to wretch. Another image, a gnarled finger pointing toward me—*You're one of us, one of us*, a voice says in the background. The branches continue to thrash my body and every part of me burns. I want to cry out, but it's as if I'm locked in, unable to move or speak.

The humidity is so thick, I struggle to breathe. I hear Nadia, her accent thickening with anxiety, telling her story of love and loss and of reinventing who she is. And a guy in never-washed clothes that smell of cigarette smoke and cheap wine pushing a shopping cart full of empty bottles. Keep things neat and tidy, he says. Teeth peeling a ripe mango, a scar between vaginal lips, my hand over a scalpel, a woman's hand over mine and the smell of almonds and fresh earth.

You're one of us, one of us.

I feel myself reaching forward, taking the mask off the wall, the huge, protruding eyes sucking me in, and the strange symbols touching my skin, pulling me into a place of darkness.

I'm on a couch, aware of Mariama kneeling on the floor by my head. Gently, she sponges my face and chest with a cool cloth. My head is pounding, and I struggle to sit. I'm wearing a *lappa*, knotted at the waist, my chest bare. I can hear chickens clucking and dogs barking and the rattling of pots and pans, sounds that I find reassuring.

"How did I get here?"

"Some of the men brought you, Dr. John. You were cleansed. Now they will come for the mask. We must stay in the house, no matter what we hear. We must not look outside."

Kabande sits beside me and places her hand on mine. "Don't worry, Dr. John," she says. "They won't come in the house. But if we look outside, they will cut off our noses."

"Kabande, what would I do without you?"

She gives me a squeeze and I respond, feeling better for it.

"I think Momodu has become a great healer," Mariama says, wringing the cloth with fresh water.

"Ah, yes," I remember, "the cleansing. I must have blacked out toward the end. I don't think I'll ever be content with a cold shower again."

Mariama offers me a gourd of water, and it is cool and delicious. I drain it, sloppily spilling much of it on my lap. "Dr. John, tonight the *nyene*, the bush-devils, will gather," she says, offering me more water. "Mohamed has put your crate on the verandah for them. Kabande is correct; we must not look out the window. It is the same for all women and uninitiated boys; no one is to look upon the bush-devils. The judgment mask will be returned to its home."

In the distance, in the direction of the sacred bush, I hear something that I take to be thunder. All sounds in the village die away except for one: the dogs. It is as if every dog for miles is howling a warning. Mariama and Kabande look toward the source of the distant sound, and I realize it is not thunder but something else—drumming and wailing. Like a wave, starting far out to sea and gathering momentum, slowly, inexorably, drawing closer, the noise builds until it feels as if it is pounding within my chest. The noise is so loud and threatening, even the dogs stop barking.

Mariama takes a blanket and hangs it across the window. On the floor below this, she places a bundle of herbs. A cacophony of drumming and wailing completely surrounds us. A scream, like a panicked animal being choked of life, pierces the night. There are more screams, and howls and whistles, that come from all directions. I hear footsteps on the verandah and a rhythmic breathing that feels like it is pulsing through the walls of the house.

Mariama and Kabande remain calm beside me, their faces serene despite the bedlam just outside the door.

I don't know if it lasts one minute or twenty, but the drumming and screaming and whimpering sounds recede as quickly as they had come. I feel a small hand squeezing mine. "He go now," Kabande says softly, "the *nyene* is gone."

I look from Kabande to Mariama. "It is gone, Dr. John," she says. "The mask has been returned to the sacred bush."

FORTY-SIX

"I was notified by a friend in the Lodge in Freetown that you had applied for a visa to return to Sierra Leone," he says.

"The Lodge? But I stayed at the Family Kingdom Hotel."

Momodu laughs so loud the chickens at our feet explode off the floor. We sit alone on the front verandah of Momodu's home. Mariama and Kabande are behind the house with Momodu's wife, Theresa, and a few other women. On the step of a neighbouring house, Mohamed flirts with a pretty girl.

"Ah, that is a good one! The Lodge is the name of the most powerful secret society in Freetown—the politicians and anyone who knows anything are members. For years we have been watching for the return of the mask. Unwittingly, you tipped off the watcher in the embassy in America—you gave my name as a local contact on the visa application, even though you had no idea where I was."

"Momodu, when I arrived at the airport in Lungi, a man who helped me with my luggage recommended me to a brother named Hussein. He drove a green Nissan."

"Ah, the green Nissan," he says, waving his hand. "For years our enemies on the losing side have kept a low profile in this country. They know the role the Tamaboro and Kamajor hunters played in defeating them the first time. They, too, have been waiting. They knew that when you returned with the mask of my father, you would lead them to this place. I do not know how they were tipped off, but I suspect someone else in the embassy, probably for a few leones. They were waiting for you at the airport—they followed you, and we followed them. After you found Mariama, we knew it was time to step on the cockroach."

I stare at my friend, a man I thought I knew. Or had known. "This still doesn't explain how they knew I had the mask in the first place," I say.

Momodu's eyes soften. "John, you made inquiries to so many people, looking for me and for Mariama. And you placed advertisements in the Freetown papers asking for anyone with knowledge of the whereabouts of Dr. Momodu Camara. I am afraid our enemies read the same newspapers—they put two and two together, it was only a matter of time."

I don't like what I'm hearing. I've been using a flashlight on a dark night, unaware that I'm giving my own position away.

"There were anonymous calls to my cell and my office phone. The voice said the mask was ready to return. Who do you think made the call?"

Momodu hesitates, his expression grave. "Hmm, okeh, okeh. John, the mask wanted to return the moment I left it with you. It is hard to explain, but we believe it will always want to come back to the sacred grove. It may even have made you sick, or anxious—again, I am sorry." He looks deeply into my eyes, weighing what he wants to say. "I did not make that call, and I do not know who did. But it is disturbing news, John—our enemies have more confidence than I thought."

The realization of what I've set in motion makes me nauseous. "I saw the bloody car, Momodu."

He regards me quietly, his eyes searching so deep I feel he is looking through me. "My friend, I owe you an apology. I chose you to bear a weight you did not ask for, a burden you could not possibly understand."

"No, I don't understand," I say. "I don't understand what a physician with your talent is doing in a village in the middle of nowhere. This country stinks with foreign NGOs, every one of them defining your people by something good they don't have enough of, or something bad they have too much of. Education? Not enough. Doctors? Not enough. Malaria? Maternal mortality? You've got it in spades. Meanwhile, you're sitting here with your shirt off, content to be one of the disappeared. You're perhaps the best physician this country has ever produced. No, I don't fucking understand anything about you."

His head nods slowly, his eyes partially closed—like a priest hearing a difficult confession. "My friend, I am a Kuranko man. We have our knowledge passed down to us by our fathers, and they by their fathers before them. Some are healers, some divine the future, but others specialize in more evil things, like curses or making poisons. My father's knowledge was for good. It helped us to win the war against evil. I promised him I would not let his knowledge die with him. It is God's will. In Kuranko we say 'wale,' work and duty. And 'latege saraka saa,' something you would call fate, but more than that. John, this is not something I chose. It chose me on the day I was born."

I watch Kabande and a strapping teenage boy draw water from a nearby well. The boy bends at the waist, muscles glistening with sweat, his arms working effortlessly. He places a full bucket on the ground and Kabande, putting a foot forward for balance, hefts the dripping load onto her head. She carries the bucket around to the back of the house and returns for another. They repeat the process over several bucketfuls, smiling and chatting.

"John, our belief about fate unites Muslims and Christians in Sierra Leone," says Momodu. "I have no sons, I am the last in my line." He pauses, his eyes darting toward Mariama and his wife. "It was my destiny to return here, and it is the duty of all Sierra Leoneans to prevent the cockroaches from returning. The men in the green car were just two—there are more lurking in the background, waiting for their opportunity. There are many unemployed young men in this country, and they are all angry. As long as this is so, there will be those who exploit them for their own purposes. It is the same all over Africa."

I feel like I'm slowly coming out of a deep hole—the world around me is starting to make sense, but there is so much to absorb. "I've missed you, Momodu," I say. "It was a good time we had."

He nods his head and his eyes soften. "John, now that the mask is in the grove, I can go where I want. I have already decided to go back to Freetown." He smiles. "I will practise medicine again, my friend, with my shirt on."

Mariama appears with a steaming platter of cassava stew. It is my favourite African dish, and the smell makes my mouth water. As she places the food between us, her eyes meet Momodu's. An acknowledgment passes between them, and it reminds me of the night in Freetown when the evening light captured her in silhouette. There is something different about her: the confident, self-assured *kpako nyaha* from Lileima looks ten years younger, her expression as demure as a young bride's.

Mohamed slows the Mercedes, tapping on the horn with his stump. A small herd of cattle, tails swishing at flies, plods along in front of us. A boy of perhaps ten or twelve deftly flicks his cane switch and the bony backsides move as one to the side of the road.

I dial the number and Nadia answers on the first ring.

"Hi, it's me."

"John, where are you?" So familiar, relaxed, like she's asking if I've left work yet.

"I'm still far away, but I'm heading in your direction. I don't know, really. Somewhere near Guinea. We've been out of cell range for a while."

"You sound different."

"Good. Nadia, I feel different. I'm coming home."

"When?"

"I'm on my way now, if these cows will get off the road. I should be in Freetown tomorrow. Can you hold off any kicking for three more days?"

"I'll see what I can do." A now-familiar pause. "John, what happened?"

"Hard to explain over the phone. I'm not really sure, but you were right, Nadia."

"Yes?"

"I needed to do this. Now I need to come home."

FORTY-SEVEN

Nadia and I have been talking. On my first night home, we talked for eight hours straight. We talked until the sun came up, and then we went to bed and made love and slept into the afternoon. She wanted to know everything—from the moment I arrived in Freetown until my last goodbyes with Mariama and Kabande. She asked about Mohamed and about the green Nissan and if I was ever afraid. And she wanted to hear everything about turning Najwa's baby. She had me describe what the birthing hut was like and what palm oil felt like on Najwa's skin.

She smiled and became animated when describing her two lunches with Bonnie. "She is like a Roma woman," she said. "In Croatia, I met others like her. Bonnie agreed that you needed to return to Africa. She told me Sierra Leone was where you became ill and it was in Sierra Leone that you would recover. Bonnie had such a nice way—I trusted her completely."

Nadia seemed most interested in Kabande. When I asked her why the little girl intrigued her so much, she shrugged and said, "Because that tells me what kind of woman Mariama is."

We talked so easily, I think neither of us wanted it to end. We spoke of the past and I asked her about her family. Her father died of cancer when she was a child and she remembered little about him. Of her mother, she said, "She sacrificed—always she sacrificed. One chicken for a family of six, and she ate the neck. She took the neck out of the pot and pretended she was being selfish by having it. Then she served the good parts to everyone else." Her mother suffered a stroke the year after Nadia entered nursing school and died a week later.

"None of the ones I loved survived," she said. Nadia loved two of her brothers, both of whom died in the fighting. She hated the other two, and about them she was characteristically blunt: "They were in a Croat paramilitary and they were as bad as the Serbs. All they knew was hatred. If they survived, I don't want to know. The wrong brothers died."

The baby kicked on my second day home. We had gone for a long walk under sunny blue skies. The street was pink with blossoms of cherry and Japanese plum. It was the kind of spring day when everyone is outside enjoying a good book and a park bench or a stroll around the seawall. We walked to Jericho Beach and didn't say a word about Sierra Leone or Croatia—we just held hands and walked and enjoyed the spring air.

We came home and made love under the skylight and took another nap. I fell asleep, my body spooning hers. I awoke when she took my hand and pressed it into her abdomen.

"She's kicking," she said.

"You're sure these are the first kicks?" I asked.

"You kept your promise, John. There was a time, when you were at Mariama's house, I wasn't sure." She pushed herself closer in to me. My hand felt a bump, then another, like popcorn popping under her skin.

"You think it's a girl?"

"It's a girl, no question."

"How do you know?"

Nadia was absolutely sure. "It is a female presence. The only male in the room is you."

She sighed, pressing my hand harder against her womb—I felt a kicking back. It was like holding hands with my little girl.

FORTY-EIGHT

My office has a hole in it, something is missing. Bonnie noticed it too. On my first day back, she dropped by and threw every inch of her five-foot frame into a hug. "My God, John. It feels like this office needs new paint or something." We both stared at the space on the wall—the paint was discoloured, the energy gone. "Do you miss it?" she asked.

"He's home where he belongs."

She took a chair and waited. She wasn't leaving until I told her about returning the mask to Momodu. When I described the cleansing and the wild night when the Poro men came for the mask, she nodded her head and smiled. Bonnie leaned forward in her chair and said, "John, this is absolutely amazing. I'm so proud of you—you returned the mask to its home. Do you have any idea what that means to those people? Now I have one more question for you. What does it all mean, for you?"

I stood and walked to the window and looked down at the street. A homeless man, Starbucks cup in hand, sat hunched at the entrance to the liquor store across the way. A few doors down, the Chinese grocer was putting out fresh bunches of flowers into buckets of water. A Brinks truck was parked in front of the bank, one guard at the back of the truck and one scanning the street from the entrance.

"It all began making sense when we left Mariama's village and I saw how the women responded to her. After everything she had been through, she never lost her sense of herself—she was the same honest, loving woman with everyone she met. I watched those women and girls stand to see her go, and I realized there was a purpose to my being there. I went back to Sierra Leone to find someone, Bonnie. And I did."

In my hand is an enlarged and newly framed black-and-white photograph of a proud African woman and her smiling daughter. I took the photo as Mohamed waited in the Mercedes, ready to leave for Freetown. Mariama had dressed formally, in the traditional way, in a *lappa* in a colourful print with a matching *docket*. Over her plaited hair she wore a head tie of the same material. Kabande wore a *lappa* and T-shirt and her hair was also plaited, with a single pink ribbon above her ear. In the photo, Mariama has her arm draped around her daughter's shoulders.

I asked Mariama about her plans, and she didn't hesitate. "I will go to Freetown now. It will be better for Kabande there." She took my hands in hers and said, "Dr. John, please remember us this way, we are happy now."

I managed a smile, not trusting my voice. Kabande came to my rescue, tugging at my shirt. "Dr. John, do you know what my name means?"

"Miracle. Your name means 'miracle'—it's a beautiful name."

I lifted the little girl, and her hug was ferocious. I held her close, my nose buried in her hair. In the background, Mohamed stood like a chauffeur beside the passenger door of the idling Mercedes. My eyes found Mariama's, and what I saw was as obvious as if she had been speaking the words: she was remembering that day—the day she took the scalpel from my hand and made the cuts in Jolie's belly. The day I lifted Kabande into the world.

A phrase comes to mind—*cutting the string*—words Mariama used to describe her circumcision. An act I cannot understand but which I've come to accept as something that has given her strength. The framed photograph feels heavy in my hands—soon, Kabande will be initiated.

I hang the picture on the wall, where the mask had been.

FORTY-NINE

May, 2009

When Dr. John come back he have an emptiness inside, so different from who he was, like a mango tree that forget how to make fruit. He have so many questions about what happen during the war—questions that fill his head. I think there is something underneath, something he carry with him, go make him sick.

When he turned Najwa's baby I see the old light in his eyes. I pray to Jesus that light help him find what he lost. Birthing is women business, that is the traditional way. But Dr. John have a healing spirit I see, and I want him to see. There is so much that go on in his head, I think he forget he have two hands. He need to feel with those hands, let his hands talk to him, then the light will stay in his eyes.

Wah! I remember the night he feel me with those hands. He was not like other men who go quick. I have not felt such love for so long. When he come back that is all I want, to wrap me in his arms and hold me again.

He is so sad about what happened to me, and he do not even know. It do not just happen to me Dr. John, it happen to everyone in my country. I am not the only woman get raped by those rebels. I have so many sisters who have the same things happen.

To us, bein a woman and feelin pain is the same thing. The same. We do not cry out when the sowei make the cut. It is not our way. If you are ready to be reborn a woman you are ready to take the pain. I do not cry for the things behind me now. I do not cry for what I have lost.

E yala yala e yalao
E yala yala nunga e yalao.
What God give to us,
He has taken away.
It is not my choice, it is his.

AUTHOR'S NOTE

My first trip to Sierra Leone was during the war in 2000. What I witnessed in refugee camps for amputee victims has stayed with me, and was the inspiration for this novel.

I have since travelled across the country on three occasions researching this story. Some terms, like "bush wife" to refer to captured women who were forced to live as "wives," are part of the lingua franca. I am aware that some scholars view this and other terms I've used in this book as pejorative. I have chosen to use the terms commonly used by Sierra Leoneans themselves.

I have attempted to use correct spellings and usage for Mende dialect. The Mende have a number of sub-dialects, however, and spellings vary across these.

So as not to confuse the reader, I have used the Mende term

"Kamajor" broadly to refer to the traditional hunter groups that formed the Civil Defense Forces (CDF) during the ten-year civil war in Sierra Leone. In fact, the Kuranko people's hunter society was referred to as Tamaboro. The CDF contained Temne and Kono hunter groups as well.

It is accepted in Sierra Leone that the Kamajors used secret medicines to make them invisible and impervious to bullets. Every Sierra Leonean I have asked, without exception, believed the Kamajors possessed such special powers. However, not all hunter groups used masks as their medicines. The use of the mask within this novel is entirely the product of my own imagination.

It is a matter of historical record that one of the most notorious rebel leaders, Sam Bockarie, referred to himself as Maskita. It is commonly thought that Maskita was eventually murdered by rivals in Liberia. Although one of my informants met Maskita on three occasions, my description of him, including his behaviour, is entirely fictional.

ACKNOWLEDGMENTS

I am hugely indebted to many who supported, guided, prodded and otherwise helped me toward a finished novel.

I owe a huge debt to Betty Tenga. A nurse/midwife who escaped Freetown with her family in 1999, Betty came to Canada as a refugee in 2001. In my research for this book, she helped me with everything from midwifery to Mende phrases and the names of traditional herbs. It goes without saying that this novel would not have been written but for Betty Tenga.

Betty Tenga's brother, Kenawa Bernard, guided me in 2009 on the first of my three road trips across Sierra Leone. Although I had written a mask into my earliest drafts, it was Kenawa who suggested the mask be a Kamajor medicine and that it would "want to return." Kenawa was also my inspiration for the character Mohamed. Tragically, Kenawa became ill with cancer in 2010 and passed away in December 2012. Kenawa, sleep well, my friend.

I've met many Sierra Leoneans as drivers, restaurant servers, informal guides and random verandah acquaintances, and many of them have become friends. Special thanks to Theresa Benjamin for her openness in discussing things Mende and Sandei, and to Jose Tenga for sharing his historical knowledge of the dark decade of 1992 to 2002. I would like to acknowledge the memory of Ed Banister for his early logistical support. I am indebted to my many Poro and Sandei friends, who will remain anonymous (secret societies are, after all, secret), and the people of Sumbuya, Lugbu Chiefdom, for taking me into their lives.

In researching *My Heart Is Not My Own*, I benefited greatly from a number of people who I have not met but who generously shared their time and expertise through numerous emails. These include: Dr. Chris Coulter, author of *Bush Wives and Girl Soldiers* (Cornell University Press, 2009); Dr. Neil Carey, author of *Masks of the Koranko Poro* (Ethnos Publications, 2007); and Dr. Arthur Abraham of Virginia State University for his kind assistance with the Mende language and culture. I thank an anonymous Médecins Sans Frontières ex-staffer for early discussions about Connaught Hospital in 1998 and '99.

I am indebted to Dr. Fuambai Ahmadu, who has shared her own initiation experience in her writings and, in telephone discussions and a series of emails, her views on the meaning and phenomenology of Bundu. I would like to thank Sandra Laframboise of the Dancing to Eagle Spirit Society in Vancouver for discussions about two-spirit people in First Nations cultures.

Thanks to Kathy Dempsey, Meghan Juby, Jean and Gary

Luthy and Don Zabloski for helpful comments on an earlier draft. Don's suggestion about changing Rourke's character from the third-person to the first-person point of view was insightful. Thanks to my writing buddy, Daryl Baswick, and fellow writers Eileen Cook and Leanne Tremblay for comments on later drafts.

I owe a very special thanks to my agent, Drea Cohane of The Rights Factory, and my editor, Adrienne Kerr of Penguin Canada, for believing so enthusiastically in *My Heart Is Not My Own*. I cannot imagine a more insightful and supportive team, and together they've brought the novel to the world. Thanks also to my wonderful copy editor, Alex Schultz; my production editor, Sandra Tooze; cover designer Mary Opper; and the entire team at Penguin.

I would like to thank my children, Natalie and Daniel. Your message to me is always the same: "You can do it, Dad!" Back at you two …

The last word, as always, is reserved for the love of my life, Shelley. She has read through every one of my many drafts and provided numerous plot and character suggestions, encouragement and unconditional support. Over my many phone calls from Sierra Leone while under a net with a headlamp, Shelley has been there on the other end of the line.

Thank you, Shelley—this is for you.